BADGE BUNNY

LEGACY IN BLUE, BOOK 1

KATYA ENSMORE

Copyright © 2020 by Katrina Moir

All rights reserved.

No part of this publication may be reproduced, distributed, or transmitted in any form or by any means, including photocopying, recording, or other electronic or mechanical methods without the prior written permission of the authors, except in the case of brief quotations embodied in critical reviews and certain other noncommercial uses permitted by copyright law.

Badge Bunny is a work of fiction. Names, characters, places, brands, media, and incidents are either the product of the author's imagination or are used fictitiously. Any resemblance to actual events, locales, or persons, living or dead, is entirely coincidental.

ISBN: 978-1-7773228-0-9 (Paperback)

Cover Design by Katrina Moir

Image by Comfreak from Pixabay

This book is currently available exclusively through Amazon.

https://katyaensmore.weebly.com/

❦ Created with Vellum

AUTHOR'S NOTE

SERIES NOTE:

This book is the first book of a series that centres on the lives of six siblings from the same family. Although it can be read alone, it is suggested to be read as part of the whole. Also at this point, the exact total of books and release dates for the series hasn't been decided as of yet, but at the moment there are books planned for each sibling.

CONTENT WARNING:

Due to some of the content of this fictional story, it is recommended for mature readers of 18 years old and above. Please be forewarned that some of the topics that may be presented (abuse, bullying, depictions/discussions of rape, violence, etc.) may cause triggers.

FOREWORD

badge bunny[1]

1. A female, usually of the barely legal age, who spends her time chasing police officers and offering them her 'services' in hopes of gaining status among her badge bunny friends.

See also: holster sniffer

---

1. Source: Urban Dictionary; https://www.urbandictionary.com/define.php?term=badge%20bunny

THE KING FAMILY

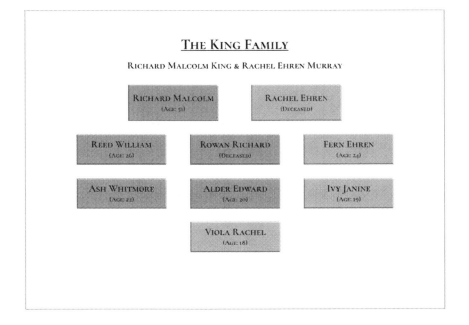

VIOLA

JANUARY

I HAD ALWAYS WANTED TO FALL IN LOVE.

Once.

Not twice, or thrice or whatever number came after that.

When it came to relationships, my sister Ivy was the polar opposite of me. I had yet to decide which one of us was north or south. Ivy and I were what people referred to as Irish twins. She was born in the middle of March, and I was born ten months later at the beginning of January. Even though we were born less than a year apart, we ended up in different classes, so she was a year ahead of me. The sibling bond we shared was closer than it was with any of my other brothers and sister, even with our completely different personalities.

Over the years, Ivy confessed to me many times, that she didn't care how much she fell in love. As long as the last and final love would be strong enough to follow her soul into the afterlife, that was all that mattered. The knowledge she did impart upon me, after several failed attempts, was to wait. Wait for that perfect person to give your virginity to, because once you made the choice to have sex, you couldn't go back. You would never be the same. She said it didn't matter what anyone said, the act of giving yourself to someone intimately changed you.

Tonight was my eighteenth birthday, and since everyone in my family had all deserted me, I decided to be spontaneous for once by making the very adult decision to give myself a birthday to remember. For once, I was going to live outside of my self-prescribed mold. My bag was already packed for the weekend and a partial plan was in place. Earlier in the day and prior to making my final arrangements to travel home for a couple days, I wrangled my friends Shelby and Chandra to be my wing women.

You see, I had yet to fall in love.

Having six older and very overprotective siblings inevitably placed a hinderance on any possibility of a love life. Being the youngest, I tended to do my own thing. After years of perfecting my wallflower state, I became silent and observant. Witnessing Ivy's failed relationships, leading up to getting back together with her ex, I feared that I might never find a love that could rock the ages. The planner in me decided it was time to bite the bullet and rid myself of this pesky v-card before I leave for university. It was common knowledge that even though I attended an all-girls Catholic school, I was one of the few that still hadn't had sex yet.

Who in their right mind wanted to be the awkward virgin after graduating from high school?

Definitely not me.

If I had learned anything from spying on my brothers, it was that no University aged male wanted to waste their time with a virgin. I also didn't want that awkward moment at the frat party where I had to explain the existence of my hymen. I didn't want some guy to turn me down after he had already seen me naked because he was scared of me turning into Clingy McClingerstein. So instead of spending the weekend at Sacred Heart Academy, an all-girls Catholic school just outside of the city, I would be heading home to our acreage.

Shelby and Chandra were already at home with their families celebrating the New Year while I had been holed up in my dorm room, waiting for the perfect moment to escape. The sisters all expect me to be here over the weekend, but I had other plans. I figured since I turned eighteen today, they shouldn't be able to force me to stay here as a minor. As it was, my dad didn't care about my birthdays, or the fact that I was spending it alone at the boarding school. So, I had taken it upon myself to fill out the paperwork to allow me full control over my residence.

Lucky for me, I had money saved up from my last babysitting job, so I was able to pay for a taxi to come get me and take me home.

NONE of the lights in the house were on, which didn't surprise me. Empty, just like it was every weekend I came home. There had to be a great comparison regarding our family dynamic somewhere in there. Considering the general lack of people occupying the space, I would have thought my dad would adopt a dog to guard the place or possibly brought home a retired police dog. It made me wonder if he only vacated the place when I came home, or if he was actually gone all the time. I tried not to feel jealous, but looking back, he seemed to be present during most of my siblings' birthdays.

I was the youngest of seven.

I had four brothers and two sisters – Rowan, Reed, Ash and Alder were my brothers and Fern and Ivy were my sisters.

Our mother was a botanist, so of course our first names were derived from plants. Mom was also the only reason dad purchased the acreage. She grew up on an orchard nestled in the mountains and wanted the same type of life. So, after my parents were married, they bought the land and built the house and surrounding buildings. She wanted a place to grow anything and everything without space restrictions. The only one of us who got the short end of the stick was Fern. The rest seemed to have semi-normal names.

Rowan and Reed, identical twins, and firstborn of the King siblings, were inseparable until Rowan died when I was eleven. Reed was younger than him by a meagre five minutes, but Rowan never let him forget it. They were eight years older than me. What I remembered of Rowan was that he was an amazing, caring older brother. He overdosed on Fentanyl and was found during a raid on a crack house. He struggled over the years with his addiction. I only wished he would have been able to escape his demons and grow older with the rest of us, instead of succumbing to them. Although he was gone, he would never be forgotten.

Reed took over the mantle shortly after Rowan died. He became our protector, and the stand in father for most of our lives. He was the first to uphold the King family legacy in blue. That was another one of the twins' differences. Reed joined the police force shortly after he graduated high school, while Rowan's addiction didn't let him keep it together long enough to finish his first semester in University. He has been on the job for seven years now and hasn't regretted the decision. The only time he had second thoughts was when he almost dropped out after Rowan overdosed. He was just a month into the academy and the grief of losing his twin in such a tragic way almost ruined his future.

Fern was the oldest girl in the family and seemed to be the biggest disappointment to our father, next to me of course. She was six years older than me and was the closest thing I had to a maternal figure in my life. She went into the police academy after graduation but was kicked out just before their final evaluation. There was an extreme blow out at our house, that resulted in her leaving town and essentially never looking back. She had been officially gone for five years, but she still visited us once a year, minus dad. They had been incommunicado since the blow out of the century.

Ash, four years older than me, was the next to join our legacy in blue. He was placed at the same precinct as Reed and as far as I knew, he had been doing well. He often suffered from middle child syndrome because he felt responsible for Alder, Ivy, and me, but he was considered a younger sibling to Rowan, Reed, and Fern. It could have been his central birth order that enabled him to be a natural lie detector. None of us could keep a secret around him even if it saved our lives.

Alder was a couple years older than me and was the first in our family to attend University before deciding on the police academy. He received a full ride sports scholarship to play hockey and was currently studying Criminal Justice with aspirations of going to law school. However, if I had to wager a guess, he would be registered for the police academy once he graduated. He was the brother I was closest to, not because of the smaller age difference, but because he didn't have some misguided sense of responsibility over Ivy and I. Sure he would likely go ape shit on anyone who caused us pain, but he was often in on some of our shenanigans rather than trying to stop them.

My sister Ivy and I had almost been in the same class at school, but I was a week later than my estimated birth date according to Fern. During our exile to Sacred Heart we were inseparable and were lucky to share a room until she graduated. I loved her to death. We saw less of each other these days since she moved in with her douche of a boyfriend. None of us were surprised when she got back together with Tyler, one of the boyfriends she dated when she was in High School. They broke up when he went away to college for football. Before he could finish his degree, he was injured. He eventually lost his scholarship due to failing grades. When he returned the year she graduated, joined the police force and they started back up where they left off.

With my dad playing the lifetime roll of my absentee father, I constantly wondered what things would have been like if my mom was still around. Over the years, my older siblings told me stories about her, but it wasn't the same as having the person present. I glanced at my phone again to remind myself that even though I had been deserted by all of them today, they still thought about me.

> Ivy: Hippo Birdy, Hippo Birdy, Hippo Birdy to you
>
> Me: You're officially a moron
>
> Ivy: Whatevs, you love me
>
> Me: unfortunately
>
> Ivy: Hey, so please don't hate me. Ty has an event tonight that I need to go to. It's important for him.
>
> Me: so, you're missing my birthday
>
> Ivy: I'm sorry, you know I'd be there if I could
>
> Me: I know
>
> Ivy: Have a blast though TTYL
>
> Me: TTYL
>
> Reed: Happy Birthday, imp. Sorry I had a shift today, otherwise I'd have taken you out for supper.
>
> Me: No prob, big bro. Keep the streets safe and come home in one piece.

Fern: Hi sweety. Happy Birthday. Sorry I couldn't be there today. They've got me at a conference in Russia this week. Know that you're loved, and I will see you soon.

Me: Cool! Bring me one of those Matryoshka dolls if you can. I've always wanted one.

Fern: Already got you one.

Me: Thanks, sis, you're the best!

It was hard not to miss my big sister. She was essentially the only maternal figure I had growing up. Sure, there were a couple nannies or caretakers, but that only lasted until I was old enough to go to school. Once that happened, Rowan and Reed were thirteen and Fern was eleven, so dad didn't need to hire caretakers. He had three, ready and willing to take care of the siblings they loved so much. When I was twelve, Fern enrolled in the police academy, against the wishes of my dad.

With dad's vehement rejection of her plan to follow the King legacy, no one expected him to lose his mind over her failing out of the academy. Yet, when she did, he made it painfully obvious that she disappointed him. Since we all still lived at home, there were several uncomfortably silent meals because they had stopped talking. Before any of us could suggest an intervention, she packed up her bedroom and snuck away while he was at work and we were at school.

Ash: Happy Birthday, imp. Sorry I can't be there to celebrate with you, gotta work tonight.

Me: Thanks bro. No worries.

Alder: Happy Birthday, imp, the troublemaker.

Me: I think you've mistaken me for Ivy.

Alder: Nope, she's Satan's little helper.

Me: Don't you mean Santa's little helper?

Alder: Satan, Santa, same letters...

Me: You're weird.

Alder: Weird, but you love me.

Me: In small doses.

Alder: Nope, definitely not small

Me: Eww, shut up. TMI.

Alder: Haha

Me: TTYL.

Alder: Ciao

It wasn't like today wasn't my birthday or anything.

Eighteen really must just a number. If no one was bringing the party to me, I was going to find one myself. Preferably one full of debauchery, because I was tired of being the perfect youngest child of Richard King. Who cares if he was the Chief of Police and had an image to uphold? With that in mind, I immediately sent a text to Shelby with tonight's action plan.

Me: Tonight's the night.

Shelby: To go all night?

Me: Can you go all night your first time?

Shelby: If anyone can do it you can, you hussy.

Me: Get your lily-white country ass over here and help me get ready.

Shelby: Be there soon.

Ten minutes later, Shelby arrived carrying a bag full of clothes and a pair of gorgeous black cowboy boots. I could always count on her to be my cohort in delinquency. I had asked her to bring something that would make me look different than I normally did. She came through on our plan, but I had no doubt in my mind that she would. She dropped everything she had in her hands on the front porch and launched into my arms.

"Hey, babe! Happy birthday!" She hugged me tight.

"Thanks!"

"Where's your dad?" she asked, even though I was sure she knew the answer. That was Shelby though, always great at pointing out situations and opening the floor for discussion. Even if I usually managed to sidestep her psychiatrist couch.

"Working," I replied with a shrug. "You know how he is."

"But you're home for your birthday weekend," she pouted.

"It wouldn't surprise me if he took a double just to avoid me."

I wished I could be one of those teenagers that could yell at their dad for being a moron, but my dad wasn't a normal dad. What he did for a living set him apart from most parental figures within my social group. He was the Chief of Police, and with that came stress, structure and an unchanging stance. However, I was sure out of all of his seven children, I was the one he could stand the least. After all, my birth meant he lost the love of his life, my mom.

"Why would he do that? You should be having a party."

"We are going to party."

Shelby never understood the distance between me and my father. She came from a two-parent household filled with love. I came from a single parent household where the parent regularly delegated his responsibilities to someone else. My sister Fern was only six years older than me, but that didn't stop him from making her the stand-in mother. Then when she no longer conformed to his ideals of the ways in which his "perfect daughter" should act, he sent the rest of us off to a school that provided dormitories during the week. So, for the last six years of my life, I spent most of my nights away from home.

My sister Ivy and I shared a dorm until last year when she graduated. She called me on the night of my birthday and apologized that she wouldn't be around when I came home because she moved in with her boyfriend Tyler. So tonight, I have a bit of a fuck the world attitude.

"Shelb, he's been avoiding me since the day I was born. It's par for the course."

"That's a shitty deal."

"Meh, I'm used to it."

My eyes burned with unshed tears. Usually I was able to push my feelings aside concerning the relationship that I had my dad, but for some reason this year it was harder. Maybe it was because I was finally an adult and he missed my whole childhood. The thought of him having the choice to be in my life all this time and he never took the chance, and now I was an adult with the ability to make the decision to cut him out of my life.

"Doesn't make it right."

"What about the rest of your family?"

"Reed has night patrol, Fern is anywhere but here, Ash is moonlighting as a bouncer at Underground, Alder is in Vegas with his buddies and Ivy just moved in with Tyler."

"Ew, she moved in with Handsy McGroperstein?"

Tyler, the creep, constantly found subtle ways to touch anything with a heartbeat, and Ivy lived in denial because she thought she was in love. Maybe she was, after all, I had never been in love. All I knew was that the person I hoped to fall in love with wouldn't feel the need to act on attraction he had for anyone but me. With that in mind, it was hard not to predict a tragic ending to their relationship. I had hoped she would see him for who he was before it got to this step, but sometimes you have to let people make their own mistakes.

"Yep."

"I thought for sure she'd be here."

"Whatevs. Ivy's in the honeymoon period of her relationship. They're probably having tons of sex." I laughed. "Now, let's focus. I have one goal tonight, and I will not fail it." I responded.

On nights like tonight, I wished my mom was still alive. A girl was supposed to share all those exciting milestones in her life with her mom. Granted, I likely wouldn't have divulged my exact plan for tonight, but I think she would have gotten a kick out of me getting ready. Especially since, out of all her girls, I looked the most like her. Some days it was a curse, however, during those moments of wondering, being her doppelgänger made up for it. Fern looked more like my Dad's mom, and Ivy didn't look like any of the women in our family.

"I hope you didn't shovel shit in these boots." I wrinkled my nose as I push my feet into the black cowboy boots Shelby brought to go with my chosen attire. I had plans for these shit kickers. I only hoped she didn't actually kick shit in them, because that wouldn't be sexy at all. I wanted to ooze sex appeal tonight, and these boots would go awesome with my daisy dukes and red corset.

"You said that you wanted authentic cowgirl."

"Authentic looking…not authentic smelling."

"They don't smell, whiny pants. I actually bought them for you for your birthday, you ungrateful bitch."

"Awe, thanks."

A moment passed where Shelby had a look across her face that I couldn't place.

"I just want to say this before Chandra gets here."

"Okay?"

"You don't have to go all the way tonight you know."

"I know, but I want to."

"We made that pact, but it doesn't mean I'm going to hold you to it. We both know Chandra wasn't a virgin anymore when she joined in. That's probably why she was so quick to jump on the bandwagon."

"I don't want to go away to University still a virgin and lose it to the first or second frat boy that I see."

"I know."

"I don't want to wake up in the morning, do the walk of shame and then have it spread like wildfire through school that he popped my cherry and has another notch on his bedpost. I don't want to have to see him in my classes after everything is done and be the laughingstock."

The last thing I wanted was to have people whispering about me when I should be focussed on classes. I wanted something anonymous; someone who didn't know that I was the Chief of Police's daughter. A man who wasn't looking to have a King daughter as a notch on his bedpost. I also didn't want some inexperienced high school jock fumbling his way through things making the night something to remember for all the wrong reasons. It might have been crazy, and I knew losing my virginity would be a big deal, but I didn't have a boyfriend and really didn't want all the hassle.

"Okay, but only if you're sure."

A knock sounded at the door, then I hear it creek open. Ivy and I have always had an open-door policy on the weekends with our friends. All they had to do was knock once and then they could enter. It's not like I have to worry about intruders here. There are guns and I know how to use them. If I can't get to them, my Krav Maga classes will come in handy.

"That must be Chandra!" Shelby squealed.

Footsteps thundered up the stairs and Chandra burst through the doorway swinging a platinum blonde wig around in circles like she was a cheerleader at the high school football game. Shelby and I both giggled at the display when the wig was launched towards my face where we both sat on the bed.

"Put it on birthday bitch. You're gonna get yourself some tonight."

"I don't know why you have to wear the wig. Your hair is awesome, and you'd look more like yourself."

"I don't want to be myself tonight, Shelb."

"Then you don't have to be, babe!"

Shelby was the only one of my friends that I confided in about my true homelife. Having a distant father and no mother could affect anyone. I wasn't naïve enough to believe that on some deeper level that I wasn't affected. Most daughters would be affected by an emotionally distant father. The one thing I had going for me was the fantastic relationships I had with my brothers. They were probably the reason I didn't dislike all men.

For one night I wanted to forget the past and the future and focus on the present. This was a night to let go of everything and be someone else.

"Then you don't have to be, babe!"

"Something borrowed…" Chandra teased.

"I'm just punching my v-card, not getting hitched."

"And here I thought you were waiting until marriage. Well at least you'll rid yourself of that pesky thing before you are all shrivelled up down there." Shelby chimed in.

"God you're crass!"

"You love me."

"Sometimes."

"Admit it, you lurve me."

"Shut up and finish helping me with this stupid wig."

∽

"Quit fucking with it Vi!" Shelby chastised me. "You said you wanted to wear it."

"But it's itchy." I whined, shifting the wig back and forth on my scalp. I knew this is going to be a horrible idea. It didn't rank as high as the pact we made last August to lose our virginity by the end of senior year, but it is a close second since I was wearing this ridiculous wig as step one in my hymen obliteration.

"You're the one that's so scared someone will recognize you."

I stopped shifting the wig covering my long straight obsidian locks. I only hoped I would still be able to get in the club using my ID while wearing a disguise. My eighteenth birthday had come and gone, so I was finally legal in every sense of the word. The main reason for this outfit was there was a photo of everyone in the family in the paper last week that was taken when my dad was recognized for his years of service with the city police. My family was well known because of who my dad was. Being the Chief of Police's youngest daughter prescribed how I needed to behave in the public eye.

Noticeably absent from the candid family photo was my eldest sister Fern. It had been five years since she got kicked out of the police academy and essentially banished from the King household. Rowan's death turned dad into a tyrant and he just wouldn't accept failure on any level. She still came to visit once a year, but we never spoke of dad and she never went to see him. I often wondered who would cave first in their never-ending battle for superiority. If I had to put money on it, I'd pick my dad. He was oblivious to most things going on around our family because he was too deeply ensconced in the politics of policing the city.

"I still don't understand why I'm dressed like a hooker. I'm also going to freeze my ass off out there. It's the beginning of fucking January, bitches."

"Bitch, those are my clothes." Shelby swatted my shoulder. "And for your information, we have jackets, chickee."

Oops.

"You say you didn't want anyone to recognize you, so we got rid of your church smocks." Chandra chimed in.

I had plenty of chances to lose it at a party with some rando from public school, but I had no desire to spend the evening with an amateurish boy fumbling in the dark. An experienced man was what I needed to rid me of the last of my innocence, and I definitely wasn't going to find him at the all-girls private school Dad enrolled me in when Ivy graduated.

We needed a bar, preferably one frequented by my perfect fantasy guy. A man with a badge. *Go ahead and diagnose me with a father complex, I don't care.* Maybe the reason I wanted a man with a badge is because my dad never wanted any of his daughters to date a cop. You know what they said about wanting something you couldn't have. Well, the Chief had a surprise in store for him because not only would I be seeking out a man in uniform; I planned on becoming a woman in a police uniform or going into criminal psychology when I graduated and eventually working in corrections.

There was an undeniable hotness factor to men in a uniform, preferably paired with a badge. My sister Fern would have said I was crazy to swoon over anyone like our dad, but he has nothing to do with my obsession. *Actually, allow me to rephrase.* I didn't now, nor would I ever have daddy issues. However, due to my enrollment in Westfall Girls Academy, the only men I came in contact with were either related to me or worked for my dad. There was no way I would be allowed to go anywhere near the officers that worked for my dad.

So, when my friends talked me into a night of debauchery, I conceded. My only stipulation was that we go to a club that I knew was frequented by the unattached men on the force frequented. My perpetual cloak of invisibility allowed me to pilfer that information from a conversation between my brothers Reed and Ash. I also knew that they would not be attending say club because they had both requested an extra shift. I only hoped I could avoid running into Ivy, and her ass munch of a boyfriend Tyler and his wandering hands.

"Ooh baby, you're looking completely fuckable. I know I'd do you, that is if I was into munching rug."

"I'll keep that in mind when I strike out tonight. Maybe I can talk you into being my first."

"Sweetheart, I've got all the wrong equipment. If it's a pimp that you're looking for, I can find a pole for your hole."

"Oh my God!" Shelby squealed. "And Vi thought I was crass."

"What?" Chandra placed her hand on her chest, feigning shock and outrage. "That is the goal for tonight isn't it? She needs a pooch for her hooch, some tail for her pail…"

"Okay we get the point." Shelby cut her off. "Now is everyone ready to go? Who's driving tonight?"

"Not it!" I yelled. "I'm planning on having no reason to come home tonight."

"What if he wants to come to your place?"

"Can you imagine? Sorry Chief, I just have to fuck one of your deputies." Chandra cackled.

"Do they even call them deputies?" Shelby inquired.

"No, they're called constables until they make sergeant." I answered robotically. There's only so many times you can listen to your family discuss police rankings before you can repeat them in your sleep.

"Whatever, ladies, let's get our jackets on and bounce." Chandra called out.

MIKE

"What an epic night," I said to Reed, my partner at District Two Police Precinct and best friend since we graduated from the police academy.

"You're still riding the high from that chick flashing her tits at us," he teased.

"They were some sweet tits. Too bad we had to arrest her for indecent exposure." I replied, recalling the perky globes and the nipples I would have loved to get a chance to tweak.

"She wasn't even drunk. Daddy will probably bail her out before princess has to spend too much time in the clink."

Reed didn't know much about my past, but I understood where he came from. So many of my friends growing up didn't have to worry about what they did because their parents had enough cash or clout to get them out of pretty much anything. It was depressing to think that some of them had enough power to even escape being convicted of murder.

"Are you from the 1950s or something?" I joked. "You weirdo."

"Fuck you, asshole," he countered.

"Are you sure you don't want to come tonight, man?" I asked, knowing Reed would probably turn me down because he had been staying home more often lately.

"No, I'm beat. I'm going to just go home, have a beer and pass out."

"Alright."

Deep down, I would like to think I wasn't losing my wing man, but the realist in me knew I was. He gradually started losing interest in casual flings a couple weeks ago. He grew more accepting of the idea of having someone to come home to. I didn't begrudge him for wanting more, but it definitely wasn't the life I wanted for myself.

Pushing a baby carriage was so far away from where I wanted to be right now that it might as well be Jupiter.

"Don't dip your wick in anything too skanky. Wouldn't want it to fall off."

"Don't you know it. I'm going to find me a nice innocent badge bunny."

He barked out a laugh. "Is there such a thing as a badge bunny that's innocent?"

"There has to be one somewhere. You know about that two sides of the same coin bullshit."

"Whatever you need to tell yourself at night to pump up your ego to conquer the masses."

"Mark my words, I'm going to be successful finding a unicorn tonight."

"I'll put a fifty down on that." He pulled a crisp, red fifty dollar bill out of his pocket and slapped it on the dash before he hopped out of our cruiser. "Just watch she doesn't poke you with her horn."

"Hope you're willing to lose your rent money, because I never strike out. When I'm on the hunt, my arrow strikes true."

"Now I know I have to leave when you start referring to your dick as an arrow."

"That's not what I meant, and you know it."

"You're definitely not a poet."

"That's only cause you aren't a chick. I'd be slinging romantic lines left and right if you had tits."

"Hardy har. Go get drunk."

"That's the plan, Stan."

"See ya."

"Have a good night."

THE SHRILL SOUND of my parent's ringtone invaded the cab of my truck. When I was eighteen, I changed it to the sound effects from an eighties horror flick and haven't had a reason to change it back. I sure as hell didn't want to answer at this time of night. Nothing good could ever come of my parents calling late on a Friday night. They were up to something and I wanted absolutely nothing to do with whatever they were cooking up. Regardless, my past experiences pushed me to answer, even if I would rather not know what their newest reason, I was a disappointment and disgrace to the Sinclair name.

"Hello," I answered using the handsfree.

My dad's voice boomed through the speakers. "Junior, your mother tells me you aren't coming to Sunday brunch at Silver Springs."

The Silver Springs Golf and Country Club was my parents' ultimate and predictable choice for brunch every Sunday. The place was like Mecca for all those who belonged to my parents' elitist society. Congregation occurred every Sunday as a means to flaunt and compare their accomplishments like two macho men flopping their dicks onto a table and measuring them.

Completely unnecessary and crude.

This same group of individuals believed it was completely acceptable for a twelve-year-old to be shipped off to year-round boarding school in another country. Sure, my parents allowed me to come home, but it was only for special events and holidays. Saving face was the only reason they retrieved me at all, with hope that it proved that they weren't a dysfunctional family.

Additionally, it was more than a little annoying that he still referred to me as junior, considering I was the eldest of three. Extremely fitting that I was also the only disappointment. The middle child, Victor, was six years younger than I was and was a self-entitled moron. Claudia was the youngest, and I was eight years old when she was born. She was the least annoying of the two, but still acted like she was a princess. I hoped she would grow out of that phase. Shortly after my sister was brought home, I was sent to boarding school.

"That's right. I have an early shift, so I can't attend." I roll my eyes, even though he can't see.

"We were meeting up with the Miltons. Cynthia just came home from Europe and she's been asking about you."

Of course she has.

"Oh?"

"I think she wants to see you."

More like she wanted to sink her harpy claws into my flesh and hang on like a scaly barnacle.

"Well then isn't it too bad that I have to work."

"I don't know why you still work there, it's beneath you, son." His gruff voice grated on my nerves. He acted this way every time we talked. "I think it's time you came to work at the business so that you're ready to take your rightful place when I retire."

He was nowhere near ready to retire considering my grandfather hadn't even handed over the reins to him yet.

"I'm not coming to work there. We've already had this discussion. I like my job, Dad. I feel like I'm making a difference."

"One person does not make a difference, son. You could be making so much more money working at the firm." I could almost see his disgust emanating through the phone.

"Look, I'm sorry I can't attend the brunch this Sunday. I'll try to make the one next week, but no promises because I might get called in."

"I'll make sure the Miltons meet us there. Your mother will be pleased," he clears his voice. "Robert, I expect you to reconsider your current career aspirations. You could be a more useful member of society, if only you would take your rightful place at the company."

"Which society, Dad?"

"The only society that matters, son," he answered as if members of his income bracket and community was the only society that mattered. "And as soon as you get that through your thick skull, your life will be much better."

"What about Victor?" I asked, hoping once again to push his focus in another direction.

My attempt to sway him had nothing to do with the animosity between my brother Victor and me. In fact, I wanted nothing more than to bury the hatchet between us. Unfortunately, due to my father's unending obsession with my future succession at the family's investment business, the relationship between my brother and I was strained. Victor had always been resentful of me. It was one thing I had never been happy about. From the conversations over the years, I could tell how close Reed was with his siblings and I only wished I had even a small percentage of the relationship that they possessed.

"What about Victor?" He repeated my words as if they we're supposed to mean something more.

"Victor is still in university, and he needs to focus on his studies."

"Dad, I think you need to entertain the possibility that I might not take over the family business. I have never wanted to run your company."

"I don't need to entertain anything, Junior."

"Dad I hate being called Junior. It's Michael, or Mike, and if I'm having a good day I might answer to Robert, but never Junior. Do you realize how demeaning that is?" I argued.

"That's just like you to focus on the wrong thing in a conversation. Let me remind you of a couple of items." He proceeded to lecture me on the importance of being Robert Michael Sinclair, the third. "Firstly, anything I say should be taken as final. As in, you will be joining the firm eventually, and you will most definitely be entertaining the notion of taking Cynthia as your bride within the next year. Secondly, how I run my household is not up for discussion. If you try to interfere with the position, I appoint Victor to once he graduates, you will keep your mouth shut. If you don't agree with who I've chosen for Claudia to marry, you will keep it to yourself."

I cut him off. "Dad, I've got to go."

Before I lost my fucking mind.

"Junior," he stressed the name, "you will join your mother and I for brunch this Sunday. You will be jovial and present for all discussions of the future, including, but not limited to your succession in the company and your upcoming nuptials with Cynthia Milton. It's time you start the groundwork for producing an heir."

"I never agreed to marrying her, and I'm definitely not going to procreate with her. Can you imagine the wretched offspring she'd produce?"

The thought of how much it would rile my parents up if I didn't produce suitable heirs was worth putting up with this ridiculously pointless conversation.

"It's not up to you to agree with your prescribed future. Your only option is to fall in line and obey." He cleared his voice. "I didn't have the choice to marry your mother. I might not have loved her at first, but I have grown to love her, and you can see for yourself how everything turned out."

"Yeah, you're the picture of a perfect marriage." I scoffed.

"Marriage aren't all perfect, they take work," he argued.

"What did Clarissa Carlton have to do with helping your marriage succeed, Dad?"

When I was twelve, just before he shipped me off to boarding school, I was at home sick and mom forgot to tell him. When I still respected my father, I liked spending time in his office when he was at work. That day I heard noises coming from his office, so I went to check what was happening and I got quite an eye full. He had Clarissa, his nineteen-year-old intern, bent over his desk and he was going to town, while she was squealing like a stuck pig.

I shuddered to think about all the therapy I should have gone through over the years. What surprised me was that I wasn't more traumatized by their antics. It was bad enough knowing your parents have sex, but to watch your forty-four year old father getting his wrinkled rocks off with a woman less than half his age on the desk you coloured on, was more than a bit disconcerting.

Nine months later, and a week before I was shipped off, Claudia appeared out of nowhere. In hindsight, they likely sent me to boarding school to keep quiet because I was old enough to know that babies didn't just appear on a doorstep. Mom has always been a svelte woman, and I would have been able to tell if she was pregnant. Victor would have been only six or seven at the time, so he had no idea where babies came from. He thought a stork dropped Claudia on the doorstep because he wanted another sibling. I overheard mom and her book club discussing the demise of that low bred trollop.

Sometimes I wondered if the reason that our mom was so distant was because we're all products of affairs. Victor's lack of height and dark complexion matched closely with my old nanny. Claudia and I both had dark hair, but our skin tone was much lighter than his.

"What the hell is that supposed to mean?"

"Goodbye, father."

I hang up on him before my response makes things more difficult. Let him stew on that statement for a bit. If only my mother would stand up for us, but she's even worse than he is.

Now I really could use that drink.

VIOLA - EDITED

CHANDRA WAS KNOWN AROUND OUR CIRCLE OF FRIENDS was known for trading sexual favours with bouncers to get what she wanted, but I had never seen her in action until tonight. She walked straight past the huge line and up to the bouncer, swaying her hips seductively the whole way. Now I knew the reason she insisted wearing stilettos all the time. She walked with barefooted grace, whereas I would have faceplanted in the first few steps. We couldn't hear what she was saying to him, but it was obvious what was happening between them. We watched as she unzipped her jacket and thrusted out her boobs, pressing them against his chest, when he leaned forward to whispered in her ear his gaze lingered on her cleavage for a moment and I knew we were set.

It was no surprise when Chandra turned around and waved us forward and we skipped the huge line. Once inside the bar, I was a bundle of nerves as we made our way through the crowd. The atmosphere and the number of people present supported my belief that I picked the best night club to search for a cherry popper. Over the years, I had overheard my brothers mention how this place was prime for the picking to search for someone to do the horizontal mambo with.

We paid the cover charge to get into the club and then dropped off our jackets at the coat check. At least there was a place to store my god-awful heavy wool coat. Chandra and Shelby stood to either side of me, threading their arms through my elbows and dragged me to the bar.

"This is gonna be awesome!" Shelby squealed over the music. "I've been waiting for you to take me up on my offer to go here for ages."

"I just turned eighteen, it wasn't possible before today," I argued.

"I know, but you could have used that fake ID I offered to get you at the beginning of the school year."

"You know I couldn't do that," I responded. Unlike my other friends, I neglected to get fake identification in order to partake in the club scene earlier than allowed.

"Yeah, Shelbs, Princess Viola can't break the law or Daddy will lock her in the Ivory tower," she joked.

"He already locked me away at a Sacred Heart, and we're not even Catholic. So really, what more can he do to me?"

Chandra cackled maniacally before explaining her train of thought. "He could always spank you."

"Eww!" I shuddered. "Seriously Chandra! Now I have to find some brain bleach to erase the visual you just gave me."

"Yeah, you sicko. Now let's get some hotties to buy us shots so we can forget all about it." Shelby suggested.

"Ooh, what about him?" Chandra pointed out a wannabe cowboy down at the end of the bar, wearing leather chaps over black jeans and white cowboy boots.

"Not in a million years." I answered, unintentionally spurring her into pointing out every possible drink purchaser in the joint.

Shelby and I cracked up when the aspiring cowboy strutted his way through the crowd towards us. He removed his hat and waved it in an extraordinarily awkward arc in our direction. Chandra fell for it hook line and sinker, letting him pull her into the crowd. Undoubtedly, the bouncer from earlier will spending tonight with his hand.

"Okay, now that Chan has thinned the herd a bit, do you see any more potentials?"

"Not exactly," I continued my survey of the room. "There's a lot of options here tonight, but I don't feel that certain spark with any of them."

"Spark? Why not take a page from Chan's book and pick any dick with legs?"

"You're bad."

"You know I love her, but you also know it's true," Shelby said.

"She likes to have a good time, nothing wrong with that. She reminds me a little of Ivy when she was seventeen."

"Ivy probably had a fake ID too," she said.

"Yep."

Chandra moved here to attend Sacred Heart when we were all sixteen and she attended school with us for exactly six months. At which point, after getting caught spending most nights out way past curfew, the school expelled her. Unlike most of the other girls from our age group, Shelby and I never once passed judgment on her. There were rumours going around school that she got pregnant, so they kicked her out, some said she was shacked up with the baby daddy, while we knew the truth. Chandra's personality didn't thrive under strict regulations, and it needed to flourish.

"I'm only pointing out that you're not going to wait for that someone special to pop your cherry. The night's not getting any younger, so pick one."

"This isn't a search for a candy bar." I laughed.

"Depends on the size of the bar," she responded.

"Well, let's hope it's just the right size. I wanna go dance, maybe I'll be able to see more of the room from the centre."

"You might even draw him to you when you shake your tush."

Shelby and I held hands as made our way through the crowd to the middle of the dance floor. My dad taught me and my siblings this trick when we were younger for when there was a large crowd we needed to walk through, to eliminate the risk of separation. It was hard not to think about the little girl who used to idolize the man who taught her tricks to ensure her safety. Deep down I knew my father loved me, but somehow down the line he forgot how.

The dance floor sunk a few feet lower than the main floor and we had to walk down couple steps to join the wall to wall people dancing. The music was infinitely louder on the lower level, likely because the speakers were placed in the corners. The moment we stepped onto the floor, Shelby twirled me, eliciting a laugh. After the drinks I had consumed the music easily moved me like I'm a marionette, and my strings are attached to the cords.

When I spotted Chandra through the crowd, I cringed at the sight of the cowboy groping her like an octopus. The look on her face was priceless, as she tried to look anywhere but at him. I made a point to try and get eye contact with her just in case she needed a rescue, but she shook her head when she noticed me a couple seconds later. The next song she unsurprisingly ditched the douche and joined us. Four songs later, I was beyond parched and needed a drink.

Shelby must have felt the same because she leaned closer and yelled in my ear, "I'm thirsty, let's go get something to wet my whistle. Then maybe he'll pop out at you."

"As long as his name isn't Jack."

After a few minutes of waiting for our drinks, I grew impatient, and was seriously reconsidering the whole evening. Then I saw him. My eyes were subconsciously drawn to across the room, to a man with dark hair and piercing eyes, towered over the other people lined up at the bar. He had to be at least six foot four, maybe more. Something in me yearned to see what shade they were while he shredded every last speck of my innocence tonight. My thighs clenched with the elicit thoughts rolling through my mind.

He moved with purpose through the throng of people drunkenly swaying along with the music. His dark red V-neck shirt clung to his body like a second skin. Everything fell around me the moment our eyes met, almost as if we were the only people in an empty room. The confidence he exuded threw me; he was a predator stalking his prey and I felt like a lamb going to the slaughter.

MIKE

WHEN I PULLED UP AT THE CLUB, AND THE PARKING LOT was packed I knew I picked the right place. There were a couple clubs I frequented in the area, but I tended to lean towards this one because of the location. It was close to the hotel I utilized for my after-hours activities. After all, what was the sense of having a one-night stand if you had to entertain them in the morning.

The concept of using a hotel being considered calloused and uncaring didn't escape me, but in practicality, it served a couple purposes. The first purpose was to remove the portion of intimacy that went with familiarity. If a woman never came to your house, they wouldn't become intimately familiar with how you lived, and hotels offer anonymity. Secondly, utilizing a hotel removed the question of whether someone should or shouldn't stay for or make breakfast. Lastly, there was the option to escape without the implication of hurt feelings.

There were a couple spots left in the back lot, so I parked there, knowing I wouldn't be getting my truck until morning. As I rounded the corner of the building, the monstrosity of the line became more apparent. Thankfully being a Sinclair had its benefits, like bypassing the line. My career in law enforcement also created opportunities because by default our paths crossed. There were times when just being a bouncer wasn't enough, things got out of hand and they needed to call the police. More often than not, Reed and I were the ones to respond because these clubs were in our district.

I couldn't believe my luck when I arrived at the club and took my usual residence by the end of the bar. Most nights it took unimaginable patience and a couple shots of whiskey to find a woman that caught my eye. The number of gorgeous women in this city was staggering, but to find the right one took just the right amount of finesse. Good things definitely came to those who wait. She entered my field of vision, and I envisioned her looking fantastic on my sheets. The revelation surprised me because my conquests never graced my doorstep. The risk of a stage five clinger encouraged me to set up my account at a hotel near the club to utilize.

She was dressed to impress in her cut-off jean shorts and a red corset that left nothing to the imagination. Just the right amount of cleavage escaped the wonderful creation made with man in mind, her miraculously generous breasts begging for my attention. Her platinum blonde hair was most definitely not real, but she wore the colour well. The disguise sent a thrill through me and eliminated the usual guilt I felt when I gave women a name I didn't normally use. In my family, the first born was always named Robert Michael, and I was the third in line for the cursed throne. So tonight, like most nights, my name was going to be Rob.

Her eyes didn't stray from mine as I meandered my way through inebriated clientele. Her brunette friend leaned over and whispered something in her ear, leaving them in a fit of giggles. I yearned to know what her laugh sounded like. I wanted to be the person to make her laugh. For the first time in a while, I felt anxious that she wouldn't choose me. Just as I reached the pair, she inhaled deeply causing her breasts to heave, and my eyes involuntarily left her face.

"Hi, gorgeous," I greeted her with my best panty melting smile.

Her eyes widen, but she neglected respond. This might just be my unicorn; shy and sweet, but hopefully nasty between the sheets. The combination of black cowboy boots, denim cut-off shorts and form-fitting corset was pure torture. The unbelievable desire to have her laid out on my bed begging for a release threw me.

Her friend shoved her in my direction, and suggested, "Why don't you two go dance?"

Before I could stop her forward motion, her face smashed into my chest, and she let out an indecipherable noise. She turned to glare at her friend, but her friend had already deserted us. By the look of her hasty retreat, she had set her sights on a conquest of her own for the night.

"I'm sorry about her," she mumbled. "She's usually not such a bitch."

"No need to apologize," I whispered next to her ear, fully aware of the effect I had on her when she shivered uncontrollably in my arms.

"Do you want to dance?" I asked, wanting to have a reason to put my hands on her body.

"Lead the way," she answered, placing her hand in mine, and I tugged her to the dance floor.

Everyone around us disappeared the moment I placed my hands on her hips, and her arms wrapped around my neck. Her soft hands caressed the back of my neck, fingers slightly grazing my hair. I imagined what they would feel like as she laid below me later this evening, calling out my name in ecstasy. The way she moved was as if she absorbed the music, and it flowed through her, choreographing every move.

Her breath warmed my neck as she whispered, "I don't even know your name and we're dancing like this."

The way the light hit her eyes gave me a moment of pause. For a second, I almost considered telling her my real name, which would defeat the purpose of a one-night stand. Plus, in my line of work, I really didn't want a stage five clinger showing up at my precinct looking to lay claim on me. That was the reason I sought out women who were badge bunnies; they knew the score. This club made picking up women like a lottery, sometimes you win, others you lose.

"You can call me Rob," I replied. "And yours?"

"Viola," she answered, "But my friends call Vi."

"Gorgeous name for a gorgeous woman," I stated.

Mid-song, she turned around and placed her ass against my cock. I grasped her hips and she hung her arms around my neck. The arch of her back gave me an amazing view of the sensational package she was hiding under the corset. Her breasts heaved with every breath mesmerizing me. The heat of her body made me anxious to worship it all night long. Hair from her blonde wig tickled my neck. Even though she looked amazing, I couldn't wait to get her alone so that I could unwrap the cover and see the real Vi she disguised underneath.

There was no doubt in my mind she would be coming home with me tonight. This might be the night I broke my own rules and took her to my place. She was the kind of person you cooked breakfast for in the morning, if only to ravage her again in the afternoon. This woman was absolutely heart-stopping and it looked like she was all mine tonight.

VIOLA

"Do you want to get out of here and go somewhere more comfortable?" he asked with his mouth to my ear, causing shivers down my spine.

"Sure," I responded, without a second thought.

"Do you want to tell your friends that you're leaving?" he asked, sounding concerned.

I followed his sightline and witnessed Shelby and Chandra stalking us from afar. I spared them a glance and they returned it with their thumbs up, then started giggling.

"They already know," I responded.

Inconspicuous, my ass.

"I'm beginning to think you planned this."

"Maybe," I answered.

I was an excellent planner, but this night was going better than I would have even imagined. He was most definitely a welcomed present for my birthday. In all honesty, although I set out to have sex tonight, I hadn't relegated my search to only this night. I still had the rest of the school year and the summer vacation to fulfill my major goal of not going to University untouched. So, if tonight goes as planned, I will have the rest of the school year to focus on my grades and forgetting all about this Adonis.

"I hope I'm not being taken advantage of," he teased.

"I hardly believe that you're the type of guy to relinquish control."

"You're right, sweetheart, I'm not," he winked. "Now I think it's time get out of here and get started on our evening together."

His warm hand caressed the small of my back as he led me through the crowd. After we both grabbed our jackets and put them on, we head to the exit. The bouncer nods his head at Rob as we exit the club into the night.

Although I had only one thing on my mind tonight, it still surprised me how easily Rob persuaded me to leave with him. Part of me wanted to blame my reduced inhibitions on the amount of alcohol I had consumed tonight, but considering I only had a few drinks that was impossible. The true reason for my inability to say no was that he carried himself and spoke in a way that made him virtually irresistible.

There were taxis parked in a line along the street next to the club as they most likely waited for their future drunken patrons. Rob waived one forward and guided me in that direction. When the vehicle ceased rolling, he opened the rear door and motioned me inside. Once he was seated in the back with me, he gave what sounded like a residential address to the driver.

Rob pulled me over into the middle seat, eliciting a squeak from me and then securely buckled me in. Leaning over me to snap the buckle gives him complete access to my ample cleavage as it rose and fell beneath my jacket, with every laboured breath. I jumped as the tip of his warm tongue placed pressure at the top of the valley between my breasts. My body shivered in anticipation as he slowly traced a line up past my collarbone and ended the journey with a kiss just below my ear.

"Are you cold?"

I shook my head.

"I'm going to rock your world tonight," he whispered against my skin leaving goosebumps in his wake.

"I sure hope so," I whispered.

"I know so, sweetheart." He kissed me again and then sucked on the spot. "God, you're beautiful."

"Yeah?"

He placed my hand over the ever-growing bulge in his pants, then confessed, "You obviously haven't noticed what you're doing to me."

The act equally terrified and excited me. None of the boys, and I used that term matter-of-factly to describe any male besides this man, ever took a chance with me. My curious nature pushed me to explore where I had never gone before. I glided my hand closer to the base, just above his balls and squeezed him slightly. When he let out a groan, I looked up and met the eyes of the driver, who I knew is completely aware of what was happening in the back of his vehicle.

His cheeks coloured enough to be apparent in the dark as he averted his eyes and returned his concentration to the road. It wasn't not like he hadn't seen this before, but a thrill rushed through me at the prospect of risqué PDA. He subtly increased his speed, either to swiftly take us to our next location or because he was excited himself. We made it to the address Rob indicated in no time flat.

"Is this your place?" I asked, surprised he directed us he to a townhouse in a swanky part of town. Part of me thought he would have taken us to a hotel, but I was glad he didn't.

"Yes," he answered.

After he paid the driver and helped me out of the car, he took my hand and guided me toward the house. He searched for something in my eyes I hoped I didn't give away, then pulled me up the stairs and inside. Once we breach the door, he stepped toward me with determination, reached for my jacket and pulled it off, tossing his and mine over the kitchen island.

He tugged me into his arms and his lips crashed against mine. They were soft and demanding at the same time. He threaded the fingers of one hand through my blonde wig, while his right hand settled on my ribcage, and his thumb caressed the side of my breast, causing my nipples to harden. When his tongue touched mine for the second time, he proceeded to devour me with his kiss, pulling me into oblivion.

An involuntary noise escaped in the form of a squeak when suddenly my back was up against the wall. A sudden ache between my legs begged to be released. His hand roamed from my breast down my side until he grasped my thigh and lifted my leg, sliding into the crevasse behind my knee. Instinctively, I ground my centre against his erection, seeking relief for the unexpected throbbing of my clit. He released my hair to hoist me up so that my legs could wrap around his waist and he pressed me harder against the wall.

He swept me into his arms, like I weighed nothing and swiftly took me up the stairs. Once we entered his room, he

"I can't wait to see what you've got under here."

Wanting to commit everything to memory, I took in the state of his bedroom. The walls were painted in light grey and his bedding matched but were in darker tones. I didn't know what to expect from Rob's room, since his was the first I had been in. Growing up I didn't have a lot of guy friends because my brothers had a knack for scaring away any guys trying to get close to me and my sisters. He watched me as I ceased my perusal and eyed his uniform in the closet.

"Do men with badges get you hot?"

I nodded, then watched with wide eyes as he pulled the handcuffs from his holster. He twirled them around on one finger as he tracked my movements to the bed.

"Are you afraid?"

I shook my head because for some unknown reason I trusted him. It wasn't just because he was a cop and likely worked with for my dad, somewhere deep inside I felt like he wouldn't hurt me.

"I need your words," he commanded.

My stomach fluttered. Nothing like knocking off three of the firsts from my sexual bucket list in one second flat. For once in my life I was going to let things happen instead of planning everything. He made me want to throw out my calendar and live for the moment.

"No, sir," I respond, making eye contact.

"I know you are, but don't worry, I'll make it good," he assured me in a husky voice. "These, however, will have to wait for later because for the first round I want to feel your hands grasping my biceps as I drive deep inside you."

He walked with purpose toward me, making me tremble with a tiny bit of fear and a whole lot of need. When he reached the edge of the bed, my stomach clenched as the cuffs clanged together. He placed them carefully on the bedside table, opened the drawer, grabbed a roll of condoms and set them beside the cuffs.

"Never know how many we'll need," he winked.

How many times can you have sex in one night?

My heart lodged in my throat wondering if I got myself into a predicament and several things ran through my mind. Odd things like baseball, and how many bases a person was supposed to work through when tonight I was just going straight for the home run. Then I pushed aside the niggle in my mind reminded me that now was the time to stop if I wanted.

The lapse my racing brain caused must have been longer than I thought because when I glanced up Rob was watching me. Goosebumps rose in his wake, as he perused me from head to toe like a painting in a museum. He was either trying to commit me to memory, or systematically deconstruct me with his eyes.

"I want to strip you bare, leaving only your boots."

My heart raced. No man had ever seen me naked. Self-doubt reared its ugly head, and a million scenarios entered my mind. What if my breasts were too small or disproportioned? Would he be turned off by the scar on my stomach from when I fell out of the tree and got nicked by a branch on the way down? What if my body wasn't feminine enough or he thought I was too muscular from all the self-defense training I took?

"You need to get out of your head," he voiced exactly what I was feeling.

How did he know?

"I'm normally not this kind of girl," I said, hoping he thought I meant having a one-night stand.

Part of me wondered if I was being deceptive by not confessing my inexperience. However, if I learned anything from being sneaky around my brothers, men were disinclined to rid a woman of their virginity because of their tendency towards what they referred to as being a stage five clinger. Which was why I was going to be cognisant of my reaction after this experience.

"This is a judgement free zone," he responded. "Besides, you only live once, right."

"Right," I confirmed.

Not knowing what to do next, I remained in the middle of the bed, with my back against the headboard and my legs crossed, awaiting whatever was about to happen. My friends had tried to tell me scandalous details of their trysts with boyfriends or fuck buddies, but I never wanted to know the play by play.

"I want you on the end of the bed, knees spread,"

He carefully unsnapped the steel fasteners on the front of my corset. One by one, they slowly revealed what lied beneath. With the material splayed open I was left bare from the waist up. My hands instinctively moved in an attempt to cover my breasts, but he gently grabbed my wrists and placed them to each side of my head. He threw his left leg over me, straddled my waist and then looked down at me with hooded eyes. The cool air puckered my nipples, drawing his attention. My back arched as his tongue swept over my left nipple. His teeth and tongue were a mixture of pain and pleasure I didn't realize existed.

Sweet torture.

Kneeling on the floor between my legs, he reached up and threaded his fingers in my wig and smashed his lips down on mine, demanding entrance. The way this man could kiss was dangerous, and exuded experience. A shiver ran through me with thoughts of what I was in store for tonight.

"A-aren't you going to get undressed?" I asked.

"All in due time, sweetheart. I'm the one in control here."

He unsnapped my shorts, then painstakingly dragged them down my legs and discarded them on the floor next to his leg. Lips feathered the inside of my knee, followed by the tip of his tongue, leaving tingles in its wake, slowly leading in the direction of the previously unexplored erogenous zone nestled between my legs. Chandra and Ivy both told me what it was like to have a man's mouth between their legs. Not knowing what to expect, I kept my eyes on him, cataloguing his every move.

I wanted to remember this night for the reset of my life.

"Lay back and enjoy the ride," he directed, the heat of his breath fanning over my panties.

Breathing deep, I laid back. My heart jumped into my throat as he placed his hands against my knees and pushed them open. The wider he went, the more on display I felt. I kept telling myself this was for his eyes only. His hands slid slowly up my legs caressing them as he leaned forward. Reaching his final destination, he ran the flat top of his tongue over my red lace panties. My back arched off the bed and I threw my arm over my mouth to muffle my moan. Tiny sparkling stars burst upon the inside of my eyelids as he pressed harder on my clit with his tongue.

I was given reprieve from the onslaught of ministrations as he pulled back to peruse me from my face down to the now very lubricated juncture between my legs. Forefingers grasped the sides of my lace panties at my hip bones as he tore them off with one yank. Open-mouthed, I watched as he tossed them on the top of the temporarily discarded handcuffs.

"Sorry, but I have to keep those for prosperity," he laughed. "I hope you're ready for this, cause I'm going to fuck you until you see stars and can't remember your own name."

My heart leapt into my throat as his fingers spread the lips of my pussy, licking from my clit to my entrance and then stuck it deep inside me. He returned to his sensational ministrations on my clit, and entered me with two of his large fingers, curving just at the right spot.

"You're nice and tight."

The rollercoaster ride of his tongue and fingers pumping brought me to heights my own fingers had never found. I bit my arm to soften the surprising sounds coming from me. He sucked my tiny sensitive bud into his mouth and held it between his teeth, causing a wave of intense heat and sparks to cascade from my nipples down to my toes. My lilting moans ceased as I floated down into my body.

He slowly pulled his fingers out and my eyes enlarged as he placed them in his mouth, licking off every last bit of my essence.

"Just as sweet as you look," he said just before he kissed me.

I wasn't sure what to think of the whole situation as I tasted myself on his lips. A million thoughts ran through my mind as he devoured me whole. Our tongues collided with purpose, a loud groan escaped him before he broke our kiss and stood.

"I can't wait any longer. I need to see if you feel as good as you taste."

He stood to remove his clothing piece by piece, revealing a body that rivalled a sculpture. His body was most definitely his temple, and he took care of it. It was no surprise that he was in shape, knowing he was in law enforcement. Cops weren't all coffee and donuts. Some of them actually cared if they could run down a suspect on foot or defend themselves against a violent offender.

My eyes roamed his body, taking in every detail and then halted when I spied the size of him stood at attention. He placed his knee on the bed and slowly crawled up until he was between my legs. He leaned back and supported his weight on his heels, displaying his manhood. The need to wrap my fingers around him consumed me. Rob closed his eyes as I reached out and used my thumb to remove the bead of precum on the head of his cock.

"Alright, sweetheart. Take a deep breath and get ready because I'm going to own your body and soul tonight," he said with a husky voice.

If I had ever imagined wanting to be owned in my life, it would have been by this gorgeous specimen of a man. He was all my fantasies rolled into one, including the ones I never thought existed, and he's all mine tonight. Something deep inside told me that I would remember my first time until the day I died.

The square foil wrapper makes a crinkling noise as he removed the condom. He sat back on his haunches and slowly rolled the condom down to the base of his penis, then squeezed it once. He grasped my knees and pushed my legs wide before he settled between my legs. He rubbed the head of his cock up and down my entrance, wetting it with my juices. He rocked the mushroom tip in and out a couple times, then he thrust deep without warning and stilled when a strangled moan passed my lips.

With one deep stroke, he obliterated my v-card. All my friends had warned me that losing my virginity was going to hurt. Yet, when his rock-hard cock stretched my walls, the only things that came to mind was an unusual fullness, followed by mind blowing pleasure. I often wondered if their pain was related to the age they were when they first had sex and who they slept with.

"Hearing the noises you make get me so hot."

Grasping my breast, he rolled my tiny nub between his thumb and forefinger and sent electric shocks straight to my core. He slowly pulled out until just the tip was still inside me and pushed back in. We instantly became one. There was no telling where he started, and I ended. I didn't know what it was, but that feeling made me overly emotional. I was amazed he didn't notice when he leaned forward and kissed me deeply. A part of me wanted to hate him for setting the bar so high for comparison to my future sexual experiences.

Moving my legs to his shoulders, he holds them together with his arm across my thighs, while he thrusts his hips repeatedly. Before I registered what happened, in one swift motion, he had pulled out, and flipped me over on my front. I glanced back, making eye contact with him while he blindly retrieved the cuffs from his bedside table.

How many times had he done this before?

My stomach fluttered and heart raced with thoughts of what I was in store for tonight. Most people would think that growing up in a house full of cops that I would have already worn cuffs, but I hadn't, so I had no idea what I was about to happen. A shiver ran through me when he brought my hands close to the headboard and snapped the cold metal cuffs into place on my wrists, effectively locking me to one of the rails. In that moment, I wanted to release the shackles of my life, and ironically allow him to restrain me.

"Hold on to the headboard." He instructed.

Grasping my hips, he instantly pushed into me so deep it felt like he was hitting the end, of what I didn't know, but it was amazing. My breasts swayed with his movements. Reaching around me he grabbed one of them and increased his thrusts. Rhythmically we moved together, the sounds of flesh hitting flesh until the familiar feeling of intense heat emanated from my clitoris down through my legs until I couldn't stand it any longer.

"Harder," I pleaded.

I jumped when his hand smacked my ass. Chandra joked about being spanked all the time, so the thought of him doing it threw me. What was usually a joke between friends became an intimate act between strangers. The thrill of wanting to know where it would take us, encouraged me to play along. My knowledge of sexual intimacy was solely based on snippets I was either told or overheard, and the details described in the romance novels I liked to read.

"Who's in control here?"

"You are, sir."

MIKE

THE NOISES COMING OUT OF HER SIGNALLED THE START of my undoing. When I entered her for the first time, she was so tight I almost came. Rocked to my core, I couldn't fathom where this woman had been hiding for the last couple years. How could one woman make me feel like I was experiencing my first time again? Like I was a hormonal teenager in the back seat of my parent's car on prom night. Everything with Viola felt like something new.

"I have no intention of stopping for a while, sweetheart. You're going to leave my bed thoroughly fucked."

Her hands held my biceps as I plunged like a piston as she moved her hips in motion with mine. My mouth found its way to her nipple instinctively as I sucked and twirled my tongue around her engorged peak. Her breasts swelled with my attention and her pussy spasmed encouraging my movements.

"Come for me," I whispered in her ear.

Her eyes closed and fluttered as I thrust harder. Her sexy black cowboy boots digging into my ass spurred me on. Her walls clenched, placing a welcomed strangle-hold on my dick. Seconds later, she came undone, calling out my name as her legs quaked from pleasure. I allowed her a tiny moment of reprieve before I withdrew completely and shoved back in, rotating my hips.

Her sounds incited me. I drove repeatedly into her and chased my own release. When she neared her third orgasm, I revelled in her responsiveness, and I wanted us to come together. I reached between us and rubbed her tiny nub to ensure mutual climax would be simultaneous. When her body was rocked with uncontrollable spasms, I couldn't hold back any longer, emptying myself into her. Collapsing beside her I glanced over, noting the glowing, fully sated expression on her face.

"That was…wow," she breathed out.

One time would never be enough to get this woman out of my system. She had buried so deeply under my skin I never wanted the night to end. In one act of mind-blowing sex, this gorgeous vixen rewired my brain. Originally, I was going to clean up, but then a sudden compulsion, like I had never experienced before, took over me.

Leaning over, I kissed her softly and then rolled to the edge of the bed. "I'll be back in a minute," I told her, as I got up out of the bed.

The master bedroom had a bathroom off to the side that I always used, so I went there to dispose of the condom, clean up and get a cloth for her. The moment I glanced in the mirror I saw a man I didn't recognize.

What was she doing to me?

When I returned to the room, she was focussed on the sheets as if they were seconds away from moving on their own. Curious as to what she was examining, I was drawn to her focal point. The knowledge of how the countless women I had taken to bed never acted in the same manner caused me to pause. In my experience, the women I had sex with in the past were well aware of what happened to the sheets when you rolled in them as much as we did tonight.

Once I moved closer, tiny spots of blood were evident, even against the dark grey sheets. As much as my instincts often pushed me to be, I knew I wasn't rough enough with her for there to be any evidence. I immediately knew this beautiful woman was hiding something extremely important. Something she should have informed me of and would have completely changed the outcome of this evening.

A deal breaker.

Our evening would have ended after a dance or two, but tonight's main course absolutely would have been unavailable for consumption.

Virgins were never an option on my take home menu.

Painstaking precautions were taken to avoid finding myself in this type of predicament. They we're clingy and demanding of my time after doing the deed, so I steered clear of anything or anyone resembling an innocent. I wanted a freak in the sheets, and that's what I thought I had. In my line of work, I needed to be concerned about entrapment. Badge bunnies didn't show their identification during the elaborate mating dance they used for a screening process, and I didn't want to be a weirdo by asking for their driver's license.

The cover definitely didn't represent the book.

What the fuck am I going to do now?

"Vi, baby?"

Her head snapped up as if it was the first time she had registered my presence.

"Yeah?" Her submissive voice escaped like a whisper in the night.

"Why didn't you tell me it was your first time?"

"It wasn't. I've done this loads of times," she gasped, while she struggled to maintain eye contact.

"That's the first and only time you'll ever lie to me." I reprimanded her.

She nodded.

"I need to have your words sweetheart."

"Yes, sir."

My dick hardened with her response, making it look like I pitched a six-man tent in my boxers. She stopped fiddling with the sheets over her chest and dropped them, revealing her miraculously generous breasts. Her eyes dropped to my cock, making it jump.

"I still can't believe that fit inside me."

"It fit like a glove. It's like you we're made for me," I answered with a wink.

Her face flushed with colour, reminding me of her innocence. I tried my damnedest to stay away from women like her because they never knew the deal. They got hooked and couldn't let things go.

Yet somehow, I couldn't turn off this road to my ultimate destruction.

"Now, first things first. Before we go any further, I need to see your ID."

"Wh-at? Why?"

"I need to know I'm not spending the rest of the night doing what I want to do with you, if you're jailbait."

She scrambled out the of bed like it was on fire and searched for her miniscule handbag. When she pulled out her ID, she held it up enough for me to see everything, but she conveniently covered her last name with her thumb.

"You're just barely eighteen."

"That's an adult," she argued, pushing me down on the bed and placing her legs on either side of my thighs.

Viola's fingers caressed my chest as she reached for me one more time and I wasn't strong enough to resist. Her eyes held mine, as I leaned down and pressed my lips to hers in a tender kiss. She moaned as my fingers stroked the side of her breast and pinched her hardened nipple. She playfully swatted my shoulder, so I quickly grabbed her. She squeaked as I flipped onto my back, taking her along for the ride. She straddled me, rolling her hips forward, the delicious friction further hardening my dick. This previously virginal goddess was insatiable.

If I was going to hell, at least I would be enjoying the ride.

The foil wrapper indicators of how many times I had taken her littered the floor.

What felt like a couple hours later, we fell asleep in each other's arms.

Another first for me.

I WAKE A COUPLE HOURS LATER, with a conscience.

Fuck, what have I done?

My previously fake blonde, de-virginized beauty, slumbered peacefully in the bed. Her platinum wig was discarded sometime during last night's festivities. Instead of remembering all the ways I had her, the only thing running through my mind is that I couldn't stay here. I needed to plan my exit before she stirred and decided she wanted monogrammed towels in our future bathroom.

This had to be a clean break, for the both of us.

Not one woman before her had made me want to flee my house so quickly. This is why I used a hotel, no hasty exits with the possibility of a clinger left in your bed. The last thing you wanted to do after a one-night stand was kick a bunny out of your bed, only to realize that she knew exactly how to find you in the future.

Sure, she acted like losing her virginity wasn't a big deal, but I knew it was. Who waited to sleep with someone and then chose a random guy? If she had indicated she was a virgin, I would have run in the other direction.

Virgins expect commitment.

No matter how hot last night was, committing to one woman was something I couldn't and wouldn't ever do. I was the last thing she needed in her life. The life that was unbelievably just beginning. Was she even out of high school yet?

I revisited the thoughts of going to hell, then I take one last look at the breathtaking image of her in my bed. Her long dark brown hair spread across the pillow. Committing the scene to my memory, with my final decision made, I made a quick exit before she woke.

I went downstairs to have a shower without the risk of waking my overnight guest. Wrapped in a large towel, I searched the kitchen for a piece of paper. I wanted to at least leave a brief note to state that I got called in to work. Fuck me. I came up short.

Maybe fate was trying to tell me something? Hell no.

Maybe I should stay and get her phone number.

Last night was pretty amazing.

I crept up the stairs and to take one last look in the bedroom door before making my final decision.

Fuck me.

The bed was empty.

She left.

Some cop I was!

How the hell did I not hear the click of the door?

VIOLA

I woke up alone, in an empty bed.

Was I really that surprised?

I was in a house I had never been to before. If I was being honest, when my older sister had parted with some of her wisdom on how I would feel this morning, I should have listened. I didn't know what I expected in the morning, but it sure wasn't an empty bed. Last night was amazing. Even after he found out that I lied about my level of experience, he treated me like I was special.

But then again, he left me.

A lone tear rolled down my cheek, betraying my attempt to remain strong. What I needed to do was get my ass out of here before he came back and saw me crying. Getting rid of my virginity like it was a pesky annoyance, was exciting, but I felt a bit like the bed. Empty.

Some mature woman I was.

I couldn't even handle the one night stand I planned out since last year's pact with my friends. I tiptoed into the hallway. The sound of running water hitting the glass of the shower in the second bathroom on the main floor made me hasten my exodus. Like a fire lit under my ass, I rushed back into the bedroom.

If he was anything like my brother Reed, he wouldn't want me here when he got back. I kept telling myself that the reason he left me alone in the bed was so that we didn't have that awkward morning after conversation. What else could explain his reason for using the bathroom downstairs instead of the one in the master bedroom?

Butterflies flitted around in my belly as I snuck around his room to try and find another exit. What if he comes back? Below the balcony there was a secondary exit to the back. I only hoped I could make it there before he shut off the shower and heard my departure. My heart raced as I scrambled around the room, collecting my discarded clothing.

Spying my shredded red lacy panties beside his bed, something naughty inside me wanted that to be the only thing for him to find. A thrill ran through me when I decided he could have them. I left my cowboy boots off to deaden my footfalls. I would put them on once I got safely to the back porch. With my luck he would probably catch me on the way out, but I needed to give myself the best possible getaway.

When I hit the bottom of the stairs, I traipsed through the kitchen, making as little noise as possible. I strained my ears and still heard the water hitting the glass. It softly echoed through the hall indicating he was still in the shower. Halfway past the kitchen I noticed my jacket strung over the chair at the breakfast nook.

Fuck me.

I almost forgot my stupid jacket!

I quickened my pace. I threw my jacket on and scrambled out the back door. After ensuring my cowboy boots were in place, I left. My chest ached with the awareness that he never noticed me leaving. Treking through the backyard, I shivered as the cool morning breeze hit my bare legs. Escaping like a thief in the night might not have been the best course of action. Then again, did I really want to wait around for a colossal rejection? If he had wanted me to stay, he wouldn't have left me alone in his bed. Mind made up, I unlatched the back gate, squeezed through, and ran like a bat out of hell down the back alley.

About a block away, when and elderly lady threw a disgusted look my way, I grasped the error of my ways. It was the middle of the winter, even if we were experiencing the warmer weather thanks to a chinook, and worst of all I was experiencing my first ever walk of shame, dressed like a streetwalker. Before I got any colder, or someone from the neighbourhood called the cops, I used my cell to order a taxi. They gave me twenty minutes for a proximate time, which meant I needed to find somewhere to keep warm. Thankfully, I spotted a twenty-four-hour convenience store near the entrance to his gated community.

TWENTY MINUTES LATER, I spotted the taxi coming down the street towards me, so I waved my hand. It's not as if there were any other weirdos wearing jean cut-offs and an outrageously huge wool winter jacket that went almost down to my knees. The cool winter morning had chilled me to the bone, but luckily, I would be in a warm vehicle in a matter of seconds. From the reaction on his face I looked even more ridiculous than I felt.

He rolled down the driver's side window, and asked, "Are you Viola?"

"Yes, I am," I replied.

He made no attempt to get out of the car to help me in. Must be because of the hour. He was an older man, about the age of fifty, dressed in a polo shirt and jeans. Thankfully he didn't' seem like he was a creep.

"I'm so glad you arrived so quickly. I don't know what I was thinking last night. I should have definitely worn jeans instead of shorts," I continued, as I got in the back of the vehicle.

"At least we didn't get that snowfall that those darned meteorologists warned us about."

"True," I agreed.

Everything got quiet after that, as we rode in welcomed silence to our next destination. From my semi-dishevelled look, he must have assumed I would rather not talk.

The whole ride home, I thought about Rob.

Some part of me wondered if last night was real, but the soreness between my legs told me otherwise. When I pondered about what happened, I wasn't sure how to feel about it. There might have been a tiny tinge of regret deep down. Out of everything, I was glad I met Rob and that he was the one. He definitely made last night the one to remember.

When I arrived home, it was around seven in the morning. There was a light on upstairs, and a strange vehicle was parked out front. Thankfully my dad wasn't at home to watch me do the walk of shame. However, if he wasn't at our house, I wondered who would be upstairs at this hour.

The driver pulled up the driveway and parked the vehicle. I tapped my debit card on his machine to pay for the ride, then got out of the back and dashed up the stairs. Before I could open the front door, it swung open. A squeal erupted from me as it nearly knocked me off the front porch and down the steps.

"What happened, Vi? Why are you home so late? Did someone hurt you?"

"Holy shit, Ives, you scared the crap out of me. What are you doing here?"

"I came to get more of my clothes. Now answer my questions," she demanded, then amended her statement, "First, get your ass inside before you catch a cold."

"Yes, Mom," I joked.

Once inside, my jacket was weighing me down, so I took it off and hung it up in the closet. She surveyed my attire, then screeched, "What the hell are you wearing?"

"Just be thankful it wasn't dad that opened the door. He would have tanned your hide for being outside in the winter dressed like a streetwalker."

"I'm not…"

She stared at me with a pointed look and her hands firmly placed on her hips.

"Well, I guess I'm sort of dressed like a hooker. I was at a club, what else was I supposed to wear?" I asked sarcastically. "I need to go upstairs and get changed. Then I need to crash."

"Okay, let's go. We haven't talked in ages and I have the car for an hour and then Tyler needs it to go out for brunch with his family."

"And you're not going?" I asked, surprised that her live in boyfriend would go for brunch with his parents and not invite her. Wasn't the purpose of moving in to solidify your life as a couple?

"No," she answered sadly.

"Oh, Ives."

"It's fine. Besides, we're talking about you and your atrocious attire. Didn't you see the clothes I left in your closet?"

"Of course I did. Shelby dressed me."

"Like a doll I suppose."

"Yep, just like her living breathing Streetwalker Nancy doll."

Ivy cracked up. "You're definitely tired when you start making sarcastic jokes."

Ivy sat down on my bed. I removed my boots and chucked them in the closet. I was about to remove my shorts when I realized that I didn't have any underwear on. I grabbed my night shirt and a pair of boy shorts and quickly changed.

"Ives, I did something stupid tonight."

Ivy shakes her head. "You let those skanks talk you into it, didn't you?"

"Yeah."

Surprisingly I didn't regret what happened, only that I would disappoint my sister. Over the years, Ivy told me how much she regretted the way she lost her virginity. She was fourteen, and he had graduated the previous year. She hasn't ever told me who it was with, only that it happened the back seat of a car after the football game. They hadn't been dating at the time, and he thoroughly spread the details of their encounter. After that night, she was approached by his brothers, who all assumed she would do the deed with them too. One of them even had the audacity to say, "sharing is caring", as if that would have made her decision.

"Someone from public high at a party?"

"No."

"Who the hell was it then?"

"A cop I met at the club."

"Oh Vi, tell me you didn't…"

"I told you I did something stupid."

She rocked me back and forth on the bed, then softly whispered. "Did he hurt you?"

I shook my head and pull back. "No, the opposite."

Ivy snickered. "Well then what's the problem? I mean besides giving up your virginity to some stranger you met at a club."

"It was hot, and passionate. I'm upset because it's over. You know how dad is about us dating cops. Plus, I didn't even tell him my name, and my wig never came off. If he knew who I really was, he wouldn't have touched me with a ten-foot pole."

"I wouldn't count on it. You're pretty hot."

"Ya right." I responded.

"Vi, you're my sister, of course you're sexy. It's in the genes."

"God, I'm gonna miss you around here."

"I'll miss you too. Just think, you'll be graduating soon and ditching this house. Who knows, maybe you'll hook up with Mr. Wonderful again and it will be a love connection."

Ivy was in love with being in love. I think that was the main reason why she was still with Tyler McGrabbypants. She just wanted to be loved and in love. It was oddly comforting knowing that I wasn't the only person my father messed up. He gave his all to the job, and nothing to us. He was all that we had, but in reality, we had nothing. Fern and Reed remembered the way he used to be, and the fun they used to have.

Dad ran our house like a police precinct. Our chores were scheduled, and it was a dictatorship. When I was eleven my oldest brother Rowan died of a Fentanyl overdose. At the time of Rowan's death, Fentanyl use had been on the rise in our city. To this day, the police were having difficulty getting a handle on it. As an eleven-year-old, I received weird looks from the librarian as I asked for her assistance in researching the drug. I found out it was synthetically made and something like fifty to one hundred times as powerful as morphine.

Rowan's death changed a lot of things in the King household. A decision was made almost overnight to enroll my remaining siblings in private school. Fern had it the hardest because she was switched with only one semester remaining in her senior year. They thought I would be the easiest to convince, but at eleven I hated everything. I refused to do schoolwork and I only wrote my name on exams.

It took almost a year and several trips to the school counsellor to make me re-evaluate my behaviour. Unfortunately, my tirade cost me a year of schooling and I was held back a grade. So, at the age of eighteen, I was still in high school, while my childhood friends had all graduated. As a result, they were out enjoying their lives and teased me about being a goody two shoes academy girl. They especially liked to poke fun at my school uniform, complete with a blazer. I was technically the last child left at home, although I spent most of the year at boarding school. My time there was drawing to a close and I had already prequalified for acceptance to the University to study criminal psychology with a focus on juvenile offenders.

MIKE

THE COUNTRY CLUB WAS JUST AS ANNOYING AS I remembered. Granted, I had only been able to avoid this hell hole for six months last year. I kept giving the same speech about work and school. It allowed me a reprieve, but once I graduated law school in December, there was only one excuse remaining. Since my parents didn't care that I worked anywhere other than the family business, my law enforcement career didn't matter.

Mandatory brunches like this made me remember how once I entered my teen years, I was brought home more frequently. During the school year, when I was away from them, was the only time I could actually breathe. My parents even brought me home for a whole summer to stay at the vacation house, but what they didn't tell me was that the purpose of that vacation was to integrate me into their society as a perspective husband for the daughters of current or future business partners. Shame on me for thinking that they actually wanted their first-born son to spend time with his family.

That summer, I realized that everything my friends had told me over the years was true. Unbeknownst to my parents, I participated in a ride-along with the local police department. Being the age of eighteen at the time, I didn't require parental consent. My parents foolishly thought I was off doing delinquent things, when I was actually finding my calling. My grandfather's brother was in the police force and retired at the age of forty-five, and whenever he was around, he would share stories. Instead of finding a future wife, like they obsessed over, I learned that I wanted to help others and provide a service to my community.

"Oh honey, you're just in time."

I took in the room and cringed.

Franklin and Marietta Milton were dressed like they had just arrived from church. Mr. Milton was wearing a grey Armani suit, and his wife, who was at least four or five years younger than his daughter, was dressed like she was getting married. She wore an ivory lace dress that hugged all her curves, accented with a string of pearls around her neck. His daughter Cynthia was wearing barely anything in her translucent black lace blouse and mid-thigh red skirt. I chuckled as I briefly imagined her being thrown out of church for dressing like a hooker.

Of course they would be here.

The Milton's were family friends of my parents. Unfortunately, they were regular guests at our family brunches and get togethers. They had darkened our doorstep with the Spawn of Satan, or Cynthia as I knew her, on many occasions. Mr. Milton, or Frank, as my father called him, went to the same boarding school as my father Cynthia was his only child, and he entertained her every whim.

My parents took every opportunity possible to throw Cynthia into my path. This society married for money, not for love. My parents' marriage was a prime example of why I should never get married. Little did they know, I would never get married. They could throw a million naked women at me in an attempt to entice me into marrying, and I wouldn't cave.

"Of course. How could I forget?" I tried to hide the sarcasm of my words.

My father, obviously ignoring my statement carried on his conversation with his chum. These two could win the Olympics of parental ignorance, while their wives earned a medal for their vows of silence. At home was another story. My mother shrieked on a daily basis. This was her outside voice. See and not be heard, and all that jazz.

"I'm hoping that we can all have more days like today. Frank, I see a bright future for our children."

"I do as well Robert," he responded.

Cynthia's eyes lit up with her father's confession.

Shoot me now.

"What is it you're doing for work these days, Rob?" Mr. Milton asked.

"I work for the police force and I am stationed out of District Two," I answered, gearing up for cross-examination.

Cynthia's dad came from a long line of lawyers that made most of their money through legal defense for some of the more notorious criminal cases in our country. His occupational background was one of the reasons that I wouldn't touch his daughter with a ten-foot pole. There was no way I could keep my current occupation if I married into that. I didn't think I could stomach sitting down to supper with someone who defended people convicted of human trafficking.

"I can see your wheels turning, Frank. I wouldn't worry too much about it, he'll be taking over for me soon enough," my father piped up.

"If working for your father's company doesn't interest you, you could always take the bar and put your law degree to good use at my firm," Frank interjected. "Although you would be required to start at the bottom so I can't be accused of nepotism." He chuckled, as if any of these people are concerned with getting a leg up because of their last names.

Being single had its perks when it came to home studying. In the time that I had been working for law enforcement, I had also completed a degree in Criminal Justice and then I completed my secondary degree in law. It was never my plan to be a lawyer, but I really liked going to school, so I thought if I had the money and the time, why not do something constructive with it.

In my father's eyes, nothing would ever be enough.

After years of these monotonous brunches, I learned it was best to smile, nod and take bites of your food often to avoid having to talk. So, as a result, sometime during their lengthy conversation, I spaced out. About the same time, I felt Cynthia's toes creep up the inside of my thigh, I knew this brunch was over. This was her modus operandi at every meal. She would take the seat opposite mine and make every sad attempt at cracking my calm façade. I was surprised I didn't have perpetual chaffing from her nails.

Since we were seventeen, she was led to believe that I belonged to her, no matter how many times I told her it would never happen. Without drawing attention my way, I moved my hand between my legs, grasped her foot and twisted her jacked up toes to the side. She squealed, bumped her knee on the table and almost knocked over her mimosa when she fell out of her chair.

"Cynthia, stop acting like a dimwit in front of the Sinclairs," Frank chastised.

"Sorry, Daddy," she apologized.

"Your Claudia isn't an airhead, is she?" he asked my father.

Claudia most definitely was the polar opposite of Cynthia in the brains department. She still had the whole sense of entitlement that comes with being the progeny of anyone from our society and sometimes she could get on my nerves. In a perfect world, my sister would escape the evil clutches of my parents and learn how to be a fully functional adult on her own, but my mom still had four more years with her at home to make the damage irreparable.

Francis Milton's obvious distain for his daughter made me think about all the lectures I had dealt with from my dad over the years. Every time my father spoke of the importance of being a Sinclair, I came close to spilling a few secrets I had harboured over the years. Most of my secrets surrounded my father's extramarital activities and my siblings. Even though we weren't close, I made a point of knowing all there was to learn about my siblings.

"Claudia has plans to apply for a business management degree when she graduates. She's skipped ahead two grades, so we're hopeful she'll enter college at seventeen."

"She sounds like an extremely determined young woman."

"She most definitely takes after my side of the family, if you know what I mean."

Frank laughed and shook his head. I often wondered if Frank knew dad was dipping it in the company ink around the time of Claudia's conception. With all his legal prowess, Mr. Milton was likely the man who paid off Clarissa so she wouldn't seek custody of Claudia or come after my father for more money. They probably made Clarissa sign a non-disclosure agreement and put a restraining order into place.

"When she gets her degree, she'll probably use it to open a nail salon or a spa, where she will work until she gets pregnant with her first child. In fact, just last Christmas, Charles Kensington and I sat down regarding his intentions towards my daughter. They haven't started dating yet, because she's still underage, but I definitely hear wedding bells in their future. They'll likely marry shortly after she turns eighteen, since his parents have expressed interest in having an heir soon."

The current secret that I didn't want to divulge was regarding my sister's future fiancé. Claudia was completely in the dark that Charles actually preferred to be called Charlene away from the office. Charles was five years younger than me, and I had known his sexual preference for years. One night when we were out at the bar, he got drunk and confessed that he was a couple months away from undergoing a gender reassignment surgery. He went along with our societal expectations so that he could gain access to his trust fund, which would be where he would be getting the money for the surgery.

"That's great news, Robert." Marietta Milton congratulated my father as if my mom didn't exist.

"What about Victor? Is he still planning on law school? Tell him to keep us in mind when he graduates. I'm sure we could use someone like him at the firm."

Victor was blessed with both sets of entitlement genes for the two of us. The only reason he settled on law school was to appease my father and try to prove that he deserved to be handed the reigns of our family's investment firm. He could have it for all I cared. I was happy in law enforcement. He was already engaged to Diana Huntington, who was sixteen and still in high school. The

Huntingtons were known for marrying off their daughters young, so there was no doubt in my mind that Diana would be married a day or so after her seventeenth birthday, whether she graduated high school yet or not.

"Victor is graduating high school soon, so I'll make sure he keeps you in mind for pointers and where to apply once he passes the bar," my dad boasted. "In fact, he will be marrying Diana Huntington next July."

"If Diana is anything like her other sisters, I see grandchildren in your near future," Frank chuckled. "If only these two could agree on a date, I know Cynthia has been keeping track of her ovulation. Lord knows she's not getting any younger."

There goes my appetite.

If memory served, I was positive that Diana's seventeenth birthday was near the beginning of July. The audacity of these people discussing procreation like it was a business transaction sent me over the edge. The only reason Cynthia was keeping track of her ovulation was to avoid getting pregnant. She was so cold towards children that I had no doubt she would secretly take contraceptives and fake infertility to avoid having to share her husband's affection with his offspring.

"I know I can't wait for the pitter patter of little feet around our house," my mom gushed.

She barely wanted to hear our little feet running around the house. How could she possible handle grandchildren?

"How about you Cynthia? Are you still in school?" dad asked.

"I graduated from cosmetology school several years ago, Mr. Sinclair. Mikey doesn't need to worry about that because I'll quit as soon as we're married," she answered, batting her eyes.

"That's wonderful news, isn't it son? Oh, and you can call me Robert."

"Thanks, Robert," she preened like a cat that got the cream.

VIOLA

Sunday evening, I returned to school just before curfew. I had spent most of the weekend moping around, and surprise, surprise, my father was absent for most of it, only coming home to sleep. Ivy had moved in with Tyler, so she was busy with him. Fern was still in Moscow, so I wouldn't be seeing her anytime soon. Reed and Ash had to work, and Alder was just starting his new semester and was deep into hockey practice, working out and games, so he didn't have a lot of time either.

After successfully dodging Shelby and Chandra's calls all weekend, I knew my luck would soon run out and one of my friends would find me. The moment I stepped foot on the academy grounds I would be cornered, and they would demand details that I didn't want to give. My bag barely hit my bed when Shelby flew in the door, the knob hitting the wall with the force. It took all but ten minutes for her to find me for interrogation.

"What the hell?!?" she yelled, pushing her way past me into the room.

"Sorry I haven't called," I responded, hoping she would drop it.

"Sorry?" she scoffed, placing her hands on her waist, just above her hips and cocking one out to the side. "That's all you have to say is sorry?"

"Yeah," I responded quietly.

"For all we knew, you could have been dead in a ditch or on some serial killing psycho's metal table being sliced and diced for Hannibal's buffet," she exaggerated, but it still hit home.

"Wow…Okay." My stomach dropped. I hadn't actually considered the safety factor of my ignoring her all weekend. We never really talked about the follow-up plan though. "I'm sorry, I never thought of it that way. I just wanted to decompress and maybe compartmentalize a bit."

"It's okay. Ivy told me you got home safe," she smiled extra big and then flopped onto my bed as if she wasn't just yelling at me.

"When did you talk to Ives?" It wasn't a big deal, but I didn't even know they had shared their phone numbers.

The reason I hadn't talked to Shelby all weekend was that I didn't want her to say anything negative about what happened between Rob and me. All weekend, I had been living in my own world of negativity and I didn't think I could handle her adding to it. Sometimes the inner monologue of disappointment was enough, I didn't need my best friend to agree with my belief of my own stupidity.

"Okay, so dish," she flopped down on the bed and rolled onto her stomach, then steepled her hands, resting her head on the peak. She looked as if she were praying for a story that I was about to spin.

"I'm not giving any specific details because I'm not quite ready for that."

"Awe, come on, Vi! How else am I supposed to live vicariously through you?" she groaned. "That was some excellent luck you had picking that hottie. I mean who does that? We were at the club for all of thirty minutes and he whisked you away to places unknown."

I barked out a laugh. "He took me to his place."

"Not to a hotel?" she asked. "I would have thought a one-night stand would take place in a seedy motel with mirrors on the ceiling."

"I don't know what kind of movies you've been watching, but I've never been in a hotel with mirrors on the ceiling."

"That's cause you've never been in a seedy motel. Silly."

"He was amazing Shelbs…not at all like I thought losing my virginity would be like," I let myself reminisce for the millionth time today.

"Did it hurt?" she cringed.

"Nope," I answered with a shiver as I remembered that night.

"He must have known what he was doing then."

"And then some," I responded. "I didn't even tell him I was a virgin."

"You didn't? Vi!" she chastised with a voice level that made me cringe. Thankfully my roommate was off with her gossip queens. That was all I needed was for her to be blabbing about my lack of virginity, or how slutty they thought I was because I lost it on a one-night stand.

"What? I wanted him to treat me like any other girl, not some precious gem he didn't want to crack."

"Still, he could have been super rough with you."

"He was, and I liked it."

"You little hussy," she teased with a gleam in her eyes. "Did you stay all night?"

"Yep," I chuckled. "We've got to talk about your choice of outfits in the winter. I ran two blocks in the freezing cold wearing a winter jacket and friggen shorts."

She cackled. "Two blocks?

"Why the fuck did you run two blocks for?"

"I snuck out in the morning."

"You didn't," she gasped.

"When I woke up and he was gone, I didn't know what to do."

"He left you alone at his house? Why didn't you stay longer and snoop around?"

"I could never do that; it'd be too weird. Besides, he was downstairs having a shower. I woke up alone, and although I didn't regret what happened, I still felt weird about it. I didn't want to stay there if I was going to cry. I didn't want him to have to deal with a regretful virgin."

"Are you really okay, Vi?" she said with concern.

Shelby had always been there for me. When Ivy graduated last year, Shelby and I became closer. Up until that moment, even though Shelby was my best friend, I shared everything with Ivy. We were only ten months apart and could have been in the same class, but because I was born on January the second, I ended up in the following year.

Shelby and I had our non-boy crazy ways in common. Sure, we appreciated the male of the species, but until this year, I had no interest in dating them. The summer of this year, Shelby and I made a pact. We both decided we didn't want to be virgins when we went away to University.

"I know I sound like I'm not." I exhaled the breath I didn't realize that I had been holding. "Honestly, I'm not sure how I feel. Don't get me wrong, it was an amazing night. One I'll never forget."

"But?" she interjected.

"But I should have maybe built up to the moment instead of just going from first base to home in one night."

"Hindsight is twenty-twenty I guess," she responded.

"Yeah, I guess it is," I agreed.

"So, it was a good night?"

"The best; he was amazing," I sighed. "Definitely the best guy for the job." I laughed at my own joke.

The door opened, and Christina sauntered in carrying her bags from Christmas vacation. She took one look at Shelby laying on my bed and rolled her eyes.

"Of course you'd be in here," she scoffed. "Don't you have your own room, loser?"

"Why do you have to be such a bitch?" Shelby taunted. "I was just leaving skank." She rolled her eyes, before getting off the bed and heading out the door.

"Lights out in fifteen minutes," Christina informed me.

I wished Shelby and I could have been roomed together instead of me and Christina. When my head hit the bed that night, I kept telling myself that I only had six more months of this and then I would be home free. Shelby and I could share an apartment with Chandra in University; no more assigned roommates.

"What's this I hear about you going to a club, Vi?" Alder, my nosey older brother, asked when I called him on Tuesday for our weekly chat.

Immediately, I guessed Ivy had been blabbing again. She was the only one who knew where I had gone on Friday night. Those two were only a couple years apart, so they tended to party together sometimes. When Ivy drank, she spilled secrets, not the important ones, but ones that she thought were funny or out of character for those involved.

"Ivy told you."

My sister was dead…not literally, but figuratively.

"Yup. She also said you went to the club Reed and Ash always go to. What were you thinking, Vi? They would have flipped their lids if they saw you at a club."

"I'm eighteen," I argued.

"I know you're eighteen, they know you're eighteen, but to them, you're always going to be a baby. Not only that, they don't want you to ever be mistaken for a badge bunny."

Little did he know, I already had been mistaken for a badge bunny.

"Why would they think I was a bunny?" I asked, wanting to know what he was thinking.

"Vi, do you know how many of my friends I had to keep away from you and Ivy?" he asked, surprising me.

"No."

"All of them," he laughed. "Every single one wanted your digits."

"Yeah right."

"I'm serious. It's rather annoying having sisters that are considered knock outs."

"That's crazy."

"You're telling me. You should have seen how many of them drooled over Fern when she worked as a lifeguard for a whole summer."

"I remember that. It was awesome because she took me every time, she had a shift."

It was the summer the year that Rowan overdosed. Fern was concerned about leaving me at home because my brother would often get high in the barn. My father hadn't completely checked out yet, but he was working hard for on a narcotics case. He was gone most nights, so Fern was my self-appointed caretaker. Reed was too busy spending tons of time with his fiancé Candi in preparation for going to the academy, so he didn't have time for me either.

"So, how's school?"

"School is school," he answered passively. He never really liked school that much, but he was super smart, so he got good grades all through high school. I doubted that had changed.

"Don't sound so exited," I joked. "What about hockey?"

Two years ago, Alder received a full ride scholarship to play hockey at the University. He didn't have any goals to play professionally, but it was a great opportunity to get his degree before deciding if he wanted to join the family business. We both knew that dad would be disappointed if he didn't, but what I didn't know is whether he had decided to yet or not. Even though dad knew that law enforcement was dangerous, he believed that it was our responsibility to serve and protect.

"Hockey is great!" he responded enthusiastically. "I'm looking forward to playoffs this year. We've got a really good team. Some of the senior players are focussed on giving it their all this year. Go out with a bang and all that."

"Cool."

"You and Ivy are going have to come to my games."

"We will," I assured him. As long as I could find a ride, and didn't have to study, I would go to his games.

"You better," he teased. "Gotta go. Night!"

"Good night, big bro," I responded.

MIKE

"Hey baby, remember me?" asked a high-pitched, adenoidal voice right next to my ear.

Katie…Catherine…Kelsey…or whatever the hell her name was, placed her recently manicured claws on my chest, and leaned forward, giving me a face full of her ample cleavage. In fact, her nipples were so hard against her halter top that I was surprised they didn't slice right through it. If there would have been enough room she probably would have slid in between my legs and pressed them to my chest to lift them even more and ensure I could feel how hard her nipples were.

Her type of women was all the same and up until now, it worked to get my attention, if only for the night. Oddly, I found that I was gradually becoming bored of the monotony of their over sexualized behaviour.

There were a couple drinking establishments Reed and I went to unwind after work. Burnett Arms was by far our favourite because of the wide selection of beer. It was also a great place to pick up women and the hotel I frequented with my chosen conquest of the night was just up the street. Most evenings, you could find some of the guys from the precinct having a beer, playing pool, picking up chicks, or all of the above. Working in the law enforcement field was taxing on the body as well as the mind.

Any given shift might end up being our last, so most of us tended to live it up while we could. Some of the guys got married straight out of the academy and started their family because they wanted someone to come home to. That was definitely not in the cards for me. I didn't want to leave anyone behind when my timecard got punched. It was a morbid thought, but I just don't want to be that guy who leaves behind his wife and kids because of some stupid traffic stop.

I gently removed her hand and replied, "Sorry, Katie, I'm just not feeling it tonight."

"It's Kayla," she corrected me, like I should already have known it and cared.

A couple of weeks ago, I would have caved without a second thought, but only so I could have dragged her out back and had my way with her in the back seat of my truck. Ever since the hot night back in January with the sexy brunette pretending to be a badge bunny, I hadn't felt like getting between the sheets with anyone else. It wasn't for lack of trying, because believe me, I made an effort to find someone to scratch the itch. Even the ladies tried to tempt me like Kayla did, but it just felt like the inevitable consumption of a stale sandwich.

What made matters worse was Vi had forgotten her wig in my bedroom, along with the red lacy panties I shredded in haste to get inside her. Like a stupid sucker for punishment I couldn't bring myself to throw out either item, so they were currently residing in my nightstand drawer. They were also most likely keeping the stack of condoms that I should be using, but probably won't, company. I couldn't foresee me using them, at least not until I got her out of my head, but women like Vi were hard to forget.

"Are you sure?" she pouted, turning me off further by sticking her bottom lip out like my little sister used to do to get her way. "I can put my ankles behind my head."

"Yeah, I'm sure."

Case in point.

In the past, I would have taken that statement and ran with it. She would have been in a hotel room in a matter of minutes to test out and make use of her flexibility.

All. Night. Long.

"Limp dick," she turned so fast her hair whipped me in the face, and I tasted her nasty floral perfume in my mouth.

Curiosity and being a hot-blooded male made me watch her for a couple minutes to see what she did next. She immediately set her sights on Devlyn down at the end of the bar. Definitely dodged a bullet there.

"That true?" Reed laughed his ass off before taking another drink of his beer.

"Shut up," I replied. "I haven't even slept with her. I hooked up with her friend Tiffany or Tina last year just before Christmas.

"You didn't want anything to do with that? I would have thought you'd jump on the chance to try out her flexibility and then brag about it at work tomorrow."

Thinking back, that would have been my norm. Following my night with Viola, I didn't even share the details. That little vixen had me all twisted up, and not at all eager to share anything about our night together.

Who knew why?

Maybe it was because subconsciously I didn't want to admit to Reed that I slept with a virgin who was barely eighteen years old. Likely cause his baby sister was still in high school. Most guys would have been shouting that from the mountain top.

What hot-blooded male wouldn't want to have bragging rights?

"What's up with you man? You haven't gone home with anyone lately?"

"I'm just not feeling it tonight," I answered.

"You haven't been feeling it for at least a month. Are you still hung up on that chick? She couldn't have rocked your world that hard."

At the risk of being accused of losing my balls, I explained, "I've never met anyone like her, and she was gone in the morning before I could even think about asking for her number."

"The self-proclaimed 'bunny slayer' gets ghosted." He cackled. "I never thought I'd see this day pass. She must have really been a unicorn in disguise. Either that or she's got a magic pussy."

I punched him in the arm. "When have I ever called myself the bunny slayer? That sounds like some vampire hunter knockoff."

"So, what are you going to do about your sitch?"

"Get over her the best way possible by getting under another bunny riding me reverse cowgirl." I lied.

"Whatever, man." He raised his glass. "To drinking ourselves under the table so we don't have to think about how fucked up our lives have become."

"What's going on with you, man?"

"Nothing I can't handle, eventually," he replied, taking a drink of his beer.

My partner and I went through the police academy. During the nine months there, sharing a bunk, we became as close as brothers. His twin, Rowan, overdosed on Fentanyl one month into our training. Reed almost dropped out, but I convinced him otherwise by using his future ability to deal with the drug problem plaguing our city. It was a shitty deal to lose your twin the way he did, but it wasn't a reason to throw away his future. The academy gave him leave for a weekend to attend the funeral, and when he returned, he was hell bent on graduating and getting out on the street.

With the way he had been acting lately, I swore he was revisiting those old wounds. There was something bothering him, but I couldn't put a finger on it. It wasn't like him to hide anything from me. Over the last week I'd noticed a difference in his attention span. He was definitely distracted enough to indicate he was going through something big. It hasn't affected our work yet, but I was worried about him.

"If you ever need to talk," I offered.

"Did she cut off your nut sack before she ran out the door?"

Classic Reed, diverting the direction of our conversation to my family jewels.

"Fuck off. I'm your partner. Your problems are my problems."

"I'll let you know if and when it becomes a bigger issue."

A couple minutes later we were joined by Reed's brother, Ash, who walked in the door and immediately headed in our direction.

"Hey, assholes! Thanks for the invite," Ash complained, then smacked his brother in the back, almost knocking over his beer.

"Watch it."

"That's for not telling me you were having beers."

"Never knew you were off shift tonight," Reed responded.

"How's the fishing tonight?"

"Mike just did an unexpected catch and release," Reed joked.

"Whatever man," I responded.

"You'll never believe what Al told me," Ash told Reed.

"What?"

"Apparently our little imp went to the club for her birthday."

For some reason these guys called their little sister imp. In eight years, I had failed to learn what their sister's name was, which I found weird. Fern and the sister they called imp was their only siblings that I hadn't met, and if the little imp was anything like Hurricane Ivy, I would rather just not meet her and pretend that I had.

"Seriously?" Reed asked. "Which club?"

"Roadhouse," Ash replied. "Seems our little sis wants to follow in our footsteps."

"You'd better be wrong," Reed replied. "Please tell me she went home at midnight. Alone."

"Ives was pretty tight lipped about it," said Ash. "You know how those two are. Al said it took a couple drinks before Ivy was loose lipped enough to blab about the imp's night out."

"What the fuck?" Reed seethed. "I'm going to have to have a long chat with her about going to that bar. I don't need anyone from the precinct screwing my little sister."

"Have another drink, man." I slid a beer his way. "You can't do anything about it now, so we might as well have a drink."

"Sure man," he replied, taking a huge swig of the beer.

I could tell he just agreed with me to try to pretend he wasn't bothered by his little sister going to the club that we went to on Fridays to pick up chicks. I would have given my left nut to see his reaction to her on the dance floor with one of our guys from the precinct.

A couple hours later when I arrived home to an empty house I wondered if my past choices had been right.

VIOLA

Almost a month had passed since the night of losing my virginity. I didn't feel any different, other than the more realistic fantasies I was left with. Up until the moment of meeting Rob and sleeping with him, all I had for sexual reference were my books and the private details from my friends' personal experiences. If I was being honest, I never actually wanted any of those details.

The daydreaming about him was getting a bit ridiculous though. I had a hard time concentrating in classes because I was thinking about what he was doing. Whether I would ever see him again was often in the forefront of my mind. Sometimes I imagined Reed bringing him to the house, him becoming completely enamoured with me and asking me out on a date.

Then when I revisited the reason, I would likely never see him again, I was left bereft. How could one night with a complete stranger make me go so crazy? It was funny because now I actually understood why Ivy was so boy crazy between boyfriends. The constant wondering and hoping would drive anyone batty.

Maybe I shouldn't have snuck out like a thief in the night. What if he was actually going to give me his number and not the brush off? He did bring me to his house instead of renting a hotel room for the night like I thought he would. I mean, why would you want a complete stranger to see where you lived unless you had plans of possibly seeing them again.

On the home front, my dad remembered a birthday card. I knew the thought was what counted, but I couldn't put it out of my mind that he was a month late.

How could you forget your youngest daughter's birthday when it was a day before your wife's death?

He was still away from home on the weekends when I visited so I started staying at Sacred Heart full-time. This was my last year at school and all that mattered was my grades. My ultimate plan would not be derailed for anything, especially a man that I had only known for a night. Who cared if that night was the source of numerous dreams staring said man?

So, just like most weekend nights for the past month, I was holed up in my dorm room studying. I was deeply engrossed in memorizing the events of World War II when my door burst open, revealing a heavily caffeinated Shelby.

"Hey, party pooper two point oh," she cackled.

"What's up?" I asked.

"Sasha snuck in some booze, so a bunch of us are going to get wasted together," she replied, bouncing back and forth on her heels.

"I need to study for history tonight."

"Don't come up with a lame ass excuse. That test isn't until next Wednesday. You're going to ace it with your eyes closed and you know it," she replied.

"Okay, I guess I can come for an hour," I answered. "But that's it. Just one hour."

"Deal. After all, that's all we need to loosen your brand of crazy."

"I'm not crazy," I argued.

I shut my textbook and stacked everything in a pile on the corner of my desk. Most people thought I was crazy because of my incessant need for order, but that's what happened when you came from a family like mine. My dad ruled the house the way he ran a precinct, and instilled military-style cleanliness in all of us from a young age.

"You've been uber-focussed since your birthday and subsequent night of debauchery."

"There wasn't really any debauchery."

"I think demolishing your v-card during a one-night stand with a sexy cop that most definitely works for your father counts as debauchery," she retorted with her hands placed firmly on her hips. Shelby could be a tad dramatic when she wanted to.

"Whatever, drama queen. Let's get to Sasha's room before those bitches guzzle all the booze."

"I think her sister Macy got her four bottles, so we should be fine for an hour's worth of drinking."

Curfew on the weekends were a bit more relaxed because of the off-campus privileges, but drinking was obviously against the rules. As such, we couldn't get caught convening in Sasha's room with alcohol, so we walked quietly down the hall to her room to avoid causing suspicion.

"I've got a good one," I said, glancing at Shelby. "Never have I ever cleaned up by piling everything into a closet."

"No fair," Shelby whined. "It was only the one time."

Everyone laughed.

"I got one," said April. "Never have I ever sung karaoke."

"Good one," I replied, taking a sip.

Sasha was next and she started with, "Never have I ever pretended to know a stranger."

To my surprise, no one took a drink. My brother Alder would have drunk to that one. He met his current girlfriend by pretending to know her to avoid talking to one of the many jersey chasers that follow him around. Jokes on them, though, because he has never been one to jump from bed to bed. Alder has always wanted to find the one and settle down. Unlike Reed and Ash, he has only had a couple of girlfriends or bed partners that I knew of. Ash was somewhat of a lady's man, and Reed hadn't dated anyone seriously since Candi.

"Well, that one didn't work," Sasha joked. "Let's try this one. Never have I ever worn sleepwear and pretended it was clothing."

Three of us drank. Who hadn't gone out of the house wearing all or a portion of their pajamas and pretended not to notice? I loved my fuzzy sleep pants and I didn't care what anyone thought of me wearing them to the grocery store.

"Never have I ever said excuse me when there was no one around," said Erika, followed by all of us drinking.

"Never have I ever had a crush on a friend's sibling," Shelby said next, followed by taking her own drink.

"Seriously? Please tell me it's not one of my brothers."

"Okay, I won't tell you," she replied.

"Eww. I think I just puked a little in my mouth."

"As if you don't know that your brothers are friggen sexy as hell, Vi," Sasha agreed.

"I can agree that they're not ugly, but I don't want to know anything about their sex lives. I heard enough stories when I was younger through eavesdropping," I confessed.

"If that's the case, maybe Viola should come up with the raunchy never statements," Erika suggested.

"Nu uh. I think we're just fine the way we are," I disagreed, not wanting to be the centre of attention.

Just when I was celebrating the absence of my arch nemesis, Vanessa, Sasha's door opened, and she waltzed in like a model on a catwalk.

"Hey ladies, sorry I'm late."

"No problem, grab some carpet," Sasha responded, then continued with, "Never have I ever flirted with someone more than 10 years older than me."

Vanessa and April took a drink.

"Never have I ever been a friend with benefits," giggled April.

No one took a drink.

"Never have I ever slept in the buff," I said.

"Eww," said Vanessa. "That's something I definitely didn't want to know about, Viola."

"These statements are so lame, let's get to the juicy deets," Vanessa clapped her hands together excitedly.

I couldn't believe that she thought it was gross to know about sleeping nude, yet she thinks the who line of statements were stupid. My guess was that she couldn't handle not having some type of leverage over the rest of the girls, so she decided to change the game in her favour.

"Sounds like fun," Sasha agreed, with an already slurred voice.

"Great! I'll go first." There was an evil glint in her eye, so I braced for total annihilation. "Never have I ever made out with someone in a hot tub."

April and Sasha took a drink.

"Never have I ever looked at naughty pictures," said April.

Shelby winked at me, then took a drink.

"Seriously?" I asked, tittering into my glass.

As the night progressed, we all started rattling off statements in order by going around our makeshift circle one by one.

"Never have I ever bought lingerie."

"Never have I ever been to an adult store."

"Never have I ever watched a movie because I knew it had nudity."

"Never have I ever played strip poker"

Thankfully I wasn't getting that drunk because a lot of the statements didn't apply to me.

Vanessa sat back against the bed and kept her drink away from her mouth, then said, "Never have I ever had a one-night stand." Surprise, surprise, she never did anything out of the ordinary, which was most likely why she had a hate on for anyone who did.

Shelby elbowed me. "April's not the only one who has to take a drink."

My face heated up at the accusation, but since she called me out in front of everyone, I had no choice but to take the drink. She was so going on my shit list after tonight.

"Oh my god, seriously? The Captain V of Virginity lost it on a one-night stand? That's so cliché."

"Whatever, Vanessa. As if you even know the definition of cliché."

"Alright, it's time for me to go."

I got up and headed for the door. I really didn't want to act like a child fighting over toys in a sandbox, but I was still sensitive over what happened between Rob and me. I was also peeved at Shelby for not allowing me to avoid the question in mixed company. Vanessa was like a dog with a bone, and I knew that the results of this game would not remain within these four walls. I gave it a couple hours and the whole school would know that I lost my virginity during a one-night stand.

"Poor baby," Vanessa taunted.

"We've all been drinking tonight, so I'm not going to dignify that with an answer," I replied, shutting the door behind me.

I was halfway back to my room when a drunk Shelby smacked into my back.

"Vi, I know you're pissed and I'm sorry," Shelby apologized.

"I'm going to give you a pass because I know how you are when you're drunk, but I want you to know that I really didn't want Vanessa to have any more ammunition on me."

"I'm sorry," she sniffed.

"You're forgiven for tonight, but please just watch what secrets of mine you divulge. You know how vindictive she can be."

After shutting the door, I got on my pajamas and fell face first into my pillow, wanting to forget the whole thing.

MIKE

"Are we there yet?" I asked for the umpteenth time. I couldn't help feeling like I was a four-year-old stuck in the family station wagon on a cross country road trip with siblings I loathe.

"We've only been in the car for a half hour," he replied. "The turn is just up ahead you big baby."

I spotted a huge black metal security gate at the end of a winding roadway to the right. Beyond the gateway stood a huge monstrosity of an institution that was more like a fortress than a school. The school reminded me of the boarding school that I went to in England. It was built of red brick with white trimming around the windows. I imagined it being defended by two guards drinking coffee and most definitely eating donuts, cause let's get serious, this whole thing looked like overkill.

It brought back memories of the school in England that my parents shipped me off to as a teenager. They wanted a well-rounded son to take over the family business. I didn't know how it escaped them that they had two more children that could do with a similar education. If they would have sent them away like they did with me, maybe my siblings would actually have a mind of their own.

"You're an asshole."

"It won't be that bad," he made a sad attempt to assure me.

"I have no idea how I let you talk me into these things. What made me think being the partner of Chief King's son a good idea?" I joked.

"It's not going to be that bad."

"I really don't feel like dealing with a bunch of hormonal teenage females, all while nursing a hangover."

"I thought you liked dealing with females."

He was right, but I had no desire to entice any of these high schoolers into my bed. That just seemed four ways from crazy. In fact, I wouldn't have taken Vi home if I would have known her actual age either.

"A school full of jailbait doesn't sound like the best way to spend the afternoon." I groaned, knowing that a gaggle of teenagers equals giggles and a migraine.

"You're the one who wanted to down a half a bottle of Jack, trying to avoid the bunny that wanted to jump your bones," Reed teased.

"You sound jealous," I retorted. "I told you that you were free to have a crack at her."

"And I've told you I don't do sloppy seconds," he responded. "Besides, she registered an eight on the crazy stalker-o-meter."

"She probably would have been a sloppy first," I responded, remembering how she hung all over Roger from Precinct Four.

"I'm not a consolation prize. Besides, I don't need your cookie crumbs to get laid. I can do that all on my own."

I laughed.

"So why did we get volunteered for this?"

"My dad wanted to make sure that we spoke to my sister's class because they are one of the largest to go through the academy in years. He said that enrollment is down across the board and we need to find new ways to recruit. So why not go to the future graduating class of one of his daughters."

"I bet your sister is going to love being singled out," I responded.

"Vi doesn't care. She loves that we're all in law enforcement. I wouldn't be surprised if she doesn't either wear the badge or marry into the badge. Either way, I think she'll do something in line with the family business." Reed responded.

Hearing the name, he just called his sister made my blood run cold. For eight years I had only heard his sister be called imp, but now she had a name and it was eerily similar to the name of the woman I took home three months ago.

It couldn't be...

WE PULLED through the gate and parked in front of the school. Walking through the hall brought me back to the time I spent in England. My parents thought that they were making me stronger by sending me away. They were, but what they didn't know was that they pushed me further away from them and made me realize that their belief system wasn't my own.

Essentially, they made me who I was today.

Strong, independent, and so sick of the elitist system that they wanted me to marry into and accept as my own.

"I just need to go and talk to the principal and then we can go and walk around until the presentation starts at eleven."

"Okay, sure man. I'll just go and walk around a girls' school aimlessly. That won't look weird or anything."

I really didn't want to walk around this school without him. Who knew what would be waiting around the corner for me? Teen girls were a nightmare, especially ones like my sister Claudia's friends. In fact, I was positive that she mentioned her friend Vanessa went to Sacred Heart. I hoped my memory was incorrect, but I doubted it.

"Don't be such a pussy. You're wearing a uniform. I highly doubt anyone is going to think that you're up to something nefarious."

"I wasn't considering them believing that I was. I was considering being accosted by these restricted Catholic school girls who would likely be obsessed with a man in uniform."

He laughed. "You're priceless. I'll be back in ten. Try not to get anyone pregnant before I get back. That would look bad on the comment card."

"I haven't heard any complaints so far. My comment cards will be stellar," I winked.

"Don't even joke like that, my sister goes to school here."

He punched me in the shoulder and then took off down the hall.

VIOLA

"Oh my God, Vi!" Shelby screeched.

"What?" I stage whispered.

"Didn't you hear?" She vibrated with excitement before bouncing into the seat beside me. I couldn't figure out what at this boring institution would get her so tied up in knots.

"Hear what?"

"Seriously! You should know this shit, with your dad being the Chief and all," she taunted.

"Just spit it out already, Shelby," I hissed. "The teacher will be here any second and I can't afford a detention."

"Two cops are coming to give the school a presentation on the dangers of university life. Kelsey said they're hot as hell. What if one of them is your Rob?"

"He isn't my Rob," I sighed. "I sure hope he's not here, cause he thinks I'm already in university."

I only assumed he thought I was in University, but the truth was that he never asked if I was. He only asked for my identification after he discovered it was my first time. I actually found it interesting that he never saw my last name on the identification. I only wished he never lied to me about his name. It made me think he had other things to hide. Like what if he was married? The thought of him finding out I was still in high school wasn't the sole reason for my fear of seeing him again.

As much as I tried to avoid my feelings, I hadn't been able to get him off of my mind for the last month, and if I saw him again, I didn't know what I would do. I knew he was a cop when I slept with him, but with the unspoken rules of a one-night stand, I doubted I would ever see him again. I was due to graduate in a few months, and I fully planned to attend a school in another province. As much as I loved my family, I felt this need to escape and alleviate the expectations of being the youngest of the King family.

Ding. A soft ping sounded, followed by the scratchy voice of the secretary making an announcement, "Viola King, please report to the Principal's office. Viola King, please report to the Principal's office."

"Ooohhhh," the girls in the class chimed.

Great, now they all thought I was getting in trouble. Maybe I was?

"Shut up you people," Mrs. Warner commanded. "Get a move on Miss King, you heard the announcement.

I sped down the hall in the direction of Principal Wexler's office. She was a stickler for schedules and hated when anyone wasted her *precious* time. With my head down, focussed on the possible reason for getting called to the office, I wasn't paying attention. I rounded the corner and ran face first into a familiar rock-hard chest. My gaze wandered over his body, committing everything to memory one more time.

Of course he's wearing a uniform.

"Hey there, beautiful, are you okay?"

The timbre of his voice sent shivers down my spine, causing me to take a moment to react to his question.

"Well, I don't think I'll need plastic surgery, at least not this time," I joked. "However, I won't guarantee my nasal structure the next time I run into your statuesque torso."

"Statuesque torso?" Rob questioned with evident humour in his voice.

"First thing that came to mind." I flashed him a huge smile.

He returned a smile so wide it reached his eyes. Deep down I hoped it was an indication that he recognized me.

"Hey, I had no idea you were one of the teachers here."

Yes! Wait...

A teacher...?

Damn.

I glanced down at my shoes, as I made the realization that even though he looked at my identification that night, I wasn't memorable enough that he could recall how old I was.

"I'm not a teacher," I replied.

A sinking feeling in my stomach made me wonder just how many women he had been with since me that he couldn't remember I had just turned eighteen the night I was with him. Especially now, since he most definitely believed I was much older than I actually was.

"One of the counsellors then?" He questioned.

"Nope, not a counsellor," I responded with a tilt of my head.

"You're not the receptionist, because I left my partner talking with her a few minutes ago," he responded, touching his chin in thought. "So, what exactly do you do here?"

"I'm a student," I answered.

"You're joking, right?" He muttered with disbelief.

"I'm not."

"Please tell me you're eighteen, at least." He ran his hands through his hair and glanced at the ceiling in distress.

"Don't worry, I'm not jailbait," I joked, not wanting to bring up the fact that he knew how old I was and conveniently forgot or didn't care. Then the green monster raised her head and had to reply, "Just how many teenagers do you have sex with that you don't remember looking at my ID that night?"

"Are you being serious right now?" He groaned, throwing his head back and looking at the ceiling like he was in pain.

"I'm sorry," I blushed. "My sickly twisted sense of humour comes out when I'm nervous."

His head turned back towards me; eyes lit up. "I'm making you nervous?"

"Have you looked at yourself?" I waved my hand from his head to toes dramatically.

"Every morning when I wake up, and at least twice more before breakfast," he replied with a chuckle.

"Hot and egotistical, excellent combination for a cop," I responded.

"So, Viola, isn't there something in the rules at this school about loitering in the hallway?" He inquired.

"Shouldn't you be reading my rights before interrogating me, Officer Rob?" I asked, putting my hands on my hips. I couldn't help but notice his eyes linger on my legs and the barely-there skirt of the uniform we were forced to wear at school. If I had my way the uniform would be much more comfortable and less revealing.

A place like this that placed value on chastity and purity shouldn't make their young girls dress in revealing skirts. I found it hypocritical and off-putting.

"Imp, why are you calling my partner Rob?" the familiar voice of my eldest brother Reed interrupted before he could answer.

Rob and I both spoke at the same time. "Partner?" "Imp?"

"Do you guys know each other, or something?" My brother asked, sounding suspicious.

"He was looking for directions to the bathroom," I quickly responded before Rob could, in order to take control of the situation and hopefully disarm my overprotective sibling.

"Uh, yeah, I gotta take a leak, man." Rob agreed.

"Okay…" Reed dragged out, as he narrowed his eyes. "Mike, you've got two minutes until we're needed in the auditorium for our presentation. Apparently, Principal Wexler heard that the Chief's son and brother of their next valedictorian would be making an appearance. She made our lecture mandatory for the whole school."

"Great." Mike or Rob, or whatever the fuck his name was, responded.

"I gotta go," I told Reed as I quickly made an exit.

Halfway down the hall, I heard footsteps behind me, but I don't think anything of it because I was at school. It could be anyone following me. Someone could be late for class and heading in the same direction. What I don't expect is for Rob/Mike to grab my arm and whip me around to face him.

"Ow…what the fuck?" I hissed.

"I didn't mean to pull you so hard," he responded, apologetically.

"I have to get to the Principal's office, and you really don't want Reed to see us talking. He's like a dog with a bone and won't give up once he gets a scrap."

"Are you okay?"

"My arm hurts, but I'm positive I'll be okay."

"No, I mean, since that night," he clarified. "You snuck out before we could talk."

"Wasn't that what you were planning to do?" I asked, wondering if he would tell the truth.

"I won't lie, that's my usual M.O. I already broke a couple of my rules that night. I didn't want to make it a trio of discretions."

"Rules?" I asked, curious as to what types of rules a man like him would have. I thought he would have been the one to throw the rule book out the window when dealing with the opposite sex. Especially if he was anything like the stories I had overheard from Reed.

"I never take a bunny to my house," he answered.

"You go to theirs?" I asked, wondering what made me different?

What would make him break one of his rules and bring me to his house?

"No, that would bring a new set of uncontrollable variables," he smirked. "I use hotels."

"How romantic," I choked out.

"I thought you knew by now, I'm not romantic. I'm just a guy who likes to fuck."

I clenched my thighs together, reminiscing about the way he talked to me the night I gave my virginity to him. He was all man, nothing like the boys I was used to. Just listening to his voice made me want to beg him to defile me in the janitor's closet. I hadn't slept with anyone else since him, by choice, but I would set aside my feelings to see if he was as good as I remembered.

"What's the second rule?"

"I don't do virgins," he deadpanned.

"Well, I think I can attest to the fact that you do them, and you do them very well."

He barked out a laugh that echoed through the hall, catching me off guard. For a moment I almost forgot I was at school.

"Fair enough," he agreed, shaking his head. "But I still broke that rule."

"I never told you that I was a virgin until after the deed was done, so breaking that rule was my fault," I giggled.

"You definitely are naughty girl." Mike winked. "Too bad there isn't somewhere private that I can throw you across my lap to spank you until you're nice and pink."

Blushing, I choked out my next question. "What's rule three?"

"I never, and I mean ever, go back for a second serving. I'll go all night and then leave before my guest wakes up, but I never go back for morning sex," he admitted. "I was going to sneak out, but after my shower I decided I wanted to get your number."

"I heard you banging around in the kitchen, cursing that you couldn't find any paper. Then I heard the shower, so I ran," I confessed.

"So, what do you think of us exchanging numbers now?" He pulled out a business card, wrote a number on the back and passed it to me. "That's my personal cell phone number. Now you have a way to contact me."

"I'm not allowed to have my cell with me during the day, but I can text you my number as soon as I get back to my dorm."

"You live here?" he asked, surprised.

"Yeah."

"Doesn't the Chief have a house big enough for the two of you?" he asked.

"Yup," I responded, heavily enunciated the p, even though I didn't want him to ask further questions.

"So, do you come home every weekend?"

"Not every weekend," I responded, glancing at my watch. I cursed under my breath. Being the valedictorian gave me a tiny bit of leeway on days like today, but I couldn't take advantage of the privileges allotted to me. I needed to get to Principal Wexler's office, pronto.

"You're late for class now, aren't you?"

"I'm sorry," I apologized, then explained further, "I was supposed to go to the Principals office like fifteen minutes ago. I'm actually surprised they haven't called me again on the intercom. Principal Wexler is a real stickler for timelines and hates when people mess with her schedule."

"No big deal. I should get back to your brother before he thinks I fell in."

I giggled. "You fall into the urinal often?"

He held his hand over my mouth. "Shush you."

I licked his hand, shocking myself.

"Get going," he gruffly responded. "I wouldn't want you to get detention for wasting time with me.

"Yes, sir," I replied, causing his eyes to smoulder with intensity. When I stepped past him, his hand smacked with my ass.

Did he seriously just spank me?

Startled, I glanced down the hall to ensure it wasn't witnessed by anyone of importance, like my brother. Then, I continued walking to the office swaying my hips to draw his attention to my ass. The newly discovered adrenalin junkie in me wanted him to know what he had been missing for the past two, almost three months, and I really wanted to entice another night or three of passion out of him. Halfway down the hall, I coyly glanced behind me, hoping he was still watching me. When our eyes met, I knew I had fallen further down the rabbit hole.

"Did you talk to him?" Shelby questioned, as we walked to the gym for my brother's presentation.

"Talk to who?" I asked.

"Your brother, silly! That's why you were called to the office, right? In Home Economics, Ms. Wilson mentioned that your brother was one of the officers coming to lecture the school on the dangers of college life. Apparently, they're also here for some recruiting? Aren't there already enough cops out there?"

"Yeah, Reed was out there with his partner." I closed my eyes, still not believing that the guy who took my virginity was also the same person that Reed had talked about for eight years.

One month into Reed's education at the police academy, our brother and his identical twin, Rowan, overdosed. It almost destroyed Reed. If it hadn't been for Mike, I think he would have quit the academy and gone into an even deeper depression. Fern and I were the only siblings that hadn't met Mike yet, which was why I had no idea who I was sleeping with that night.

"Who's his partner?"

"Rob, or rather Mike is my brother's best friend and partner."

"Shut up!"

"Yup. Rob's name is actually Mike and he's been my brother's partner on the force since they graduated from the police academy."

"Girl, you really stepped in the shit this time."

"I didn't even know who he was," I replied. "That's the point of a one-night stand. Or at least I thought that was the point. Now I'm not so sure. Everything's changed now that I know who he is."

"So, are you gonna do him again?" She asked, almost jumping out of her skin.

"Maybe," I answered, not sure of what would happen.

What if the only reason he gave me his number was because he didn't want to offend his partner's youngest sister?

"Wait, Vi!" Vanessa disrupted my revelry like she suddenly had an epiphany and invented the vaccine for cancer.

"What?"

She pointed to the stage. "That's your brother up there, isn't it?"

"Yeah, why?" I asked, bracing for the worst.

She tugged the sleeve of my school cardigan. "You have to introduce us."

"Why?" I asked, hoping she wouldn't go the direction I thought she was going. There was no freaking way I would allow her to sink her claws into my brother.

"Because! If you introduce us, and say that we're friends, then he'll be more receptive to my advances."

"Aren't we friends?"

Deep down I knew weren't, but now I was having some fun with the audacity of her train of thought. In fact, I wished her train would derail and take her bitchy ass with it. May a fiery inferno rain down from above and smite this fake plastic tree from the planet. Some people shouldn't procreate; her parents should definitely have used a contraceptive.

The whole spit versus swallow debate was fresh in my mind, and her mother most definitely should have spat her nasty ass out before she was conceived.

"Of course we are!" She gushed. "Vi! I can't believe you think we aren't friends. We're two steps from being BFF's."

Shelby failed to hide the sound of her retching.

MIKE

Annoying giggles echoed throughout the room.

"All right, quiet down everyone," commanded the prim and proper woman standing at the podium, dressed in a black business suit. Immediate silence followed.

"Thank you, Principal Wexler." Reed addressed her.

Ah, that was who she was.

I couldn't believe this old crone was the one who hit on Reed. When he came out of the office, he confessed she had laid it on thick and he couldn't wait to get out in the hall. He had been known to take home questionable women, but most definitely had never taken home someone close to his mom's age. There was no way he was into stuffy women who lived and likely slept in her business suits.

"When I approached Chief King, he offered two of his finest officers to come and give you a special presentation about the dangers facing female students at post-secondary institutions. I realize not all of you will be graduating this year, but I believe the information can also be applied to your daily lives since we live so close to a heavy populated city. Now I'll hand the floor over."

Reed moved up to the podium and set down his notes, then addressed the room. "My name is Officer Reed King, and this is my partner Officer Michael Sinclair. We've been on the force for seven years, and I've lived in and on an acreage near the city all my life. I'm proud to say that my youngest sister Viola, who is set to be valedictorian, will be graduating from this fine institution this year. My sisters Ivy and Fern also previously graduated from this academy."

Viola blushed a perfect pink, reminding me of the shade her ass cheeks changed to when I spanked her that night.

"I have ten ways that you can all increase your ability to stay safe while at school, or even during normal activities away from your school environment." Reed began.

Why the Chief thought two male law enforcement officers would be the best choice to make a presentation to an all-girls school was beyond me. I understood the concept of appealing to their demographic to fill the ranks, but the task would have been better suited to female officers than us. Rather than listening to the dangers presented from drinking at college parties and walking home alone, they were ogling Reed and me. I also felt that female officers would be able to explain what it was like for them.

"The most important thing to remember is to be aware of your surroundings at all times. In a time of technology, it's crucial that you don't allow that next text or cat meme to cause you to get distracted. Wearing headphones will limit your ability to hear a stranger or would be attacker to gain an advantage."

"I'd love for one of them to take advantage of me," a familiar tall blonde in the row below Viola said to the girl beside her.

My gaze strayed to Viola, just in time to see her roll her eyes, bringing a curve to my lips. The first woman to bury herself under my skin proceeded to dig her hooks in further. I broke more than three of my rules when I took her home. If she kept eyeing me like she was, I would have to switch spots with Reed behind the podium to hide the evidence of what she was doing to me.

I chanted over and over in my head: wrinkled grannies, Reed punching me in the balls, losing my job…and so on…

The crazy thing was, Vi was probably completely unaware of the effect she had on men. Like a horny little pimple faced teenager, I almost came in my pants when I ran into her in the hall. I didn't know why I thought she was a teacher, wearing that ridiculously sexy school uniform of hers. For some reason, when I saw her, I completely forgot that I already knew and was hung up on her age.

I interrupted and then suggested, "You should all consider carrying pepper spray, a whistle or taking a self-defence course from your local martial arts facility."

Reed added, "If you haven't taken it before, I wouldn't expect for you to achieve a black belt in Krav Maga like my sister Viola before you graduate, but any form of self-defence would be helpful for anyone. I'll have pamphlets to hand out after this presentation."

Reed succeeded in embarrassing her again and she became even more badass in my books.

If I couldn't stop my eyes from drifting in her direction, Reed would learn our secret in no time. I had already made enough mistakes. How I missed what her last name was on her identification that night is completely beyond me. She was my best friend's baby sister for fuck sakes. Why couldn't I stop thinking about finding the nearest janitor's closet, bending her over, flipping up her plaid skirt and losing myself in her while she continued to wear the knee-high stockings.

She was a fantasy come true, and I needed to get as far from here as possible. I glanced at the generic round white faced clock and realize only thirty minutes had passed since we came here. Reed continued to talk about the dangers of college life, while I surveyed the crowd.

"Female college students between the ages eighteen and twenty-four are three times more likely to be sexually assaulted than other women."

"He can assault me anytime," whispered the same blonde from before.

"Shut up, Vanessa." Viola's friend from the club hissed at her.

Of course, this girl had to be named Vanessa. Now that I looked closer at her, she was the same Vanessa that Claudia had over to the house on several occasions. More than once, she tried to coax me into having sex with her by creating suspiciously convenient moments where I caught her naked. The week before I moved into my new townhouse, I was staying in the pool house. I came home one night to find her sleeping in my bed, completely nude. She made up some excuse that Claudia said she could spend the weekend in the pool house to escape her overbearing parents.

"Robbie! I can't believe you're here!" Vanessa squealed, and made an attempt to touch me suggestively.

She was closely followed by her friends, which explained why she was so exuberant with her greeting.

"Robbie?" Reed eyed me with a raised brow.

"Ness, you know I don't like being called Robbie."

"But that's what your name is, silly," she responded.

"Because you know me so well," I replied sarcastically.

"I've been naked in your bed; I think that qualifies as knowing you well."

All of her friends sighed dreamily in envy. I couldn't let her get away with what she was insinuating though. She was still under eighteen and there was no way I would let her endanger my employment or get me charged with some ridiculous statutory rape charge. Especially when I had never, nor would I have ever touched a hair on her head, or any skin on her body.

"What is your problem?" I growled. "What exactly are you trying to accomplish? Do you realize what you're implying by twisting your words into blatant lies?"

"You and I both know it's the truth," she answered, as she pulled her sweater down by the bottom hem, so that her cleavage was on display.

All of her friends giggled in hysterics.

"Okay, Vanessa. Let's get something straight. You and my sister Claudia are friends. You and I don't really know each other at all."

"I've known you my whole life, Robbie," she argued.

"Firstly, If you'd known me your whole life, as you claim, then you'd definitely know that I never go by my first name. Secondly, you break into the pool house when I'm staying there, stripping off all your clothes and crawling into my bed doesn't count as us knowing each other in the biblical sense."

She immediately switched tactics and sets her sights on Reed.

"What about you, Reed?" She perused him like a side of beef hanging from a hook at the butcher shop. "I've definitely known you all my life."

"I highly doubt that. Vi didn't start going to this school until seven years ago. I don't know what kind of math they're teaching at this school but seven doesn't equal seventeen," Reed responded. "Seventeen most definitely isn't an age that I'm interested in. Now, if you don't mind, we need to get back to our presentation."

"Awe, guys," Vanessa whined, jutting out her hip and chest.

"Come on Vanessa, let's just go," one of her friends begged. "I don't know what you're trying to do, but I don't' want to get arrested for harassing the police. I also don't want to get detention for annoying guests of Sacred Heart. Principal Wexler would blow a gasket."

"Fine. I've tired of this. Let's just go," Vanessa huffed, then turned and marched away, followed by her gaggle of geese.

Reed laughed and then said to me, "That chick is super annoying. She's right behind Vi in the race for valedictorian, and she does everything possible to discredit Vi. I also have a suspicion that she's bullying her, but Viola would never tell me if she was."

VIOLA

Seeing Vanessa draped all over Mike in the hallway was the last thing I wanted to witness when I came out of the gymnasium for our break. I immediately dragged Shelby in the other direction to avoid being jealous.

"What are you doing, Vi? Why are we going this way? Don't you want to talk with your brother and Mike? You know you wanna," she teased.

"I don't need to have yet another discussion with Vanessa and her lemmings," I responded with distain. I was so sick of her attitude.

"Don't let her get to you. You've already had him once," she teased, elbowing me in the side.

"Well, that is an accurate statement." I laughed.

Giggles flooded the halls as the other girls went in their perspective directions for our fifteen-minute break. What I really had wanted to do was talk to Reed and Mike. That wouldn't be happening with Vanessa there. The combination of me being at boarding school and Reed working a full-time shift work for law enforcement meant that it had been a while since I had seen Reed. I felt it was ridiculous since we lived in the same city.

When Shelby and I finally made it to the bathrooms, she went straight for a stall while I leaned against the sink. A sudden wave of uneasiness flowed over me, so I held my hand to my face and noticed it felt clammy. Leaning over the sink, I splashed cold water in my face and breathed deeply. Thankfully the feeling passed quick, but not before Shelby noticed I had the water running.

"Vi, what's going on?" she asked coming out of the stall.

"Nothing."

"Why'd you run the water?" She looked closer at my face. "Why are you all wet?"

She just barely got the words out when I hightailed it into the stall and emptied the contents of my stomach. Thankfully I hadn't opted for the full meal deal this morning, otherwise I would have been evacuating bacon and eggs. Something about the smell of the cafeteria had set me off this morning, so I went back to my dorm room and had a mango Greek yogurt from the mini fridge.

"Don't you dare give me the flu." Shelby held up her fingers in the form of a cross, as if to ward off the ailment. "My sisters are taking me to Cancun for spring break. I can't afford being holed up at home while they're having the time of their lives."

"It must have been something I ate last night. I wasn't feeling well this morning when I woke up," I responded.

"If you're sure," she replied with hesitance.

"I'm sure," I responded. "We should get back to the gym before Wexler has a canary."

"Yeah, let's go."

"OMG. Vi!" Shelby shrieked as she elbowed my arm.

"Shelby! Shush!" I chastised. "Quit taking the name of the Lord in vain. You know what Sister Mary Francis did to you last week."

She cringed, then continued. "But he's staring right at you."

"He is not!" Vanessa argued. "I think you need your bifocals checked, dearie, cause that tall drink of water is mine."

Shelby rolled her eyes, as Vanessa droned on, as usual, with no end in sight.

"He's been totally eye-fucking me throughout the whole presentation. I'm friends with his sister, so we go way back. When I talked to him during the break, he kept finding reasons to touch me." She closed her eyes, tilted her head back and sighed dramatically. "I'm telling you, gals, he totally wants to fuck me. I'm going to give him my number after this presentation."

"If you go way back like you're obviously suggesting, then wouldn't he already have your number?" Shelby asked.

My jaw suddenly ached from clenching my teeth. Vanessa had always found a way to put me down, undoubtedly because we were racing neck and neck for the valedictorian position. She had this misconceived notion that 'daddy' could donate enough money to make up for the five grade points that separated us. I didn't have the heart to tell her that a wallet book wouldn't fix her grades, and that unsurprisingly, she actually had to study for that shit.

"Shut up, loser," Christina snapped.

"Viola, do any of you have a question for us back there?" Reed called me out, putting me on the defensive.

Before I could respond, Shelby waved her hand in the air. "I apologize for disrupting the presentation, Reed, but Vanessa here has been begging Vi for Reed's partner's phone number instead of learning the dangers of frat boys."

The shocked look on both Vanessa and Reed's faces were priceless. Vanessa most definitely had the look that she would be planning Shelby's imminent death. Reed glanced at me and gave a subtle look of disappointment. If I hadn't experienced that expression from him before, I would have missed it. It made me feel guilty that I had placed the suggestion in his mind that Mike had been hitting on Vanessa. When he swung his attention toward his partner, Mike held up his hands in surrender.

"Shelby, you can meet me in my office after this presentation," Principal Wexler reprimanded.

"Yes, Principal Wexler!" she agreed, then saluted. "Ma'am."

"Alright then ladies, we should let these fine young officers head back to their busy lives. I think we've kept them away from protecting the public long enough," said Principal Wexler. She then turned to my brother and continued, "Please tell your father how much I appreciated him setting this up."

After my brother and Mike walked off the stage and exited the gymnasium, we were sent for lunch.

Another meal I didn't feel like eating.

VIOLA

MARCH

Mike's first text came through at around midnight on Friday. After two weeks of waiting for Mike to contact me I had all but given up. Spring break had come and gone, leaving me bored out of my skull. Both Shelby and Chandra went with Shelby's sisters to Cancun. They had a blast; many debaucheries to be had since all four of them shared a room.

My father banned me from leaving school grounds for some reason unbeknownst to me. It didn't matter that I was eighteen already, or that I had the best grades in my graduating class. Nope. Apparently, I was sequestered to Sacred Heart until at least two weeks from now. My thoughts are that it might have had something to do with Ivy's inability to keep things quiet when she was drinking. He told me, and I quote, *You need to focus more on schoolwork and less on parties and friends.*

Whatever that meant.

I wanted to yell into the phone, *I'm currently a shoe in for valedictorian you dictator.* We all knew how that would have went, which was why it only happened in my head while I was sitting on my bed and nodding incessantly. Luckily my dorm mate was with her friends, who unsurprisingly were not my friends.

I was just putting pyjamas on when my cell beeped. Christina, my dorm mate flashed me a dirty look when I grabbed the phone. I refrained from hitting her with the same stink eye. It wasn't like she hadn't gotten a text this late before. I wished we could pick our own roommates, but the only time they do that here is if there are siblings. Ivy and I had the same room until she graduated last year. My dad likely pulled some strings for that arrangement to happen.

Mike: I hope I'm not messaging you too late. I just got off of my shift and wanted to say hi, so…Hi.

Me: Nope, I was just getting ready for bed.

Mike: Really?

Me: Yes, really. So how was work?

Mike: A dozen speeding tickets and a B and E.

Me: Sounds boring.

Mike: Definitely wasn't exciting, but I'll take an uneventful night like tonight anytime.

Me: What's an exciting night for you?

Mike: With a legacy like yours I'm sure you've heard all the exciting stories.

Me: I've heard a few, but I want to know what you find exciting.

Mike: Oh?

Me: Yeah. Tell me.

Mike: That night we met, your brother and I arrested a chick for flashing her tits.

Me: That's what you label as exciting? I thought you'd say high speed chase or a bank heist.

Mike: High speed chases get the adrenaline going for sure, but they aren't exciting for me. I'm too scared of having an accident or injuring the public to enjoy the ride. Never dealt with a bank heist.

Me: So, you're a careful adrenalin junkie?

Mike: I'd hardly call myself careful, considering I'm texting with my partner's sister…that's rather dangerous, knowing your brother.

Me: True. So why do it?

Mike: Call me crazy, but there's something about you that makes me want to know you more.

Me: More than just in the biblical sense?

Mike: Exactly. Although knowing you biblically was pretty awesome.

My mind immediately went back to the night we met. The way that he claimed me and how amazing it was for my first time. Even after he found out that I lied to him about my experience level, he treated me like a goddess. Deep down, I knew we were playing with fire communicating like this, but part of me wanted to see where it would go.

Mike: You still there?

Me: Yeah, sorry. Just thinking.

Mike: About?

Me: That night. I can't get it out of my mind.

Mike: Me neither. No matter how much I've tried.

A thrill shot through me at the thought of him trying to get me out of his mind. Then the logical portion of my brain reminded me of all the times I had heard my brothers talking about getting over someone. Reed, especially after his fiancée left town, was all about the best way to get over someone is to get under someone else.

Me: You've tried?

Mike: Tried and failed. One thing keeps bugging me though.

Me: I'm sorry I lied.

Mike: That's not what's bugging me.

Me: Then what is it?

Mike: Why did you leave without saying goodbye?

My heart leapt into my throat. In that moment I was glad that he couldn't see my face. How was I supposed to answer that question without sounding like the needy little virgin that he probably thought I was. The last thing I wanted to do was scare him off when he finally showed some interest in talking to me.

Me: When I tell you the reason, you're going to think I'm a chicken.

Mike: Doubtful

Me: After years of listening to my brothers' escapades, I assumed you were downstairs to avoid me in the hopes that I would leave, and we wouldn't have an awkward morning after conversation

Mike: I've got to admit, it's the first time that's happened to me

Me: So, I guess I was your first?

Mike: haha…nice one

Me: I'm here all night, folks.

Mike: It's late, I should let you get some rest for school

I glanced at the clock and realized how late it actually was. Even though it was a Friday night, Christina must still really hate me for texting most of the night.

Me: Um, it's Friday. But if you need to go, that's totally cool. TTYL?

Mike: Sure. Goodnight.

Me: Night.

After I finally wiped the goofy look off of my face, I closed my eyes and had one of the best sleeps.

MIKE

A COUPLE DAYS AFTER MY FIRST TEXT CONVERSATION with Viola, Reed and I were out on patrol when a domestic violence call came over the radio. We were in the vicinity, and I absolutely despised spineless wife beaters, so I pushed for us to take the call. Ten minutes later we found ourselves chasing down some asshole that had beaten his wife bloody and then hopped into his car and sped away.

"What is it with these morons that they think they'll get away?" I shook my head and then redirected my eyes to the road.

"I think you summed it all up with the label of moron. It's not like we haven't already run his plate, or that emergency services didn't get his ten-year-old daughter's frantic call about her mom bleeding out on the kitchen floor."

He led us on a high-speed chase down one of the busier city freeways. We followed as close as possible as he weaved in and out of traffic, causing absolute mayhem during the evening commute. Thankfully, the majority of rush hour traffic had receded, but a number of hazards still remained on the road. To top it all off, numerous motorists neglected to either stop or move out of the way when they saw the flashing lights or heard the sirens. It was like somehow, they forgot everything they had learned during their driver's education classes.

During our calls for accidents, it was not uncommon for emergency services to dispatch another unit because of the rubberneckers that just *had* to take another look, lost control of their vehicle and crashed into another motorist doing the exact same thing.

"We're almost at the corner of Memorial and tenth. It looks like he's heading into the downtown core."

"Where the fuck is this guy trying to escape to?" I asked. "There's nowhere for him to go.

Reed picked up the radio for dispatch, then said, "1-2-1-9, we're in pursuit of the suspect involved in the 10-11, suspect is heading south into the downtown core."

"He's doing what morons do," Reed responded. "Up ahead, he just turned left down eighth avenue."

Reed then repeated the directions to dispatch. Hopefully one of the guys from district one would be responding soon.

"Thank God it's not the middle of the day," I responded.

Eighth avenue was closed in certain sections for pedestrian traffic during the day. It was open to vehicles only from 6:00 p.m. to 6:00 a.m. If this idiot would have driven down the road during the day, we would be looking at multiple injuries to the people who walk there. It made me imagine one of those police shows where the evading suspect drove up onto the sidewalk and took out fruit stands and pedestrians in his wake.

It never turned out well for the citizens, or the perpetrator. I often wondered if these guys had ever taken a moment to watch one of those live police shows.

"Over there! He just jumped out of his vehicle and ran into the building."

"1-2-1-9, suspect exited his vehicle and entered the Telus Convention Centre at eighth and first."

We parked our vehicle and chased the suspect on foot into the building. People screamed and mother's with strollers ran out of the way. Another patrol car responded and came in from the back to block off his exit. Lucky for us this time we apprehended him without incident. When we finally got a look at the guy, he was covered in his wife's blood and the buttons on his dress shirt had all but popped off.

When we got back into the patrol car, I said the first thing that came to mind. "I need a drink."

"Me too, brother, me too," Reed responded.

I wondered if he would feel the same if he knew I was talking to his sister behind his back.

The three hours we still had remaining in our shift was filled mostly with traffic violations, and a couple drunk and disorderly. At the end of our shift, we followed up on the wife beater case. We had a bad habit of not letting things go when we clocked out, so sometimes we had to see the case to the end. It wasn't good enough to just make an arrest and fill out the reports. I needed to know that we were making a difference.

It turned out the husband worked at a bank in the downtown core and had lost his job. The wife reported that when he came home, he was drunk and started in on her about the disarray of the house. It likely hadn't been the first time, and I knew if she wasn't willing to press charges or file a restraining order, then it wouldn't be the last.

～

"Have a good night. Try not to spank it too much or you might not have enough tadpoles for the future," I told Reed.

"I come from a huge family, man. I doubt there's any problems with tadpoles from the King descendants. I just hope our girls don't produce multiple eggs at one go," he visibly cringed.

When my mind immediately went to Viola, I mentally slapped myself. Why the hell was I thinking about viola and babies in the same moment? That woman was under my skin further than I thought anyone could ever get.

"That would eliminate the need for multiple pregnancies. Although, I don't know why anyone would want to have seven kids. You guys must have driven your dad nuts."

"He was barely around to be driven nuts. He checked out after mom died. Rowan and I were left to pick up the pieces."

"But you were only eight years old."

"There's a lot that two eight-year-old boys can do if they put their minds to it."

"I suppose," I replied, wondering what type of hard ass expects their young children to fend for themselves after losing their mother. "Look, sorry for bringing it up."

"It is what it is. Sometimes you win, other times you lose. It's how you play the game that matters. All of us might be a bit fucked in the head, but the one thing we've got is each other. I would walk over a thousand burning coals or past African porcupines throwing their quills if it meant saving any of them from pain."

The thought of Viola going through that sort of upbringing made me more interested in seeing what made her tick. Her childhood wasn't much different than mine when it came to parents. Although, I think her dad probably loved her but just checked out when his wife and eldest son died. He was a hard man, but even I could see how involved he was in Reed's career.

"Man, I wish I was as close with my siblings as you are."

"You could be, you just have to work at it. From what you've told me there's already a common ground for you to work from. Your parents sound like they're a piece of work."

"True," I responded, trying to think of a way I could start some sort of dialogue with my siblings. We shared common ground when it came to the completely cold parental units we had.

"It's not going to happen overnight. You have to work at it."

Reed and I spent the rest of the evening drinking and talking about work. Around midnight I decided to call it quits and take my drunk ass home. The taxi ride from the pub took a little over twenty minutes, and the whole time all I could think about was talking to Viola again. The moment I got in the house, I turned on some music and flopped on the couch, then texted her.

Me: Are you awake?

When she didn't answer right away, I texted again to ask another question. I figured if she noticed the text she would answer, if not, then it didn't matter.

Me: Can I call?

Vi: Sure

Me: I had a hard night tonight…

For some reason I just wanted to hear her voice. Never in my history of interactions with women did I want to talk to someone I had slept with. It could have been because of my aversion to relationships, and my I didn't want to discuss the wife beater with her; I wanted her to make me forget all about the scene. I dialed her number, and it only rang once before the call connected.

"Hello," she answered with a sleepy voice.

"Hi," I replied. "I hope I didn't wake you up."

"No, you didn't. I was just reading."

"Studying?"

"No…" she drew out the answer so much that I wanted to tease her to find out exactly what was occupying her time.

"What are you reading?" I asked, then had an epiphany. "No wait, I want see your beautiful face when you answer the question. Let's video chat."

The truth was it had been too long since I'd seen her at the school that I really wanted to. Somewhere deep down I didn't think it was a good idea for us to meet up. The fear of being discovered by my partner lingered in the back of my mind. A part of me didn't trust myself to meet up with her in person, so this was the next best thing.

Or so I thought.

Because the moment she answered, my heart stopped. She was wearing a barely there, skintight tank top and the rest of her body was buried beneath the blankets.

"Okay, now answer my question," I demanded playfully.

"Promise you won't laugh," she responded with a serious face.

"Why would I laugh?"

Colour flooded her cheeks and I immediately knew she was reading some kind of smutty romance. Now, with how cute she looked blushing, I really wanted to hear her tell me.

"My older brothers always bug me about what I read," she confessed.

"Let's just agree that brothers can be jerks, and then you can tell me."

"It's a new genre of romance called reverse harem."

My sister and her friend were discussing new paranormal romance novels and how interesting it was to read. Most of the time I think people read to escape their own world for a moment or two, so why not read a book about relationships that you might not necessarily want for yourself, but that you would find interesting to read about.

"Let me guess, it's called a reverse because instead of a man having the harem, the woman does?" I asked, wanting to see if her face would flood with colour again. She was unbearably cute with a flushed face.

"Yeah, how'd you guess?" she giggled, and it was like music to my ears.

"My sister reads them," I replied.

"You have a sister?" she asked.

"Yeah, I have a younger sister named Claudia."

"Seriously?" She got lost in thought with a faraway look in her eyes. "Actually, I think I might have met her. She was hanging out with Vanessa at the last party I went to."

"Yeah, my sister likes to be out there. What about you? Do you go to a lot of parties?"

I was curious to know just how much of a partier she was. I had a sneaky suspicion that the sweet little Viola that Reed thought she was might have been a bit of a stretch. To me she seemed a bit closed off to certain people, but to others, not so much.

"Yeah, I go sometimes," she responded. "However, apparently since my sister can't keep her mouth shut about me going to the club for my birthday, my dad has removed my off-campus privileges until next week."

"Are you sure she told him?"

"Someone let it slip." She ran her hands through her hair and sighed. "I haven't even gone out anywhere since that night, so the logical explanation is that he found out about my birthday. Which is completely mental considering he forgot about my birthday and didn't give me my card until a month later."

"Seriously?" I asked. My parents were assholes, but they had never forgotten my birthday.

"Yeah. When he called a couple weeks ago, he basically told me that I need to focus more on schoolwork and less on parties and friends. If he truly cared, he would have known that I am the top mark of my class at ten points ahead of Vanessa for the spot of valedictorian."

"That sucks."

"Yeah," she responded. "But enough of my home drama."

"Alright. So, you're reading a book about a pack of shifters getting it on with one woman?"

"Maybe."

Before my eyes, her nipples hardened as she answered, drawing my attention to her chest. She immediately noticed my shift in gaze and pulled her blankets up over her chest to hide the evidence of her arousal. I couldn't choose which picture elicited more desire because I instantly became hard. In that moment I was thankful I was calling her from my couch and not in the patrol car with Reed.

"That right there is one way to make me forget everything that happened tonight."

"Shush, you," she replied shyly.

"It's nothing I haven't seen before," I teased.

"That was different," she responded, loosening her grip and then smoothing out the blanket. By the look on her face, she still had every intention of hiding her goods for the rest of the conversation.

We talked for several hours about everything and nothing. When I hung up the phone, I knew I had to see her again in person, but I just didn't know how I was going to make it happen. My relationship with Reed would likely not withstand the budding relationship with his sister, so I had to tread lightly. My mind kept telling me that I needed more time with Vi to decide if it was worth it, even if my heart told me to go full steam ahead.

When my head hit the pillow that night, I had one of the best sleeps ever.

VIOLA

"Okay, that's it!" Shelby groaned theatrically and threw her pillow across the room. "We're going to a party tonight."

"I don't feel like going," I sighed.

For the past couple days, I hadn't been myself. It felt like I was coming down with a bug. I really didn't want to attend a party and spread whatever was wrong with me to a bunch of people who were drinking. It was easier to avoid going out when we were at Sacred Heart. The curfew and recent random bed checks tended to make it more difficult to leave or get out of line.

"Come on Vi!" Shelby whined. "You've been nothing but a bump on the log for the last week."

"He hasn't called since last week," I whined.

"He'll call again," she reassured me.

"What if it was something I said?" I asked, not really wanting her to answer. I recalled seeing Mike for the first time in a couple months when he was at the school. Then my negative self-esteem raised its ugly mug. "Maybe he didn't like what he saw?"

"Vi, you gorgeous, colossal idiot. First of all, you've already seduced that sexy hunk of a man once. Secondly, he was the one who initiated contact again. Thirdly, if he doesn't call again, then it's his loss."

"You really think so?" I asked.

For the first time ever, I second guessed everything I said and did. I only seemed to do that when it came to him. I was normally a confident and headstrong woman with a plan. My next five to ten years were planned out, then he showed up and smashed through all my defenses. Mike turned all the self-confidence I built over the years up on its head. I was falling for him, hard. I honestly didn't think I would ever see him again after he took my virginity. When I did, I started to believe there could be more between us than that night. Sure, it was a problem that he was best friends with my brother, but I hoped what we could have would transcend that tiny detail.

"I know so. You're smart, beautiful and funny. Who in their right mind wouldn't think you were a fabulous catch?" she responded.

"With that glowing review, I'll say yes to your request."

"Is he the only reason you don't feel like going out tonight, Vi? You seem a little pale."

"I just feel like I have a little stomach thing, no big deal."

It actually was beginning to be a big deal for me, but I wasn't about to admit it to Shelby. For the past week or so I had been extra tired and occasionally I had nausea with the lovely side effect of vomiting. Like a moron I didn't go and get my flu vaccination this year, so that was probably the reason. I couldn't afford to miss any classes, so I had been a trooper and kept attending no matter how I felt.

"Are you sure? Cause I'd feel like a huge bitch if I forced you to go to a party and you spent the evening yakking in the bathroom."

"I haven't thrown up yet, it's just a weird feeling, that's all."

I hadn't thrown up yet, today that was. At least I hoped it was just a weird feeling and that it would go away as soon as it came. The people at the party wouldn't appreciate their hangover being served with a side of the stomach flu.

"Ok, if you say so, let's get you looking cute."

Shelby launched off my bed and buried her head in my closet. Thankfully, most of my clothes were here because we were required to wear uniforms at school. Even If I was fully capable of dressing myself, having Shelby here felt like my sister Ivy was still around. Ever since she moved in with her boyfriend Tyler, she had placed all of her focus on him. Just like when Ivy was dating him in high school, she threw everything she had into their relationship to the detriment of all of her other relationships. I didn't really have any examples of healthy relationships to compare to, but it seemed wrong to cut off everyone in your support circle to devote all your energy to a boyfriend.

While I reminisced about Ivy, it didn't take Shelby long to find the ensemble she had in mind. She picked a pair of black skinny jeans and a light blue halter top I didn't even know I had. Fortunately, it wasn't the same clothes she dressed me in for Operation V-card. My phone dinged with a text while I was getting dressed, but I ignored it.

"You deserve a gold star," Shelby commended.

"Why?" I asked, perplexed.

"Because you didn't dash over and grab that phone to see if it was him," she laughed. "But that doesn't mean I can't check to see if it was him."

"Go ahead," I responded, knowing that if she looked, she would tell me everything, but still hold my phone hostage so I couldn't respond.

She glanced down at the phone and entered my passkey. Shelby and Ivy were the only two people who knew it because I trusted them with my life.

"It was him; do you want me to read it?" Shelby asked.

"Nope." I made a popping sound as I emphasized the p at the end.

"He said that he's sorry for not texting."

"I don't want to hear it." I held my head high.

I totally wanted to hear it.

"Awe. He said he misses you, but he's been working doubles all week."

"Shelby!"

How could I remain mad at Mike when he sent a text like that?

I thought he was giving me the brush off because he lost interest. I mean, why would a guy like him want to continuously hang out with me? I was an introvert at heart. The type of person to walk into a room and take the chair in the corner so I could people watch. I kept considering all the more experienced women he was spending his time with. We were only meeting for coffee, and each time couldn't have been more platonic.

"What?" she asked innocently.

"You know what!"

"Oh, are you referring to how your mope fest can end now and turn into a reason to celebrate."

The party was packed with teenagers encompassing all ages, some of them were girls I recognized from Sacred Heart, while the rest must have attended public high school. Chandra stood next to one of her friends over by the kitchen island, drinking out of a red plastic cup. I couldn't believe the number of hard liquor bottles, beer and variety of mixes that filled it. She was dressed in a skintight white tank, short red and blue plaid skirt and black fishnet tights. She looked over, saw us, and waved us in her direction.

When we reached the island, Shelby grabbed us both a couple of those cheerful red cups, passed me an empty one and filled hers with a bunch of vodka and a dash of juice. When I filled mine with only orange juice, she gave me a dirty look. I took a big gulp of juice and then stuck out my tongue at her.

"Seriously?" she asked.

"I'm really not feeling well. I only came because you wouldn't shut up about it."

"You're acting like I kidnapped you," she guffawed, and started giggling as if she had been drinking for hours. I honestly didn't see it as that funny, but whatever floats her boat. When she finally got control of herself, she took a huge swig from her cup.

"Well, didn't you?"

"I thought I made a compelling argument as to why you should come tonight," she joked.

"It was compelling enough to be considered felonious." I laughed.

"Oh, shut up, Officer King." She smacked my shoulder, almost spilling my drink. "Let's go get our party on."

"Yippee," I overemphasized with fakery.

"How about once more with feeling?" she replied, then laced her arm with mine and pulled me into the fray.

LATER IN THE EVENING, after spending several minutes praying to the porcelain gods and emptying my stomach, I emerged from the bathroom to be met with a line of teenage girls.

"Oh my God, she was ralphing in there," a high-pitched voice cried out in disgust, grating on my already frayed nerves. "There is no way I'm going to bathe in her putrid party puke stench."

"Grow up," I responded as I knocked my shoulder into hers and pushed my way past her.

"Ru-ude!" I heard one of the mean girls rejects exclaim when I reached the bottom of the stairs.

The bizarre desire to turn around, march back up and give her a piece of my mind surfaced abruptly. With my emotions all over the place I must really be sick. Exhaustion pushed me to search for my friends so that I could get a ride home. My dad was working again, so I couldn't call him. That and he would kill me if I asked him to a pickup at a high school party where there was teenaged drinking.

After combing through the main floor of the house, Shelby and Chandra were nowhere to be found. Ready to give up, I finally spotted one of Chandra's friends leaning against the wall with a beer in her hand. I made my way in her direction.

Maybe she would know where my ride was.

"Vi, hey, how's it going?"

"I'm fine," I replied. "Sorry to bug you, but have you seen Shelby or Chandra?"

"Ah…Shelby's the girl that came with you and Chandra?" I nodded. "She left about a half an hour ago when she couldn't find you and," she leaned closer. "Chandra is in one of the upstairs bedrooms with Jake the snake. I wouldn't go in there if I were you."

I shuddered. "Believe me I won't."

The noise and overwhelming smell of booze wasn't doing me any favours. I needed to find a way out of here and fast. Surprised and a little miffed that Shelby would leave me here after forcing me to come out, I pulled out my cell phone with one person in mind. The decision to call Mike undoubtedly came in my moment of weakness considering I had already dialed his number before I had a chance to second guess myself. I almost hung up, but he answered on the first ring.

"Hello."

"Hello, Mike?"

"Hi, Vi," he replied.

"Hi, can you come and get me?" I asked in a quiet voice, not once considering his ability to hear me would be impeded by the volume of the music in the house.

"I can barely hear you. Where are you calling from?" he asked with concern in his voice.

"I'm at a party."

"Vi, you're at a party? Are you drinking? Are you safe?" he fired off the questions so fast that I couldn't even answer the first one before he got to the next.

"Wow, okay."

"Sorry for the interrogation, I'm just worried about you."

"For the record, I didn't want to come tonight, but Shelby talked me into it."

"Where's she?"

Considering his level of concern, he was not going to like my response. However, since I was calling him for a favour it seemed bad taste to be deceitful.

"When I was getting sick in the bathroom earlier, she left, thinking I had already gone home."

"Vi, did you drink too much? Is that why you were throwing up?"

"I've only had orange juice tonight. I wasn't feeling well earlier today but came anyways when I really should have stayed in bed."

"Okay, that's good. Where's the party?"

"I'm at a house party over near Signal Hill. I'll text you the address."

"I should be there in fifteen. Stand inside in a well-lit area surrounded by people, but near the door. Don't come outside until I text you.

People looked at me funny when I took my place near the door. I felt like a complete moron standing by the door and not drinking while I was supposed to be at a party. Every once in a while, I would move the curtain and glance outside, even though Mike said that he would text me when he got here. With Shelby gone and Chandra getting busy in the upstairs bedroom, I really didn't feel like being at the party. The last thing I wanted was to have to fight my way to the bathroom if I had to throw up again.

The queasiness I had felt earlier kept coming and going, so I hoped Mike wouldn't take too much longer. Chandra still hadn't appeared from the upstairs bedroom, so I doubted it would happen anytime soon. Deep down I knew it was a bad idea to call him to come and get me, but I didn't want any of my siblings to know that I went to this party. Especially considering I was supposed to be at the academy this weekend and some of them have loose lips. If my father found out I left Sacred Heart to go to a party, he would lose it and I wouldn't be allowed home until after I graduated.

Mike's text came through ten minutes later and I headed outside to meet him. When I spotted the police cruiser, I stopped in my tracks. I was shocked to say the least. My heart leapt into my throat as I thought about Reed knowing that Mike was here at the party to get me. When his eyes met mine, I broke out of my trance. As soon as I took my first step forward, he climbed out of the car and opened the passenger door.

"Never thought I'd be getting into the front seat of one of these." I climbed inside.

Before I could, he pulled the seatbelt over me, lingering for a moment and then clicked it in. The breath I was holding finally released when he closed the door. He tapped the hood, walked around to the other side and got into the vehicle. Feeling eyes on me, I glanced back to the party and saw several of the teens looking out the window. I was either going to be the talk of the town because they thought I was being arrested, or I was suddenly a trollop.

"Your dad and your brothers never took you in one of their squad cars?" he asked with confusion evident in his voice.

A lot of people were surprised that I hadn't been in a cop car, or even to the precinct. My dad didn't exactly want his girls involved in law enforcement. He seemed willing to support Fern's application to the police academy. However, after she dropped out, his opposition to us joining the force escalated. It wasn't that he was against female officers, he just didn't want us to be cops. The only things he supported was us learning how to handle a gun and self-defence.

"Dad didn't really want us involved."

"I find that odd, considering he sent Reed and I to Sacred Heart for that presentation. However, I don't think I would want my sister involved either, so it's understandable."

"Yeah, everyone thinks it's weird, but that's our family. Sometimes we're a bit strange and unusual. Thanks for coming to get me."

"No problem." He smiled. "Besides, your brother would kill me if anything happened to you."

"Does he know that you came to pick me up?"

"No."

"No?"

"Vi, how do you suppose I would begin to tell your brother that you not only went to a party, but that you called me to come and pick you up? You technically shouldn't even have my number. Nor should we be texting. He would flip his lid."

"I just assumed that since you picked me up with your police car that he probably knew where you were going."

"I dropped him off at home and I was just returning the vehicle when I got your text."

"I really appreciate you coming to get me so late."

"I'm glad you thought of me to come get you. Not that I mind, but why did you call me? Why didn't you call one of your siblings?"

"I wanted to see you again."

"You did?"

"Yeah."

"Where are you staying tonight? Are you at the farm?"

"Yeah. There's no way they would let me in at Sacred Heart after curfew. I only hope my dad is either in bed or not at home."

"He sleeps through you guys sneaking in and out?"

"He barely knows I'm there half the time."

"I doubt that's true."

I gazed down at my hands. "Can we talk about something else?"

After his eyes scanned my face, he responded, "I'm sorry, Vi. I didn't know."

"It's alright."

"Okay, changing subjects. How's everything going with school?"

"It's going great. I'm not sure if I'm ready for adulting, but I do know that I can't wait until I graduate. The one thing I think I'm ready for is to start my next chapter in life."

"I know how that is."

"Yeah? What was your high school like?"

"My school was nowhere near here," he responded. "My parents sent me to boarding school in England."

"Cool. I wished that I could have gone somewhere like that. Sacred Heart is a good school but being surrounded by girls all the time can really grate on your nerves."

"I can get that. The only thing cool about being at my school was that I didn't have to live with my parents. They only brought me home once a year for a couple weeks during the summer."

When we ran out of things to talk about, we drove in silence until we got to the turn off by my family's acreage. He turned and we drove down the long winding driveway, then pulled up in front of the house. Every light in the house was on, but there were no vehicles anywhere.

"Are you going to be okay?"

"Sure," I mumbled.

He reached over and put his fingers under my chin, turning my face towards him.

"Call me if you have any problems. I don't like that you're not feeling well and you're alone in this house without a vehicle to get anywhere."

"I'll be okay. It's not the first time I've been alone and sick."

"That doesn't mean that it's right."

"I swear, I'll be fine," I responded, then asked, "When can I see you again?"

"I don't know if us seeing each other in person is a good idea."

"Why not?"

"Your brother," he replied.

I thought about that for a minute and couldn't see myself giving up on getting to know him. Not for any reason, just because of my brother. We could at least be friends, and that didn't mean that we had to be anything more.

"We're friends, aren't we?" I asked.

"Look, Vi," he sighed.

From the sound of it, I knew exactly where this conversation was going. I really didn't want to hear it. If he didn't want to see me, then why did he come and pick me up?

I held up my hand. "Save it."

"I'm sorry, but I don't think that we should."

"Not even just for coffee?" I asked.

When he shook his head, the finality in it was obvious. I didn't wait for him to say anymore. Without looking back, I got out of his vehicle and went inside the house. The second I shut the door I wandered into the kitchen and glanced out the window over the sink. The police cruiser sat motionless at the end of our driveway just before the tree line. He was halfway out of our yard, and I wondered if he was leaving or coming back.

My feelings were fifty-fifty on the situation. If he came back, it would mean that he wanted to be around me. If he didn't, then it meant it was over. Either way I was scared of the possibilities.

I had never met someone like him.

The vision lasted for only a moment. His vehicle started moving, further away from me, and even further away from the possibilities of our future.

I had never felt so crushed by anyone like him.

MIKE

A COUPLE OF WEEKS LATER, FOLLOWING SEVERAL LATE-night texts that bordered on what could be considered as elicit, my need to see Viola in person was unbearable. First, I had to get through my shift so I could text her again, without Reed looking over my shoulder. I already put her into my cell phone as Cowgirl. I just hoped she never texted anything that could be easily identified considering notifications came up on the screen of my phone and sometimes Reed saw them.

So far, so good, but I couldn't even begin to think of the jabs I would get if he saw the identification come up as Cowgirl.

Then if he ever found out who Cowgirl really was…World War III.

"So, what's been going on with you lately?" I asked my partner.

"Nothing."

"You've been a bit spaced out lately? Is everything okay with your family?"

I didn't know what was going on with him, but I had known him for almost eight years, and he was acting weird. A couple of times when we were out for drinks, he took off just after receiving a text or a phone call. The crazy part of everything was that he left the room when he received the calls. He never did that before. That right there made me realize he was hiding something.

"My brothers are all doing great, not too sure about my sisters though."

Sisters?

I immediately perked up.

Was there something going on with Viola that I didn't know?

"What's with your sisters?"

"Fern barely ever comes home, and my dad doesn't say a word about it to me. Ivy has distanced herself from us by throwing herself into her relationship. I give it another month before her putz of a boyfriend screws things up again. Then there's my youngest sister. She just turned eighteen and it's like everything with her behaviour has changed. She's going to the clubs we go to, house parties, and leaving school without my dad's permission."

"I can't believe I've never met Fern. What's her deal?"

"Well, you know that we only see her twice a year."

I nodded.

"I thought by now she would have come home permanently, but instead she's travelling the world doing who knows what. She's really quite secretive about everything. I can't help but wonder if she's doing something that she's ashamed of and doesn't think that she can come home."

"Do you really think after being raised like you were that she would be a criminal?"

"Not necessarily. Although there are similar situations where women that haven't had a good male role model in their lives can turn to others to seek out that relationship. I've done some checking into the places that she's been, and they have high rates of organized crime."

"You think your sister's in a gang?" I couldn't help but to laugh.

"Now that you say it that way, maybe I'm just losing my mind."

"It's understandable, she's your sister."

"It's not that she has to live here or anything, but it's been five years."

"I'm sure it will figure itself out eventually."

"Yeah," I agreed. "About Viola…maybe she's learning who she is without everyone. Last year she had Ivy to keep her company at school and now Ivy is living with her boyfriend."

"You obviously don't know Viola." I schooled my features. "She's a planner. Her only goals in life have been written down and planned out at least for the next five to ten years. She's got a timeline printed on her wall at home, which no doubt has been duplicated on her dorm room wall."

"People change," was the only way I could reply.

There was a point when I was a teenager that I thought I couldn't escape the plan that my parents had for me. Then I came home an spent a summer at our vacation house. Instead of partying I spent my grandfather pulled some strings to get me the placement at the police station volunteering. So, in the evening when my parents thought I was misbehaving, I was doing something productive. Something that led me to the person I was today.

In fact, that exact placement was the reason why I loved my grandfather and respected him as much as I did. He didn't care if I kept up with the family business. He wanted me to do what made me happy. He was the only one who showed up to my academy graduation.

LATER IN THE DAY, when I walked into Java the Hut, I immediately spotted Viola. My eyes were drawn like magnets, unable to ignore her beauty and innocence. She was sitting at a corner table, facing the door, with her head in a book, completely oblivious to all that was around her. She didn't even look up, until after I sat down. Then she did a double take.

"I hope you weren't waiting too long," I inquired.

"Time tends to get away from me when I'm reading, so I have no idea," she responded. She placed a bookmark in her novel and set it face down on the table.

"I've already seen the cover, no use in trying to hide it now." I teased.

"It's just so embarrassing."

"Has anyone told you that you're cute when you blush."

"No," she responded, then looked down at the book.

I glanced at the empty table and asked, "You didn't buy a coffee yet?"

"I don't drink coffee."

"You don't drink coffee?"

"Coffee gives me headaches."

"So, what are you going to drink then?"

"Tea."

"What kind can I get for you?" I asked, getting to my feet.

"Chai Latte, please," she answered with a smile that could light up the darkest room.

"Coming right up," I told her as I headed to the barista to place our orders.

After placing the order, I stood to the side to wait. The whole time I couldn't keep my eyes off her. Viola didn't even notice that I was captivated by her presence. It was beyond me how she turned out so introverted when the rest of her family was so outgoing. She was bookish but wasn't representative of the nerd class. She was a living oxymoron; a woman who at one moment, like the night I met her, was outgoing and the next moment, like right now with her head hidden in her book, was closed in on herself.

I was a complete extrovert. My personality could be traced back to the moment I was shipped off to England. For the length of time I spent there, it was a miracle I didn't come back with an accent. My father likely would have lost his mind and sent me to some voice coach or something as equally absurd. Standing here, watching Viola, I realized we didn't have a lot in common, but something inside of me was willing to try to figure her out.

The barista called my name, snapping me out of my revelry. Viola never stirred at the mention of my name; her head remained firmly planted in the pages of her book. I walked over, placed our cups, Americano for me and Chai Latte for her, in the middle of the table. She still remained engrossed in whatever she was reading. Just before I sat down across from her, I glanced at the cover. Sure enough it was one of those paranormal romance books my sister always read.

"More smut?" I whispered in her ear, causing her to jump.

"Oh my god, don't do that!" she whispered loud enough for the tables next to us to hear.

I chuckled at her reaction, but I wasn't alone in my amusement. By the time I took my seat, her book was hidden from sight and her face was flushed with embarrassment.

"You're still so innocent."

"What do you mean?" she asked.

Pushing her hair back around her ear, I leaned forward and whispered, "I still can't believe you let me, a total stranger, handcuff you to my bed, but you're scared to admit you're reading smut in the middle of a coffee house."

Colour flooded her cheeks.

"I don't know what you're talking about," she responded defiantly, then lost all seriousness as soon as she started giggling. "Leave me alone."

"You're just too easy to bug," I teased. "Besides, I love making your face go all pink when you get flustered."

"Glad I'm here for your entertainment," she responded crossing her arms in front of her. The motion drew my attention as she unknowingly causing her breasts to push out, giving me a little show.

"That you are, sweetheart. More than you know," I responded with a smirk, then quickly glanced back at her chest.

She followed my gaze, then reached across the table and smacked my arm. "Behave," she said.

I feigned injury and held my hand over the area she hit.

"Watch the guns, Rocky."

She threw back her head and laughed. "I hardly even touched you. Believe me, you'd know if I actually hit you."

"I believe it, especially if what your brother said about your self-deefense classes."

She blushed. "I remember watching ultimate fighting on television when I was younger. I don't know what it was about the sport, but it drew me to learn how to protect myself. Plus, ever since I was a little girl, I wanted to be a cop. I thought, hey, why not learn Krav Maga from a young age and then I won't have to worry about it later. Even if I don't become a cop, I don't have to be afraid that I can't defend myself if I ever needed to."

"I wished my sister wasn't such a prissy girl. The only thing she cares about is getting her nails done and going to parties."

"I never was a girly girl. Neither was my sister Fern. I think sometimes I take after her because we are both into reading books and learning new things. She was actually the one who registered me for the classes and took me at the same time as she went every week. She's six years older than me and since she was responsible for me most of the time, she ended up taking me to a lot of those types of things."

"It's cool. What about Ivy?"

"Ivy only went for a couple of years and then quit. She would still come with us, but she usually just watched. She's the only girly girl out of our family. It's weird that we're so different considering we're only ten months apart."

I couldn't help but laugh. For how close they sounded, Ivy and Viola were definitely opposites.

"How many years difference is there between you and your siblings?" she asked.

"Victor is the same age as your brother Alder I think, so six years younger than me, and Claudia is your age, which means I'm eight years older than you. I'm the same age as Reed."

"Wow, you're old," she teased, not realizing she had pointed out one of the many things that was wrong with this situation.

"Definitely too old for you."

"Not if we're just friends," she responded coyly. "We are *just* friends, right?"

"Of course," I responded, then looked at the time. "Sorry, Vi, I have to get to my shift. You going to be around tonight when I get off? Can I call you?"

"Oh, yeah, sure."

After we left, I spent the night trying to focus on someone or something else while I was in the vehicle with her brother.

MIKE

APRIL

Reed looked like he was deep in thought after ending whatever call he was on, so I tapped on the hood to get his attention. He jumped slightly and faced me, something in his eyes betraying his normally calm demeanour.

"Hey man, you mind if we make a short stop?" Reed asked.

"Nah. I've got lots of time on my hands," I responded, knowing he probably had something important to do.

"We need to make a stop at central booking," he replied, shaking his head.

"Why?"

"My sister got arrested last night."

"Viola's been arrested. Is she okay?" I hoped he didn't notice the concern in my voice.

"Viola's fine. It's Ivy that's been arrested."

"That makes sense," I answered. "Vi doesn't come across as the type to get arrested."

Viola and I had been meeting for coffee regularly for the last month. I felt like an ass for keeping things from him, but I couldn't bring myself to break things off with her. Over that time, I had come to know her more and I definitely liked what I learned. She was focussed and determined. She had a plan, and nothing was going to stand in her way. She almost reminded me of myself when I decided to go against my dad and not go into the family business.

"You're definitely right there. She's got charts and schedules drawn up for the next five years of her life. She would never allow an arrest on her record to derail any of her plans."

"What did Ives do to get arrested?" I asked.

"Trashed her boyfriend's car," Reed answered with a smirk.

"Not the Shelby?" Thinking about how obsessed Tyler was with his car I had a hard time holding back my sarcasm. "What a tragedy."

"The real tragedy is that it wasn't Tyler she trashed."

"What does she see in that schmuck anyway?" I asked.

Ivy had been dating Tyler for a couple years. In that time, Reed had introduced me to her. I think he was hoping we would hit it off, but we didn't. There was still doubt in my mind that he would be okay with me and Viola dating though.

"I'm convinced she's obsessed with the idea of being married and having a family, and Tyler is likely the first guy that's been willing to offer her dreams up on a silver platter. I'm almost positive that he's keeping her around until something better comes up."

"That's a shit thing to say about your sister, even if she is freaking annoying."

"You're hearing me wrong. Ivy's a catch for the right guy, even though she's got her quirks. I'm just saying that Tyler set his sights on her when she had barely turned eighteen, knowing that she was the daughter of the Chief of Police. He's got his sights set on some kind of crazy promotion that is never going to happen. That's not the way my father works, and if he did, I'd likely be off the streets and working homicide in a suit."

VIOLA

When Ivy called and informed me that Mike was helping her move home. I couldn't stop the green monster of envy from raising her ugly head. For the last month and a half, I had been meeting him in secret. Yet, she had the ability to spend time with him in the open. They didn't have to hide their friendship. In fact, Reed was the one who introduced them, and part of me wondered if he did that so they would hit it off. The kicker was that I was also keeping it a secret from my sister, the one I kept very little from.

A freight train filled with a million questions drove through my head.

Did she want to be his girlfriend?

Did he find her wildness sexy?

Was I seriously too young for him?

As I stirred the final cup of sugar into the delicious lemonade I prepared to the exact directions of mom's recipe, Ivy stormed into the kitchen. She was on a mission, and I wasn't quite sure what I did to deserve her current focus. I hoped she didn't notice and take offense to my delight over her moving back home. Ivy deserved more than she was getting, and I only wished that this break from her ex was forever. She neglected to tell me anything regarding the reason for her moving home, so I didn't have any idea what happened between them. My only wish for Ivy was to find someone who genuinely cared about her the way she deserved to be cared for.

"What's going on with you and Mike?" Ivy whispered in my ear.

"I don't know what you're talking about," I denied all accusations as I watched the liquid swirl in my pitcher.

"I think you've mixed that enough," Ivy shouldered me, almost making me knock over the whole pitcher of lemonade.

"Watch it, lady," I hip checked her as soon as my hands stabilized the liquidy goodness.

"Tell me the truth, Vi.

"Nooo…" I replied.

"Methinks doth you protest too much," she teased.

"I protest just enough, thank you."

"If nothing's going on, then why can't you two keep your eyes off one another?" she pushed for answers. "All day you've been sneaking glances. If I've noticed, don't you think Reed's noticed?"

"We slept together," I responded, knowing she wouldn't stop until the whole crew heard every word she was saying.

"What?!?!" she screeched.

Mike gazed our way and his eyebrows rose as if questioning what was going on. He could just barely see me through the kitchen window. I shook my head hoping that he would drop it. Seeming satisfied with our non-verbal exchange, he turned back toward his conversation with my brothers. Immediately, I breathed a sigh of relief.

"See, that right there is what I'm talking about." She pointed between the two of us, making a scene. Thankfully her craziness was out of my brothers' line of sight. If only she would shut up.

"Keep it down!" I smacked her arm repeatedly. "What if they hear you yell and come running in here? You know I can't lie to Ash. He's the human lie detector."

Out of all of our siblings, Ash was the only person that could tell when any of us were bullshitting. As a result, my dad would often approach him with the goal of gaining any and all pertinent information. We all tried to steer clear of him whenever we had something to hide.

"Are you sure you know what you're doing, Vi?" she asked, the concern evident in her voice. "Just because you lost your virginity doesn't mean you need to hop in and out of bed with a bunch of different men."

"I'm not." My hackles rose at her accusation.

"You just said that you slept with Mike," she argued. "That makes two guys in a matter of four months that I know of."

"Mike is the only guy I've ever slept with," I countered, hoping she would drop it.

"But that would mean…" she paused, finally grasping the meaning of the situation.

"He's the one that took my virginity," I cleared it up for her. "Now would you shut up about it?"

"Who lost their virginity?" Ash asked, making us both jump sky high.

Ivy's eyes widened in reaction to his sudden appearance. It was just my luck that Ash would overhear the last part of our conversation. Now he was set up with all the ammunition for years of blackmailing if he so desired. After all, that was what siblings were for, blackmail.

"I did," Ivy answered, in a sad attempt to draw his attention away from me.

The kicker was, we all knew when Ivy lost her virginity, and it wasn't yesterday. When she lost it, our dad raged on for days about finding used condoms in his office in the basement. The only reason I never got grounded was because I was at my Krav Maga tournament and he had to come pick me up at the bus station the night after his discovery. That didn't stop him from questioning me to see if I knew who the offending party was.

"Ugh. I don't need a reminder," he groaned. "I walked in on you and Kurt in dad's office. I searched the house high and low for bleach to wash the scene from my eyes."

"You're the one that asked, moron," I pointed out.

"I was only confirming that our sweet little imp hadn't given up the goods yet." He looked me straight in the eyes, trying to disarm me. "Cause if you have, I'd have no other choice than to tell our brothers, and then hunt the bastard down to perform the ultimate smack down."

"Ash, you're a cop now," I laughed. "You can't rough anyone up, no matter how pissed you are at them."

"Vi, grab the lemonade. Those guys out there are probably thirsty after moving all of my shit," Ivy clutched my hand and directed me towards the counter, then took off back outside.

While I gave the lemonade one more stir, to dissolve more of the sugar, I could see her laughing and carrying on with the guys. Watching her outside, I envied the way she floated around without a care in the world. It wasn't that she didn't care, it was more that social situations didn't faze her. I was the type of girl to go to parties and become a wallflower. If I was with my friends, I would at least have someone I knew to talk to. Outside, with Mike standing around, I was nervous about doing or saying the wrong thing.

Even when we would meet for coffee or talked on the phone, I couldn't help being nervous. I wanted to make a good impression. It didn't matter that he only wanted to be friends; if that was all we could be, I didn't want him to think I was boring or a loser. I also didn't want to come across as annoying. My brothers often brought home their friends when they were in high school. They enjoyed teasing me about my being aloof because I tended to be around but didn't insert myself into conversations. I was often shy, until I got to know the people around me.

Ash pulled me aside after I served up the lemonade and whispered quietly. "I sure hope you know what you're doing."

"I don't know what you're talking about."

"Don't act stupid, Vi. Do you think it's a good idea to continue a relationship with Mike when you know that Reed is going to flip his shit when he finds out that he popped your cherry?"

"We're not in a relationship," I responded defiantly. The last thing I needed was for Ash to tell Reed about my illicit relationship with Mike.

"I heard everything that you and Ivy said inside. On top of that, I'm not blind or stupid enough to ignore the lingering looks being exchanged between the two of you, but I sure hope Alder and Reed are. You know Alder can't keep his mouth shut, he never could.

He'd use this information to rile Reed up the moment he gets a chance."

I glanced down at my cowboy boots, and couldn't hold the smile in. In my haste to get dressed, I subconsciously pulled on the same boots I wore the night Mike and I first met. Maybe that was the reason his eyes widened when he saw me.

"What was that smile for?" Ash asked.

"Nothing," I responded, giggling.

"Eww, Vi, TMI. I don't want to be around when disgusting sex memories go through your mind."

"TMI? Are you channelling the twelve-year-old girl inside you?"

He sputtered, choking on his lemonade.

"Shut up."

"That's not what that was. Besides, when am I not allowed to smile."

"When you're thinking about your oldest brother's best friend, and partner. You know, the one you shouldn't have seduced into popping your cherry. That one."

"I didn't know who he was when I did it."

"And that makes this all okay? You knew who he was when you continued the relationship."

"How do you know we continued the relationship?"

"I saw you at the Java the Hut, Vi. You guys were making googly eyes at each other from across the table. There may or may not have been a hand caress or two."

"So now you're following me?"

"I had to meet one of my confidential informants there."

"You meet them at Java the Hut? That seems a little not so confidential."

"I love how this conversation digresses from your risky behavior into me putting someone else at risk. I've been at the job for a while now Viola, I'm pretty sure I know how to keep my informants safe."

"You're right, and I'm sorry. I'll try to make it less obvious, but I won't stop seeing him just to appease Reed."

"If you plan on continuing on with this illicit affair, then you both need to think long and hard about how and when to tell Reed the truth. Don't leave it too long, because sometimes you just can't come back from deception."

"I know."

"If you know, then why are you doing it? Why haven't you marched right up to him and told him the truth about your relationship?"

"I'm not going to tell Reed that I had sex with his friend."

"Of course not, you dummy. That would be ground zero for the beginning of the next Apocalypse."

"When was the first?"

"So not the point, missy."

"I get it."

"Do you really? I don't think you were old enough to remember what all the lies did to Reed. All those times he covered for Rowan; the times Dad covered for Rowan instead of getting the help that he needed?"

"I remember."

"Then how in your mind is this any different? You and Mike having a relationship effects Reed. Whether you can see it or not, it does. Mike was around to pick up the pieces when Rowan overdosed. They have a close enough relationship that could make him more of a brother to Reed than I am. Now tell me what you think will happen when Reed finds out that his best friend is hiding something this significant from him? What will that do to him? What will Mike lose in the process?"

"What am I supposed to do? I really like him, Ash. I think he could be the one."

"The one? Sis, you're only eighteen," he replied in disbelief.

"When you know, you know," was the only way I could reply.

"If he's that important to you, then you need to tell Reed, and I mean yesterday."

"Okay, I will."

"I'll hold you to it. Now let's go join the crew." He threw his arm around my shoulders and ruffled my hair. I swatted his hand away in annoyance.

"Vi, get your butt over here." Ivy called.

Walking back over to join the group, I fixed my hair by pulling it back into a bun. Glancing up, I saw Mike watching us. My stomach fluttered, wondering if he remembered what it felt like to have his hands tangled in my wavy hair while he drove into me repeatedly. Mike smirked as the heat rose to my face. If he didn't know what I was imagining before, he did now.

"Yeah?" I asked, my voice quivering a bit.

"We were having a bit of a discussion," she answered.

"What about?"

"Are you going to carry on the great King legacy or not?" she asked with a wink.

"Why would you guys be discussing that?"

"We were talking about Fern and how she went to the academy but didn't graduate. Ivy won't be following in our footsteps, so you're the only sister left on the docket," Ash replied.

Mike's attention was solely on me, as he waited on bated breath for my response. It was like my response meant more to him than it did to everyone else. I kept my focus on anything and anyone besides him when I responded. We had already played with enough fire today. It didn't matter that we hadn't had a conversation; it was more than obvious that people were taking notice to our interactions.

"I'm not sure what I'm going to do yet. The only thing I know is that my future employment will have something to do with the justice system. I'd like to become a police officer, but if I don't decide to enroll in the police academy, then I will be going to University to take my Criminal Justice degree."

"See guys, told you she's a planner," Ivy commented.

"What's wrong with knowing what you want to do for the next five to ten years?" I asked, curious as to her response. Ivy had never been the type to plan and usually lived a life of spontaneity.

"There's nothing wrong with planning," Mike responded. "I have a degree in law that I don't use as a lawyer, but I wanted more education, so I went for it."

"Doesn't that take like seven years of school?"

"Yes, it's technically seven years of school, but I finished in five," he agreed.

"How the hell did you do that and work full time?" I asked, completely flummoxed. If he finished basically two degrees and worked full time for law enforcement, he was seriously disciplined.

"He's a machine," Alder responded.

"I'm sure he is," Ivy whispered in my ear.

"I didn't have a life for the two years it took for me to complete the law degree. I completed it via correspondence through Nottingham University in England, so I was able to move mostly at my own pace," Mike responded, thankfully completely ignoring Ivy. "For my first degree I had already done several advanced education courses that qualified me for University credit, which reduced the number of credits required for my undergraduate degree."

"That's crazy. I think I really do want a degree, but I don't know if I have the determination to work as a police officer full time and take school full time."

"You can do whatever you put your mind to," Mike assured me.

"I like to fly by the seat of my pants," Ivy cut in. "I have no idea what I want to do. Before today, I wanted to get married and become a stay at home mom. Now I am single, free to roam, and have no clue what the future holds."

"That doesn't mean you can't have some sort of plan," I argued.

"My whole life just went topsy turvy. I'm totally not going to do anything but apply for new jobs and look for a rebound."

"Why would you want a rebound?" I asked, curious as to what her answer would be.

"Cause the best way to get over someone is to get under them," she replied giggling.

"Yuk. Didn't we just have this conversation ten minutes ago? I don't want to know who you're getting jiggy with."

"I never told you who I was going to blow, just that I was going to do it soon," Ivy taunted. Ash immediately gagged dramatically and bent over like he was going to hurl in the grass.

Reed moved behind me and covered my ears. "Guys, young impressionable mind over here," he admonished the group.

I grasped his wrists but didn't remove his hands. "I can hear everything you're saying big bro."

"Ignore them, imp. You don't need to be getting on, or under anyone for another ten to fifteen years."

"You're saying it like I'm going to be incarcerated for ten to fifteen," I responded.

"Then my best advice to you would be to not bend over and pick up soap while your gone," Ivy cackled.

"Ewww, Ives."

"What?" she shrugged her shoulders. "It's legitly good advice."

"Are you speaking from experience based on your one night in lockup? Or were you just watching a marathon of 60 Days In?" Alder teased.

"The answer is no to both of your silly questions," she replied. "I'll have you know I can read too."

"Oh? When did you start that?" he asked, poking further. "It's obvious you have no clue that legitly isn't even a word? How's the Hooked on Phonics working for you?"

"Whatever, you knew what I meant."

"Just because we've all learned how to translate Poison Ivynese, doesn't mean that you should continue speaking it."

Mike's phone rang, so he stepped away to take the call. I couldn't keep my eyes off of him as he had a heated conversation with the caller unknown to me. The giddy schoolgirl inside of me was overjoyed at the knowledge that the person on the other side of the call wasn't a girlfriend.

"Whatever Jerks," Ivy responded, drawing my attention away from Mike. "Thanks for helping me to move. Now I just want to sleep the rest of the day away."

Mike re-joined the group. "Sorry, guys. I've got to go. Parental issues and all that."

"Sure, no problem," Reed answered. "We were all going to disperse since Princess Ivy wants to go up into her tower and have a sleep."

"You're a princess," Ivy argued. "A big burly princess named Regina, pronounced like a part of the female anatomy."

"Ok, Ives is obviously tired. Thank you for all your help with her emergency move," I directed my appreciation to Mike. "I didn't want her to be around that asshole any more than she needed to."

"No problem," Mike responded, then waved as he made his way to his vehicle to leave.

MIKE

As much as it pained me, this journey needed to end. A week passed since we were all at their farm to move Ivy home from her old apartment. I couldn't stop replaying the conversation I overheard between Viola and her brother Ash. I had just dropped off the last box and was walking from the house when I heard him tell her that her and I shouldn't be together. Uncharacteristically, I found myself looking forward to these clandestine meetings we had been having. Although, since hearing that Ash frequents Java the Hut, I decided our final meeting needed to be more secluded.

There was no escaping the reality of what had to be done. We were already playing with fire by meeting every weekend. Reed's suspicion as to why I wasn't up to my usual parade of one-night stands was escalating at an alarming rate and on more than one occasion he almost caught me in a lie. Viola and I hadn't been intimate again since the first night we met back in January. However, the other night when I kissed her we came close to crossing the line again. Something about Viola made me come unhinged, like a teenager discovering his first crush. With that in mind, I felt it was wise to do the mature thing and end things before they went too far.

Before neither of us could reverse our actions.

The conversation we needed to have shouldn't have an audience, and it couldn't wait any longer. Since it wasn't the weekend, I had to find a way to meet up with her at the school. It was a risky move, but to delay the outcome would only result in more heartache. I recalled the stories from Ivy about sneaking out to see her boyfriends and using a pass, so maybe Viola had access to the same privileges.

Me: Hi, you busy?

Vi: Nope.

Me: Are you able to meet tonight?

Vi: I'm at the academy.

Me: Is there a way I could pick you up so we could go for coffee?

Vi: Sure, you can pick me up at the gate.

Me: Will it be okay with the school?

Vi: I'll get a pass, but I need to be back in time for curfew at 8:30.

Me: Perfect. Be there in 20.

The drive took me fifteen minutes, and Viola was waiting at the gate when I got there. She wasn't wearing her school uniform, which was a plus for me, because I didn't think I would get through this night without making another huge mistake. If she was dressed in that skirt and knee highs, I wouldn't be accountable for my actions.

Go ahead and call me a predictable horny male.

I parked my truck off to the side of the road and hopped out. My hand instinctively sought out the small of her back, just above the waist of her skin-tight jeans as I guided her toward the passenger side of the truck. She was definitely not short, but there was something primal about holding a door open and helping a woman into my truck that boosted my ego. It also gave me the perfect opportunity to touch them, not that I should be trying to find any way to put my hands on Viola.

Maybe just one more time?

She blushed and hopped into the truck, quickly securing the seatbelt. I walked around the front of the vehicle, watching her face the whole time, committing it to memory. I knew I would probably see her again after tonight, but it wouldn't the same. She would return to being Reed's youngest sister, and not my anything. Whatever the hell she was now, would cease to exist. The journey to the next town over took us about twenty minutes, after I get in and start driving. No one knew us here, so it was the perfect spot to have our private discussion.

"Why'd we come this far?" Vi asked, sounding curious more than anything.

"I thought we could spend some time together without having to worry about anyone we know coming through those doors," I explained, turning off the vehicle. Viola unclipped her seatbelt and reached for the door. "Wait, and I'll come around and help you out."

"You don't have to do that," she replied softly.

"I want to." *Anything to delay the inevitable.*

"Okay," she responds softly.

Jumping down, I slowly made my way around to her side, then opened the door. She slipped her soft hand into my outstretched palm, sending electricity through my veins. Helping her out of the truck, I fought the extreme desire to pull her into my arms and kiss her until she couldn't even remember her own name.

Why did something right feel so wrong?

When we reached the front door of the coffee shop, I fought the need to convince her to get back into the vehicle. Subconcioulsy admonishing myself, I shook the feeling off and opened the door for her to go inside. The café was virtually deserted, which is perfect because I didn't want to embarrass her by making a scene. We headed up to the barista to placed our order. We both called out our order for chai lattes at the same time, causing us both to laugh.

It's like this woman was made for me.

The chasm in my chest grew infinitely larger.

"What's wrong? Why haven't you said anything?"

"I'm not sure where to start."

"Why not from the beginning?"

"I'm not sure it's that simple."

"All you have to do is say something. That seems fairly simple," she responded softly.

"Let's wait until we get our drinks and sit down."

As soon as our butts hit the chairs, she beat me to starting the conversation. "Spill. What's going on?"

I sighed.

"Seriously, I can tell something's wrong. Might as well spit it out."

"Vi, I'm sorry, but I think this has to be the last time we meet in person."

Her eyes snapped up to mine in surprise. "W-what? Why? Did I do something wrong?"

"No, Vi, that's most definitely not it. You've done nothing wrong. If anything, I'm the one who's doing something wrong."

"I don't understand," she responded, lacing her fingers in front of her and hunching over slightly as if bracing for impact.

How could I have possibly thought anything would work between us when there was so much stacked against us?

"After spending time with your brothers during Ivy's move back to the farm, it feels wrong to keep such a big secret from my partner. Reed's been my best friend since the academy, and I've betrayed him more than once by continuing to have a relationship with you."

"You were the one who pursued this."

"I know, and I can admit now that I was wrong."

"How can you meet with me every weekend for the last month and think that what you did was wrong? Wouldn't you have known that at the beginning?"

"I had a niggling at the start, and I ignored it because I wanted a chance to get to know you."

"And so now that you know me, you don't want to know me?"

"That's not it."

Viola finished her drink and stood up, "Let's go."

"Are you sure?"

"Yes," she replied. "What's the point in dragging out the evening if it's just going to end the same way? No matter what I say to you, you're still going to say goodbye forever when you drop me off at Sacred Heart."

"Okay, let's go."

We walked out to the vehicle in silence. Once we got inside the truck, I drove us back to Sacred Heart, unsure of what else to say to her. There wasn't much I could say. There had never been a reason for me to let someone down easily. I had never found a woman that I had cared about enough about to be concerned with how I broke things off. There was never anyone to break things off with before. Sure, I had dealings with Cynthia, but I honestly could care less what she felt or thought about our relationship, or lack thereof.

When I parked the truck, I turned to address her. "I'm truly sorry for everything, but I need to do the right thing and stop this before it goes any further."

"I don't understand why we can't just tell them. It's not like we're doing anything wrong. We're just friends, aren't we?"

"I don't think we were ever meant to be friends, Viola." I muttered. "I was concerned that this relationship was detrimental to your development."

"Development? I'm not a child anymore, Mike. You of all people should know that."

"You're not a child, but you have definitely not lived long enough as an adult to know exactly what you need or who you should want."

"What if I don't care?" she asked, reaching for me. When I shrunk back, pain flashed in her eyes momentarily and was gone quicker than it had appeared. I hated to be the one to cause her pain, but in the future, there would be more pain if we dragged things out.

"I'm not going to change my mind. Once you get to University, I'm sure you'll find someone else, closer to your age who will sweep you off your feet and you'll forget all about me."

"I'll never be able to forget."

"With time the façade of me that you've built up in your mind will fade away."

"If that's what you want, I'll just go." She opened the truck to get out of the vehicle. When she was halfway out, a moment of regret has me lightly grabbing her arm. "Don't make this harder than it needs to be, Mike."

She twisted her arm out of my grip. Then she used the momentum to hop out of the vehicle, before slamming the door. I let her go without a fight, subsequently watching her walk out of my life forever.

The sharp, stabbing pain in my chest was like nothing I had ever experienced before. All I wanted to do was make it go away with a couple of drinks or ten, so I headed straight for Reed's house. When I pulled into his neighbourhood, every light in his house was on, so I knew he should be awake. Either that or he was gone on a completely improbable bender and he was passed out on the lawn thinking the lights of the house would somehow give him a tan.

I pulled my vehicle into his driveway, shut it off and then went up to the front door. After knocking once, he immediately opened the door, as if he had been standing beside it.

"Hey man, what are you doing tonight?" I asked.

"Nothing."

"Grab your wallet, we're going for a drink or twenty."

"Sounds ominous," he laughed, as he grabbed his wallet and put on a black leather jacket.

"I just need to drink this day away," I responded with a sigh. There was no way I would be able to tell him the truth of why I was upset.

"I'm game if you are."

"Perfect."

VIOLA

"What do two pink lines mean again?" I asked my sister Fern, throat constricting because I already knew the answer, but hearing the words from my older sister would cement the truth in my mind.

Harsh reality stared at me with defiance in the form of a white plastic stick, the two pink lines like a beacon in the night.

I was having a baby.

With my brother's best friend.

The same best friend who only just last week told me he wanted nothing to do with me because I was too young and inexperienced. The same man who was convinced I would find someone more appropriate when I attended University in the fall. The same one who was convinced that being with me was detrimental to my development. I laughed aloud as I considered what he would think having a baby would do to my development.

"The same thing it meant on the last five tests, Hun." She responded, with a laugh.

"This isn't a laughing matter, Fern," I responded.

"It most definitely isn't, but what did you expect. Weren't the first four tests positive too?"

The weekly call from Fern happened at the exact moment I needed to talk to someone. When I saw her name on the caller ID, I immediately picked up. I didn't care that I was currently in the bathroom, staring at the fifth pregnancy test, waiting for my life to change. This morning, I decided to crawl out of the river of denial I'd been living in. I borrowed dad's truck and drove to a neighbouring community and bought a couple boxes of pregnancy tests.

There was such thing as a false positive…I needed to be sure.

For the first time ever, my period was late. It had been like clockwork since my first menstruation. Since I had been stressed out over getting into college and everything that an almost graduating person freaks out about. Stuff like: would I make valedictorian, would I get into the University I chose, where was I going to live, etc. There were just too many things on my mind. Even the breakup or whatever that was between Mike and I weighed on my mind. Reed still didn't know about our mini relationship and his reaction worried me, even if it was over.

The flu like symptoms, followed by incessant hunger for the last week and a half didn't sway me from my self-diagnosis. It didn't take a genius to figure out what the cause is. In my mind, the precautions we took made pregnancy seem impossible, but a quick internet search illuminated the truth that condoms were only ninety-eight percent effective. Lucky me…I seemed to be in the two percent. It was as if the world was punishing me for my choice to lose my virginity to my brother's best friend.

"This can't be happening," I groaned.

The irony of being an unwed mother while attending a girls only Catholic high school didn't escape me. I was a teenage statistic.

I would always be a statistic.

"I hate to break it to you, but you're experiencing one of the consequences of having premarital sex."

"I appreciate your wisdom, Einstein," I responded.

"Considering it took five tests for you to figure out that you're pregnant, I'll take the nickname."

"As if you haven't already had sex, you old fogie." I joked.

"I haven't," she deadpanned, her response almost knocking me off the toilet seat. Here I was dealing with the aftermath of hastily getting rid of my v-card, and my sister, six years my senior, was still a virgin.

"What do you mean, you haven't? Aren't you twenty-four years old? How is it possible you haven't done the deed yet?"

Not that there was anything wrong with it.

"For the exact same situation, you find yourself in. My lack of a steady boyfriend," she responded.

"But, you're you. I find it hard to believe you haven't had a steady boyfriend. All this travelling around the world and you haven't found a sexy foreigner to hit the sheets with?"

My sister had been in more countries than I could begin to count. She was tight lipped about the work she did, but I knew her work was important to her, so I never gave her a hard time about the secrecy.

"I've been on dates, but nothing amounted from them. Although, I'll be honest with you about one thing," she responded, laughing. "I had the same hairbrained scheme planned out as you did. It ended with me being rejected and sobbing my eyes out in the bathroom."

"What happened? Who in their right mind would reject you, you're gorgeous?" My sister Fern was the trifecta of a girl next door: sweet, smart and beautiful. I always looked up to her and was beyond devastated when she moved away.

"It was the graduation party, the final one of the year. I had a crush on this guy from public high school. He was a total bad boy and had slept with a lot of the girls from my class. So, I thought, why not ask him to take my virginity," she sighed, obviously remembering the past.

"Did you actually say, 'take my virginity' to him?" I asked.

"Yes. Like a moron. I had been drinking, and dancing, and later in the evening, I approached him. You know they used to call him the devirginator? That's why I wanted to ask him to do it. He obviously had no issues with having sex with virgins, so why was I any different?"

"What happened?" I asked, wanting to know the whole story.

"We went into one of the bedrooms and started kissing. It was my first kiss too. To this day I wonder if he thought that I sucked at it and that's why he said no," she explained, getting sidetracked for a moment. She took a deep breath and then continued, "so, yeah, we were kissing, and I reached for his belt. He asked what I was doing, and I said I want you to take my virginity. I said I didn't want to go away to school a virgin and that I had always wanted it to be him."

"What did he do?"

"He said that he just wanted to see if I was a good a kisser as he had been told. He said that he never wanted me that way, and that I should find someone else to do the deed, cause he wasn't going to be the one to pop my cherry."

"That's just mean."

"I don't know what I was thinking when I went into that room with him," she confessed.

"First of all, you'd been drinking. Second, you had a crush on the guy, and he seemed like a done deal. It's the same reason I went to Roadhouse. I knew from all of Reed and Ash's conversations that they had no problem picking up women there, so I figured I wouldn't have an issue finding a guy who was interested in sleeping with me," I laughed, looking down at the two pink lines on the plastic stick that would forever change my life. "Now look at me."

"Yeah, I think I'll pass. I couldn't imagine getting pregnant the first time."

"Tell me one thing and then I'll drop it."

"Okay?"

"What's this jerk wad's name?" I asked. I needed to know because obviously this asshole had hurt my sister. If I ever met him, I would punch his lights out for taking away her confidence.

"Jaxon Carter."

I tapped my head. "It's in the vault now."

"Why would it be in the vault?" she asked, laughing.

"Cause if I ever see that sorry sack of shit, I am going to knock his block off for hurting my sister. No one lays a finger on my family and gets away with it."

"Okay, back to your sitch. How are you going to tell dad?"

"I'm not sure," I responded.

Considering I had just confirmed the pregnancy, I had no idea what to do. I planned everything in my life down to the minute up until I met Mike. It all went out the window the night I turned eighteen. I had been spiraling out of control, and it was all because of a boy.

A man.

"Well, you're going to have to think of something soon."

"What am I supposed to say? 'Hey dad, remember the weekend I came home from the academy and you had to work night shift instead of celebrate my eighteenth birthday…well, I got dressed up in skimpy clothes and went to a bar. Oh, and by the way I lost my virginity to a cop. We aren't dating, but you're gonna be a grandpa.' Something like that?" I scoffed.

My father was going to kill me, then Mike. That was if Reed or one of my other brothers didn't beat him to it.

Fern coughed, obviously trying to hide the laugh that almost slipped out. Freaking siblings, always the first in line to laugh at each others' misfortunes.

"Well, obviously you're not going to say that. Are you going to keep it?"

"I don't know yet."

"You don't have much time to wait if you're not."

"I can't have an abortion."

"Okay, that's your choice. What about the father? Are you going to tell him?"

"Yes, but I don't want him to think I got pregnant to force him to be with me. Mike and I are only friends, as he so painfully made aware last Saturday."

"What did he do?"

"I thought he was going to kiss me, but then he didn't. He told me that I was too young to be in a relationship with him, and that it wasn't right for us to pursue anything further than friendship."

"I'm sorry."

"It is what it is, sis. You can't make someone fall in love with you if they aren't willing to."

"That's true."

"Yeah."

"Well, I think you should tell him right away, so he doesn't think you've been hiding things from him. As for dad, you can take some time to figure out what you're going to say to him. There is a timeline, but obviously you're going to have the baby either way, so you have some time, but not a lot of time because you're going to start showing."

"I wish mom was still here." I sob into the phone.

"I know honey, I do too. If I could be there, you know I would."

"I know." I sniff. "So, how's Germany?"

"Okay, I guess. I've mostly been to a lot of boring meetings."

"You haven't seen any sights?"

"It's not all fun and parties, I'll tell you that much. I've been stuck in a conference centre for the most part. We went out for beers at this cool little pub down the street from the hotel. I had a huge stein, but that's all."

"What about the men? Any gorgeous hunks with brother-in-law possibilities?"

"I think you've had enough thoughts of men to last you, hmmm, let's say eighteen years?"

"Hardy har."

"It got you to laugh, didn't it?"

"Yeah, thanks for listening," I sigh. "I really needed to hear your voice."

"I love you, sweetie. Everything is going to work out, I can feel it."

MIKE

My mother's complaining could be heard at the front entrance of the restaurant. How these servers put up with her every weekend was beyond me. They never got paid enough and I knew for a fact that my parents rarely tipped the wait staff. They ran on the absurd assumption that their membership dues supported the employees' wages. In fact, I think the only time I had ever seen my father tip someone here was on the golf course when he had other people watching him.

"You're late," my father greeted in his usual overbearing and judgmental way.

My siblings, to my utter surprise, gave me looks of pity. The first thing I noticed was that family had been placed at a table with place settings for eight people. Which could only mean one thing. My parents had invited the Milton family, which to my utter dismay, included Cynthia. For the past four months I had successfully dodged most of her calls. For some reason, she had it in her head that we would be engaged soon. Likely because my parents invited her to my first brunch of the year.

"It's only eleven thirty," I countered, then took the seat next to him at the table, across from my mom.

"You were advised to be here at eleven," my mother reprimanded me like I was a five-year-old child.

"Well, I'm here now, so why don't we just get on with it," I replied with ire.

"You should have checked your attitude at the door, Junior."

My parents had been pulling stunts like these for years. Like a sucker for punishment I continued to subject myself to their antics. Maybe it was the sad little boy inside me that craved parental attention. Regardless, I wasn't about to change my whole life and do what they say just to get positive attention. Parents should support and love their children regardless. I seriously used to envy the defendants in courtrooms that had their parents sitting on their side, ready and willing to provide support regardless of the charges levied against them.

"So, Vic, how's school going?"

"It's okay," he responded with general disinterest.

"Claudia, what about you? Still on track to graduate?"

"Yep," she replied without raising her eyes from the screen on her phone.

It wouldn't surprise me if she stared at it during the whole meal. Then again, it seemed that this meal was about my future, and not theirs.

Lucky them.

Considering the last conversation about my siblings, I knew their futures had been all planned out. It wasn't my place to tell Claudia that her prescribed future wouldn't be working out as planned. I wished Victor would show more interest in school in front of our parents. It might provide me with enough leverage to give him access to the position our father wanted me to take.

"Sorry we're late," Mr. Milton said as he made it to our table.

"You're right on time," my mother cooed.

Of course, they were right on time, but only ten minutes ago I was late. Cynthia spotted me like a mosquito discovering an all you can eat buffet at a nudist beach. She immediately took the seat next to me. It was more than a bit obvious that our seating arrangement had been pre-planned by my parents and everyone else seated at the table fell in line like the lemmings they were.

"Frank, we're so glad that you and your family could join us today."

"We thought it was a great idea to get together. It's been a couple months and I'm sure we have a lot to discuss," Mr. Milton replied, his eyes hovering on me and Cynthia. If I had to hazard a guess, this brunch was going to be all about the nuptials that would never be happening.

"How's the firm? Have you had any interesting cases lately?"

"We ended up with two cases out of one," he explained. "Our client was charged with spousal abuse, and once we prove his innocence, he wants to file for divorce and sole custody of his three children."

I recognized the client's name immediately. He was the same wife beater we went on a high-speed chase to arrest last month. This type of case was the prime reason I didn't want to work for Milton LLC. Being a lawyer was never in my plan, but even if it was, I wouldn't be caught dead defending a wife beater. If someone didn't want to be married and treat their wife with respect, they should just stay single. It didn't surprise me that his firm was representing the man we arrested last month for beating his wife. What did surprise me was that he was unemployed when he had such an influential family at his beck and call. He must have clout if he obtained Mr. Milton's firm to represent him.

"I thought most of your cases were high profile criminal trials," my father commented.

"Normally we don't take domestic violence cases like his, but it turned out that the client is the grandson of one of the Huntingtons, so they called in a favour," he responded, "Actually, Mike, you and your partner Reed King were listed as one of the arresting officers."

"Yes, we did arrest him," I agreed, knowing it was part of public record that we were the arresting officers. However, if his line of questioning got more precise, I wouldn't be permitted to say any more.

"What can you tell me about the wife? Did she seem mentally competent?"

"You know that I'm not allowed to discuss anything pertaining to your case."

"Sir, if you'd like me to make a statement, then you'll have to subpoena me for the trial," I responded.

"Frank's basically family, Junior. You should tell him everything he needs to know. It won't matter either way. I'm doubtful that a Huntington would ever deserve to be convicted for this type of crime. It's just not in them to hit a woman."

"That's neither here nor there, father. You know that I cannot legally discuss the intricacies of a case, especially with the lawyer for the defendant."

"It's okay, Robert. We actually have more important matters to discuss today."

"Of course, you're right, Frank. We need to start making arrangements for the wedding."

"What wedding?" I asked, feigning ignorance.

"Our wedding, Mikey." Cynthia cut in and then rubbed her hand up and down my arm. "Don't be silly."

Trying not to make too much of a scene, I subtly removed my arm from her clutches. "We're not getting married, Cynthia. No matter how many times you call my cell phone or show up at my house unannounced."

Just last week, Reed told me that she showed up at the Burnett Arms, of all places, looking for me. I thought she would have been scared to catch a lurid disease from the booths there or something absurd like that. One of the reasons I liked going to that bar was that people of my parent's caliber never set foot inside the doors.

"Junior, if you don't marry Cynthia, then we'll cut you off."

"Like that's supposed to scare me," I replied.

Claudia glanced up from her phone, eyes wide, her hand flew to her mouth and my brother stared off into space as if he was trying to hard to portray his lack of interest in the train wreck rapidly developing at our table.

"Don't raise your voice at your father," my mom chastised.

Yet again, we became the drama at the Country Club.

"You both realize you're making a scene in the restaurant again?"

"I think you've done enough, Junior. Why don't you do us a favour and leave?" directed my father, making my exit from the train wreck that was supposed to be my family brunch even easier.

"Gladly," I responded, then addressed my siblings. "Have a great rest of your day. Hopefully they don't drive you batty."

"Bye, Mike," Victor responded.

Claudia didn't even glance up from her phone, but I did notice a slight nod of her head.

VIOLA

MAY

My morning classes at school dragged by so slowly I was thankful for the weekend to begin in a couple of hours. I would finally have a couple days off to rest and focus on the reality of my current situation. This was my last semester! I always thought there had to be so much more out there than the life I had been living. I could hardly believe another chapter in my life was about to close. It was laughable that the impending epilogue was about to be a doozy.

Maybe fate dealt me this new hurdle to enable me to think of what I really needed in my life.

Originally, I had intended to carry on the King family's legacy in blue and follow in the footsteps of my siblings. Enrolling in the police academy and becoming a police officer had been the plan following graduations. However, my recent findings of impending parenthood (not to be confused with impending doom) would delay my chosen career path. As a secondary option, if my original dream didn't come into fruition, this time next year I would almost be finished with my first year of Criminology at the University.

Two weeks had passed since the day in the bathroom when my life changed completely. Fern was the only one who knew what I had been going through because I wanted a clear head and no external opinions steering or hastening me to make important decisions for the wrong reasons. I needed to figure this out on my own, and I was now confident with my decision. It would take a lot of work, but I believed in time I would be able to get my goals on track. My plans for securing my future would be delayed for a year or two. Out of all the scenarios I explored, keeping this baby was the only solution where I could live my life without regret. Sure, I was young, and possibly a bit naïve, but I knew what I could live with.

If there was one thing that I was sure of it was that I couldn't live with ending this pregnancy or handing over a piece of myself to a stranger. Fern was completely supportive of my decision when I explained what I was thinking over the phone. She warned me that our father would most likely blow a gasket, but that sometimes it was worth it to piss him off. Secretly I hoped this pregnancy would give him a reason to finally pay attention to me, as stupid as that line of thinking was.

Now I just needed to figure out a way to inform my family of my predicament. I only hoped that once they got over their initial shock, that they would support my decision to keep my unborn child. More importantly, I wanted to figure out a way to tell Mike that he was going to be a father. As I took a deep breath, I stared down at my phone. He hadn't texted or called since he told me we couldn't keep meeting up. Now I had this huge secret and I wanted nothing more than to hear his reassuring voice.

But what would he say if he knew I was pregnant?

From the stories I had overheard from my brother, he was a playboy. So, I doubted the last thing he would ever want was a child. In the prime of his life, why would he want to be saddled with responsibility? So, where did that leave me?

The last class before lunch had just ended and I was putting my books in my locker. I grasped the door of my locker as my head swam. If only this nausea would cease and desist long enough for me to finish my applications and essay submissions. The rollercoaster currently using my stomach as its own person fair ground, made me want to avoid the cafeteria. For the last month I had successfully avoided the room full of students and smells that assaulted my senses. Instead of staying for lunch and risking impending purging of said lunch, I preferred to go back to my dorm room so I could lay down for at least thirty minutes.

Just as I emptied the last of whatever I had managed to eat this morning, the door of the bathroom banged open.

"Vi, are you in here?"

"Yeah," I answered as I exited the bathroom stall. I walked over to the sink and tore off a paper towel. After running it under cold water I wiped off my face. I doubted I had anything on there, but it felt good to have the cold against my flushed skin.

"What's going on with you?"

"Nothing."

"Do you have the flu or something?"

"Or something," I answered.

"Holy shit!" she screeched.

"Keep it down!" I hushed her, not wanting anyone else to hear her and come running into the middle of our conversation. All I needed was for Vanessa to hear what was being said and it would be all over the school by the end of lunch hour. I still hadn't discussed my situation with the faculty yet. I had no idea how I was going to broach that subject. Nothing like a teenager who attended an all-girls Catholic school getting pregnant by an older man.

"You're pregnant?!?!"

"Yes."

"What are you going to do?" she reached over squeezed my arm.

"I'm going to keep it."

"Are you sure?"

"Yeah. I've had a month to think about it, and I've decided. I can't go through with an abortion and I don't think I could live with myself if I gave a piece of me away."

"Yeah, me neither. I would always wonder."

"I would also worry that I could never have another baby again. There would always be the chance that it wouldn't happen. Then I would have given up something that I had always wanted because it didn't fit at the exact moment I planned."

"Are you going to tell Mike?"

"Eventually. I keep picking up the phone to call him and hanging up."

"Don't wait too long," she warned me.

It had already been a little over five months since we had sex. I was already starting to show a tiny bump and I wouldn't be able to hide my condition for much longer.

She suddenly gasped. "What about your dad?"

My brother was going to kill Mike and my dad was going to kill me.

"He's either going to be another sort of crazy or maybe he'll pull his same old ostrich routine and stick his head in the sand."

"Maybe he'll surprise you."

I wished she was right, but unfortunately, I believed this was going to be a tough month, maybe even year. If there was one thing I knew about my father, it was that he didn't deal with disappointment in his children well. He ran Fern off and kicked Rowan out of the house. Even if he felt guilty about the results of Rowan not having anywhere to go, he still kicked him out.

"I've never known my dad to be accepting of our failures. There's a first time for everything I guess."

"Do you need anything?"

"No, it will be alright, eventually. There's nothing I can do about it now. I just have to live with the consequences and try to come out on top."

"If there's anyone who can, it's you," she replied.

The only thing I could do now was hope that she was right. Hopefully the only way to go was up from here. After all, maybe I deserved a bit of a break.

VIOLA

"Viola! What the hell is this?" Dad shouted from the top of the stairs, waving what was definitely one of the five pregnancy tests that I used a couple weeks ago. My heart leapt into my throat. He knows. For the life of me, I couldn't recall exactly what made me keep the test, but I definitely should have hidden it in a better place. Of all the damned times my dad had to be a detective, he finds the one thing I wanted to hide from him.

Not only that, but he was never at home. Why of all nights did he have to come home and go snooping?

Of course, he would be the one to find the cause of all my current stress.

"I didn't know how to tell you." I whispered, circling my arms around my waist in a sad attempt to console myself or maybe create a shield for the onslaught of anger he was undoubtedly about to unleash.

"How long?"

I flinched with the level of unfettered rage in his voice. It was the first time in a long time that my father had shown any level of emotion. He never even cried when Rowan died. The last time I saw him this angry was when Fern left.

Then again, in order for me to see any sort of emotion from him, he would have to be a regular fixture in my life.

"What do you mean?" I asked, confused by his line of questioning. Did he want to know how long I had known, or how long ago I had sex?

"How long have you conveniently forgotten to clue me in to your present condition?" he pressed.

"A month, maybe more."

"Who's the father?" he asked. "Or better yet, where's the sack of shit that knocked up my youngest daughter? Is he so much of a loser that he doesn't have the balls to face me?"

"I don't know," I responded, even though I had only slept with Mike. I wasn't about to tell my dad that the father of my baby was my brother's partner. I most definitely was not going to confess that I had gone to a bar with the specific goal of losing my virginity, went home with a police officer and let him screw me seven ways from Sunday.

Who knew what fresh hell that would unleash?

Mike could lose his job, or even worse, his head.

"Great. How are you supposed to get him to take responsibility for your situation if you didn't get his name and have no idea where he is? What type of a moron did I raise?"

I shrugged.

If my father wanted to think I was an idiot, he could go right ahead. I wasn't going to add any more fuel to the fire that was already burning in his eyes. I never thought it would have been possible for a person to have both ice and fire in their eyes, but I was positive he did right now.

"I don't even know who you are right now. The level of irresponsibility you've shown by having sex with and getting pregnant by a stranger is exponential."

"I'm sorry," I responded.

"How far along are you?" he pressed.

"I don't know," I whispered, not knowing anything about being pregnant. I hadn't even had a chance to go to a doctor yet, and I could only think of an estimate of time, not an actual time. Also, I didn't exactly want to confess to my father the day that I lost my virginity. This conversation was enough to send me over the edge.

This whole ordeal made me wish my mom was here.

"What do you mean you don't know? Are you having that much unprotected sex that you don't know when it would have been possible for you to conceive a baby?"

"Five months, I think," I responded, shaking. My hand instinctively went to my stomach to cover my barely-there baby bump. I didn't know if the reason I wasn't showing yet was because I was in good shape or not.

"Five months!" he roared, throwing the test down the hall. "I should have known something like this would happen. I swear you three girls will be the death of me. Ivy's out throwing tantrums and getting arrested, Fern is god knows where; she doesn't even pick up the phone and call me. Don't even try to lie about how she visits you all twice a year but doesn't have an ounce of respect left in her to visit her own father."

"I'm eighteen, Dad," I argued suddenly losing my usually sound sense of self preservation.

"So what? You think because you're eighteen you're an adult now?"

"I can vote," I responded defiantly. Being the barely teenager that I was, it forced me to act in an unruly fashion. There was something about him finally showing interest in my life that finally irked me.

How dare he act like he cared now!

"Oh, well then that makes this situation completely normal," he replied, his voice back to the familiar calm and collected, better known as unfeeling. I hoped it wasn't the calm before the storm. "If you want me to treat you like an adult I will."

"Thank you."

"You shouldn't be thanking me so soon. Get up those stairs and pack your bags," he responded, eyes filling with malice.

"W-what?"

"You heard me. Get your suddenly all grown up behind up those steps and pack a bag. You don't want to follow my rules, then I won't force you to. However, you are not going to remain under this roof," he pointed to the ceiling for effect, "and continue to not follow those rules. The first rule being that my youngest God damned daughter isn't going to end up knocked up by some loser and have to drop out of high school."

Where the hell was I going to live?

"Where am I going to live?" I echoed my thoughts out loud, grasping for a lifeline.

"I don't care where you live, as long as it's not here," he replied.

Tears filled my eyes as I leaned against the wall, the weight of my newfound reality causing me to slide to the ground, where I buried my head in my knees. Heavy footsteps signalled my father's return to my bedroom. I couldn't tell how long I remained with my face down, but when I heard what sounded like hurricane Richard had struck my room, I got up. Before I made it to the base of the stairs, he suddenly re-emerged, red faced, and carrying an overflowing hockey bag.

I began to sob uncontrollably, the reality of the situation striking home, as he tossed my hockey bag over the railing, and it landed at my feet. One inch more to the right and it would have knocked me over.

"Dad! What the hell are you doing?" Ivy yelled from the entry way; the sound drew my attention. It was no surprise that through all the madness, I failed to hear the front door opening and my sister arrive home from work.

"I'm getting control of this house!" he bellowed as he paced back and forth on the top landing. "My eldest son overdoses in a crack house, one daughter drops out of the academy, stops talking to me and disappears to who knows where, you go and get yourself arrested for vandalizing one of my officer's vehicles."

"But Daddy, he was…" Ivy interrupted to argue.

"I don't give a fuck what that sorry excuse of a man was doing. You were arrested Ivy!" He roared, turning his face red with anger. "What kind of example are you setting for your sister. Not a great one, because your sister has now gone out and gotten herself pregnant."

"That's no reason to throw her out on the street," Ivy replied, glancing my way for a moment, the surprise clearly evident on her face.

I hoped my sister knew enough not to divulge Mike's identity. Mike and I hadn't spoken, so I didn't have time to tell him. What a surprise that would be for my father to show up on his doorstep and ream him out for getting me pregnant, especially with him not knowing.

"My house, my rules," he replied with distain.

Who knew my own father despised me so much? My heart raced and my skin grew clammy. All I wanted to do was curl up into a ball on my bed in my room upstairs and cry. Yet, according to my father, that bed was no longer mine to use, and I no longer had a roof over my head to shield me from the coming storm.

"At least let me drive her somewhere." Ivy suggested.

"You won't be taking my truck anywhere. I approved the use of it for work or school, not for cruising around the neighborhood. She's made her bed and she can lie in it."

With his pan-ultimate decree delivered, he turned and headed to his master bedroom. Ivy and I jumped as he slammed the door, conversation dismissed.

"I can't believe you never told me that you're pregnant," she accused with pain in her eyes.

"I only told Fern. I wasn't sure what I wanted to do yet, so I didn't want it to get around the family too much."

"But I'm your favourite sister," she teased, having accepted my explanation.

"You may be my favourite, but you also have a tendency to get loose lips when you drink. Especially around Alder, and you know how he can't keep anything to himself."

"Yeah, I guess you're right," she relented.

The seriousness of the situation hit me even harder. I was essentially homeless. "What am I going to do, Ives?" I sobbed.

"Why don't you go stay with Reed or Ash and Alder?"

"You know why."

There was no way I was going to go live with my brothers. Firstly, I never wanted to admit to Reed that his best friend got me pregnant. Secondly, all of them needed their space to sew their wild oats. Thirdly, I never wanted to hear any of the previous statement happening.

Ever.

"He's going to find out sooner or later. You know he'll flip either way, you might as well pull the bandage."

"That wouldn't be fair to Mike," I replied, imagining all the ways in which Reed would kill the father of my child.

"Mike rocked you and dropped you, girl."

My sisters were the only ones who knew that I was pregnant and who the father was. However, they weren't the only ones who knew that Mike and I had been hanging out. Thankfully the third person was Ash because he was like a steel trap, when it came to things, we had confided in him. The only time his steel trap opened was in the case where the information was detrimental to our overall health.

"That's not exactly what happened," I argued.

"Let me get this straight. You guys had sex, then hung out and texted non-stop, and then he dropped you like an old dish rag."

"He didn't drop me like a dish rag."

He so dropped me.

I refused to utter the truth of her statement out loud, and part of me was regretting ever telling Ivy what happened between Mike and me. At the time I didn't know that I was pregnant, so I didn't see the harm in telling her. However, now she had a preconceived notion of just how much of an asshole he was for treating her baby sister like a hit it and quit it girl.

"Whatever you want to call it. I know you're hurting and a little bit in denial," she softened her tone. "However, both of you are at fault for this. I think Reed has a right to know that his partner was diddling his little sister and knocked her up."

"That's why I can't go there yet. I think I need to go and see Mike, even if he doesn't want to see me. I need to explain the situation to him before Reed goes over there and kicks his ass for getting me pregnant."

"So, are you going to go there tonight then? Isn't it a bit late?"

"Better late than never," I replied.

"Well obviously the King and Chief stated that I can't give you a ride, but I can give you cash for a taxi."

"I've got enough to cover the ride to his place," I answered solemnly.

"You're going to need a lot more than taxi fare to take care of that kid."

"I know."

"You are going to keep it, aren't you?"

"I know you're going to think I'm crazy, but I can't give it up because the baby is a part of me. I'll always wonder where they are or whether they're okay." I place my hand on my stomach.

She grasped my hand and pulled me over to the couch, sitting next to me. Then she took a deep breath and proceeded to tell me something I never thought I would hear from her.

"I've never told anyone this, but I got pregnant the year I turned sixteen."

"What? Why didn't you tell me? Or Fern?"

The better question was how I could have missed it, considering we shared a room at boarding school. How did I not notice her getting sick? How did she hide it from all of us? It wasn't the thought that she left me out of the situation, it was that she had been alone through it all, when she didn't have to be…but then that was how Ivy was. It was always her against the world and a constant show of independence.

"I was ashamed, and I didn't want anyone to talk me out of the decision I was going to make."

Even when we were younger, she wanted to be treated like she was much older than she really was. It showed in her choice of boyfriend, the way she dressed, talked and her mannerisms.

"I was ashamed, and I didn't want anyone to talk me out of the decision I was going to make."

"What happened?"

"When I went to talk to Tyler about the baby, his parents were there. His mother took me into another room and persuaded me that an abortion was the right decision. Tyler planned on going to university the next year on a full ride football scholarship, and he didn't have the time or the money to take care of a baby."

"Oh, Ives."

"Then when Tyler and I went upstairs to his bedroom, he said that we would have more chances to have a baby later. I stayed the night at his house, and the next day we went to the clinic."

"Where was I?"

Again, I was struck with the disbelief that she had gone through everything alone. We were supposed to be close. I wasn't hurt that she kept her pregnancy from me; I only wanted to be there for her when she went through with something so emotionally traumatic.

"You were all away for a Krav Maga tournament."

"I'm sorry."

"Don't be. I wouldn't have told you until I decided what I wanted to do."

"That doesn't make it okay. I would have been there for you. You're my Irish twin. We're supposed to share everything, even clothes. Although your legs are a bit shorter than mine." I tried to lighten the mood with a lame joke.

"Hardy har," she replied, sticking out her tongue.

"So, what happened with you and Tyler then?"

"The day after I went for the procedure, I caught him coming out of a fitting room at the mall, followed by Helen, the town bicycle. The buttons on her shirt were mismatched in haste, and his pants undone, and he was doing up his belt."

"Dick."

"Looking back, I know that I made the right decision for my fifteen-year-old self. Besides, who would have wanted to be stuck with Tyler for the rest of my life. Yet, right now, my nineteen-year-old self wouldn't be alone if I had the baby."

She was saying the words as if they had been rehearsed over and over in her mind until she believed it. However, I knew her almost better than she knew herself and I could tell by the look on her face that she regretted it. Since we were children, the only desire Ivy expressed for her future was to be a wife and a mother.

"Ives, you're not alone. I know it seems like too much shit has happened in your life and now you're back home. But, don't you ever think that you're alone. You have me, and the rest of our rowdy siblings."

I pulled her into my arms and squeeze tight.

"Thanks, Vi," she wiped a stray tear off of her cheek. "Now, you should get going before the King returns and it's off with your head."

I picked up my discarded hockey bag, which was overflowing with whatever my father deemed essential. Then I went and sat in the truck while I waited for the taxi to arrive. Praying the whole time that the tyrant wouldn't look out the kitchen window and see me sitting there.

MIKE'S TOWNHOUSE was just how I remembered it. Although, I hadn't taken the time to appreciate it when I scurried out the back door the morning after my birthday, like my ass was on fire. I only hoped Mike didn't turn me away like my father had. The whole interaction with him left me feeling conflicted. He had never been so angry with me, but at the same time it was nice to see him actually show that he cared what was going on in my life. If only he had shown a minuscule amount of caring towards me growing up, maybe wouldn't have felt so disregarded my whole life.

He was detached with my siblings too, but as I got older, it seemed like he wasn't around as much. Maybe it was because he thought he could trust us as teenagers, or maybe it was because he didn't really want to be around me. Often, when my dad looked at me, he seemed in pain. I didn't know if it was my presence that saddened him or if he blamed me for the loss of his wife.

The taxi dropped me off at the start of the cul-de-sac, as instructed. It took me seconds to arrive at the destination that will either be my salvation or damnation. I couldn't predict which one. My feet weighed a ton as I slowly trekked up the front steps. Hands shaking, I raised one and took a deep breath before I knocked three times on his door. If he turned me away I would have nowhere to go until school on Monday. My brothers really didn't need me invading their bachelor pads and they really didn't deserve to be saddled with me and my mistakes.

My heart pounded as I waited; my damnation or salvation just on the other side of the door.

"What are you doing here?" He eyed the duffle bag hanging from my hands with suspicion. "I thought we agreed that it was better if we didn't see each other anymore."

"I know I shouldn't be here," I agreed with a shaky voice. "But we need to talk."

"We have nothing to discuss."

"Can I please come inside?" I asked. "I'd rather not do this out here for everyone to see."

He glanced down the street and then stepped to the side, allowing me to walk through the entry and into his living room.

"Thank you."

"What's this about?" He asked as he shut the door. "And why do you have what seems to be more than just your brother's hockey bag?"

"I think you should sit down," I replied, not correcting him on the ownership of the bag. This was not the time or the place to teach him a thing or two about women being able to play hockey.

"Just spit it out," he told me as he crossed his arms and leaned against the kitchen island, effectively placing a barrier between us.

I steeled my back and replied, "I'm pregnant, and it's yours."

"That's impossible. We used protection."

"I hate to break it to you, but I've recently discovered that condoms are only ninety-eight percent effective, and in most cases they're only about eighty-five percent effective."

"You weren't on the pill?" he asked pointedly.

"Virgin. Remember?" I responded.

The only reason I wasn't on the pill at the time was that my dad would have blown a gasket if he saw them come up on his health insurance. I also really hadn't planned on having sex the moment I turned eighteen. I should have had time to get a prescription when I turned eighteen. He probably still believed Fern was a virgin, and she was twenty-four years old. If he had his way, we would all be in living in a convent far away from any men who could corrupt us. After all, we weren't even Catholic, yet he had me and my sisters there while our brothers went to public school.

"Fuck," he ran his hands through his hair, causing it to stick up in an odd pattern. "I need something stronger than this."

He tossed the coke can into the sink and grabbed a bottle of bourbon off the top shelf of the cupboard by the sink. He poured himself a small glass, and then immediately tossed it back, swallowing every last drop. He repeated the process once more and dropped into the chair across from me. The calm and put together guy I had known for the last four months disintegrated before my eyes, into a pile of nerves within a matter of seconds. His reaction was completely understandable, considering I collapsed into a puddle of tears last month when I saw those two pink lines, on every one of the five tests that I took.

I had already had the time to digest the fact that I was carrying his baby, so my shock at the news had mostly dissipated for me. To be honest, I had already accepted it and was looking forward to the baby's arrival, even though I was currently homeless. When I had decided to come here, I wasn't sure what I should have expected. I only hoped that the guy I had fallen for would be willing to give me a place to stay until I could find something more permanent to raise our child in.

MIKE

"You're sure it's mine?" I closed my eyes and then shook my head as I quickly re-examined my words. "Forget I asked. With my luck, of course it has to be mine."

"What's that supposed to mean? With your luck?" she asked through gritted teeth.

Reed was going to kill me. Unknowingly, I had been walking the line and heading to death row since January. Now he was going to be presented with undeniable proof of my betrayal in the form of a baby. There was going to be a massacre at District Two. He would be painting the walls in crimson. They were going to be scraping my blood and guts off the locker room floor at work when he found out I knocked up his baby sister.

What the hell was I thinking?

Oh, I knew what I was thinking. I was thinking with my dick. I just had to take her home and fuck her all night long. Even if I hadn't known who she was at the time of the incident, later it was undeniable that I knew her. Especially when I decided that I had to keep seeing her and eventually develop feelings for her. All of that was supposed to be over. The sole reason I broke things off with her in April was to avoid intertwining our lives any further than they already had been.

"I told you before, I'm not the right guy for you. I'm not looking for a relationship now, nor will I ever want to be in a relationship."

This was one hell of a noose to tie around my neck.

Forget the ball and chain. Let's just find out what was behind door number two: eighteen years of child support, being forever tied to my best friend's little sister, and who knew what else would be drummed up as a bonus prize.

"Be that as it may, I'm still pregnant," she retorted with her hands on her hips.

"The solution to our situation isn't going to be solved," I glanced at the clock, "at eleven thirty-five on a Friday night."

"I know. We have a lot to talk about. I wanted you to know before anyone else finds out."

"I appreciate that you wanted me to know first so that I could prepare for impending doom. However, you still haven't told me the reason that you brought an old hockey bag to tell me the news. Are you going somewhere?"

"I would explain, but I don't want to cry," she sniffed.

"Then don't," I responded.

"If you make me explain my hockey bag, crying will be inevitable. I'm not even sure if he packed the right things for me, he did it so fast."

He?

My stomach clenched at the thought of another man packing her bags for her. The agony in her eyes made me want to go out, find the man who hurt her and make them feel the same pain. I stood silently for a moment not sure what to say or do. Then when the fog of my temporary insanity cleared, I reminded myself she still lived at home with her father on the weekends. That meant the he she was referring to is likely him.

Then it hit me like a punch to the gut.

He kicked her out.

"You don't have anywhere to go, do you?" I asked, softening my voice.

Her own father upon finding out that his youngest daughter was pregnant, just closed the book on her. Gave up.

WTF?

Viola glanced down at her clasped hands. Her hair fell like a curtain across the front of her face, as if it was sentient and wanted to hide her shame. If there was one thing I understood, it was the feeling of having the only parent or parents you knew, shipping you off to boarding school and forgetting that you existed.

"No," she replied so quietly I barely heard her.

I knew Reed and Ash lived together, so I imagine she thinks that she would be a hinderance to their single lives. Ivy is obviously back at home, since we all moved her there a couple weeks ago. She's mentioned her older sister Fern in the past, but I have no idea where she lives. Alder definitely wouldn't want his pregnant baby sister crashing at his dorm room. She really doesn't have anywhere to go, and I wasn't going to put the mother of my unborn child out on the street. Not to mention Reed would undoubtedly murder me if I was so cold.

"Then you'll stay here." I suggested.

"Are you sure?"

"I'm sure. I have an extra room that you can use. There's even a bed in there. The closet's empty so you'll have room for all of your stuff."

"Thank you. I know you probably don't want me here, but until Monday morning I need a place to stay."

"You're still going back to the dorm on Monday?"

"That's the plan. I've only got a month and a half left of school until I graduate."

Of course.

How was it that every time I was around her, I forget she's still in high school?

"What about the baby?" I asked.

"I have morning sickness, but I can't afford to miss any school, or they will take away my valedictorian status. I'm required to have perfect attendance for all of my classes."

"Are you sure that you want to stay there?"

"I think it's best, since you really don't need a teenage girl cramping your style."

"You're pregnant with my child. I'll be helping you out, but you won't be cramping my style," I responded.

"I still think that I should stay at the school. I'd hate for people to get the wrong impression of you because I'm living here."

I had no idea what an all-girls Catholic school would think of having an unwed, pregnant teenager living in dorms. At least she would only have another month or so left of school before she graduated.

What the hell was she going to do after?

What the fuck did we do?

I took a deep breath to calm my nerves from spiralling out of control. I had never felt so out of control of my life. From the moment my parents shipped me off to boarding school I knew I was fine with being alone. All of the fights my parents had, the cheating that I knew my father did, and the subsequent parading of their eldest child like I was a stud out to pasture proved that my life would be better alone.

"Viola, we're going to have a baby. I think the time to be worrying about the impression we make on society has passed."

She laughed.

The first real laugh I had heard from her in almost a month. It was like music to my ears. I had come to the terms that I would never be close enough to her to hear it. The moment I broke off all contact with her after we moved her sister Ivy back to the farm, I knew I would have to make a point to avoid her at all costs.

There was no way I could be in the same room as her and not want to touch her.

To kiss her.

"Do you want to keep the baby?" I asked, not sure of the answer I desired. I never in a million years saw myself as a father, likely because my parents were so cold and calculating.

"Yes, I am going to keep it," she replied with confidence. "I know it's probably not something that you want, so if you'd rather not be involved, I completely understand."

"I want to be involved," I immediately responded. "Vi, if you allow me to be, I won't let you down."

"That's more than I could have ever hoped for," she responded.

"Okay," I sighed, thankful she wasn't going to keep me away from my child. Even if I was scared shitless, I still wanted to be in his or her life. "If you want, you can hang your jacket in the closet in the hallway."

She went in the direction I pointed. I listened as she opened the closet door, rattled the wooden hangers and then closed the door again. Her sock feet barely made a sound as she made her way back to me.

"Thanks," she replied

"No problem," I responded. "You're probably tired after everything that happened today."

"Yeah," she replied timidly.

"I'll show you your room," I told her, leaned down, picked up her hockey bag and headed in the direction of the stairs.

"I can take it," she objected, then reached for the bag.

"I don't think so." I shook my head and held the bag out of her reach.

Then, before she could take the bag from me, I ran up the stairs. My reaction wasn't because I believed she could actually physically wrestle it from me. However, as she reached the top of the stairs and entered the bedroom, the look on her face made me question the validity of that statement.

She stood in the doorway of my spare room with her hands on her hips. "You know, I'm pregnant, not an invalid," she retorted.

The motion drew my attention to her midsection, which had changed in the last couple of months. I didn't know how I never noticed it when she came in. She had started to develop a little more of an hourglass shape as her body prepared to carry our unborn child. She even had a tiny bump that was visible due to her tank top. Her tiny pink flamingo covered shirt.

What the hell was she wearing?

"Um, what are you wearing?" I asked as I tossed her hockey bag on a chair in the corner of the room.

She blushed. "It's eleven at night. I was getting ready to go to bed when my dad discovered the pregnancy test. I was just downstairs to get a drink of milk when he screamed from the top of the stairs."

"Your dad found the test? How did that happen?"

How long has she known that she was pregnant with my child?

"I have no idea why he was in my bedroom. He must have been rifling through my drawers. That's the only explanation for why he found the tests," she answered, shaking her head.

"Tests, as in plural?"

She nodded.

"Just exactly how many tests did you have to take to find out you were pregnant?"

She blushed. "I didn't want to believe that I was. We were careful, and it didn't make sense. I thought it was a false positive."

She looked around sheepishly, then eyed the bed. I stepped closer to the closet and waved my hand toward the bed. My spare room was fairly sparse, but it had a double bed and a chair. I used the closet for my spare uniforms and a couple of my suits so that I didn't have them in my closet. I never brought girls home, except for her, but I still didn't want anything in my room just in case they snooped. If she planned on staying here longer than the weekend, she would need a desk and maybe a dresser.

WTH? Was I actually thinking about her staying?

"Have you gone to the doctor yet?"

She sighed, "Yeah, and let me tell you, that was probably the most invasive medical exam I've ever had. Wow."

"Really?" I was curious and a little jealous about the appointment that I missed.

"They checked everything. They examined my cervix, took my blood pressure, listened my lungs, and a bunch of other stuff. They also checked me for STDs, which I was completely cleared of, FYI. At the end, she went through importance of eating well, exercising, and taking prenatal vitamins during the pregnancy."

"I'm clean. I get checked regularly because of work."

"Oh," she responded, surprised like she hadn't considered it a hazard of law enforcement.

"How long have you known?"

"My appointment was in the middle of April."

I tried not to let it bother me that she waited almost two months to tell me that she was having my baby.

"Did they do an ultrasound?"

"Yeah, I got to hear the baby's heartbeat." She smiled, then a tear rolled down her cheek. "You know what's the hardest part?"

It sounded more like a rhetorical statement, instead of a question, so I glanced at her and waited for her to continue.

"I was actually going to talk to my dad about everything the next time that he came home. Joke's on me though, cause he came home and ransacked my bedroom like I was one of his criminals. Then when he found the contraband in the form of a pregnancy test, he blew up and kicked me out."

"He'll come around."

"You didn't see his face."

"Give him time. He runs a tight ship. He seems like the type of man who strives for control in all aspects of his life. You, my dear, have thrown a huge wrench in all of his plans."

"Maybe."

"Well, I'm going to grab my stuff out of this closet and let you get to bed. I have a morning shift with Reed

LOUD BANGING against the downstairs door startled me from my sleep. I hope to hell it didn't wake Viola. She had told me that she has been having a rough time with the morning sickness. She said that her doctor told her the most important thing was rest. After all, she was growing another human in there.

"Open the door, you fucker!" Reed bellowed from the front step.

I opened the door and he pushed his way past me, his shoulder knocking me to the side.

"Did you think I wouldn't find out that you were shacked up with my baby sister?"

Fuck!

In all the commotion tonight of her telling me she was pregnant, I never once asked her if anyone else knew where she was. I should have been the better man and just called him to confess everything before it got out of hand. He was going to find out sooner or later and it really should have come firsthand from me.

"We wanted to talk to you together, once the dust settled."

"Where is she?" He seethed.

I did the most immature thing I could have done in the moment and shushed him. The look on his face was priceless.

"She's sleeping."

"She better not be up there in your fucking bed!" He started up the stairs and I grabbed his arm.

"She's not in my bed. She's in the spare room," I told him. "We've known each other for eight years, man. Do you really think that little of me?"

He started pacing.

"I don't think I even know you. The guy I knew wouldn't get some high school girl pregnant and then take her away from the only family she's known when she needed them the most."

"You're wrong."

"Oh, so you didn't get my sister, who's in high school, pregnant with your child?"

"That's not what you're wrong about."

"Enlighten me then."

"Your dad threw her out, man."

"He would never do that."

"She finally got up enough courage to discuss her situation with him, but before she could, he searched her room and found the test. Then your dad waited a whole two seconds before he told her to pack up her bags and get out," I explained. "Apparently, his exact words were that if she wants to behave like an adult, then she would have to live like one. When she was done packing her bags, there was a taxi waiting for her outside, ready to take her wherever she wants to live."

"I knew something was going on with the two of you. The way you guys were looking at each other at the farm."

"We shouldn't have hidden it from you."

"It shouldn't have happened!" he yelled.

I cringed when I heard Viola's bed creak upstairs.

"You woke her up, asshole."

"I'm the asshole."

"Yeah, you're being a ripe old asshole, big brother." Viola called from the banister just outside her door.

"What the fuck, imp?" Reed asked his sister.

"Dad kicked me out."

"No shit, Sherlock. Ivy called Alder in tears but wouldn't tell him where you went. So, when he called me, and said he didn't have any clue where you were, I started driving around looking for you. Ash got home from his shift to Alder freaking out asking if he knew anything. Ash immediately called me and told me where you might be."

"Oh," Viola whispered.

"Yeah…Oh…Why the fuck aren't you answering your phone?"

"I turned it off."

"Why the hell would you do that?"

"Because I'm fucking tired," she yelled.

"Whoa, okay you two, you need to calm down." I looked up at Viola. "It's not good for the baby for you to be upset."

"A fucking baby?" Reed turned beet red in the face. In fact, his whole body was lobster-esque. "Tell me you're joking Vi."

"You mean Ash told you everything but didn't tell you why I got kicked out?"

"Yeah, he wasn't very forthcoming on the rest," Reed responded tilting his head to the side. "What exactly do you have on him that he kept your secret?"

"I have nothing on him. Mike ended it shortly after my first conversation with Ash regarding our situation."

"Ash knew you were having sex with my sister?"

I held my hands up in surrender when Reed glanced at me. "This is the first I'm hearing about Ash knowing anything. As far as I knew, we weren't telling anyone."

"Reed, you know how Ash is; he figured it out when we moved Ivy back home."

"Of course, he did," Reed responded, shaking his head. "He didn't tell me that you're pregnant, though. How long has this little arrangement been going on for?"

"We aren't together, Reed." She answered sheepishly.

"Well that's just great. It's his kid, right?"

"Of course it is!"

"Well, you never know with the way you've been acting lately. This is totally unlike you, imp," Reed responded, clearly disappointed in Viola.

As soon as I saw the hurt in her eyes, a streak of protectiveness ran through me and I had to shield her from any negativity in her life.

"I would appreciate it if you wouldn't talk to her that way."

"She's my sister. Just because you're suddenly fucking her, doesn't mean that you get to control how I talk to her."

"We're not fucking," I argued.

Reed redirected his anger toward me, but before he said anything, I rushed to tell him more. "I'm not going to lie to you and say I never slept with your sister. Obviously, I did considering she's carrying our child."

"It's true, Reed. The first thing he did was offer me his spare room. Do you think if we were fucking, that I would be in a different bed?"

"You must be telling the truth; Mike only fucks his women in hotels or back seats of cars. He never brings them home with him."

Viola visibly winced. We weren't in a relationship, but the last thing I wanted was for her to think I was a complete manwhore.

Reed then turned and addressed me. "Head or gut?"

"Reed, don't do it." Viola called our and started down the stairs.

"Stay up there, Vi. It's okay," I assured her. Whatever Reed wanted to dish out, I deserved. "Gut."

"You know what. None of this shit matters. I'll put in for a transfer by the end of this week."

"Reed, don't be like that man."

"You slept with my sister. Not only did you sleep with her, but you knocked her up. She's in high school, asshole."

"He didn't know I was in high school when we met," she argued.

"Good luck with this asshole, imp. You're going to need it."

With that, he walked out the front door.

"Well, he's pissed," I commented to Vi.

"Yup," she answered. "I think I'm going to go and lay down again."

"Okay," I replied. "If you need anything, I'm just down the hall."

"Okay," she replied meekly, then went back into her room and shut the door.

After that I didn't last long downstairs. I cleaned everything up, had a shower and crawled into bed. All through the night I tossed and turned, unsure of what my future would hold. I didn't want to lose Reed as a partner or friend, but there was no way I could turn my back on Vi and our baby.

It was a double edge sword, either way I would lose, either way I would gain.

VIOLA

My heart raced and my palms were sweaty, as I waited to be called in for my scheduled appointment with the guidance counsellor. Considering my pregnancy would affect my future studies, I knew I needed professional advice on what my options were for the first semester while taking care of my baby. I wouldn't let me having a child affect my education. It was going to be a difficult road, but I wasn't going to let it derail my plan.

I wouldn't be admitted to the police academy like I had originally planned, but I could and would be able to go to University and major in Criminal Justice so that I could still make my mark in something to do with law enforcement.

"Miss Rudolph will see you now," the secretary motioned toward the counsellor's office.

"Thank you."

"Ah, Miss King, welcome to my office."

"Please call me Viola." The formal manner in which the teachers and staff spoke with students seemed odd to me, and I would rather be called by my first name.

What the fuck was wrong with me?

My hormones must really be all out of whack today because I felt snippy in my mind. Hopefully it didn't actually come to fruition out of my head.

"Okay, Viola it is then. Please take a seat." She gestured to the only chair in the room.

As if I had a choice.

"What would you like to talk about today?" she asked, clasping her fingers together on her desk.

As much as I didn't want to discuss the exact motivation of why I had decided to see the counsellor, I knew it was better to just rip off the Band-Aid. So, I went straight to the reason for my visit.

"I recently discovered that I am pregnant and that I'm due in the middle of October. It shouldn't have any effect on this school year, but obviously it will have some conflict with my first semester in University."

Her eyes widened, but she quickly schooled her features and replied, "It sounds like you're dealing with a very stressful situation. What do your parents think?"

I tried not to let the way she was ignorant of me not having both parents get to me. In my mind, it was her responsibility to have general background knowledge of the students that visited her office. I would have assumed that if she didn't know my whole background, that she would have at least reviewed my file before this meeting. There probably wasn't a lot of information in there; it couldn't have taken her more than a few minutes to skim over.

However, I knew those basic details were in there because I was present when my dad filled out the paperwork. It was just after my brother overdosed, so it was a memorable time in my life.

"My dad isn't very happy at all and the moment he discovered the positive test, he asked me to move out of the house."

"He did?" she asked with surprise in her voice.

"Yes, he did." The more she continued to repeat my words, the more it sounded like an echo and the rapport she hoped to facilitate by enticing me to repeat everything I told her was receding by the minute.

"You must have really disappointed him to make a mistake like that."

"No shit." The answer slipped out before I could stop it.

"Viola, language."

"Sorry, Miss Rudolph."

"Now, where was I?" She reviewed her notes as if we had a huge conversation instead of me saying just a few statements. I tried not to let the fact that she had parroted everything back to me and still forgot it cause me to lose my temper any further.

She looked at the ceiling for a moment and tapped her pen on her chin then continued.

"So, where do you stay on the weekends if you can't go home? I can see by the records that you haven't been spending every weekend at Sacred Heart."

So, she had time to review my attendance record, but she couldn't review what was the most important?

"The father of my baby is letting me stay with him," I responded.

"Do you think that's wise?" She made no attempt to mask the judgement in her voice.

"I'm eighteen and I have nowhere to live. It seems like a great idea to live with the father of my unborn child."

"I see." She tapped her lips with her pen. "What about your mom?"

Even though eighteen years had passed, and I didn't really know her, the question of Mom's whereabouts never gets easier.

"My mom died a day after I was born."

She gasped.

So, she didn't know about my mom's death, which should have been in my file, but she somehow memorized my whereabouts every weekend? What was with this chick that she didn't already know that? She'd been a counsellor at the academy for four years. I would have thought it would be part of her mandate to review the records of any and all students enrolled here.

"Oh, sorry," she replied.

She hummed lightly as she skimmed the top page in the manila folder on her desk. I leaned forward slightly in an attempt to see where she was looking, and I was flabbergasted by what I saw.

"That's right, I must have missed it, but that note is right here in your file."

Yup, right there under the right yellow highlighting, you daft cow.

"So, what exactly are you hoping to gain from this meeting?"

"I was hoping you could give me some options on what I can do to still take classes while I'm at home with my baby for the first semester."

"Do you think that's your best option?" she asked with a judgemental tone.

"I realize it's not my only option, but I was hoping that you could help me see all the possible options before making a concrete decision."

Right after I saw those two pink lines…First I had a bit of a mental breakdown. Then, the planner in me completely raised her head. I picked my ass up off the bathroom floor, went into my bedroom and started researching online classes. What I needed from the counsellor was a bit of real-world knowledge and support external to my interpersonal relationships. Considering the first part of our conversation got off to an absolutely fabulous start, I highly doubted I would be getting anything I wanted out of this session.

"Don't you think you should stay at home and raise your child?"

What was this? The 1940s?

"Um, no." I argued. "I think I should keep my career aspirations like I planned and also raise my baby."

"In this day and age, sure, you could do both. But the bigger question is, should you?"

"What do you mean by that?" I was becoming increasingly agitated.

"Research has shown that there are numerous benefits to raising your children at home. Children who are raised at home experience less stress and are less likely to display aggressive behavior."

Who was this lady?

"I'm sure there are also articles that state children in daycare are better socialized and less dependent."

"Of course, there are, but do you want to take a chance? Isn't it a bit like Russian roulette?"

Russian…fucking…roulette? WTF, Batman?

"Are you seriously comparing raising a child to shooting yourself in the head during a stupid competition?"

"U-umm, no-o, that's not at all what I was saying."

"Then what were you saying, Miss Rudolph?"

"I think you should seriously consider being a stay-at-home mom."

"I'm beginning to think that this appointment isn't going to go in the direction that I wanted."

"What exactly are you implying Miss King?" she asked with bite.

"It seems as though our ideas of what is appropriate for my situation completely clash. I'm not so sure this avenue is the best route for me to be made aware of all of the options available to me."

Her mouth dropped open, agape.

"I wanted to thank you for your time, Miss Rudolph." I had finally stopped the echo, but I was not a complete bitch.

A FEW MOMENTS later I left, feeling completely unresolved in my future. I stepped out of the guidance counsellor's office and ran right into Vanessa.

"Oh, sorry Vi, I didn't see you there. Are you okay? I didn't injure you with my clumsiness, did I."

"Uh, no. I'm okay, thanks for asking."

Hell hath frozen over. Either that or it was an invasion of the body snatchers and Vanessa was their first candidate. I walked out of the office and over to my locker in a daze.

"What's wrong?" Shelby asked.

"Umm…I just had a literal run in with Vanessa and she was acting kind of strange. I think she could be up to something."

"Like what?"

"I don't know. Do you think she could have been listening in on my counselling session? She seemed excessively close to the door. It was the only explanation for us bumping into each other."

"She wouldn't be above listening in on any of our sessions in hopes that she gets some sort of ammunition on one of us to use at another time." Shelby responded. "Why? Was there something you discussed that you really didn't want Vanessa to know about?"

"Yes."

"Do I already know?" She asked.

I still hadn't told Shelby about the pregnancy because part of me was worried about her passing judgement. I knew she was completely on board with operation v-card elimination, but I also knew that she was still a virgin. What if she thought badly of me because I had chosen to have a baby just after high school? When we were younger and talked about our future families, we joked about trying to have our babies at the exact same time. I knew that our dream was completely absurd, but it was still in the forefront of my mind every time I was about to make a confession.

"No, I haven't told you yet."

A pained expression crossed her face momentarily, but it disappeared quickly. Throughout our entire friendship, there was very little I had kept from my best friend.

"But I totally want to!" I tried to assure her.

"Why haven't you? You know I can keep a secret! I didn't tell anyone that you wore the same socks for a month in grade four."

"Okay, let's forget that ever happened. Remove it from your memory database stat."

She twisted an imaginary key on her lips and threw it across the hall. "Done."

"I promise I'll tell you soon."

"You better," she responded as she looped her arm through mine and dragged me to our next class.

MIKE

JUNE

"Come on, don't transfer," I begged Reed. "I know you're pissed. I broke a thousand bro codes by getting with your sister."

"I don't want to talk about this."

"Come on, man."

"Mike, I'm still pretty pissed over everything," Reed replied, pulling the patrol car over to the side of the road and putting it in park. "I don't want to talk about it because I don't want to get into a fist fight in the middle of shift. We've got a job to do, so let's just do it."

"Okay," I held my hands up. "We won't talk about your sister, but we should talk about the transfer. I don't want a new partner. I trust you to watch my back, implicitly."

"The problem is, Mike, I don't know if I can trust you anymore."

"There's no way I would let anything happen to you. Just because I got your sister pregnant doesn't mean that I wouldn't take a bullet for you," I argued. "Besides, I've stepped up and taken responsibility for everything with Viola."

"You've taken responsibility for her, but you still don't get what's wrong with this whole picture."

"You don't think I can't figure out what's wrong with this? I know I fucked up. You've got to understand though, I had no idea who she was when I took her home that night."

"Do you realize you haven't even apologized?" he seethed. "I get that you made the mistake of sleeping with my sister. Sure, I want you to apologize for that, even if it wasn't technically your fault. I know how she can be when she has a plan."

"I'm sorry, I really am." I responded.

"The issue I have is the fact that you carried on a relationship with her in secret and the only reason I even found out was that you got her pregnant."

He had me there, I knew I was in the wrong for keeping things from him. In all honesty, I didn't think we would go this far, which was why I ended things with Viola in the first place. Regardless, all the reasons in the world still didn't make the situation any better.

"You probably wouldn't have known anything about it, that's true. We were both in this, but I take full responsibility. I should have never indulged the relationship."

"It didn't really matter if you indulged the relationship or not. She was already pregnant," he shook his head. "This is just fifty ways of fucked up, you know that?"

"Yeah," I agreed.

"I always promised myself whoever ended up with my baby sister, they're lights would be punched out, regardless. Then here you come, my best friend, partner and as good as a brother, and you get her pregnant. The kicker is, she's still in high school."

"She can still finish school. She can even go to University. We haven't discussed anything yet, but I was thinking of changing shifts while she's in University, if that's what she still wants. I can look after our child while she's going to school and then she'll be at home while I'm at work. If that doesn't work, you know I have enough money to pay for a full-time nanny for her. I want them both to continue to live with me because I need to be able to see my kid, and Vi needs to be comfortable. I don't want her to have to worry about anything while she's in school or even after."

"What if she doesn't want to stay with you?"

"Then she doesn't have to. I'm not going to force her to stay, even if I want her to. I just think it will be easier when it comes to raising our child. We have no animosity between us. In fact, I think we're pretty good friends considering."

What I didn't want to admit to my partner, was that sometimes I envisioned us as more. Having her living with me was definitely blurring the lines. I just had to be strong and not let it affect us. Our child was more important than us being more than what we were.

"So, you're going to try the co-parenting?"

"What more can we do?" I asked him, not really wanting an answer. "I think it will work."

"And that's all you want with my sister?" Reed asked. "I don't think I can handle anymore lies, so if there's something more, you have to tell me."

"I won't lie, I'm attracted to your sister."

What I wasn't going to tell him was that I had to jack off in the shower every night just to keep from inviting her into my bed. It didn't escape me that I hadn't had sex in six months either. Nor did I want to have sex with anyone other than his sister. Which made things all the more complicated.

"Of course, you are. Just perfect." He threw his hands up in the air dramatically.

"I'm not going to let my attraction to your sister to affect or influence the relationship that her and I have right now." Adding sex to our unorthodox relationship would complicate things more than they already were. It didn't matter that we already had sex. Starting anything with Viola before we figured out what was between us would be a recipe for disaster.

"Okay."

"Okay?"

"Yeah, okay," Reed repeated. "I'll pull my transfer papers, but we might revisit this conversation later."

"Okay."

Reed pulled back onto the street and we reported for our shift.

THE NEXT MORNING, the faint sounds of Viola moving around in her bedroom drew my attention. It was like the moment she moved in, I turned hypersensitive to her movements and mannerisms. Never in a million years did I think I would have a woman living with me. I glanced at the clock and took note of the time. She was definitely not a morning person when she rolled out of bed just before noon. Then again, she was pregnant.

Wow. Pregnant. With my baby.

A month ago, if anyone had predicted I would be shacked up with my partner's little sister and expecting our first child, I would have laughed them right out of the joint. A relationship was never in my future. This was most definitely never in my plans. Regardless, there was nothing that could ever make me regret our child, or the gorgeous woman willing to bring him into the world and my life.

"Good morning, sleepyhead," I called from the base of the stairs. The other thing I had noticed since she moved in, was an almost instinctual desire to protect her from anything that had the potential to cause injury.

"Morning," she groaned.

As she stretched her arms above her head, the movement drew my attention to the skin being revealed and the ever-growing baby bump. If there had been any doubt in my mind that she was truly pregnant, it was more than obvious seeing the evidence of our union.

"How did you sleep?"

"Better than I ever did at the Academy," she replied with a yawn, then slowly descended the stairs and made her way over to me.

"That's good. Are you hungry? I can make you something."

"You don't have to do that," she responded. "I can feed myself."

Viola blew everything I had ever thought about women out of my mind. Any of the women my parents had introduced me to were cold, calculating and had this sense of entitlement that was a total turn off. They had been bred to marry rich, procreate and visit spas while the help looked after their offspring. The women I used to sleep with were only after one thing and would do just about anything to get it. Once they dug their hooks in deep, they changed into the cold and calculating women I had avoided all my life.

She was nothing like them. Viola, without me sounding like a complete pansy, was a breath of fresh air. Even though she was the youngest of seven, she never acted like a spoiled brat, like my sister Claudia sometimes did. When I came home from working a long shift, the house was never a disaster, even on days when I didn't have housekeeping done. When she was awake, she was constantly studying, and could carry on intellectual conversation without breaking a sweat.

"I know you can but let me take care of you for once. I have some breakfast left over that we could heat up or I can make something."

As if spurred on by my suggestion, her stomach growled. Colour rose to her cheeks and she replied, "I could go for some bacon."

"Great. One package of bacon coming right up."

"Not the whole package, silly."

"My bad. I thought you were eating for two."

"That's just an excuse everyone uses to overeat. Don't get me wrong, I'm hungry, but not that hungry."

"Alright, have a seat and I'll whip something up for you."

She immediately hopped up on the tall chair at the breakfast nook. She had an air of maturity about her, but every once in a while, her age shone through. Thinking back on all the reasons I ended our contact; I knew it was the right thing to do. I wasn't looking for a relationship, so why would I continue to subject myself to the farce or lead her on any more than I already had.

Sometimes I wondered if meeting her was fate. It was almost as if destiny was giving me a swift kick in the nuts.

VIOLA

After a week of gruelling school, it was finally Friday afternoon and I was feeling giddy just thinking about seeing Mike again. We've been living together for a couple weeks now, and it feels like we might be on the verge of an actual relationship. Part of me is still worried I'll wake up in the morning and this will all be a dream, but even if it is, at least I got something good out of it. Sure, me being pregnant in high school wasn't part of my overall plan, but I was going to make it work.

It had to work.

I was just about to take my seat in history class when the bell sounded to indicate there was going to be an announcement. Somehow, I just knew they were going to call out my name. It was just the way my day would go.

"Viola King, please report to the Principal's office."

Of course.

A gaggle of oohs and ahhs echoed throughout the room, almost sounding like a herd of cows.

"Shut up, you people!" Mrs. Warner boomed loud enough it bounced off the walls of the classroom. I swore that was her favourite saying. I hoped she was close to retirement, as I wouldn't want her to blow a fuse before she got a chance to experience it. Even if I doubted she was the type of person to spend time on the beach. Fern used to tell stories about a teacher she had that called the students in her class 'you people' all the time when she was mad. I used to laugh about it, and then I ended up with Mrs. Warner, leaving me with a funny suspicion the Academy would be her haunt for a while.

I picked up my things and headed to Principal Wexler's office, not wanting to piss her off. She had been a bit of a bear to me lately, especially since my brother came and did his presentation. It made me wonder what happened between them. Maybe she hit on him and he turned her down. I wasn't blind; I knew how women look at my brothers. It's the same way they look at Mike when we're out together. They perused him like he was a piece of meat, and failed to realize I was with him. Some of them would even touch him, as if being there wasn't even a blip on their radar.

I took a deep breath and walked through the doorway and up to the secretary's desk.

"Miss King, they have been waiting for you. You can head right in."

I knocked once, then pushed open the door, finding Principal Wexler seated behind her desk. Miss Rudolph stood like a sentinel in the corner of her office. Who knew what the hell she was doing in the room?

I cleared my voice. "Principal Wexler, you wanted to see me."

"Yes, Miss King, please take a seat," she answered, motioning to the chair across from her desk. "It seems we have a lot to discuss today regarding your future."

"Okay…" I glanced at Miss Rudolph. "Is that why she's here?" I winced as the question involuntarily slipped out more like an accusation.

"In a way…"

Miss Rudolph cut Principal Wexler off and explained, "I'm here as an observer to ensure that both parties are properly represented."

Considering our last meeting for counselling, I doubted that Miss Rudolph had my best interests at heart. My hackles immediately rose.

"So, are you here to represent me, or the academy?"

"Both."

"Seems more like a conflict of interest to me," I challenged, knowing full well this meeting was not going to go well for me. There was only one reason they would call the school counsellor in, and that was because they were considering suspension or expulsion. "Considering you are employed by this institution; I think it's in my best interest to have a representative of my own."

"Well, since you're now legally an adult, you do not require a representative like a parent or guardian. We thought Miss Rudolph would be a welcomed third party." Principal Wexler responded, failing to prove her point.

"We, as in the school board or as in you and Miss Rudolph?" I asked.

Neither of them responded, so I just cut in. "Let's get on with it then. You're going to kick me out, aren't you?"

"Let's not be hasty, Viola." Principal Wexler tsks, then shook her head. "In light of your present condition, we've decided it would be beneficial for you to

"But if I miss classes I won't be eligible for the valedictorian candidacy."

"That's correct," she agreed with me as if she didn't have her hand on the hammer, putting another nail in my coffin.

"That's not fair! I worked hard as a volunteer and even harder to keep my grades high enough to qualify and now you're telling me because of a technicality, I'm disqualified."

"Miss King, life's not fair." Principal Wexler agreed. "I think this will be a great lesson that there are consequences to every action."

"So, you're telling me that because I had premarital sex and accidentally got pregnant, that I deserve to be punished."

"That's exactly…"

Miss Rudolph interrupted her before she could finish her statement, although I could predict what her next words were.

"Susan, I can't let you finish that statement, no matter what your belief system is."

If I didn't feel like crying, I could have laughed out loud considering that statement was coming from the same person who told me I would be playing Russian roulette with my child by choosing to have a career and sending them to daycare.

"We work for a Catholic charter school Janet; I think it's obvious what belief system we should follow. This young girl needs to realize that sins don't go unpunished," Principal Wexler stated vehemently.

"I thought that God forgives sins," I argued, thoroughly disgusted with the ways in which people bastardized religion for their own desires.

"Some sins are too great to forgive."

I turn to Miss Rudolph. "She's talking like I murdered someone. I'm pregnant. That hardly spells eternal damnation."

"It's pretty close in the eyes of the lord."

"Doesn't Genesis 9:7 say something about repopulating Earth? Seems to me if God wanted people to repopulate the earth that he wouldn't damn the souls of mothers willing to do just that."

"This is not a theology lesson, Miss King," scolded Principal Wexler.

"I thought since you were spouting nonsense about the sins I've committed and how they'll never be forgiven that I could interject with my own beliefs."

"Regardless of your own beliefs, I have a school to run. I can't have students at this Catholic institution believing that it is okay to be pregnant. You've been showing for a couple weeks now, so I think it's time for you to physically withdraw from this school. We'll have five more girls pregnant by the start of next year if I allow you to stay."

"I'm having a baby; I'm not infected with a rare communicable disease."

"Regardless," she reached in the bottom drawer of her desk and pulled out a stack of papers. She then placed them in a folder and passed them to me. "Now fill all of these out and bring them back on Sunday. Once we've received them, we will enrol you in your new online educational system."

"How will that work?"

"You'll do all of your studies online and then need a webcam for the proctored final exams. If you focus on your studies, it's possible for you to finish as early as July 15."

"July!?" *Unbelievable!* "I was supposed to graduate with the rest of my class on June twentieth."

"Considering you're likely not attending University in September, why does it matter when you graduate?"

"My transcripts are due to the University on June thirtieth. I can't believe you are doing this to me."

"I'm sorry, but our hands are tied."

I scanned through the paperwork quickly and noticed they included a preliminary list of my grades. A plan slowly unfolded in my mind of what to do with this proof of my exceptional educational competence. There was no way I would allow them to dictate my life anymore. The moment I crossed the threshold of the security gate, I promised I would never return.

They could go to hell for all I cared.

"Once I leave, I'm never setting foot in this institution again. I'll courier the paperwork back to your office and ensure that it's here by Monday morning. You won't have to harm your delicate sensibilities by gracing you with my presence again."

I couldn't believe it took only a week for the school to be alerted to my pregnancy. The only people I confided in at this school was Miss Rudolph and Shelby. Shelby would never betray my trust, and based on her reaction to my pregnancy, she was actually the only one happy for me. Even Ivy, the romantic, expressed concern when she found out. When I thought of Miss Rudolph, it just left a bad taste in my mouth.

Prior to my visit with the counsellor, I was under the impression that what was being discussed during the session was confidential. None of the issues I discussed were life threatening; I didn't express suicidal or murderous tendencies. Everything I said within the confines of her office, should have stayed there.

The moment I exited their office, I walked up to the secretary.

"Ms. Jameson, could you pass me my cellphone, please."

"I'm sorry Miss King, but students are not permitted to have access to their phones during regular school hours."

"It's a good thing I'm no longer a student here, then." I sneered. "Now give me my god damned phone."

"There's no need to swear."

"I'm sorry. I don't mean to be rude, but I've had a really bad morning and I need to call someone to come and pick me up."

"Are you going to be okay?" She asked as she handed over my cell.

How did she not know what just happened in there? I thought the secretary was privy to all actions in the Principal's office.

"Eventually."

As soon as I crossed the threshold of the office, I headed straight for the bathroom. I barely ever cried, but ever since I got pregnant it was like I was competing in the waterworks challenge. Let's see how much I could cry in one day. I put the phone to my ear once I was secured in the bathroom and dial Mike's number.

"Hello," he answered on the third ring.

"Mike." I sniffed.

"What's wrong, Vi? Is it the baby?"

"Can you come and get me?"

"Sure, I'll be there as soon as I can. Which door should I pick you up at?"

"Can you pick me up at the dorms? I'll have some bags to bring with me."

"Is everything okay?"

"Everything is most definitely not okay," I sobbed. "I don't want to talk about it on the phone, though. If I do, I don't think I'll be able to stop crying. I want to be at home on our couch before I even begin to explain all the ways my day has sucked so far."

"Are you sure?"

"I'm sure. Please hurry. I don't want to be here any longer than I have to."

"What should I tell your brother?"

"I'm not ready to talk to anyone else about this. Just tell him I'm not feeling well so I'm coming home to stay with you for a couple days."

"But will it be more than a couple days?"

"Yes," I whispered, not wanting to admit the reality.

"Okay, baby, I promise I'll be there as soon as I can."

"Thank you."

"Anytime, baby."

The moment we hung up I dissolved into a puddle of tears.

Fuck my life.

I WAS PACKING up the rest of the items from my locker, trying not to break down again. I did enough of that in the bathroom when I called Mike. As much as I want to be done with school, I've lost more than the last month spent with my classmates. They took away my valedictorian status because of my condition. Who does that?

"What's wrong, Vi?" Shelby asked as she was getting her textbook for the next class. "You didn't return to history class."

"They're kicking me out, Shelb."

"You can't be serious! Those fuckers! You've only got two weeks of school left."

"Serious as a heart attack, which is what my dad will have if he finds out."

"Why would he find out? He hasn't talked to you in over a month."

"I swear Principal Wexler has him on speed dial, either that or he has spies here."

"So, you're not going to graduate?" She chewed her lip.

"I'll still be able to graduate, but not with you. I'll get the diploma in the mail and I won't be valedictorian."

"They can't do that!"

"They just did."

"You can fight this. It's not right."

"Shelb, I'm so tired of fighting with everyone. My father refuses to take my calls and Reed isn't talking to me either. He won't even talk to Mike. They have shifts together and the only words he says to him are work related. He's won't talk to me about it, but I can tell that he's pretty bummed out. They're best friends. I'd lose my mind if you never wanted to talk to me again." I sniffed.

"Awe, hun...I'm so sorry." Shelby wrapped her arms around me, causing my shirt to ride up.

"Look at you," a familiar and extremely annoying voice cooed from behind me.

"Vanessa, I'm not in the mood for whatever it is that you want." I braced for her wrath.

It was already embarrassing enough to be asked to leave school early because I was pregnant. I wanted to make this exit as painless as possible, which was why I hoped I could be quick enough to leave before the next break between classes. Based on the current situation, that was not going to be possible.

"Why would you think that I want anything from you? I was just handed everything I ever wanted."

"This is a private conversation, so why don't you just move on?" Shelby seethed.

Vanessa straightened her spine and looked between us, clearly assessing the situation. "Do you have a new stylist? Have you done something different with your hair?"

"No..."

"It must be the extra weight. Did you hop off the bulimia train?"

"Bulimia train?"

"You know...all the throwing up you've been doing lately. I noticed you've stopped running out of homeroom to puke."

"I never had bulimia, Vanessa."

"Oh, that's right. You've got a bun in the oven," she sneered. "You know...I can't believe you. You and Shelby made me feel like I was a total loser when I said I wanted to have sex with that hot cop.

The joke's on me though, right? A loser like me could never get a guy like that to want me."

"It wasn't like that," I responded.

"Then what was it like, Vi-o-la? Was it because you were already fucking him? Obviously, hat must have been the reason. Unless you're just a fatty," she leered. "Ever hear of how someone wouldn't buy a cow if they got the milk for free? You'll never be good enough for a guy like Robbie. Guys of his caliber would never sink low enough to be with you."

Tears streaked down my face as I pulled my t-shirt over my barely there baby bump.

"Get the fuck away from her you whore!" Shelby yelled.

"I think your whore's right here, Shelby." Vanessa retorted.

"I think you're getting a bit green with envy. It's not Vi's fault he wouldn't touch you. A man's got to have standards, right?" Shelby turned to me. "Did you know she didn't stop with her quest after she hit on your boyfriend? Did she tell you that she also tried to slip her digits to your brother too?"

"Shut up, Shelby. You don't know what you're talking about. They were both extremely interested in what I had to say and eagerly asked for my number."

"Melissa told me everything. She told me you undid the top four buttons of your blouse, rolled the waistband of your skirt over to make it shorter so that your ass cheeks were almost showing and then pretended to drop one of the pamphlets Mike and Reed were handing out in the hopes they would check you out."

"Shut the hell up Shelby!" Vanessa shouted in outrage. "No one asked for your opinion."

The look in Shelby's eyes made me realize she was going in for the kill. Normally I didn't participate in or condone bullying. However, at this point in time, I really needed someone to have my back, and I could always count on Shelby.

That was what best friends were for, right?

"She laughed about how you were shot down both times."

"What the fuck ever," Vanessa put her hands on her hips and leaned forward for effect, spit spraying with every inflection. "You're probably just as big of a whore as Vi is. Did you both fuck him at the same time? Or did you get even more kinky and have her brother in the same room to watch?"

"What kind of fucked up sex fantasies do you have?" Shelby retorted. "Are you into incest or something, you psycho? Do you kiss your mother with that mouth?"

"I'm just glad I told Principal Wexler and the Sisters about your current condition before you could continue to make a mockery of this holy institution."

The smug look on her foundation caked face fueled my rage.

"You did what?" I yelled. "Do you realize what you've done?"

"I'm completely aware of what I've done." She flipped her hair back haughtily. "You see, after you left the office I was called in and notified that you've been taken out of the running for valedictorian, and now I'm currently seated in the top spot. With only two weeks left of school and finals, I'm a shoe in. I guess you being a slut and fucking the man of my dreams worked out for me."

"You can't seriously believe that Mike was the man of your dreams? That seems a bit stalkerish, don't you think?"

"At least I'm not a whore. I guess you are a little like your sister Ivy after all. Although I hear Tyler didn't stick around to send out invitations to their wedding. Are you sure he's even your baby's daddy?"

"Grow the fuck up, Vanessa." Shelby yelled.

"Ladies, do we have a problem over here?" Principal Wexler interrupted. "Shouldn't you be heading to your next class?"

"No ma'am, there isn't a problem." Vanessa responded. "I was just telling Viola good luck and that I wish her all the best with her pregnancy on my way to the next class."

"I hope you don't think I'm that stupid, Miss Cruxton. I didn't tell you the good news about your status as valedictorian for you to immediately turn around and present yourself in a manner unbecoming of a young lady meant to represent this prestigious academy." She smiled. "Now you ladies head to class. Miss King has to continue packing.

I barely contained the desire to roll my eyes. Prestigious institution, my ass.

"Principal Wexler is right. I'll catch you later, Shelby."

"I love you," she responded.

"I love you too, and this isn't goodbye, chickie."

"I know, but I'll miss your ugly mug around here."

"I'll send you selfies every day."

"I only want belly shots."

I snorted. Leave it to Shelby to make a weirdo comment.

"Ladies, it's time to go. Viola, you are no longer a student here, please vacate the premises as soon as possible."

"I'm going."

I threw my backpack on and headed to the dormitory. I wonder what the weight restriction was on what a pregnant woman could carry. I pondered over a million nonsensical things while walking over to the dorm for what would be the last time. Cause I sure as hell wouldn't be sending my daughters to this two-faced institution to be spit out like mindless drones. The ranting in my head must have been making me crazy because I was sure I can hear my name being called.

"Viola."

Yep, I had officially gone insane.

A tap on my shoulder mades me launch into the air and scream. A familiar chuckle brought me back and drew my attention.

Mike.

"Viola, I've been calling your name and walking behind you for a while now." He smiled. "Didn't you hear me?"

"I didn't expect you to be here so soon. I honestly thought I was going crazy."

"Makes me wonder if you were paying attention when we gave our presentation on College safety." He tapped his chin. "What was the most important rule Reed brought up in our presentation?"

His taunt made me realize that he didn't know that I was the one who did all of the research for Reed's presentation as part of my University entrance essay for the Criminal Justice degree that I wanted. Ironically, my dad was so impressed with my research that he requested I put together a presentation for his officers to give at high schools. It was one of the few times that my dad had paid attention to anything that I had done.

"The most important thing to remember is to be aware of your surroundings at all times." I reiterated word for word.

"Wow, do you have an eidetic memory or something?"

"Nope,' I laughed. "That was my presentation."

"We used your presentation?"

"Yeah. I did a bunch of research on the dangers of life at University for the entrance essay for my Criminal Justice degree."

"And Reed stole the info for his presentation?"

"Dad read my essay before I submitted it and was beyond proud of all the research I did and how well it was organized. He said that he'd been trying to put something together for the precincts to use as an excuse to get out and recruit new officers. He had me design the presentation and everything."

"Wow."

"Yeah, it was the one and only time I felt like I had his complete attention. It's too bad I had to gain his attention by research on the number of rapes and occurrences of violence at University."

"I know how you feel. So, tell me, why were you so spaced out?"

"Principal Wexler and her cronies," was the only response I could commit to at the moment without having another breakdown.

"Must have been quite a morning."

"It was the morning from hell. How about if we keep walking and you can tell me about yours?"

I pointed in the direction of the dorms. At this point I didn't care what they thought about me having him up there. I would need his help to carry some of the things anyways.

"Well, I had to lie to and ditch Reed, which doesn't raise me up on the deserves to be forgiven scale."

"I'm sorry."

"You're more important."

"I don't want you to lose your close relationship with my brother to be with me."

"You should know better than most how stubborn your brother is. I'm sure he'll come around eventually, we just have to give him time. He still hasn't gotten over the secrets about Rowan and what they did to your family."

"I know, but it's still hard to not be able to talk to him. He's been avoiding my calls as well and I miss my brother. He was more of a father to me than my own was."

"Really?"

"Yeah. Even though my brothers were twins, dad expected Rowan to be the sole caretaker of his siblings. I think it might have been too much for him to handle. When Rowan died, Reed almost immediately stepped into his role. Reed and Fern took on the role of parents to all of us, even to my older brother Ash, who was closer in age to them."

"That's crazy. I couldn't imagine having to look after my siblings, and there are only two of them."

"It is what it is I guess."

"Yeah. How much farther to your room?"

"How'd you know that's where I was taking you?"

"Well, I didn't think you were going to take me somewhere to have your way with me," he responded, then quirked his brow. "Or were you?"

I blushed. "Can you imagine what the teachers would say then?"

"I can imagine. Although that Principal Wexler seems like quite the cougar."

I threw back my head and laughed. "Cougar?"

"She totally hit on Reed when we came to do the presentation."

"Okay, that's just gross." I gagged. "She went on a couple dates with my dad. What was she trying to do, finish the set?"

"Wow, okay," he chuckled. "So, when are you going to tell me what happened this morning?"

"They kicked me out of school."

"They can't do that. You've almost graduated."

"Those bigots can, and they will."

"Bigots?"

"They basically told me I was going to hell because I'm pregnant with your child. Principal Wexler is of the opinion that I'm going to spread the disease of pregnancy to the rest of the student population and that there will be an increase in teenaged pregnancy at this institution if I'm not removed before I start showing."

"Seriously? She dated your dad then hits on your brother and somehow you're a bad influence?"

"Oh, and according to the guidance counsellor, I'm playing Russian roulette with our child by considering placing him or her in daycare while I pursue my degree."

"Wow. I don't know what to say to that. Did she use those exact words?"

"Yup."

"Then I'm glad you're no longer enrolled here. They can go to hell." He stopped us and grasped both my cheeks, raising my head until our eyes met. "You're going to be okay." He kissed my forehead. "We're going to be okay."

"You really think so?"

"I know so," he responded with confidence. "We haven't really had a proper discussion about what we're going to do when the baby arrives, but I think we need to because I have some ideas about how to make having the baby and you going to University work."

"Really?"

"Really."

"Thank you."

"For what?"

"For the talk, for you dropping everything to come and get me with short notice, just everything."

"It was my pleasure."

It took the two of us thirty minutes to pack up everything in my dorm room. The whole situation seemed surreal as I reluctantly closed the next chapter in my life. Mike's mention of making University work gave me the hope to get through this dark moment.

After we packed my meagre possessions into the back of his truck, he drove us home.

Home.

It was hard to believe that two months ago we were meeting for coffee and now I was living with him. My situation could have been worse considering the circumstances. Sure, I could have gone and lived with one of my brothers, but neither of them likely wanted or needed their pregnant sister cramping their style.

Shortly after we unloaded all my things into my room, I headed back downstairs, flopped down onto the couch, and pulled my ice-cold feet up under my butt. I started flipping through channels while I waited for Mike to come back down. Two minutes later Mike appeared beside me again.

"Are you going to be okay here while I take a quick shower?"

"Definitely."

I couldn't help feeling disappointed when fifteen minutes later, Mike came back down the stairs fully clothed. He had mostly kept his distance since I moved in, but occasionally, like earlier, he found a reason to touch me. I longed for those moments when his resolve slipped, and he instinctively pushed a stray hair behind my ear or tenderly kissed my forehead.

"I'm going to head out for a few, but I'll be back soon. Why don't you take a nap? You've had a long day." He leaned forward and kissed my forehead with so much tenderness that it almost brought me to tears again, but this time in a good way.

Sometime later when Mike's key turned in the lock I woke from my nap. I looked up to see Mike coming into the room carrying a bag from the local convenience store. I watched as he pulled a big tub of vanilla ice cream out of the bag along with a bottle each of caramel and chocolate syrup.

He was a man after my heart.

"How long were you gone for?"

"Only fifteen minutes."

"Wow, I must have slept like the dead. It felt like two hours."

"That's good, though. You need your sleep."

"I guess."

"Want some ice cream? I got your favorite."

I laughed. "You got vanilla."

"Correction, I got you French vanilla and what looks like a jug of chocolate syrup."

"Yum."

"Well, do you want some?"

"Hell yes," I moved both hands back and forth towards me.

"Okay, cutie. Go and get your pajamas on and come back down and we'll watch a movie together."

"Awesome," I jaunted up the stairs as quickly and as safely as I could.

Mike glanced up from the two bowls of ice cream he dished out while I was getting dressed. When I walked back into the room, his eyes scanning me from head to toe. I shifted with his non-subtle scrutiny.

"It's too tight isn't' it?" I pulled at my shirt. "I really need to go shopping for more clothes."

"I think it's cute," he replied.

"You think me getting fat is cute?"

"Vi, you're pregnant with our child, not getting fat," he corrected. "If you want, I can take you shopping tomorrow."

"Okay."

"Great," he patted the cushion beside him. "Now sit your cute butt down and have some ice cream."

I settled down beside him and he lifted a spoon of chocolatey covered goodness into my mouth. I barely contained the moan as the flavours exploded in my mouth.

"Good?"

"Um...hmm." I smile.

"Great."

We finished feeding ice cream to each other, then spent the rest of the night watching movies while cuddling on the couch. For the first time since the morning, I finally felt like everything might be okay.

MIKE

Reaching for a glass for my beer, I noticed Reed pull up and park on the street in front of the house. He stomped up the front door like a herd of elephants, the total opposite of stealthy. I was happy he didn't apply his actions to work because there was no way we would sneak up on a suspect we were trailing.

Before I could make it to the front door, he knocked. I went over and opened the door, wondering what made him stamped up the front steps. It had been a week since Vi was kicked out of school. I had actually expected him to show up that night. She was so ashamed of everything that she didn't want to tell any of her family about what happened. She preferred to have some sort of solution before she confessed.

"Hey man, how's it going?"

"Same old, same old."

"Cool. Come on in."

"What's this I heard about Vi getting kicked out of school?" he asked, leaning against the kitchen island.

"You wouldn't believe what those bitches said to her while they were ruining her life."

"I can only imagine what that battle axe said. The whole time my dad was dating that Principal, she couldn't stop telling him what he should do to keep his house in order. I think they likely broke up because of their controlling ways, but he still sent all three of my sisters to that school after Rowan overdosed."

"She told Vi that she was basically going to hell. She implied there was no forgiveness for her sins, and her choices would create a deviant child. The counsellor told her that going to school and working while having a child at home was like playing Russian Roulette."

"Russian roulette and deviants? That doesn't surprise me. Some people take religion to the extreme. People like her make everyone distrust religion. It's just a nasty situation all together. I hope you told Vi not to listen to a word those morons said."

"She's been pretty hung up on it. Then they destroy her chance of becoming valedictorian of her class like she knew she could, and hand it off to her nemesis and bully Vanessa."

He slumped down on the couch. "Shit."

"Yeah." I sat in the recliner and put my head in my hands. "I try my best to ensure Viola forgets all that crap, but it's weighing on her. She wanted to graduate with her friends and get a degree. You know how much of a planner she is."

"Yeah," he laughed.

"I bought her a huge cork board for her bedroom wall," I laughed. "She filled it in less than a week. It was three feet by four feet."

"Where's Vi?"

"She's at the library, finishing her entrance essays for her University applications and trying to find a solution to her high school completion problem."

Viola had been gone to the library for a couple of hours. When she came home last week freaking out about her future, I didn't know what to do. I knew how much she wanted to graduate on time and go to University. She was now six months pregnant and didn't need the stress all of this was putting on her. Tonight, she was moping around, so I suggested she go do some research at the library after we finished eating. We both agreed that she should continue writing her entrance essays, and then we could figure out what she would do about graduating high school.

"At least you haven't completely fucked up her life."

We remained in silence for what felt like an hour, I got up and handed him a beer.

"Thanks."

"She should be home in a bit if you want to talk to her."

"Why didn't you tell me?" he asked suddenly. We both knew he wasn't talking about how I didn't tell him she would be home soon.

"Honestly?"

He nodded.

"I thought you would shoot me in the leg or something and make it look like friendly fire."

He laughed and took a drink.

"I really do care about her." I confessed to him for the first time.

"Are you in love with her?" he asked, even though I was sure he didn't want to hear the answer. To be honest I had no idea what I felt for her and I didn't want us having a baby together to blur the lines. I wanted to know I was in love with her and that it was separate than the feelings I had about becoming a father for the first time.

"No, but you remember that woman I couldn't get out of my head?"

"That was her?" he asked in disbelief, knowing exactly how his little sister had affected everything. I didn't want to carry on the way I had in the past. It was like my player ways took a one eighty and all I could focus on was finding my mystery girl. The truth was I had looked everywhere for her, but I thought she lied about her name. We didn't exchange numbers and she was gone in the morning.

Why would she be any different than another person on a one-night stand?

Now I knew what the answer to that question was, but at the time I just thought I had met my match. Finally, I was outdone by a woman got one over on me. What I didn't expect was to meet her when we moved his other sister home. Who knew the one woman to rock my world would be the younger sister of my best friend?

Karma definitely had it out for me.

"Yeah. So, are you gonna wait for her to come home?"

He nodded.

"Alright. I'll get you another beer and put on the game."

He seemed deep in thought, so I didn't say anything more. I passed him his beer and sat in the recliner. I only hoped my confession would settle the storm enough that when Vi walked in the door, she didn't get blown away. Reed had been under a lot of stress lately, but he never confided in me what was going on. Over the past month he rarely joined the after-work drinks with the other guys at the precinct. We fell into a comfortable silence and watched the game. Once in a while we would yell at the referee making a stupid call, but essentially, we didn't say much to each other.

This was what men did; we bonded over hockey.

Once we approached the second intermission in the game I felt as though maybe we had made some headway. I didn't want to sound like a pansy, but I missed my partner and best friend. At work we had been going through the motions, but we didn't joke or carry on like we used to, and it was starting to get to me. Being with Viola was something I wouldn't change because she was giving me something, I never knew I wanted, but losing Reed as a friend was a steep price to pay for happiness.

The front door clicked closed signalling Viola's arrival. She walked around the corner and her eyes widened at the sight of Reed drinking a beer on the couch. She dropped her backpack on the chair in the corner of the room and approached like Reed was a skittish bird. Like somehow, he was going to fly away.

"Hi, guys. Everything okay in here?" she asked.

"Yeah, I was just telling Reed how his favourite team was going to lose."

"They are not," he replied in disgust. "Your team sucks. Why would you cheer for another city's team when there was a team in the city you're from?"

"Cause your team is full of pansy asses."

"Whoa, don't come to blows over there," she teased with a laugh. "I've already come to terms with this house cheering for the other team."

"Traitor." Reed accused.

"Nope. I just know when to pick my battles."

"Speaking of battles," Reed changed the subject. "What's this I hear about you getting kicked out of school?"

"Those women are bitches."

"Imp."

"Reed." She whined with the voice of a three-year-old.

"What happened? I'd rather hear it from you than Dad."

"Dad told you I got kicked out?"

"Yeah, he called to reem me out for not making sure you were doing well."

"Like you could make sure I remained in that school," she scoffed.

Reed might not have noticed, but Viola was putting on a front. Considering I knew she felt horrible for the way she was treated and how it cost her something she worked so hard for, she was doing a good job of making him believe it didn't matter.

But it did.

Those women took away more of her dreams this week and made her feel like a leper while doing it. Like somehow her going to school was going to make the other girls *catch* pregnancy. As if it would run rampant through the halls and they would have a whole graduating class of mothers.

"Just tell me what happened," Reed pleaded.

"They basically told me that I was going to hell, our child would burn forever in the fires of damnation and that I was a bad example."

"Seriously?"

"Without all the extra fancy words, yes," she replied, crossed her arms and flopped down in the recliner.

I addressed Reed, "I had never wanted to ring the neck of a nun before, but the day she came home I did."

Another reason religion and I didn't mix. In fact, authority figures of any kind and me didn't mix. It likely stemmed from the parenting I received at home.

"I can't believe they did that."

"Susan told me sins don't go unpunished and when I mentioned God was there to forgive our sins, she said some sins are too great to forgive. As if me having a baby and not being married was just as bad as murder. She then told me that if she allowed me to stay that next year there would be five more pregnant girls enrolled at school."

"That's bullshit."

"That's exactly what I told her. She can fuck our dad for weeks on end, but somehow me having sex is opening a portal to hell."

"When I was at your school for that presentation, that bitch hit on me too," Reed told her.

"She used to hit on Alder when Dad wasn't looking too."

"You've got to be kidding me."

"Nope. I think that's why Dad stopped seeing her. It didn't stop him from sending us to that school though," she shook her head in annoyance.

"So, what are you going to do about graduating?"

"I'm calling the Director of Education."

"Going straight to the top?"

"Reed, they can't do this to me! I only had a couple weeks left of school at the most. All my classes had the highest grades out of my graduating class. They could have just given me credit. Even if I would have failed the finals, I would have still had the marks to pass everything. Instead they told me I would have to do everything online and wouldn't graduate until the middle of July if I was lucky. Everything!"

"Then that's what you need to do."

"Repeat everything?"

"No, you need to call the school board. All they would need to do is look at your current transcripts and they could see how well you're doing. They're all electronic, so you have proof of your standing."

"I have copies of my draft transcripts I was using for my University applications."

"You're still going to University?"

"That's the plan," I answered for her. Viola was excited about going to the library tonight, so I wanted to give her the support she needed to keep going with her plan to go to school. I knew we could do it. I had enough money to afford a nanny if we needed one to help us through the first couple years while she went to school.

If I had anything to do with it, Viola would not have to give up any more of her dreams.

Having our baby shouldn't mean a shackle.

VIOLA

"I CAN'T BELIEVE YOU'RE LIVING HERE, WITH HIM!" Shelby exclaimed as she bounced into Mike's townhouse the next afternoon after she finished classes for the day. Her energy was infectious.

"I'm so glad you came," I hugged her tightly, not wanting to let go. "I've missed you so much."

"I've missed you too, sweetie." She pulled back and looked at me. "Oh my god, look at you and your cute little baby belly."

Ever since I left Sacred Heart All-Girls' Academy, I'd inadvertently lost touch with my friends. They were all preparing for finals while I was baking a very large bun in my oven. Even though I tried hard not to focus on the fact that most of my friends would be leaving for college in a couple months without me, it still bothered me. Getting pregnant had changed my original plan to go to the police academy, and I most definitely wouldn't be leaving town to attend a post-secondary institution. Luckily, we were a big enough city to have two Universities, so I had my choice of school between the two. They also both had daycare if I needed it. At least that part of my future plans hadn't changed.

"So, how are you feeling?" she asked as she sat down on the couch with me.

"Not sure how I'm going to handle the next three months if he keeps growing like this."

"It's a boy?"

"I don't know, I'm only guessing."

"Are you going to find out?"

"I've got an appointment coming up with the doctor, so if Mike wants to know, we'll find out. I don't exactly care either way, although it would be nice to know since it's my first. After that it probably won't matter as much cause of hand me downs."

"Is he going with you?"

"I haven't mentioned to him yet, but I'm hoping he will want to go."

"I'm sure he'll go," she assured me. "So, are you guys in the same bed yet?" she asked while wiggling her eyebrows suggestively.

"No," I blushed.

"Get on it, girl."

I glanced down at my ever-growing baby bump. Mike constantly told me how cute it was, but sometimes I was self-conscious about gaining weight. Before getting pregnant, I participated on several sports teams and competed in Krav Maga. I was sure that most pregnant women felt the same way. Being pregnant was a beautiful thing, but what it was doing to the overall shape of my body was scary. Sometimes I wished I could pick up the phone and talk to my mom about what I was going through.

"Oh my god, woman! Don't you dare be thinking what I think you're thinking. You're not fat, your pregnant."

"I wasn't thinking that."

I totally was.

"You were so."

"What if he doesn't want me anymore?"

"You know he does. He wouldn't let you stay with him if he didn't care about you."

"Caring and wanting are two different things."

"I know. You should deal with one thing at a time and possibly let the other thing evolve. Let's just think of the situation this way," she explained. "Number one, you're having his baby. His. Not anyone else's, but his. Secondly, when you showed up on his doorstep, he let you move in with him without a fuss. That has to say something about the way he feels about you. He could have just told you that he wants a paternity test and then told you that he would give you money once you had proof, but that he didn't want anything to do with you until the baby was born."

"What if the only reason he's letting me stay here is because he feels responsible, or worst, he doesn't want to piss my brother off?" I asked.

"Vi, if he didn't want to piss your brother off, he wouldn't be shacking up with his baby sister."

"True."

"Plus, you guys weren't just a one-night stand. It might have started that way, but after you met up again you hung out and talked on the phone for over a month before he chickened out about Reed."

I laughed at the visual of a man like Mike being a chicken. He didn't seem like he was scared of anything. Not even my brother.

"What did Reed the rhino do when he found out you're living here?

"Rhino?"

"Cause he's big and gruff and has a long hard horn."

"Eww. Seriously? Shelby! I don't to hear long and hard used in the same sentence as my brother."

If there was one thing, I never wanted to experience was women hitting on any of my brothers. As far as I was concerned, they were all celibate and would be until the end of time. It was as cringeworthy as imagining your parents had sex. We all knew that they needed to, otherwise we wouldn't exist, but we all convinced ourselves that storks dropped us on the doorstep.

It skeeved everyone out.

"You can't tell me that you don't know that your whole family won the genetic lottery. Even your dad is a silver fox."

"Shelby."

"What?" she feigned innocence, when we all knew she was the devil in disguise.

"Changing subjects. How's school going?"

"You mean how annoying is Vanessa now that you're gone?"

"Sure."

We talked for the next hour or so about how big of an ego Vanessa had now that I lost my valedictorian spot. It still urked me that they took that chance away, especially considering there was only a couple weeks left of school. Surely, I wouldn't have shown that much by then or at least I could have hidden it with a big shirt. They could have let me take my homework home and write my exams via proctor. Anything besides what they decided to do.

"She's spreading rumours about you too," Shelby confessed.

Of course, she was.

THE FRONT DOOR SLAMMED SHUT, cutting off our conversation. My mouth went dry when Mike walked in the living room wearing his uniform. Uninhibited, I perused him from head to toe. When I met his eyes again, he winked, well aware of what I had done.

"Ooh…" Shelby teased.

I smacked her arm. "Shut up."

"How are you ladies doing today?" Mike asked. "Are you feeling okay, babe?"

Babe?

"We're good, I'm good." I rubbed my stomach."

"He was kicking a bunch today." I told him.

"You think the baby is a boy?" he asked.

I blushed. "Isn't that what you want the baby to be?"

"As long as he or she is healthy I don't care if you have a whole hockey team in there."

"Are you saying I'm fat?" I teased.

"What? No!" he argued.

"I'm just pulling your leg."

"When you should be pulling on something else," Shelby whispered under her breath.

I blushed again when I saw the look on Mike's face. He had definitely heard her.

"I should get going," Shelby told me as she gathered all of her things and started for the front door.

"Don't leave on my account," Mike replied.

"I'm not. I've been here for a while and I have to go back to dorm before they have a conniption."

"Thanks for coming." I hugged her again.

"Take care of my little niece or nephew in there."

"I will."

LATER THAT NIGHT I couldn't wait to tell Mike what happened when I called the school board earlier in the day before Shelby showed up. Surprisingly everything worked out the way I wanted to. The vengeful part of me wanted to shove it in the faces of the faculty at Sacred Heart because I would be graduating before the rest of my class. When I called, I kept getting transferred and eventually ended up on the phone with the Director of Education.

"I spoke with the Director of Education today."

"Oh? How'd you get straight to the top?"

"Because I don't take no for an answer."

"That you don't," he responded, then winked. "So, what did he say?"

"Yup. He's pretty pissed at Principal Wexler. He sounded as though he might be making an appointment to speak with her about her rash decision to blatantly break the law based on religious views."

"Really?"

"He said that because the student handbook and policy manual doesn't explicitly state that pregnancy was grounds for expulsion that they are violating the Education Board's mandate regarding access to education."

I recalled the anger in his voice. "He sounded like he truly believed in access to education for all youth, no matter their circumstances. He said that he's on the board for a program to ensure that all juvenile offenders have adequate access to educational programs whether they're in a group home or detention setting."

"Really? You lucked out with who you got to talk to."

"I think it helped that I'm the daughter of Richard King. I think this is the one and only time it paid to be his daughter. He was appalled that the daughter of the Chief of Police had been kicked out of high school with only two weeks left. He also mentioned that my expulsion would look bad for the school board statistics because they have to report everything."

"That's good. So, what's the plan then?"

"He took a look at my transcripts and decided on the spot that he would graduate me based on my academic standing thus far. He said that because I was already on track to be the valedictorian that I should meet all the requirements for graduation."

"Which is exactly what they should say. You attended every class until the moment that they kicked you out. Reed said that you were the smartest out of all of your siblings," he praised. "What are the next steps?"

"He just needs me to come down and fill out the appropriate forms next week and then he'll give me my diploma." I breathed a sigh of relief. Out of everything that had happened, I couldn't stand if my choices caused me to have to repeat a year of school.

"That's fantastic news."

"I thought so. He's already faxed my transcripts to the University as a final record of my grades. So I'm all set to go to school in the fall, if everything works out."

"I'm sure it will. We'll make it work."

"We will?"

"We're in this together. I can take a different shift at work, or we could get a nanny for the times when you're attending classes or need to have a study session."

"Really?"

"Vi, I don't want us having a child to destroy the future you had planned for yourself. It might take a bit longer to get there, but you'll graduate and have a degree."

I smiled at the thought of being able to have everything I wanted. Almost everything.

"Just imagine me sitting in the front row holding our child as we cheer for you walking across the stage."

That night when I went to bed, I considered the words he used. It was difficult for me not to get my hopes up as I read between the lines.

Could he want more than just the baby?

VIOLA

STARING OUT THE WINDOW OVER THE SINK, I FOUND myself imagining Mike pushing our kids on a swing set in the back yard, while I was in the kitchen making supper. Since I was a little girl, I always imagined having a huge family, even bigger than the one I came from. Most people would assume having seven children was an absurd idea, but not me. Granted, these thoughts are before I went through the delivery of my first child.

"What's wrong?" Mike's voice broke my concentration.

"I made another doctor's appointment today," I replied.

"You did? Is there something wrong with the baby?" He set down his coffee and stood up. "Is that why you're so spacey this morning?"

"Spacey?" I repeated.

"You've been staring out the window for at least ten minutes. I think the toast has already popped up," he teased.

"Oh!" I turned around and grabbed the slice. "Shit, it's cold."

"Just pop it back down for another few seconds to heat it up," he smirked. "So...the doctor's appointment?"

"Will you come with me?" I asked timidly. Deep down I believed that he would want to go, but I wasn't sure how these things normally went. We weren't together-together, but we were having a baby, so I figured that he would want to see the sonogram and hear the heartbeat.

"I wouldn't miss it for the world. I appreciate you including me," he smiled so wide his eyes shined.

"You're the father, of course I would include you." I responded, surprised he thought I wouldn't ask him to go with me.

"What time is the appointment?"

"Two o'clock," I answered.

"Sounds good," he responded. "I don't have a shift today, so it actually works out pretty great."

"That's why I scheduled it for today," I confessed. "I saw your schedule up on the fridge, so I made sure that you had the option to attend the appointment with me."

"I'm glad you did," he responded and then asked, "what would you have done if I didn't go with you? How would you have gotten there?"

"The bus or a cab."

"Promise me that you'll let me know whenever you need to go to the doctor or any appointments. I'll either take time off or I'll arrange to get you there. I know Reed isn't really talking to you right now because he barely says a word to me unless it's work related."

"Yeah," I responded.

"You will not be alone in this, Vi. I promise you that for as long as you allow me to be, I will be there for you. No matter what."

I breathed a sigh of relief. I had been planning to ask him to go to the appointment with me for a couple weeks now but didn't know how. The fear of rejection constantly lingered in the back of my mind. Reed still wasn't talking to me. It took him a week to talk to me after he found out about the baby. He had just began to come around and then I got kicked out of school and the silent treatment started again. I assumed the same went for him and Mike at work. The worry of Mike choosing his relationship with my brother over me and his baby constantly hovered over my head.

Like waiting for the proverbial ball to drop.

∽

"Mr. and Mrs. King?" The bubbly receptionist called.

"Oh, we're…"

"We're right here," Mike cut me off, the excitement evident in his voice. It was more than obvious because he would have never cut me off before.

"You don't have to come in with me." I tried to give him an out, just in case he wasn't interested in going in.

"I'm not going to miss a minute more of this pregnancy," he surprised me.

We followed the receptionist into the examination room. The walls were filled with pregnancy information, and posters for prenatal and post-natal classes. It was comforting to see all of the information on the walls.

"Dr. Kensington will be with you shortly."

My hackles raised as she unabashedly perused Mike from head to toe, like I wasn't even there. Then placed my chart in the holder beside the door frame, before leaving the room.

The moment the door closed behind her, I asked. "Does that happen to you often?" The jealousy in my tone caught me by surprise.

What was wrong with me? We're not even dating.

"Does what happen?" He glanced at me, oblivious that he had been objectified.

"She just checked you out and didn't even hide it." I shook my head. "Who does that? Checks out a person that she just insinuated was married?"

"She does I guess," he answered.

"It's just wrong. I mean, at least don't make it so obvious."

"You're cute when you're jealous." He kissed my temple.

"I'm not jealous," I muttered under my breath.

"Whatever you say, sweetheart," he chuckled.

The door opened, "Viola King?" The doctor smiled at me, then glanced at Mike. "Robert?"

"Mark?" Mike responded, with obvious confusion. "You're a doctor now?"

"As of two years ago, yeah. What about you?" Dr. Kensington, or rather, Mark, asked.

"I'm in law enforcement," I replied well aware the disapproval in his voice.

"Oh, for real? What do your parents think?"

"I don't really care what my parents think."

"And you're going to be a dad? What about…"

"Yes," Mike cut him off, responding with pride in his voice.

A niggling in my mind made me wonder what the doctor was about to say before he was interrupted. I tried to push it out of my mind and tried to focus on the situation at hand. It was more important for me to see how the little one was doing than it was for me to figure out what Mike was trying to keep from me.

Was there something he was trying to keep quiet?

"This might be a little cold. We try to keep it relatively warm, but it all depends on the person it's being used on," warned the doctor.

A whooshing sound filled the room as soon as the wand touched my baby bump.

"There's your baby's heartbeat," the doctor confirmed. "Nice and strong."

Tears filled my eyes when I saw our baby on the screen. It wasn't the first time I had seen it, but for some reason this appointment meant more. I was further along, so we could see much more of the baby and we might even find out what the gender was.

Even if I was on the fence about finding out…

"I can't believe that's our baby," Mike said as he squeezed my hand. He leaned closer to me and kissed my forehead once. "Thank you."

What was he thanking me for?

The doctor cleared his throat and continued, "You're about twenty-five weeks along, which means there is around fifteen weeks left in your pregnancy."

"It's going by so fast." I commented.

"Have you felt any fluttering in your stomach yet? The baby should be moving around now."

"Yeah, I thought I felt something last night."

"That's your baby," the doctor confirmed.

I looked over at Mike. "Do you want to know what the baby's gender is?" I glanced at the doctor, "We can do that right?"

"Sure, if you want to find out, I'll let you know. Some parents can't agree on whether they want to know or not. In that case, I can have my receptionist write it on a piece of paper and put it in an envelope for you to take home. Then you either look or you don't. Totally up to you."

"What do you want?" Mike asked me.

"I almost want to know because it's our first baby. It might make things easier for getting things," I admitted. "We won't have to worry about spending too much money."

"Don't worry about the money, Vi. I've got you covered."

"Yeah, don't you know…" the doctor began, stopping before he finished his statement. I glanced over at Mike and noticed the ending of the look he had given to the doctor. The kind of look that told someone to shut up.

Several things went through my mind, even though I tried to shake it off. *What wasn't he telling me? Did it have to do with money? Would he ever tell me what this secret was?* Maybe I hadn't seen what I did. The hormones running through my veins were making me a bit wonky. Maybe I was seeing things.

"I think I would like to know what we're having." Mike finally said.

"Great," the doctor replied. "Let me just see here. It looks like you are having a baby boy. Congratulations!"

"You're happy?" I asked Mike.

Tears shone in his eyes when he answered. "More than you could ever know."

MIKE

WE WERE HAVING A BABY BOY!

A son I wouldn't repeat all the mistakes of my father with.

Before, when she had asked, I told Viola the baby's gender didn't matter. It truly didn't, because all I wanted was a healthy baby. However, when I thought about having a girl, I didn't look forward to the nightmare of raising a daughter and dealing with the teenage boys. Now I couldn't wait to play catch with him in the summer or teach him how to skate in the winter.

Never in a million years did I think I would ever become a father. The plan for my life since I was younger, was to remain single. In that plan there definitely wasn't any children running around. I never wanted to have children; I wouldn't do that to them. The parental role models I was dealt were horrific examples of proper parenting, and perfect providers of the cold shoulder. Sure, my siblings and I never wanted for anything that could be bought with money, but as the saying went, it couldn't buy love.

The whooshing on the speakers was the new soundtrack of my life. Everything changed in one moment and there was no going back. So many questions started rolling through my mind as soon as I heard the sound of my baby's heartbeat. Major questions like how was I supposed to be a loving father when my own used his offspring as pawns on a chess board? Until I heard that heartbeat, I didn't even know what I wanted. The past couple months with Viola had been amazing, but sometimes I still doubted that I was what they needed. Inevitably, I fucked up everything good in my life, so what made this situation any different?

What if Viola woke up one morning and decided that she couldn't handle her life with me?

If I were to let her in all the way, then she would have the power to wreck me. No other woman before her had been close enough to.

I couldn't believe how fast the switch inside of me was flicked when I saw the life we created on the screen. It was like the baby was evidence of everything I felt the morning after our first time together, when she left without saying goodbye. Until that moment, nothing was real, but when I heard the heartbeat, my life changed completely. Everything after would be all for them, my family. Tonight, things were going to change, starting with our sleeping arrangements.

After we left the doctor's office, I took Viola for a milkshake because she was having a craving for peanut butter and bananas. She was becoming predictable with the cravings. She didn't know it, but I kept Rocky Road, her favourite ice cream, stocked in the fridge in my garage just in case she ran out. She never went in there because it was technically my beer fridge, even though I'd been having less friends over in trade for more time with her. She had slowly worked her way under my skin and seeing our child on the monitor made her cemented in place.

On our way back from the drive through, we drove past a couple maternity and toy stores. I couldn't help but notice her eyes drifting to the side.

"Do you want to go and get some things?"

"No, that's okay."

"Are you sure?"

She shook her head, but I knew she wanted to go. So I pulled into the parking lot at the next one I saw. Her eyes widened when she realized what I was doing.

"I really don't need anything."

"What about some clothes? Something comfortable."

She blushed.

"Don't tell me you like wearing my sweatpants."

"Okay, I won't," she beamed. "Really, it's okay. I'm going to wait until Fern comes next month to go shopping with her. She really wants to take me and make a day of it."

"If it's money you're worried about, I'll buy everything you and the baby need."

She shook her head. "No, that's not it. I have some money saved up. I just think there's no point in shopping twice for clothes that might not fit in a month. Unless you don't want me to wear your clothes."

"Believe it or not, I love coming home and seeing you wearing my clothes on the couch," I smirked.

There was something about a woman wearing your clothes. Even with the baby bump my shirts all hang loose on her. The sweatpants are baggy in the legs, but they fit her around the waist, which is why I think she enjoyed wearing them. Knowing how in shape Viola used to be before her pregnancy, it wouldn't surprise me if she felt self-conscious about the weight gain regardless of the reason. Most women would, even if it was completely absurd to believe growing another human being wouldn't add pounds and inches.

"Then it's settled. I'll wait until Fern comes. I think she feels guilty that she's not here with me. She sounded sad on the phone the last time I talked to her."

I shifted the truck into drive and headed in the direction of home. I wouldn't know the first thing about maternity clothes anyway.

"Knowing what I do about your family, she probably misses everyone. Do you think she'll ever move back here?"

"It would take a miracle to get her to move home."

"She's so secretive about what she's doing. She travels all over the world for conferences and work but won't tell me what it is.

"Maybe she's a spy."

"Yeah right."

"She could be working undercover, you never know."

Viola shook her head. "My dad would have known if she was. He was so mad when she quit the academy. I remember the last argument they had before she left. It was a drag down, knock out fight."

"Yeah?"

All I knew about Fern was that she had planned on becoming a police officer just like her dad and brothers. One month before she was set to graduate, she dropped out. There was some fall out between her and her dad and she moved away. She had been gone for five years now but visited as often as she could. Just talking to Viola made me realize how much she missed her family. It was evident in the far off look she got in her eyes.

"Dad was livid that she quit considering the last time he checked her marks were top of her class. Somehow just before she graduated, she started failing classes. I remember overhearing Reed telling Ash something about her partying all the time. It was completely absurd. Fern hardly ever went to parties in high school. In fact, I think she only went to a couple of the end of the year ones, like graduation. What would make her go crazy there, especially when it was so important to her to pass?"

"Maybe it was the stress of upholding the King legacy. It's tough living up to your parent's expectations."

"You find it tough?"

"Every day."

"Oh."

"Yeah." I didn't really want to get into the reasons for my parental anguish, so I was thankful we had pulled in front of the house and could stop the line of conversation. "Wait," I told her as I jumped out of the truck to help her out. She was precious cargo; I didn't want to chance the big step, even if she was tall.

When we got back into the house, I went upstairs to the bedroom. I reached up into the top of my closet to pull down the gift bag. Inside was the small picture frame I got her from the Hallmark store earlier in the day. I wasn't sure what possessed me to get it, but I knew we were going to get a sonogram picture. It had a silver frame and on the bottom was carved with *Baby's First Photo*. Something just told me she would like it.

"I got you something," I said as I reached the bottom of the stairs.

"Really?"

"It's nothing big. I saw it and thought of you." I held out the small gift bag I had stashed the frame in. Having separate rooms made it easy to hide things like this, but everything would be changing tonight. I was tired of sleeping alone in my bed, and part of me was worried I would miss something. I wanted to be able to roll over in the middle of the night and know she was there, and they were both okay.

She peeked in the top of the bag and gasped. "I can't believe you got me this," she said as she pulled it out.

"Like I said, it's nothing big, but I thought you'd want to display the first ever picture of our baby."

"Definitely!" she squealed, kissing me on the cheek. "Thank you!"

She immediately pulled out the photo from her purse and placed it in the frame. "Where should we put it?"

"What about on the coffee table?" I suggested. "That way whenever we're on the couch we can see it."

"That's perfect."

While she went and did her thing, I heated some of the soup I picked up at the farmer's market earlier in the week. It was something small and simple considering we both had ice cream after the doctor's appointment. I knew she wouldn't be hungry for anything substantial. The soup was hearty and filling, so she would like it. I heard her shuffle into the living room, and I could hear her rearranging the magazines I had on the coffee table to make space. She returned a couple moments later and took a seat at the table.

"Supper will be ready in a couple minutes."

"I hope you didn't make anything big, I'm not that hungry after that milkshake."

"I'm reheating one of those Thai chicken soups you liked from the farmer's market."

"Yum."

"I figured you'd approve."

"Definitely. It's got just enough spice that it won't give me heartburn."

"Do you miss being able to eat almost anything without issues?"

"Yeah, sometimes. I'm so glad the morning sickness is over."

"Was it really bad?"

"Not like some of the stories you hear, but I couldn't go to the school cafeteria. Sometimes when I walked by the doors, the smell would seep through the cracks and send me into a hurl fest."

"That sucks."

After we had a small supper, we settled onto the couch and watched a movie. It was some kind of romantic comedy Viola wanted to watch. An hour into the movie, I was surprised when she shuffled over, placing her head on my chest and I put my arm around her. We just sat there and watched the movie. So many times, I felt my eyes drawn to the picture on the table in front of us. I couldn't believe we created a tiny little life on that first night. We both thought we were getting one night to remember, then we were dealt with a lifetime of memories to share together. When it got to a particularly sappy point, I heard sniffles beside me.

"You okay?"

"I hate these hormones. I'm all over the place. One moment I'm happy, then the next I'm crying. I never cry. He just got her a puppy for frack sakes."

"Puppies are pretty cute. It almost made me tear up," I teased her.

"Yeah right," she slapped my stomach, then when she realized what she had done she tried to pull away, but I wouldn't let her.

"You're staying right where you are," I whispered in her ear and kissed the top of her head.

"What if I have to pee?" she joked, eyes twinkling with mischief.

"That's one of the very few exceptions to the rules."

"Okay," she responded, sighing softly as she curled even closer into my side.

It was crazy that six months ago I never would have been caught dead watching a romantic comedy cuddled on the couch with a woman who was more than just a one-night stand. Low maintenance and a great return policy. I definitely wouldn't have been living with one, ready and willing to start a family. This beautiful, sexy woman was changing all the rules to my game and I had never been more ready to see what passing go looked like.

When the movie was over, I helped her off the couch. I walked up the stairs holding onto her arm because she was groggy and I didn't want her to fall. When we reached the top of the stairs, I told myself it was now or never. She started towards her room, but didn't make it too far because I pulled her back in the direction of my room. Reaching my door, I stopped and glanced down at her. Confusion was more than evident on her face.

"You're not sleeping in that room tonight," I startled her with my gruff voice.

"I'm not?" she whispered.

"No."

"Where will I sleep?" she shied away from me, like I was giving her the rejection she expected when she first told me I was going to be a father.

"With me of course."

She tilted her head. "I don't understand."

"I want to fall to sleep with my arms around you. I want to be able to wake up in the middle of the night and place my hand on our child so that he or she knows I'll always be there for them…there for their mother."

"But we're not having sex?" she asked with innocent hesitation.

"Not tonight," I responded. It wasn't that I didn't want to have sex with Vi again. I just wasn't sure if she was there yet. Everything in our lives was changing; I didn't want her to feel rushed into anything. We already lived together and now I was asking her to share my bed.

Our bed.

"Really?"

"Yes…now get under the covers." I smacked her ass causing her to yelp. "You need your rest because you're growing a human being in there."

"Okay."

She shimmied back on the bed. I perused her, imagining our last time together in this bed, I wanted nothing more than to feel her walls wrapped around me again. Once she was situated on her side of the bed, I turned off the light. After I stripped off my clothes, I crawled into the bed beside her and pulled her into my arms, breathing in her vanilla scent and committing it to memory. She let out a dreamy sigh the moment she placed her head on my shoulder. It wasn't long before her breathing evened out and I knew she was asleep.

Lulled into sleep by having everything I would ever need snuggled beside me in the bed, I drifted off only a second later.

VIOLA

MIKE CHANGED VIRTUALLY OVERNIGHT.

Since we went to the doctor together and saw our son on the monitor, he made every effort to be more attentive. He constantly asked how I was feeling and made late night runs for my wacky cravings. One night he was out for several hours just to find a pail of tiger tiger ice cream. Who knew a pregnant woman would crave orange and black licorice ice cream?

Lines were getting blurred.

I had to constantly remind myself that we weren't a real couple. My experience with relationships had been limited and most definitely dysfunctional. Between Reed and Ivy's cheating exes and my father being a widow, I had no idea how to deal with our possibly budding relationship. All I knew was that he was making an effort, so I wanted to meet him halfway.

Me: Hey big bro

Reed: Hey kiddo, how are you feeling?

Me: The puking is over and now is the time to become virtually the size of a small killer whale

Reed: That's what happens when you get knocked up

Me: Yeah, yeah, I know. Is Mike with you?

Reed: Last time I checked he's still my partner and we're currently at work, so yeah

Me: Alright smart ass. Don't tell him but I want to make him something special tonight.

Reed: la la la la…I don't want to know

Me: Argh. What's his favourite food?

Reed: corndogs

Me: Seriously!

Reed: steak, chicken, I don't think it matters since he's a warm-blooded male

Me: Okay, so what time do you think I should expect him home?

Reed: Around 7, unless something happens

Me: Thanks, big bro

Reed: no problem…get some rest and take care of my nephew

Me: Mike told you?

Reed: He couldn't keep it a secret even if he wanted to…he's such a girl these days

Me: Be nice.

Reed: You first

Me: Whatevs. Gotta go. Be safe.

Now that I had a plan, it was time to call in a favour from one of my siblings. Considering it was the middle of the day, the only one with a relatively relaxed schedule was my brother Alder. I only hoped he didn't have a lecture or something.

> Me: Al? Can you talk?
>
> Al: Yep.

I dialed his number and put it on speaker.

"Yello," he answered.

"You got plans? I asked.

"Nope. Got milk?" he responded.

"Shut up."

"Ooh, testy," he teased. "Whatcha want?"

"Can you either take me to the grocery store or go and get me something?"

"I can grab you something, as long as it isn't too much since I only have an hour break between lectures."

"You're the best!"

"Remember me when you're naming your child. I expect to be a namesake cause I'm the coolest uncle," he joked.

"Sure, whatever."

"Not whatever, sis."

"Please," I begged.

"With sugar on top?"

"Yep."

As much as my siblings gave me a hard time, I was pretty spoiled. Being the youngest afforded me some special treatment, even if I was only younger than Ivy by ten months. She always acted older than her age, except during her moments of emotional rollercoaster freak-outs. Then Ivy was the equivalent developmental age of a three-year-old in a sandbox fighting over toys.

"Okay, since you asked so nicely, what can I pick you up?"

"I need two steaks, asparagus, and some of that premade garlic toast that you can buy."

"You're the best, Al. Love ya."

"Love ya too sis. Be there in thirty."

After Alder dropped off the groceries and I had everything prepared for supper, I sat down on the couch. My feet were aching and swollen so I needed to take a load off. Getting sleep was a challenge these days, as our son was becoming more active day by day. It made me realize how little I actually knew about Mike's past. When the baby kicked his feet, I wondered if Mike used to play hockey like my brothers all did. With the amount of weight, I had already gained and the size of my baby bump I already imagined he would be the size of his daddy.

I placed my hand on my stomach at the exact moment he became active again. I could feel his tiny little feet pushing against my palm, filling me with crazy amounts of love. Sometimes I believed he was reacting to my moods, except at night when I was sleeping, and he started bouncing around. One thing he really seemed to enjoy was the sound of Mike's voice, whether he was speaking directly to him or just talking nearby.

A couple times over the last month, first thing in the morning before Mike gets ready for work, I had woken up to soft sounds of him talking to our baby. The first time he did, I was filled with so much love that it moved me to tears. I pretended to be asleep until I heard the front door close and then I let them fall. I didn't want to freak him out with my crying because I thought what he was doing was so sweet.

I AWOKE to the door opening in the kitchen. There was no doubt in my mind that I fell asleep after prepping the supper. I glanced over to the cable box to check the time.

Fuck.

7:37 p.m. Four hours later…

Baby – 1, Mommy – 0.

"Vi?" Mike called out, followed by the sound of his keys hitting the counter. He was late coming home, so I hoped nothing bad happened on patrol.

"In here," I replied, slowly moving to a sitting position. At twenty-five weeks, I wasn't moving as well as I used to, and if I set up too fast, I experienced temporary dizziness.

"Hey, baby," Mike said from the archway between the kitchen and the living room.

"Hi," I responded, pulling down my shirt over the baby bump.

My shirts always had a mind of their own. I had already resorted to stealing some of his shirts for during the day. I was at home all the time, so I didn't really care whether I looked okay or not. Especially when I was this damned tired.

Growing another human being was serious work.

He stepped toward the couch and knelt on the floor next to me. Butterflies took flight at his closeness. He leaned forward and kissed my shirt over the baby bump. I had never experienced anything so sweet in all my life. That was the moment I realized that I was doomed. I was so deeply in love with this man that I feared the second that he decided he no longer wanted this life we were building. We hadn't had the talk, but I knew at the very least we were co-parents. Deep down I knew if we never became more, I would need help mending my broken heart.

"How's Thumper doing today?"

I laughed. He kept changing his nickname for the baby as he grew. So far, we had used bean, peanut, spud and squash. The only name he refused to use was junior, but he never divulged the reason why. It was likely something to do with his childhood, but even Reed never knew the reason. I hoped he eventually felt comfortable enough with me that he would share that side of him with me.

"Kicking up a storm. Did you play soccer or something when you were younger, by chance?"

"Hockey. How do you know he's not following your fancy Krav Maga pants?" He smirked.

"Nope. Nu uh." I shook my head. "I need to be able to blame his hyperactivity on you."

"I'm predicting the start of a new trend," he teased.

"I'll try not to pin everything on you," I promised. "In fact, I'm predicting that all of his acceptable behavior will be my fault."

"Sure, likely story." He stood up, held out his hand and pulled me to my feet. "Now, what were you making me for supper?"

I blushed. "I had every intention of having it ready on the table for you when you walked in the door."

"No big deal. You're growing a person in there. It just means I get to watch my woman cooking supper for me."

His woman?

I tried not to read too much into the possible slip of the tongue. Lines had a tendency to get blurred in situations like ours. I had no intention of tacking my heart on the dart board. Yet I couldn't help but question him on it.

"Your woman, huh?" I prodded.

"Caught that, did you?"

He reached out and tagged me in his arms and kiss me like a man dying of thirst and I was his only salvation. When he pulled away, I was thankful his arms are still around me because his kisses made me weak in the knees.

"I've wanted to do that for a while now," he confessed.

"Me too," I agreed. "Now let's go finish making supper or Thumper will revolt."

Mike laughed as the loud rumble of my stomach effectively killed the mood and embarrassed the hell out of me. He kept his arm wrapped around my waist and led me into the kitchen.

"I've got steaks marinating in the fridge if you wouldn't mind barbequing them? I already started the baked potatoes in the oven before I passed out so elegantly on the couch, and the remaining items to bake are the asparagus and garlic toast."

"You've been busy, sweetheart," he commented with a raise of his eyebrows.

"I wanted to do something nice since you're always working so hard and I'm not doing anything now that I've graduated."

"You don't have to do anything but grow our baby. Out of the two of us, that's the most important job."

"I feel so useless," I complained.

Mike never wanted any money for rent. He paid for all of our groceries and bills for the house without asking for anything in return. He even had a cleaning lady come once a week to tidy up and do our laundry. I wasn't used to being a kept woman and it made me feel bad. I knew he felt that I was his responsibility, but I wanted to feel like I made a contribution of sorts. This meal was the first of many ways I wanted to say thank you to him for taking care of me. The night I told him he was going to be a father; he could have turned me away and denied any responsibility.

It took twenty minutes to cook our meal. While I worked on the asparagus and twice baked potatoes, Mike barbequed the steaks to perfection. I loved that our meal became a joint effort and we executed our tasks perfectly. My only concern going forward was whether we could apply the same synchronicity to raising our son.

"What's on your mind?"

I jumped, spinning toward his voice.

"Sorry." Mike held his hands up in surrender. "I could hear the gears turning from outside."

"What if I fail at being a mom because I never had one of my own," I spewed out without thinking.

"You won't," he responded with confidence.

"How do you know?"

"I've seen your heart," he answered. "When your sister was going through her breakup, you called her every day and answered her calls no matter the hour. I know for a fact when your brother Rowan died, that you checked on Reed as much as you could."

"He told you?"

"Sometimes when your text messages would come through, I forced him to read them. Even when he was lost. What eleven-year-old does that?" He shook his head in disbelief.

"Me, I guess," I answered, remembering all the texts and calls I made to Reed in the months following Rowan's overdose. Sure, he was my brother and I lost him too, but he was Reed's identical twin, the other half of his soul. No one went through a loss like that and came out on the other side whole without the love and support of family or friends.

"See, there's your answer," he assured me.

"Thanks," I smiled.

The oven timer went off, indicating our garlic toast was ready. Mike beat me to the stove and grabbed the buttery goodness I had been craving for a week.

"You've really out done yourself," he praised.

"I tried."

"You hit this one out of the park."

"Great!"

He sat back down, placing a piece of toast on my plate, followed by a steak on top. I didn't know how he figured out my love for steak sandwiches, but I couldn't help feeling impressed. It wasn't our first meal together, but they had been few and far between because of his shifts. Most times I would eat alone because of my new baby-induced appetite.

"Have you thought about doing some courses online?" he startled me, breaking the silence.

"Sorry?"

"You could work towards your degree during the summer and then when the baby is born, you won't have such a heavy course load," he suggested.

"The financial assistance and scholarships I applied for don't come through until the fall. With my dad's radio silence, I can't exactly phone him up and ask for him to pay for it."

"I'll pay for the classes," he offered.

"I can't ask you to do that," I responded, shyly.

I appreciated the sentiment, but I never wanted him to give me money for anything. Above all, I didn't want him to ever feel like I was using our child to take advantage of him. It would kill me if he resented our son for anything that occurred between us.

"I don't want you to ever blame me or our child for preventing you from pursuing your dream," he echoed my thoughts.

It was almost as if he had read my mind.

"I could never do that. I love Thumper with all that I am."

"I remembered how much you planned out your next four to six years of academia. I think you would be great at whatever you decided to do. If in a year or two you wanted to enrol in the police academy, I would support you. I'd be with you every step of the way. This baby was meant to add joy to our lives, not hinder our future."

"He could never be anything more than a blessing. The moment I saw those two pink lines, something clicked inside me. It was like I was born to be his mom. Nothing else mattered anymore. If I become a young offender advocate in four years or ten, I will be happy. If my life is fulfilled through being Thumper's mom and nothing else, then I will still be happy."

"Are you positive?" he asked, the uncertainty evident in his eyes.

LATER THAT NIGHT, following a nice hot shower to loosen my achy muscles, I glanced in the mirror as I gathered the towel to wrap around me. For the first four or five months of the pregnancy, my growth was gradual. In the last week or so it seemed like I had tripled in size. My previously athletic body was gone and had been replaced by a sight I hardly recognized.

A knock at the door had me scrambling to cover myself. Mike hadn't seen me without my clothes on since the first night we had sex. We had been sleeping the same room since the night of our first ultrasound. Although we shared a bed, we would go to sleep on our perspective sides of the bed. He was being respectful of my space, yet every night like clockwork, sometime during the night, we would end up in each other's arms.

Once I secured the oversized bath towel around my ballooning body, I padded over to the door and slowly opened it. The lust in Mike's eyes when he saw what I was or rather wasn't wearing, was instantaneous. His attention brought colour to my cheeks.

"God you're beautiful."

"Really?" I was unsure of his attraction for me because I was no longer the same short sexy skirt, corset wearing woman that he took to bed seven months ago. After all, we had been sleeping together for a month, and he hasn't made any sexual advances. Most days I could be found wearing my comfortable stretchy maternity pants and a loose shirt, that usually belonged to him. Secretly, I imagined he wanted me to wear his clothes. He always got this smile on his face when he spotted me in them.

"You become more gorgeous every day," he responded.

The look in his eyes as he scanned my towel-clad body ensured he was being honest. I may have been sexually inexperienced, but there was no mistaking the desire they portrayed. His eyes weren't the only telling part of his body, as I performed my own perusal. If the bulge in his jeans was any indication, this gorgeous specimen of a man wanted me, and the hormones coursing through my veins obliterated my remaining inhibitions.

His eyes followed my hands as I gave a gentle tug on the towel. It cascaded in slow motion to the floor and I stepped over it, moving closer to him. His eyes widened as I bravely placed my hands on the waist of his pants. He didn't make a move to stop me as I undid the button and slid my hand into his boxers. Grasping his hard, velvet shaft near the base, I slowly stroked. I smirked as the sounds from him urged me on.

His warm hand wrapped around the base of my neck, tilting my head up. He crashed his lips onto mine, plundering my mouth. My knees, weak and weighed down by the baby, almost went out from under me. In that moment, I wished I could get down on my knees and show him just how much I appreciated him. However, my ever-growing baby bump would most likely trap me down there, or make my movements so awkward it would no longer be considered sexy.

So instead, I rolled my thumb over his mushroom tip and spread his precum around and then gently fondled his balls. He groaned and gently pulled away.

"It's been a while for me, so if you keep going, I'm going to come before any of the fun begins," he explained. "I hope you had a good nap before I got home, because for what I want to do to you, it's going to take most of the night."

My brain short-circuited on his comment regarding how it had been a while, and how he was going to take all night.

MIKE

Viola's towel dropping to the floor instantly made my throat go dry. Not even the Sahara Desert could rival the feeling. I mentally kicked myself for being so respectful of her space over the last month. In fact, it almost took everything in me not to show her exactly what I felt inside. It was a tumultuous rollercoaster of emotions. Don't get me wrong, I respected Viola with everything that I had. I could still respect the mother of my child and rock her world at the same time.

After all, I was known to be adept at multitasking.

The night I moved her into my bedroom, I planned to eventually escalate to this point. Yet, every night we went to sleep together, the innocence hovering over her made me want to take the time to make her comfortable. To take the time that she should have been allotted before losing her virginity. Thinking back, I still had no clue what made her choose me. Maybe it was the anonymity, maybe it was fate. Even to this day, something indescribable zinged between us during every touch.

It was electrical.

When she entered a room, I could easily zero in on her location. If I wasn't right next to her, I could almost feel her reaching out to find me. I had been with a lot of women over the years but none of them measured up to her. Her beauty was inside and out. She loved her family to the ends of the earth, even her absentee father was held in high regard. She would forgive him in a second if he only picked up the phone.

She was the exact type of woman I wanted to raise our child.

Literally every day, the proof of how good we could be together was growing inside her. Never in a million years did I think that being with only one woman could make me this happy. I spent years avoiding any form of relationship because of the dysfunctional example of marriage that my parents provided. The night I met Viola, I instinctively knew something was different about her, even if I couldn't place it. Then the next morning, when I returned to the bedroom to find her gone, I experienced a moment of emptiness that I never knew.

Hollowness that was almost immediately alleviated when I ran into her months ago at her school. My biggest mistake was letting my friendship with Reed get in the way of us exploring our relationship more. To think that she had to go through finding out that she was pregnant alone, made me feel a level of regret I couldn't even begin to describe. Now that I had her, I wanted to show her exactly how she should be cherished. After tonight, she would know I wanted all of her, not just the baby growing inside of her.

With my zipper undone and pants hanging open, I wrapped my arm around her waist and led her to the bed. The feeling of her warm supple flesh provoked the caveman buried just below the surface. The man who wanted to take her and make her know she was mine.

To claim her.

"I've been reading some articles on pregnancy and sex," I confessed.

"You have?" Her face lit up.

"Don't sound so surprised," I teased.

I wouldn't admit it to anyone other than her brother, but I had spent the last month reading any books I could get my hands on. When I first pulled them out in the cruiser, Reed became uncomfortable. Though, lately, he had taken to asking me questions. When I got to the section about sex and pregnancy, I deliberately read it when Reed wasn't around. I didn't want to get punched out on the job. There was no way in hell I would want to know if someone was having sex with my sister, so I wouldn't inflict the same thing on Reed.

"I can see you reading about sex," She paused. "I can't even begin to tell you how it makes me feel to know that you've been reading about pregnancy."

"I told you, we're in this together," I replied. "Now let's do something else equally as pleasing."

"I had no idea how we were going to do this," she confessed.

"This is going to be a first for me too, but I'm sure we'll manage." I responded.

She nodded.

"I want you to lay down on your back in the middle of the bed and spread your legs for me," I instructed as I shucked off my pants.

She made her way over to the end of the bed. My boxers hit the floor at the same time as her knee was placed on the edge of the mattress. I wrapped my hand around my rock-hard cock as I watched in anticipation. She crawled to the exact place I directed and laid down. Once she was situated, she shyly regarded me. She placed her hands over her breasts, while she zeroed in on my hand.

"Hands." I told her as I continued to stroke, but she quickly obeyed the request. Slowly she moved her hands and let me see her swollen globes. Her nipples were hard with anticipation of the main event. Slowly scanning her body, I squeezed my dick and commanded one more request. "Now your legs. I want to see the pretty pink pussy that I'm going to pound with this cock." Her eyes widened.

I relinquished my hold, knowing if I kept going, I would make a mess of myself before I got to do what I dreamed about doing to her. She watched unabashedly as my cock bounced with every step. When I got to the end of the bed I stood for a moment, feeling her eyes as they roamed my well-toned body. She blushed the cutest shade of pink when she realized I noticed what she was doing.

I knew I looked good, but it didn't hurt to know she thought I was attractive.

I wasn't a narcissist when it came to how I looked; I was pragmatic. There was no way I would survive as a police officer if I stereotypically ate donuts and couldn't jump over a fence while chasing down a perp. People could die if I wasn't in the best physical shape possible. I could die. Now more than ever I had reasons to remain this way.

Viola's delectable, naked body, swollen with my child was almost too much for me to handle. She bit her lower lip as she watched me with lust in her eyes, and I almost came undone. There was something about the way she was shy one moment and a vixen the next. Strong and vulnerable at the same time.

Perplexing, and yet such a complete turn on.

She was so far from the women I used to waste my time with, my head was spinning. Maybe the sole reason I wasn't ready to settle down was because I hadn't met my soulmate yet? If there was such a thing, I was realizing she might be mine.

She let out a giggle as I knelt on the bed and slowly prowled towards her. I ran my hands up both her legs starting with her feet, caressing and massaging the whole way. When I approached the juncture between her legs, I ran my finger between her lips, coating my digit with her essence, ending the tease by lightly flicking her clit. Her hips bucked and she moaned as I repeated the motion.

"Are you ready for me, sweetheart?"

She nodded.

"You still remember my rules?"

She nodded again. *So that's how it was.*

"I need your words."

"And I need you inside me now."

"You're an impatient little vixen, hmm?"

"Uh huh," she replied, pinching both her nipples and causing my cock to pulse.

I crawled over her, careful to not put any pressure on her stomach. Placing my forearm on the bed I hovered over her. I pulled her up toward me as I grasped the back of her neck, pressing my lips to hers I kissed her hard and fast. I couldn't hold back anymore, and I couldn't wait to show her what it was like to be worshipped.

Releasing my hold, I licked and kissed my way down her neck, sucking on one nipple and then the other as she arched her back with my ministrations.

When I reached her stomach, I placed a soft kiss on our son, who was the one responsible for tossing everything in my life all to hell, in the best possible way. Her eyes glistened with tears when I glanced up. I kissed her belly one more time for good measure, making her to laugh.

A laugh that quickly transformed into a moan as I took her clit in my mouth and sucked. Her legs suddenly boxed in the side of my head as she arched her back. Flicking my tongue repeatedly over the bundle of nerves, I was still amazed at her responsiveness. At the most inopportune time, my mind went to the article that I read on hormones and sex drive with pregnancy and wondered if maybe there was a bit of truth to the sensitivity that pregnancy created.

Her walls clenched around my fingers as I thrusted in and out, while sucking on her clit. She moaned and writhed on the bed as I kept taking her to the next height. She called out my name as she came, letting out a sigh as I withdrew my fingers. Her face was flushed with colour, making me want to watch her come as I looked into her eyes.

"Roll onto your side," I directed her, knowing the position would probably more comfortable for her and I wasn't about to throw her onto her hands and knees just yet. The night was young.

Laying on her left side, she peered down at me and watched as I crawled onto the bed. I lifted up her right leg and bent it, sliding over to straddle her left leg until I was between them. Rolling my thumb over her clit, I slowly rocked my hips forward. Her breathing hitched as the tip of my cock breached her entrance, shallowly thrusting in and out. It took everything in me to go slowly when all I wanted to do was take her hard. It had been seven months since we had both had sex, so I wanted to take it easy.

"Mike…I need you," she pleaded.

All my control faded as I gave her what she wanted and slid home. Seated deeply inside her I revelled at the way she felt as her walls closed around me. She was a dream come true in a sinfully sexy package. Like we were made for each other. All the memories from the first night with her crashed into me. In the next moment I finally realized how lucky I was.

Lucky to have a second chance. One that wasn't hidden from her brother, like a dirty secret.

We didn't last the whole night like our first time, but we managed to wear each other out thoroughly. She called my name over and over as I showed her how much her body deserved to be worshiped.

We held each other for the rest of the night, spent in each other's arms. Until Viola I never found pregnant women sexy, but with her growing round with my child inside of her, she was everything and more. Something primal inside of me wanted to shout from the mountain tops that I was the one who put the baby in her. My virile seed was too much for the condom to contain.

I was beyond over the moon about having a son, but I wouldn't have minded a little mini-Vi either. A girl with her cute little smile, hair up in pigtails running around the back yard. Until this moment I hadn't seen the wife or the child. Now when I closed my eyes at night, I was seeing a future of us on a porch swing, surrounded by our children, even our children's children.

My life had infinite possibilities, and it all begins and ends with this woman.

The love of my life.

VIOLA

JULY

Mike left early this morning for his day shift, so I was happy when Fern stopped by to take me to the mall. With the baby coming soon, he was picking up extra shifts to pay for whatever we need to prepare for his arrival. I had been feeling a little sorry for myself since school ended and my friends were planning their futures. I guessed that was part of growing up, but it didn't suck any less knowing the reality of my current situation. The baby would be born in October, which meant I would miss out on the first semester of my program.

After that, I didn't care what anyone said, I planned on registering for the winter semester. Even if I had to only take three courses on one day.

The University had a great program for parents who required childcare during their classes. I fully intended to make being a mother just part of who I was. My baby would know all the love I had for him, and I would have the ability to support him with my chosen career path. There was no way I would be solely dependent on Mike for our wellbeing. Obviously being pregnant hindered my ability to attend the police academy and follow in my family's footsteps. The more I thought about it, my abilities were better focussed on helping juveniles before they became hardened criminals.

I was sure there were other teenagers out there with a similar home life to mine that could use some guidance. With the lack of parenting, or rather absentee parenting, I could have turned to a life of crime. A lot of disenfranchised youth turn to gangs for the acceptance and belonging that a family was supposed to provide. I was one of the fortunate ones who had six other siblings who shared my homelife and could fill in the huge hole my parents left.

"I can't believe the size of this store!" I exclaimed, not having been in a baby store before. All the furniture, clothes and accessories blew my mind. How would I be able to afford all of this? I was living with Mike, but what if he changed his mind and decided he didn't want a baby? What if I was left alone to raise him?

"I know it's crazy isn't it?" Fern grabbed my elbow. "Now let's go and find you some baby stuff."

"This is too expensive."

"Don't look at the price, I can afford to spoil my first niece or nephew."

We hadn't told anyone the sex of the baby yet because we just learned the sex of the baby last week. I didn't know when I would see Fern next, so I wanted her to be the first person to know.

"I'm having a boy," I gushed. The moment I found out that I was pregnant; I knew I wanted to have a boy first. I wanted our son to be the first of many children I had, whether I stayed with Mike or not. Having a son first would be a built-in protector like I had. I loved having older brothers, even if they did put a damper on my love life.

"Oh my God! Seriously? A nephew!" She drew the attention of the shoppers near us with her excitement.

"Shh. People are staring." I hated to be the centre of attention.

"This is great news. Have you told anyone else?"

"You're the first to know."

"Ooh, I've surpassed Ivy as your new confidant."

"Ives is just too busy with her new boyfriend, or whatever River is."

"I actually talked her into joining us for a spa day!"

"Really?" It had been a while since I had talked to Ivy. She had a new guy already and I wasn't sure what to think about her rebound, if that was what it was for her. She was a serial monogamist and even if I thought she should take a break and be single for a while, Ivy was going to do what Ivy did.

"She's going to meet us there."

"That's why you were all texty earlier."

"Texty?"

"You know what I'm talking about."

We ended up buying quite a bit of baby clothes and accessories like a diaper bag and genie, whatever the heck that was. I left the furniture because I wanted to shop for those with Mike. I didn't want to leave him completely out of everything; I wanted his input. After we were done shopping, we loaded everything into Fern's rental vehicle and drove to the spa.

God, I needed this.

The last time I saw Fern was before Christmas, and I wasn't sure when I would see her again, so I soaked everything up. She was evasive when I asked about what she was doing, but I didn't let it bother me. Somehow, I knew if she could tell me she would. Which made me even more suspicious of what she was doing and if it was safe. I couldn't lose another sibling. When I told her as much, she just waved her hand dismissively and said she would be okay.

I wasn't a girly girl, but before I ballooned, I regularly went for pedicures. It was relaxing and a way to pamper myself. It used to be me, Shelby and Chandra in the salon, but both of them have gone away for school. They wouldn't even be here when the baby was born. They both sent me texts about how awesome their apartment was, and I felt a momentary pang of jealousy because it was supposed to be us three living there. Then I reminded myself that I was going to be a mother and even if our paths went in separate directions, we would still continue to be friends.

Ivy met us at the Spatastic Salon, and we spent the afternoon talking about boys and having babies. It was nice to have all the girls together again. Everything was changing and I didn't want to miss out on a thing. The ladies at the spa fawned over me and my more than evident baby bump. I was seven months along and hotter than hell in the middle of summer. Spending time in a spa, getting a prenatal massage and having someone paint my unreachable toes was heaven.

By the time we all left a couple hours later to go home, I felt pampered and more relaxed than I had been in months.

MIKE

"How's my sister doing?" Reed mumbled under his breath.

"Why don't you call and ask her?" I countered.

Reed was still having some issues in his relationship with Viola. He seemed like he was still uncomfortable with the whole situation. The only reason I was sure of this was because it had been a couple weeks since they had spoken to each other. She told me that they used to call or text twice a week before everyone knew she was pregnant. I was a little pissed at him on Viola's behalf, but I still understood it from his side. This was a lot to take in, and Reed didn't deal well with change.

"I will," he responded, appropriately chastised.

"She's getting bigger."

"That's what happens when a woman's pregnant, dumbass."

"I know that dipshit. It's just all surreal. I can't believe I'm going to be a father in a few months."

"Do you think you're ready?"

"Is anyone ever ready to become a parent?" I pondered aloud. "I didn't plan on ever having kids, so it's going to be a bit of an adjustment."

It seriously didn't matter how many books I read; I was still not prepared for our son to come home. Even though we were only at seven months, we had our go bag ready by the door and we had gone through the steps we planned on taking before we left and after we arrived at the hospital. Yet, no matter how many times we went through the plan, it didn't feel like it was enough.

"Just make sure it's what you want before you allow my sister to fall for your sorry ass."

"I know."

"Do you?" he asked, examining me for any sign that I wasn't being honest.

"Your sister is amazing. I thought I would hate the domestics of having a live-in girlfriend."

"You mean you've actually decided to date her now?" he asked.

"We're going to have a child together. I already knew I felt something for her back when we were texting and seeing each other as friends," I answered, then clarified, "you know, before she found out she was pregnant."

"I'm not so sure I want to hear any of this. It's impossible for me to imagine that my baby sister has a sex life. Especially with my best friend."

"Don't worry, I won't kiss and tell," I teased, enjoying watching him squirm. Even though I made a joke of things, I didn't blame him for the way he felt about knowing there was anything more than platonic between me and his sister. There was no way I would want to imagine Claudia having sex with anyone. As far as I was concerned, she would remain a virgin for the rest of her life. I most definitely wouldn't want to imagine her sleeping with any of my friends.

"La la la la...I don't hear anything," Reed comically plugged his ears and shook his head back and forth, like a three-year-old.

"I don't want to rush anything."

"A little late for that," he mumbled. I knew he wasn't angry anymore, just scared about what would happen if this all blew up in our faces.

Hell, I was scared.

I had more to lose than just the love of my life. She was carrying my child and where she went, our son would follow. Sure, I would get visitation, but for the most part I would miss out on key moments in his life. There was no way I would take away custody from her, so I doubted that was a thought that had crossed Reed's mind.

"I already told you I had no idea she was only eighteen when I slept with her before. Now that I know her age, and what's at stake, I want to take this at her pace," I responded. "So, yes, we are sharing a room, but only because I want to be beside her for everything."

"So, you have lost your balls."

"Fuck you, man. I can't wait until your sorry ass finds a woman you can't live without."

Something told me he had already found someone important to occupy his time, but I didn't want to push.

"So now you can't live without her?"

"What can I say?" I shook my head. "I finally found my unicorn."

LATER THAT MORNING, when we were wrapping up our shift, I decided to ask Reed for help with turning the second bedroom into a nursery. It had been on my list of things to do and today seemed like the most logical solution to the problem. I knew if I did everything while Viola was there, she would feel guilty and I would miss out on being able to surprise her.

Just seeing the look on her face would make my day.

"What are you doing this afternoon?"

"Why?" Reed questioned with a quirk of his brow.

"I was hoping you and your brothers would be willing to help me move some furniture from the guest room that Vi was sleeping in down to the basement."

Viola informed me earlier this morning that her sister Fern was in town to visit with plans to take her shopping. She was excited to spend time with Fern since she hadn't been back to town for a while and she missed her. If I had to hazard a guess, Vi probably missed her sister even more now that she was pregnant with her first child. From everything she had told me over the past few months, Fern was the closest thing she had to an actual mother.

"Why would you do that?"

The tone of his voice made me cringe. He seriously didn't have any faith in our relationship lasting. By the sound of his voice it was like he was waiting for me to tell him that Viola was moving out. Boy was he in for a surprise when he learned she had been sleeping in my bed for almost a month now. Waking up beside her was by far the best way to start the day.

If she would have me, I planned to spend the rest of our lives waking up next to one another.

"Fern took Vi shopping and I wanted to clean out that room for the baby and the load of stuff I'm sure she'll bring home," I explained. "She hasn't mentioned it, but I know she's wondering where the baby will sleep when it comes. She likely assumes he'll sleep in the same room as her, but he won't."

"She doesn't have much money for the things she'll need."

"I gave her my credit card," I responded. "I've also taken care of the main furniture. I have a crib downstairs to set up and I ordered a changing table and nice rocking chair for the corner of the room that will be here in a at the end of the week."

The look on Vi's face when I handed her my high limit credit card was priceless. Since moving out of my parents' pool house, I had lived well below my means and did for multiple reasons. The first was that I didn't want anyone to treat me different because they knew I had a high bank balance. Secondly, I had enough women throwing themselves at me because I was a cop, I didn't need more with dollar signs in their eyes. I already learned my lesson about the consequences of that particular type of knowledge when I was younger.

"Ooh, big spender," he teased.

"Nothing is going to be too much for my child." I replied with confidence. My son would be taken care of and if I decided to spoil him, I would still make sure that he understood the value of money and how not to allow it to corrupt him.

"I'm happy to hear it," he reached into his pocket for his cell. "Let met text Ash and Al, and one or all of us will show up."

"Cool. What do you think of having a BBQ tonight while Fern is still in town?"

"That would be awesome."

"Tell the guys to bring a friend if they want, invite Ivy and River, and we'll make a family event of it. Vi's been missing your family something awful and most of her friends have moved away for school or are travelling the world for the summer."

"Are you sure you have the room? We're a rowdy bunch."

"I've got a huge back yard that I've never used. It would be great to use it before we have to move."

"You're moving?"

In my spare time at home, usually while Viola napped, I had been checking listings for places to live. I hadn't broached the subject with her yet because I didn't know where we stood or what was going to happen in the future. I also had no idea what type of home Viola would want to live in. Ideally, I would like to find an acreage like her parents had and build to my own specifications. A house big enough for more than one child, a place to build a future.

"Eventually. It depends on how many children we have." I was shocked at my abrupt confession.

I couldn't believe I was seriously considering having more children before the first one arrived. Even though I had made my mind up I frequently had questions of doubt filtering through my mind. The one at the top of the list was always what if I sucked at being a parent. What if Vi finally figured out that I wasn't good enough for her and left? Reed's distraction with texting his siblings to rope them into my plan allowed me a moment to ponder the situation. After his initial text, his cell blew up, vibrating across the dash in between his responses.

"Your phone's blowing up," I mentioned, with a chuckle.

"The family," he responded, as I secretly wished my family was as close as his. "We have a group chat going where everyone can say hello or air their grievances."

"Ah...Did you remember to tell them about the BBQ?" I reminded him.

"Shit," he snickered. "One second."

His fingers flew over the screen with my final request. I really hoped they can all attend. In the past we had drinks with Ash because he works at the same precinct and often has a similar schedule, but I hadn't met Alder yet. He was just finishing up his degree Criminal Justice at the university, so he often didn't have the time to hang out. He was too busy either playing hockey or studying.

"There," he tossed his phone in his bag at his feet, then turned to me. "You're full of shocking information today. I don't know whether I want to punch you for insinuating your plan of knocking my sister up repeatedly or hug you because I'd love it for Viola to find someone worthy of her devotion," he exhaled. "You really do care about her, don't you?"

"Of course, I do," I responded. "Did you think I only cared about the baby? Or that I only kept her around out of some form of responsibility?"

"I hoped you wouldn't be the cause of more heartache for her. Her life up until now has been hard enough. Vi's strength is what draws people in, but beneath it all she's in pain, even if she never shows it."

"What do you mean?" I asked in surprise, ready to put a beat down on anyone who hurt my girl.

My girl?

"You know that our mom died a day after Viola was born. I know our dad never blamed her for the death of his wife, but he distanced himself from all of us," he lamented. "With Viola, he couldn't have been farther away. It wouldn't surprise me if the night that baby was conceived was another birthday in the long line of birthdays he avoided."

"That night was her birthday?"

"You didn't know?"

"No, she never told me. We haven't talked about birthdays. We've been too busy talking about the baby and trying to live together."

I thought back to the conversations that we'd had and realized that there was a lot of things we hadn't discussed. We had been so focussed on the future that we didn't take a lot of time to get to know each other. If we were going to have the future, I believe that we could, then I needed to know what her favourite colour was. I need more stories of her childhood.

"That's probably because she's so used to not celebrating, that she refuses to acknowledge the day even exists."

"That's a sad state to be in," I replied. "As much as my parents suck, I never had a birthday that I didn't feel like it was a celebration. At least when I was at home."

"It is what it is. Each of us has a painful memory that dictates our actions. I also don't like to celebrate my birthday, but that's because of the loss of my twin. It's not that I don't want to remember the date. The reason I don't celebrate our birth, is that I don't want to do it without him."

"I can understand that, but to never make your daughter feel special on her birthday. Who does that?"

"Our dad."

"Never again," I vowed. "That day gave me them. So, as pissed as it makes me that he's neglected her over the years, his mistake is what gave me a family."

"Ok, lover boy, let's get that nursery ready for her."

I looked at the vehicles parked in front of our house and mentally prepared myself for all of her brothers to be in our house. The only one who had really seen us together was Reed, so I wasn't sure how to act around the others. I felt like I might be signing up to run the gauntlet or something equally scary. They had already accepted me as a friend and co-worker but being their baby sister's significant other carried other expectations. When we pulled into our spot, everyone got out of their vehicles.

"Yes, let's."

It took us a little over an hour to move all the furniture to the basement and for me to make sure the room was vacuumed. Thankfully I had enough room in my small basement to store everything. The only reason I even had my guest room set up with a bed was for when my buddies from high school came to visit. Now that I was going to have a family, their visits would likely be less frequent.

"I'll be right back," I called out to the guys.

I ran back down to the basement and grabbed the large box I had hidden away in the storage room. A week after Viola confessed that I had gotten her pregnant, I went out and bought the most functional crib imaginable. It cost a pretty penny but didn't even put a dent in my savings. I hadn't touched my trust fund since it was released to me at the age of twenty-one. I only hoped she liked what I bought as much as I did and wasn't disappointed that I excluded her from the decision.

When I finally lugged the box up the stairs to the nursery, the guys all whistled.

It was a three-in-one that could be altered based on the life stage of your child. It went from a crib, to a day bed suitable for a toddler, and finally the headboard for a double-sized bed. I knew Viola liked the bedroom set in my room, so I picked the same dark cherry colour for our baby's bedroom set. The matching changing table, and a rocking chair I commissioned from a local furniture maker would be here on Friday.

Reed was the first to talk.

"Man, you've got it bad," he teased.

"I'm happy that my baby sis found a guy worthy of her affections." Ash slapped me on the back, then continued, "However, if you hurt her, I will hunt you down and make you wish you were never born."

I swallowed. "Thanks for that."

All three of them busted up laughing and slapped me on the back as they all went down stairs to wait for the ladies to arrive from shopping.

VIOLA

When we pulled up outside of the townhouse, everyone was stationed outside, I immediately knew something was up. The sight of Mike and all my brothers was the least inconspicuous thing imaginable. They were up to something. My brothers schooled their features to hide the knowledge that lied beneath.

Fern and Ivy launched out of the vehicle and started piling up our bags. Mike was the first to approach the vehicle. He opened my door, held out his hand and helped me to my feet. After he shut the door, he possessively wrapped his arm around me and placed a chaste kiss on my lips. When he pulled back, I couldn't help but glance at my brothers to gauge their reactions. To my utter surprise, they all appeared relaxed.

"Awe…" gushed my sister Ivy, who stood directly behind me.

"You guys go inside; we've got enough hands to get all the bags," Reed directed.

"Are you sure?" I asked.

"Go," replied Fern, with a wave of her hand.

"Come on, I've got something I want to show you." Mike grabbed my hand and walked me up into the house.

With my hand held tightly in his, he guided me upstairs, then into my old room. Once he flicked on the light, my jaw dropped. Somehow over the course of one day, or rather a couple hours, he had completely emptied the guest room and set up a gorgeous dark cherry crib. A mobile with animals attached to strings hung over the top. A small nightstand, matching the crib, had been placed in the corner of the room. A stencilled light that I had seen in one of the baby flyers was placed on top. I liked how when it was turned on, it rotated, lighting up stars on the walls and ceiling.

The sight of everything all set up brought tears to my eyes. I wrapped my arms around his waist and gazed into his eyes. "Thank you so much for setting everything up."

Mike smiled, leaned forward and pressed his lips against mine. "Anything for you and our son."

The gesture reminded me of a question that had plagued me over the past month. The question of where I would continue to sleep and if it would be in Mike's arms. Even though every night for the past month and a half I had slept in his room, we hadn't actually had the discussion about what it meant and if it would continue. The only thing I knew for sure was that I had completely fallen in love with him. It would be a dream come true if he felt the same way.

It seemed like the perfect time to confirm my thoughts, regardless of who would overhear us, so I asked, "I didn't know you wanted me to move into your room permanently."

"Where else was the baby going to sleep?"

"I thought the crib would just be set up in there with me," I replied.

"I don't even want to think about you guys sharing a bedroom. What goes on up there, stays up there. TMI and all that shit," Reed almost begged.

"Everyone, meet Reed, the romantic," Ash joked.

"I'll have you know I'm very romantic when the situation calls for it," Reed argued.

"As romantic as a dung beetle," Alder replied.

When my brothers started roughhousing, Mike guided me to the hall, shielding my body from my absurd siblings. He held up his hand when we reached the top of the stairs, and looked grateful when I took it so he could assist me with the stairs. Over the last couple weeks, he had been extra careful with me. Most of the time I hated to be treated like a fragile female, but never made me feel like I was weak. He made me feel like he cared for me and wanted me to be safe.

A COUPLE HOURS LATER, when everyone had left, Mike helped me sit down on the couch. He quickly grabbed a blanket, covered me with it and then gave me the remote for the television.

"I can't just sit here. It was my family here, so I should help you clean up." Even though he had been taking care of me over the past few months, I still felt uncomfortable with him doing everything.

"You should just sit right there and rest," he argued. "You've been on your feet all day at the mall and you never had your nap."

My feet were killing me, but I didn't want to be lazy and make him clean everything up.

"When you mention me having a nap it makes me sound like a toddler," I laughed, secretly mooning over him noticing my routine.

"You're definitely not a toddler," he replied. "I know you hate feeling like an invalid, but you would be doing me a favour by relaxing while I clean up the mess. It was my idea to invite your family and I had a great time."

"Okay, I'll be here watching a movie while you clean."

Mike kissed me on the temple. "Thanks babe."

Mike left the room and I turned on a movie. It didn't take long for my eyes to grow heavy. I had just barely leaned my head back on the couch when darkness took me.

"Vi," a familiar voice whispered next to my ear.

"Hmmm."

"Time to go to bed, sweetheart," Mike said.

I slowly opened my eyes and took in his smile.

MIKE

"There's my boy." My mom cooed. I would probably visit more often, if this welcome were more genuine. She's definitely up to something. This is standard for my siblings, who follow the family motto of seen but not heard, and a future that is entirely out of your control. Since childhood we were groomed to be the perfect children. The only one who dare to step out of line, away from the prescribed path, I would never be allowed to forget it.

So, my mom's actions today automatically make the hair stand on the back of my neck, as if to scream danger, danger, get out of here now before it's too late.

Yet, like a moron, I stay to find out her next plan of attack, naive enough to think she would be anything other than maternal.

"Hi, mom." I would have hugged her, but any show of affection was deemed a weakness.

"Your father is in his office; he's been expecting you." I dreaded going in that office, but I thought it was time to tell them they were both going to be grandparents.

"Mom, actually I was hoping I could talk to both of you."

"Oh, honey," She gushed. "Do you have some sort of announcement to make?"

"Yes, actually I do." I hoped her head didn't explode when I told them the news.

"Why don't we meet in the sitting room? I'll have Marta bring us some tea and cookies."

"I don't plan on staying long."

I might as well have been talking to the wall because my mom ignored me and headed in the direction of the intercom. I hated that thing. Growing up it was fun to play with, but once I entered my teen years and they used it to call me for breakfast at the break of dawn, my hatred developed. I made my way to my father's office to inform him that plans had changed and that we would be meeting in the sitting room instead of his stuffy office. I knocked on the door and awaited his response.

"Enter."

"Father." I greeted him.

"Robert." Argh, I hated when he used my first name, which egotistically was also his first name. At least he didn't' call me Junior this time. "Well, don't just stand there with the door open. Have a seat."

"It's Mike and Mom wants us to gather in the sitting room instead because I have something to tell you both."

The sitting room was just a fancy name for a boring, barren room with uncomfortable chairs to sit on and pictures decorating the wall. My mom preferred to use what she considered as sophisticated words to refer to rooms and things to do with the house. Like instead of wrap-around porch, she would use veranda. The basement was the family room, even though our family rarely used it, and could hardly be labelled a family.

"Tell your mother I will be right there. I need to wrap up the paperwork for our latest merger."

Of course, he did. This was the reason I didn't want anything to do with the family business. Law enforcement had long hours and somewhat lousy pay, but at least when I was at home, I would be spending time with my family rather than working in an office. Maybe ignoring his family was what my father thought of as providing, but that wasn't me. My children would not be going to boarding school in another country, nor would my daughters attend Sacred Heart like their mother.

They would spend every night under our roof, unless they had a sleepover with their friends. The house would not be a mausoleum, it would be lived in and thoroughly trashed by the children as they had a blast just being kids. Shit would be out of place, clothes strewn everywhere, and the memory of a loving family found in every single corner.

"Thank you." He would make up any excuse not to do exactly what I wanted at the moment he was asked.

I walked into the sitting room like a convict to the firing range. This visit had been a long time coming. Since I refused to attend Sunday brunches with them after the last one, they threw at me, I also hadn't come to visit. Plus, I had been living with Viola and the reality of becoming a father for the past four months. It shouldn't have made a difference, but deep down I was still a little boy wanting mommy and daddy's approval. I sat down in the chair nearest to the door to make a quick escape if need be.

The ninja, better known as Marta, my parents' housekeeper set a coffee in front of me without making a sound. "Nice to see you again, Master Sinclair."

"Please, Marta, you've seen me in the bathtub." She blushed. "You can dispense the formalities and call me Mike."

"You know Mr. and Mrs. wouldn't like that."

"How's Eli and Marisol?"

Eli and Marisol, Marta's twins, were raised along with Claudia. Following the Clarissa debacle, my mom refused to have another nanny. Instead she had my dad hire a housekeeper and add additional duties to include looking after my siblings until they were old enough to go to school. Then she would only be responsible for meals and such. For her troubles, Marta was given the guest house, and my parents approved her bringing the twins, who were closer to Victor's age at the time.

"Both in university now," she beamed. "I'm very proud of both of them."

"Congratulations," I replied.

She placed the tray of tea on the coffee table and swiftly left the room, just as quietly as she had entered.

My parents entered shortly after. My father bypassed the tea and poured himself a glass of bourbon from a crystal decanter that was kept in the corner of the room. I chuckled under my breath when I recalled the summer I came home when I was sixteen. My parents had done something to piss me off, I couldn't exactly recall what the kickoff was. That summer they threw a lot of shit my way in relation to our societal standing. One night while everyone was asleep, I drained his alcohol into a pop bottle for a party I was going to the next night. I replaced his bourbon with apple juice from the fridge.

He was beyond livid.

Apparently, the night of the party he had the Miltons over and they were discussing my future. The whole plan was that Cynthia would be presented to me at supper, but I put a kybosh on the whole thing when I disappeared for a whole weekend of camping with my friends. I got so shitfaced I lost my virginity with the nineteen-year-old daughter of my dad's secretary. Then the next night she brought a friend. Anyways, my father gave old Frankie boy a glass of what he thought was bourbon. He took one drink and sprayed it all over his wife.

The only reason I knew what happened was because Claudia couldn't shut up about it at supper the next week. Then she ratted me out as the person who stole the alcohol, cause the little sneak had spied on me. A month later I learned the dangers of women when not one but both of the women I screwed when we were camping came to my parents for a payoff because they claimed I had impregnated them. My father told them to fuck right off, fired his secretary and sent me back to boarding school early.

A couple weeks after that, my father flew to London on business. He sat me down and explained the perils of women. He told me that he knew I would continue to have sex with women, but that I should be careful. He also had a well-rounded speech prepared about which lawyers to use for a nondisclosure agreement and which doctors to go to for a hush hush abortion. I never wanted to clean my brain with bleach more than I did after that conversation.

It was ironic that my brain went back to that particular moment in history considering I was about to tell him that his worst nightmare had come to fruition. He was about to be a grandparent, and the woman was not one he had vetted himself. It wouldn't matter to him who Viola's father was or how influential he was in his own right. As far as he would be concerned, she would be considered no better than trailer trash.

Which was one of the reasons I dreaded having this conversation. The only thing that worried me more was someone else telling them and the shock of it all causing them to lash out inappropriately.

"Well, what's so important you had to come by unannounced?" My mother looked at me expectantly.

"Did you finally come to your senses and propose to Cynthia?"

I barked out a laugh then replied, "hardly."

"Well then, what is it?"

"I'm going to be a father."

"I can't believe you'd do something so foolish, junior." My dad chastised me. "At least tell me the mother is Cynthia, or someone of similar standing and background."

"The mother is the daughter of my boss."

"That flitty woman who works as a waitress at Alfredo's?" mother gasped. "Why would you sully our name with her?"

"It wasn't Ivy. It was her younger sister Viola."

"Just how young are we talking, son? You're not going to lose your job over statutory rape charges, are you?"

"What?" I shook my head. "No."

"Tell her to get rid of it," my mother demanded.

"I will not tell her to kill my first-born child."

"You'll have other children. Children who are deserving of the Sinclair legacy."

"What's that supposed to mean?" I knew exactly what she meant, but I wanted to hear her utter the words. For some reason I needed more fuel for the fire. More reasons to step out the front door of this hellhole and not look back.

"She isn't of proper breeding."

"What exactly is proper breeding mother? Missionary Position?"

She gasped. "You don't have to be so crass."

"You don't have to be so ignorant."

"Don't talk to your mother that way!" my father cut in.

"She just suggested I kill my own child; I think I have a right to address her in the way I see fit. Where does she get off?" I seethed.

"She was right about what she said. It's the exact same thing I was about to tell you."

"It's not going to happen."

"If it's the conversation you don't want to have, then let me go and talk to her. I'm sure we could come to an agreement. I'm sure someone like her would appreciate some monetary incentive to rid herself of the burden."

"Do you even listen to yourself talk?"

"He's rather articulate, don't you think?" my mother pursed her lips.

"If you call spouting bull shit and nonsense being articulate, then I guess he is."

"We're getting nowhere with this conversation. I suggest we revisit it once we've had a chance to cool down and you've had a moment to come to your senses."

"I don't need a moment. I'm going to be a father whether you like it or not. You don't have to be involved in our lives; I want nothing from you. I just thought you would like to know you're about to be grandparents."

"Hmpf," was the only response I received from my mother.

Even though the conversation went exactly how I predicted it would go, I was still disappointed. There wasn't much left that could be said, so I made my attempt to leave. When I reached the doorway, I glanced to the right, surprised to see there was more than just my parents and I in the room. I hadn't even noticed my grandfather had taken a seat in the corner of the room to watch the spectacle go down. It was hard to believe he was a powerful businessman in his time considering he liked to be more of a wallflower. He was an introvert at heart and preferred to be off to the side watching everything and cataloguing each moment. More so now that he had retired and became a widower.

"Sonny boy, before you leave, I want to have a discussion with you," he told me as he got up out of his chair and waved his hand in a motion for me to follow him.

"Sure grandpa," I replied, following him back in the direction of his room.

Shortly after my grandma died, grandpa moved into the house with my parents. He had just turned eighty and grandma was seventy-three. She had a fluke accident in the back yard and ended up breaking a bone, which punctured her femoral artery and she bled out internally. He once told me he didn't want to live in an empty house with all of those memories and the ghost of his wife. I couldn't imagine losing someone you had spent the majority of your life with.

"I have something I want to give you. I don't want Estelle to get her greedy mitts on."

When I barked out a laugh, he looked back and regarded me with a twinkle in his eye. There was no love lost between those two. I didn't blame him considering she was so manipulative. If my mom had her way grandpa would be in a home waiting on death. There was one thing I knew about my father and that was that he wouldn't pay for a home. He likely also feared being cut out of the will because grandpa was wile with the legality of his financials.

I watched as he went into his walk-in closet and heard shuffling of boxes. "You need some help?" I asked. He was making quite a racket that I hoped he didn't hurt himself moving things around.

"Nope, I think I've got it," he called out. A couple moments later he stepped out with a small black box in his hands. Without him telling me, I knew exactly what he had.

My grandma's engagement ring.

The exact piece of jewelry my mom had blathered on about. Apparently, it had been passed down through the family to the eldest sons and each of them had added their own twist to it. There was a jeweler that they used for everything. For all the talk about the ring, I hadn't seen it. Curiosity got the best of me as I opened the box. I was blown away by the size. It wasn't as extravagant as I believed it would be. I was imagining a huge diamond, but there was just a small one in the centre with sapphires on either side of it and the band had smaller diamonds around it. Sleek and stylish, and I immediately imagined it on Viola's finger.

"Are you sure?"

"Never been surer of anything in my life."

"Why didn't you give it to my dad?"

"Your father has always been a gigantic pain in my ass. I don't think now is the reason to tell you everything, but just know that you're the one who deserves it the most."

"Okay..."

"Was it because he was an only child?"

"More than likely. I think my wife babied him a little too much. He expects to be catered on, and to have everything given to him without working for it. Not you though. You're just like my brother."

"You think so?"

"Yes. I have no idea how you turned out okay. When I see your siblings and how they act, it makes me glad they sent you away to boarding school. It was a horrible idea at the time, but I think you being away from this train wreck of a family was just what you needed to grow into the man you are today."

"I'm glad you think so."

"Someone has to tell you that they're proud of you," he sighed. "Beyond a doubt, I'm proud of everything you've accomplished. Your schooling, your career in law enforcement, and the family you're creating to carry on the name."

"Thanks grandpa."

He touched my arm affectionately. "I know you'll put the ring to good use. I hope to meet your other half soon. I'm very excited to meet my first great grandchild. I could care less what his mother's family tree looks like. All leaves have the possibility of falling off and going rotten, no matter how special the tree is."

I laughed at his analogy.

"I promise you'll meet her soon," I assured him. "I'll come and get you for supper one night before the baby comes."

"That sounds like a great idea. Tell everyone I've retired to my room for the night."

"Okay," I replied, turning toward the main hall. Now that he was in his room there would be no one I wanted to speak with, so I could leave without insulting anyone of importance.

I walked down the hall towards the sitting room, and past my father's office. He and my mother were engrossed in some sort of discussion. Rather than interrupt I decided to hasten my exit. Just before I opened the front door, Marta touched my arm. "Going so soon Master Sinclair?"

"I've had enough of the family for one night, Marta. Would you be so kind as to tell my parents that grandpa has retired to his room for the night and I got called into work."

"Oh, you did?"

"No. I just can't stand one more moment here. I really only ever come back for the old man," I told her with affection for my nickname for grandpa.

"Master Sinclair, did I hear you right? You're going to be a dad?"

"Yes Marta, I am. His mother is a very beautiful woman, inside and out and I can't wait to hold my child in my arms."

"I'm sure you'll make an excellent dad," she said as she patted my arm and returned to the kitchen.

I was still reeling when I got into my vehicle to drive away. I couldn't believe he gave me grandma's ring. My mother had asked about it on numerous occasions, but I distinctly recalled my father telling her that it was lost. One night she got rip roaring drunk and droned on and on about how it was rightfully hers. When my father finally told her that it was lost, she stopped asking.

But it wasn't lost.

Grandpa just didn't want her to have it.

What that said about my mother I would never know.

VIOLA

A knock sounded at the door. I had been feeling slothful lately and was still dressed in my pajamas from the night before, so I quickly threw on Mike's robe, then waddled my whale of a body down the stairs. Knowing he would be pissed if I opened the door without checking, I peered through the peephole first. A well-dressed woman, with bleach blonde highlights carrying the latest Gucci bag, stood off to the side tapping her red stiletto. I took a deep breath and opened the door a crack.

"Can I help—" the blonde Barbie cut me off as she forced her way past me into the house. I stumbled back, only gaining my footing when I leaned into the bannister. Her heels clicked on the hardwood as she made her way deeper into the house.

Who the hell was this bitch?

"I don't know who you think you are, but you need to get out of my house."

"Where is he?" her hyper-nasally voice grated on my already frayed nerves.

"I don't know who you're looking for, but if you don't get out, I'll call the police."

"Your house? That's rich," she cackled, "This is my fiancés house, you little brat."

My heart leapt into my throat.

"Your what?" I gasped. Fiancé? He was engaged. The first thing that came to mind was Ivy and what happened with her boyfriend. Every one of her dreams came falling down around her, just like it seemed mine were going to.

"Did I stutter, trailer trash?"

I didn't know where she came up with the idea or the accusation that I was trailer trash. How could Mike be with someone like her? She was so cold and unfriendly. She was gorgeous, I would definitely give her that. I had been steadily gaining weight and we hadn't had sex in a couple days, maybe that's why he was with her.

"I don't know who you really are, but you need to leave. If Mike wanted you here, I would have known you existed."

"Of course, he wants me here. We discussed it at brunch last week." She tapped her French manicured finger on her top lip. "Oh, that's right, you weren't there. In fact, you've never been there. I wonder why that is."

As if to shield my unborn child from her venom, my hand fell to my huge bump.

"If anything, this works out perfect for me. My figure won't be ruined to provide him his first heir. We can get married earlier than planned and then pretend that we're doing the world a favour by adopting an unwed high school student's baby so that she can go onto college and have the life she originally planned."

"You're delusional."

This woman was completely off her rocker.

"You'll be provided with substantial compensation of course," she responded, obviously ignoring my statement. "My daddy's lawyers and media relations specialist already have the papers drawn up along with a heartfelt release for when the baby is born."

"Get out!" I yelled.

She had to think I had a backbone. There was no way I was just going to back down and roll over like a dog. I already knew I wouldn't stay here after this. Not if women from his past are going to start popping up around me. That was no way to live. I refused to live my life wondering when the next attack would arrive.

"I think it's you who should get out." She shook her head dismissively. "I give him a minor grace period before we get married and not only does he shack up with, but he knocks up a gutter rat."

"Who are you calling a gutter rat?"

"You. Did you really think this was forever? He told me all about you. The only reason you're here is because of guilt. Once you pop that little parasite bastard out, he'll send you packing, and we'll raise him ourselves without your ill-bred background tainting his future. When he's old enough I'll convince Mike to ship him off to boarding school and then we'll raise our legitimate children far away from your demon spawn."

"Get the fuck out," I yelled at her.

"Why, how dare you! You nasty cunt."

"Get the fuck out, before I call the cops."

"Like that would do you any good."

"Shows what you know."

She stepped out the door and placed her hand against the frame.

"I know quite a bit, honey. I'll leave, but you'd better not get too comfortable. You're due in October, right? That's just next month. Your ass will be out of here the day your little bastard is born. He won't even call you mom; you'll be so far from here shooting up with drugs that he won't even know you exist."

"Fuck you." I slammed the door in her face.

Her irritating squealing and cursing could be heard from the other side of the door. I watched as she stomped down the front steps and threw herself into her red Mercedes like a child throwing a tantrum. Secretly I hoped she would smack her head getting in, but alas, my day wasn't going to go at all like I wanted.

As soon as I heard her car drive away, I started packing. Over the months I had been staying here, I had accumulated a lot of items. There wasn't a portion of this condo that didn't look like I lived in it. Tears streamed down my face as I thought of everything. He let me decorate his living room with accent pillows. To most, I knew that wasn't a bit deal, but to me, it was everything. Here I was, eighteen, pregnant and homeless, and he gave me a place to stay and let me make it my own.

Why would he let me move in and get comfortable if his intentions were to marry that fake plastic barbie? Was I so wrong in my judgement of our situation? Maybe all these double shifts he had been working to prepare for our son's arrival, were actually nights he spent with her.

Once my bag was packed, I picked up my cell and dialed my brother. He was always the first person I thought of when I needed protecting. Even though he was angry and disappointed with my current situation, I knew I could count on him. He had been more of a father to me than my absentee dad ever was.

"Reed, can you come and get me?" I sniffed.

"Why? Where's Mike?"

It surprised me that he didn't know where his partner was, but I pushed it under the rug in order to deal with the task at hand.

"Just come and get me. Please!" I sobbed.

"Okay, Vi, calm down. I promise I'll be there in fifteen."

"Thank you."

After placing my call, I rolled my small bag down the stairs slowly. At my pace it would probably take me fifteen minutes to get from our or should I have said Mike's upstairs bedroom to the front door. The sound of the bag hitting each step mimicked the noise my heart made in my chest as I walked right out of the first place, I called home. I waddled my way to the door and peered through the slats of the blinds, waiting for Reed.

He pulled up outside, parked and came up the front steps. He opened the door just as I made it there with the suitcase. My back ached from all the packing and moving around. It didn't matter how much in shape I was, being seven months pregnant made for a more strenuous time dealing with normal tasks.

"Why didn't you take the truck?" he asked.

I straightened my back and rubbed my hands on my lower back. The movement caused my baby bump I liked to call my huge belly to stick out and almost hit him.

"I can barely fit behind the steering wheel with this huge belly."

He patted my stomach affectionately. "You're not huge. That's my nephew in there. The one I am going to teach how to play hockey."

"Don't tell me you've already got him some skates and a jersey."

"Maybe." He smiled, but it didn't reach his eyes. "What happened Vi?"

"I don't want to talk about it right now. I just want you to take me anywhere but here."

"But you will talk, right?" he asked with concern in his voice.

"Later," I told him, wanting the conversation to end and for us to get to his house before Mike came home.

"Alright. I just want to know who I need to murder so I can find an alibi."

"You shouldn't joke about shit like that, Reed. You're a cop."

"That just means I know how to hide the body."

We pulled into the garage and he closed the door. I followed him into the house and watched as he set my bag by the door.

Reed still lived in the house that he bought as a surprise for him and his fiancé Candi. I had always envied him knowing exactly what he wanted, even though he was so young. He planned for them to move in after they were married, but that never happened. I only wished she hadn't been a backstabbing cheater. When she left town without letting him know, he was devastated. We were surprised he had kept it, but I guessed since she never lived there it didn't possess any of the memories of their relationship.

It was a four-bedroom, two floor home with a garage and a fully developed basement. The gorgeous backyard was landscaped to perfection. The house was white with green trim around the doors and windows. It was the type of house I would have wanted if I didn't already live with Mike. Or rather if I hadn't been living with Mike. Because that was all over now. What an ironic occurrence. The house I had adored for the last six or seven years, I was now living in by default. Even if my Dad had been answering my calls, there was no way he would let me move back home.

If and when I was able to afford a place of my own, I would want something similar, only large enough to add a couple more children, because I wasn't going to stop at one.

A pang in my chest reminded me that Mike wouldn't be the father of the rest of my children. Our son would have other siblings from him, but they would be Cynthia's children, not mine. I took a deep breath and refocussed. The last thing my brother needed was a blubbering mess in front of him. I would wait until he left me alone to fully come to terms with the status of my relationship and the future of my family.

I unhurriedly followed him up the steps to the second floor where all the bedrooms were located.

"Sorry about all the stairs, but you weren't going to sleep on the couch. You can stay in here."

He pushed open a door to reveal what I would have labelled a man cave. The room was decorated in the colours of his favorite hockey team. The walls had a jersey that was signed encased in a frame, and the border on the middle wall was a stripe of blue, white and copper. There was a navy-blue fabric couch in the corner of the room and a murphy bed with an NHL comforter on top.

"What are you going to do when you want to watch the game and I'm sleeping?"

"I haven't watched a game in here since Al moved out."

"I thought you would have been watching with him."

"He was always bringing his puck bunnies over here, and I had no intention of catching crabs by proxy."

That was news to me. I never had any idea that Alder was into puck bunnies. Or maybe that was before he met his current girlfriend? Ash was the one I had heard wasn't into relationships. Except it seemed that all of my siblings were now finding their special someone and I just lost mine. Yet as low as I felt right now and knew I would feel for a while, at least I got one good thing out of all the heartache, and that was my son. I just had to remind myself that we would be just fine without Mike in our lives.

"What about your bunnies?"

"They never interested me. Not their cute tails or buck teeth."

"Come on. You don't have girls over?"

"Definitely not girls."

"You know what I mean," I replied, wanting to smack him for being such an evasive asshole.

He cocked an eyebrow. "What do you mean?"

"Shut up." I punched him. "Just tell me if I need to make myself scarce. I don't want post-traumatic stress disorder from walking in on you getting a blow job on the couch."

"That won't be happening."

"Whatever you say, Casanova," I teased him.

"I'm serious. I haven't brought a chick home in a while. Ever since you moved in with Mike, we haven't gone out to the bar."

"Do you think that's why he is bored with me? He wants to go out and look for bunnies again?"

"What makes you think he's bored?"

"He's been working a lot of hours and hasn't been home much. Then this girl comes over and says they're engaged."

"He's not engaged."

"She had a ring."

"We've been partners for five years. I think I would know if he was engaged."

I broke down and told him everything. I continued the story even when his face changed from a shade of pink to a more pronounced red. He stood there, with his fists clenched to his sides while I told him how she insinuated I was trailer trash and after his money. I told him that I never knew that Mike had any money, so there wasn't a reason to think I was a gold digger.

After I poured my heart out, I crawled into bed and passed out from exhaustion.

MIKE

TWO HOURS EARLIER...

After a rough day at work, I counted down the minutes until I clocked out and could go home to Vi. The past few months since we decided to give our relationship a fighting chance had been some of my best. I never thought it was possible to be in a committed relationship with anyone, but she made it easy. My only issue was how to use those three words to express what she meant to me. As something that was never said in the house growing up, I had never uttered the words to anyone before, not even my siblings.

Since her early graduation, Vi was focussed on her future career and with her marks she could get into University without a problem. It was my goal to enable her to follow her dreams while we raised our child. I never wanted her to regret anything. Earlier in the week, after a lengthy discussion with Reed, we decided to switch to predominantly night shifts. I spoke with my shift manager and made arrangements to start the new shift while she attended classes so that someone would be at home with our son.

My son.

In just over a month, I was going to be a father. I would no longer be known as the perpetual bachelor. I still couldn't believe it. When I round the corner and approach the front of the house, I spot a familiar red Mercedes parked in the driveway.

What the hell was the she-devil doing in my area of town?

Nothing good could come out of her being at my house. My sweet Viola didn't stand a chance against her, no matter how strong she was. Cynthia would eat her alive.

After quickly parking the truck, I took the steps two at a time and entered the house. Cynthia was perched at the island with her legs crossed, still wearing her red stilettos, undoubtedly worn to gain the attention of every male in her general vicinity. I immediately knew something was wrong. I ran up the stairs to the nursery and checked Viola's closet.

Every trace of Viola had been obliterated from our room.

After checking all the bedrooms and the bathroom, I made it back down to the kitchen in record time. Cynthia sat in the same place I left her, filing her nails as if she was dying of boredom. If anything convinced me she was a sociopath, it was that. Who came into someone's home uninvited, wrecked their life, and then sat at their kitchen island dressed to impress and filed their nails?

Cynthia, that was who.

The sight of her blasé attitude enraged me to the point of wanting to punch a hole in the wall. I wasn't a violent man, but something about this twit, whipped me into a craze.

"What did you do?" I gritted out through my clenched teeth.

"What you didn't have the balls to do! Seriously!" she screeched. Her voice was like nails on a chalkboard. "You knocked up one of your badge bunnies and then moved her in? I thought you were more intelligent than that."

"Vi's not a badge bunny. She's far from it."

"Whatever." She waved her hand flippantly. "Are you seriously planning on signing over half your trust fund to a trailer trash whore?"

"Don't call the mother of my child a whore!" I yelled.

If I had ever had the desire to hit a woman, it was now. I wouldn't, obviously, but Cynthia really needed to have some sense smacked into her. She was a spoiled little princess who always got everything she asked for and it was time for her to learn that she didn't deserve it.

"Time to stop dicking around and accept your place at your daddy's company."

"I'm not now, nor will I ever take over that pompous windbag's company."

"But Mikey," she whined. "You promised. I've waited half a decade for you."

I hated her nickname for me more than I hated my parents calling me Junior.

"I've told you a million times I don't want to be entrenched in that world. When are you going to get it through your thick skull that you and I will never happen? We dated for a matter of seconds in high school to appease our parents."

Somehow because I dated her for two months in high school, she thought she had some sort of claim on me. We didn't even have sex. However, she had no problem fucking her way through my friends while she supposedly 'waited for me'. Not that I had anything against women experiencing the pleasure of sex. The one thing I did have an internal regulation about was women who thought that sleeping their way through my friends would somehow garner my attention.

Sharing was not for me. Hell, Reed and I never fucked the same badge bunnies. Once he laid claim, if they approached me after they did the deed, it was a hell no from me. On a couple occasions when he wasn't interested in a conquest, he would give me a nod, and I would stake my claim, but that was not sharing. I didn't want to dip my wick in anything he had. It was too close to a having a sword fight than I wanted.

"Robert Senior is going to write you out of the will." She taunted, likely hoping that I would take the bait.

Little did she know, my grandparents set me up with a separate trust fund years ago when I joined the force. My grandpa, also named Robert Michael, knew that my dad would never accept my choice of law enforcement as a career. His respect of the badge and the fact that his brother was a police officer for twenty-five years was one of the things that drew me to the career. He was a self-made man and didn't subscribe to all the political notions that my father obsessed about.

"I don't care!" I bellowed. "I can't believe I thought you were above such a petty act of blackmail or that maybe we had a chance to still be friends."

"Mikey, why are you saying things like that?" she sniffed, as crocodile tears rolled down her cheeks. "We are friends."

"If we were such great friends, you'd know by now to never call me Mikey."

"I can't believe you're picking her over me."

"It wasn't even a competition. Viola is eons above you."

"She'll never be able to satisfy you," she sneered. "She doesn't know you like I do."

"Don't let the door hit you on the ass when you leave." I pointed to the front entry way.

There was no point wasting precious time arguing with a self-entitled waste of space like Cynthia. I needed to go and get my family back.

～

It took everything in me not to break every traffic law imaginable to get to Reed's house, the first place I needed to look. I wouldn't do my family any good by getting in an accident or arrested.

Reed opened the door before I had the chance to knock.

"You can't be here," he told me, barring my entry into his house.

"I'm going to be wherever she is," I replied.

"She doesn't want you here. You need to leave. After everything that woman said to my baby sister, I want you far away from her. She's eight months pregnant, Mike!"

"I know that! I've been there for her through everything. I never wanted anything to do with Cynthia."

"That's not what it sounded like. She told Vi that you were betrothed or some medieval bullshit."

"That's not true."

"Is there any truth to anything that she said?"

"The reason I never talk about my family or where I came from is because my father is an abusive prick who sees his progeny as pawns for his business deals. All of my siblings have their destinies plotted out. My mom, who was a pawn in a political plan, was brought up by a pair of conniving parents, so she never saw anything wrong with it."

"So you've never had anything to do with her?"

"We dated for two months over a summer while I was in high school. I never slept with her, and never gave her the impression that we would ever be more than friends."

"Yet she's got this claim on you. I can't have Viola around someone like that. She can't have the stress while she's pregnant."

"I agree."

"Then you'll understand when I ask you to leave."

"You're not going to let me explain things to her?"

"My sister just cried herself to sleep a half an hour ago. I don't think we should wake her up for anything. If she wants to talk to you and give you a chance to explain, that's up to her."

"I don't know what to do."

"If you truly love her, like somehow I think you do, then you'll turn around, get into your truck, and go home," he told me. "Give her time. Her world has just been turned upside down."

So, I did what he asked me to do.

Even though it killed me inside.

VIOLA

THE SOUND OF FAMILIAR VOICES RAISED IN CONFLICT downstairs woke me from a deep sleep. My heart ached when I remembered where I was and how I was truly not at home. I thought back to everything that happened just hours before and wondered how I could be so stupid to think that Mike actually wanted to be a family. I was so naïve; hellbent on the perfect life. If I had anything to do with it, it was never happening again.

If he wanted to spend time with our son, I wouldn't keep him away.

If he married that vapid bitch, I would bite my tongue.

Regardless of the circumstances, our boy would be loved with everything I had to the ends of the earth and back. This book I read a while ago had a quote about how a parent who truly loved their child would march straight into hell and take on the Devil himself, and if they weren't willing then they didn't deserve to have a child. Thinking back, even when I felt neglected by my Dad, somewhere deep inside I knew he would take down the Devil for any one of his children. I could only hope that Mike was willing to do the same, even if that Devil was a skanky hoe who wore Prada.

I pulled the covers over my head and buried myself in the bed, in every attempt to escape what was probably happening downstairs. There was no way Reed would let Mike come upstairs to talk to me, so I knew I wouldn't have to face him until I was ready. Because if there was one thing my older brother was, he was his siblings' protector.

The one man I knew I could count on until the end of time.

Cheesy, but accurate.

"For the record, I believed he had changed, Vi. He was looking forward to becoming a dad. In all the years I've known him, he never once mentioned anyone named Cynthia to me. Most likely that was because he didn't like the world that he came from. All I knew was that his parents had some outlandish expectations for how he should live his life ad they never accepted his profession as a police officer."

"Reed, I get that he's your partner, but I don't think I'm ready to talk about him yet," I sniffed.

"I'm sorry, Vi. I'll be here for you whenever you're ready to talk, and I don't care if he's my best friend. You're my family, and you come first."

"I know. I think I just want to sit here and watch some asinine action flick and forget about the world and all my problems."

"So, I know that pregnant women get cravings. What are you craving right now?"

"Sweet and salty! Popcorn with a ridiculously huge glass of coke."

"Your wish is my command, sis." He kissed my forehead and went into the kitchen for movie watching supplies.

MIKE

THE NEXT PEOPLE ON MY SHIT LIST THAT NEEDED A talking to were my parents. Something about Cynthia's visit to my house reeked of my father's involvement. There was no way she could have known about Viola's pregnancy, unless either he or my mom told her. My wager was on my dad, but my mom could be a conniving woman. I barely made it through the door before I was confronted by my father's disapproving scowl.

"What's this about you threatening to have Cynthia arrested?"

"She broke into my house," I argued. "People who break and enter deserve to be charged with the crime, no matter who their daddy is."

"Your mother gave her a key," he explained.

"First off, how the hell did she get a key?"

"You're cleaning company is the same one we use for our house."

It looked like I would be searching for a new maid service in the morning.

"Why the hell did she think Cynthia needed a key?"

"Cynthia wanted to have an interior decorator come in while you were at work and take a look at the place. You know she'll want to put finishing touches on it, so it feels like a home to her too. You can't have a man cave forever."

For a moment I had actually deluded myself into thinking they were above petty manipulation.

"You knew full well that Viola was staying with me at the house. What was your plan? I can't believe you guys are so petty that you would stoop low enough to use Cynthia to scare her away."

"That girl is not of the same stock as us, what did you expect us to do?" My mom chimed in from the hall. "She doesn't deserve to bring our heir into this world. If you would have been smarter, she would have been in the clinic the moment she told you the news. Either that or you should have had our lawyers draw up papers and then you and Cynthia could raise him as your own."

"That isn't for you to decide, Estelle." From this point on, my mother wasn't my mother. My parents could go to hell for all I cared. "Not only that, how the hell did you know I was having a boy?"

"Your doctor of course."

"Well apparently he's losing a patient. Don't you people realize that you're breaking the law?"

Not only did I have to find Viola to convince her of my feelings, but now I had to look for a new family doctor for us. One preferably not under the thumb of my meddling parents. He should have known what fresh hell he brought by informing my mother that a woman who was not of the Sinclair standards was pregnant with a son to carry on the Sinclair name. All of these rich snobby assholes always stuck together.

"What's the good of having money if we can't use it to find the information we need?" she replied haughtily. "Besides, Cynthia is a perfect match, and knows our world. She would make an excellent mother to our grandson."

I was just about to storm out of the house for the last time when I heard shuffling. Suddenly, my grandfather called out from the other room, "Estelle, your true nature is showing." I watched as he got up out of the chair by the fireplace and made his way in our direction.

"Hi, Grandpa." I greeted him, ashamed that he had to hear our argument. "Sorry you had to hear the things I was saying to them."

"Oh whatever," he responded, cutting my apology off with a wave of his hand. "What did these two morons do now?"

"Dad." "Robert." My parents pleaded at the same time.

"Be quiet. I'm asking my grandson a question," he regarded them with a pinch of malice.

"I wanted to come and tell you my news in person, but since you're here and I need to explain things, I'll start at the beginning."

"Hold that thought. Let's go into the study," he suggested.

I immediately followed him into my father's office, while my effectively chastised parents trailed behind us like a pair of sheep. My grandfather, spry for an eighty-three-year-old man, sauntered around the mahogany monstrosity my father called a desk, and sat in his chair. The look of displeasure on my parent's face was unmistakeable.

"Wipe that scowl off your face, son. This room once belonged to me, so I have just as much right to it as you do. Now stop acting like a spoiled brat and sit in the chair opposite me while I learn what occurred to cause my grandson to be so angry with the two of you."

"Over the years I've talked to you about their obsession with me marrying Cynthia Milton and how I wanted nothing to do with her," I began.

"Yes, you have." He steepled his hands under his chin. "I gather you haven't changed your mind."

"No, I haven't. In fact, when I dated her for only a couple months in high school to appease them, we had absolutely zero chemistry."

"Marriage isn't based on chemistry, junior," my father cut in.

"Your mother and I had chemistry, Robert," Grandpa admitted.

"Viola and I have chemistry."

"Who is this Viola? I've heard her name a couple times."

"She's the younger sister of my partner Reed, the daughter of the Chief of Police, the mother of my unborn child, and most of all the love of my life."

"That's quite a list, son."

"That doesn't even begin to describe who she is as a person," I replied.

"How is she doing?" Grandpa questioned.

"She's eight months pregnant with my son. Up until last night, she was living with me and thanks to these cold, calculating individuals, she left me." I hung my head in shame.

"When will you realize that she will never be like us?" my mother asked.

"You would know all about that, wouldn't you Estelle?" my grandfather addressed my mother with contempt.

"Dad, don't," my father pleaded.

"It's time this wife of yours gets off her high horse." My grandfather stood up behind the desk. "She was undoubtedly the penultimate reason your first wife was pushed to suicide. She was always jealous of her sister. That sweet woman, and the love of your life, ended her life just under a month after giving birth to your son...yes, Mike I am talking about your birthmother."

"Why how dare you!" My mother, I mean aunt, stormed out of the room in a tizzy, followed by my father.

What the fuck just happened?

I wished I could be thankful for the sordid truth. Instead it left me with too many questions to count. No wonder she never loved me. She probably moved right in and removed every piece of evidence that my real mother had lived in this house. The whole ordeal made me question if Estelle birthed any of my father's children. It would explain why she was so cold and distant.

With the room cleared, grandpa continued the story.

"I wasn't living here at the time, but I was getting ready to hand over the business to your father. Your mother, Erika, was suffering from a horrible case of postpartum, and Estelle was staying here. She swore it was to help her sister, but really she wanted to hook a big fish, and your father just happened to be that fish."

"But he was already married."

"When has that ever stopped a woman from going after what they wanted, especially when they are manipulative and callous?"

"How did she cause my birthmother to commit suicide?" I asked, not sure if I really wanted to know everything.

"Erika had a hard time getting out of bed, so Estelle would go and get you out of your crib so that your mother could feed you. She really had us all fooled." He shook his head in disgust. "It started with little things. If Erika made it out of bed, Estelle would make a point of flaunting her relationship with you and your father. She would place lingering, albeit platonic, touches on him and when it came to you, Estelle would refuse to hand you off, citing some ridiculous reason, like her needing to eat or that you had just gone down for a nap."

"How would that push her to take her own life?"

"You have to understand, especially now that you're about to be a father, postpartum can be a serious concern for new mothers. It can make them feel very sad, hopeless, and worthless. They may even have trouble caring for and bonding with their baby. No matter how strong a woman may seem, the risk will always be there."

I had read a bit on postpartum in the books I had on pregnancy. It was one of my worries because of the subtle depression Viola had been experiencing due to her ultimate abandonment by her father. Being a single, pregnant eighteen-year-old would affect even the strongest of individuals, and Viola was most definitely strong. Tack on the distant relationship she already had with her father, and it was a recipe for disaster.

"Estelle came home with your mother from the hospital. She inserted herself into the household, and systematically attacked your mother with her passive aggressive behavior. She made Erika believe she was an unfit mother and wife. Two days before your mother committed suicide, Estelle paraded her eighteen-year-old body, scantily clad in a string bikini, around the house."

"How could my father marry her?" I asked with disgust. How could a man not notice that his wife was being undermined and harassed by someone who was supposed to be her family. Even my own siblings wouldn't have been so callous.

"Once your mother died, Estelle stayed on to help him with you. In your father's grief, it was quite easy for her to push her way into his bed."

"My father is a weak man," I told my grandpa. "He couldn't even be faithful to his second wife."

"You know," he stated with surprise.

"That Victor and Claudia aren't Estelle's children, yep."

"When did you figure that out?"

"I wasn't sure about Victor, but Claudia appeared about six months after my nanny Clarissa disappeared. That and I saw Dad going to town on my nanny in his office."

He laughed. "Definitely not the answer I was expecting."

"Shortly after Claudia was brought home, I was sent to boarding school to protect the charade."

"They should have told you the truth from the start."

"Not like it would have made them better parents. Estelle is a bitter woman and Dad is a complete megalomaniac."

"We've had this conversation before. Your dad was spoiled.

Everything I knew from when I was younger was a lie.

I drove home in a daze.

VIOLA

"It's been a couple weeks, why don't you give him a call?" Reed randomly suggested.

"Why would I want to talk to him?" I asked.

"Because you're devastated and moping around like the world ended. I can only take so much female emotions. Maybe you'll feel better if you were to talk to him. Get closure or open another door."

"Okay Dr. Phil, I'll get right on that." I huffed as I went up to my room to make the call.

It had been a couple weeks since I heard from him. Every night for a week straight he knocked on the door and called me. Eventually, after gaining no headway, it seemed that he had given up all together. To be honest, I wasn't sure what I wanted; whether I wanted him to leave me alone or continue to hound me into submission. Either way it could be seen as not caring or caring too much.

I dialed his number and waited a couple rings.

"Hello," a female voice answered the phone. I almost hung up, but I needed to see it through.

"Hi, is Mike available?"

"Sorry, he's in the shower. Can I take a message?"

Of course, he was in the shower.

"No, that's alright. I call back sometime after never." I hung up the phone and sobbed into my pillow.

A couple minutes later, there was knock on my door, followed by Reed asking, "Can I come in?"

"Sure."

The door opened and I looked into sad eyes that were so much like my own. It was amazing what you noticed when you paid attention for a moment. I hadn't realized Reed had been gifted with mom's eyes. I had seen them in pictures but didn't notice it until right now. It made me wonder if my son would be gifted with her eyes as well, since they were also my own.

"Did you get a hold of him?"

"He was in the shower."

"How'd you know that? Did he answer in there or something?"

"No. The woman who answered his cell phone told me he was in the shower."

"Shit."

"Yeah and I'm not stupid enough to believe that he would take a shower with a strange woman in his house."

"I don't know what to tell you, imp."

"Well I guess I got myself some closure."

"That's not what I thought would happen."

"What did you think was going to happen? There had to have been a reason you wanted me to call him."

"He seemed down at work, like he missed you."

"Does he talk about me?"

"No, he doesn't, but I always thought that was because he was scared to rock the boat. We finally got back to a place where I wasn't wanting to punch him repeatedly."

"And now?"

"I want to punch his motherfucking lights out for hurting my sister."

A WEEK OR SO LATER, Reed was getting ready upstairs. He had been going out sporadically since I moved in. Something told me the reason he was leaving tonight was for a date. A date with someone important because I knew him, and he usually picked up women at the bar. Sometimes when we watched movies together, he would get texts. I couldn't see the conversation, but he would get this smile on his face that I hadn't seen in a long time. Whoever he was seeing was changing him for the better, and I couldn't be happier for him.

He didn't date anyone, at least not seriously after Candi. His relationship with his fiancé Candice ended around the time of Rowan's overdose. He never talked about what happened. All I remembered was that she was here hanging out at the house one moment, the next she was gone, and never returned. I was happy for him to find someone new, and have no intention to interrogate him, even though I truly want to find out who this special woman was.

"I finally understand why you were willing to pursue your relationship with Mike behind my back." Reed mentioned as he came down the stairs.

I struggled to pull myself up into a straight sitting position on the couch. I had a little more than a month left in my pregnancy and over the last week my baby bump had ballooned to epic proportions.

"Why do you say that? You're not dating Candi again, are you?" I asked even though I was pretty sure he wouldn't be that stupid.

"I wouldn't touch that chick with a ten-foot pole. Besides, I haven't seen or heard from her in seven years."

"So, who are you dating that you don't think I would approve of?"

"First off, I'm not dating anyone, yet. I'm also not ready to talk to anyone about her, but I promise you'll be one of the first people I tell. After all, you and my nephew will be living here and eventually if things work out between us, I'll bring her here."

"I hope you know that as long as she makes you happy, I'll accept her. If she hurts you, that's another matter altogether."

"All right, Rocky."

"You deserve to be loved, Reed. In order to do that, you need to move on."

"I'm not going to have a heart to heart, imp."

"Oh, I know you won't, cause you're a manly man, right?"

"You know me well," he answered with a wink.

"You are my brother."

"Exactly. So, don't make me talk about feelings."

"Ok, fine. Who's the chick?"

"I'll let you all know once I'm sure of where this is going."

"I'm going to hold you to that."

"Sure, whatever," he responded, then walked towards the front door. "Don't wait up."

VIOLA

SEPTEMBER

ONE MONTH LATER...

Sunday morning, I woke to the sound of knocking on the door of my not so temporary bedroom in Reed's house. After another fitful sleep, I wanted to throw my pillows at whoever dares to disturb my beauty sleep. The person on the other side, who was about to breathe his last breath, didn't wait for my response before they pushed my creaky door open. Unsurprisingly, I was met with my brother Alder's cheery face, illuminated by the morning sun shining through the slats in the blinds, peeks around the frame.

"Wakey, wakey, eggs and bakey," he sang out as he threw open the curtains, blinding me. Alder had always been the morning person in the family, likely from years of devotion to hockey.

"Go away." I pulled the heavy blankets up over my head to block out the offending daylight as if I was a vampire avoiding my final death. "Don't you have a ball to throw somewhere?" I groaned.

Except, I felt more like the oversized Halloween decoration emulating Count Dracula, with all the weird cravings and fear of the sunlight touching my skin.

"Very funny, don't give up your day job for stand up just yet. Time to get ready, little miss bed head. I'm taking you for Sunday brunch."

His footsteps got louder as he made his way further into the bedroom and yanked the blankets out of my hands and flung them off to the side of the bed, much farther than I felt like going to retrieve them. Thankfully, I was wearing my shorts and a t-shirt I stole from Mike's closet. I don't know what possessed me to take the shirt. I just wanted to feel close to him whenever I wore it, even if he was not around.

"Get up before I need to resort to methods that are likely to launch you into early labour. I'd hate to spend today in the maternity ward."

During my childhood, while all our older siblings were trying to sleep in on the weekends, he was looking for creative ways to get them out of bed. On several occasions, he ensured their school day alarms were turned on, waking them at seven in the morning. One time, before Rowan's drug use escalated and he was thrown out, Alder crept into the twins' room and grabbed the edge of his mattress and shook it, screaming earthquake at the top of his lungs. Reed and Rowan launched to their feet and chased him out into the barn, where his only method of escape was to crawl into the hayloft and pull up the ladder to restrict their access.

The thought of being the mother of a rambunctious boy like Alder brought a smile to my face. I rolled to a sitting position and held out my arm for Alder to help me to my feet. This baby was making things increasingly difficult in the mobility department. The momentary smile was replaced by a pang in my chest reminding me of the heartache of losing Mike when all I wanted to do was curse him for putting me in this state.

He should be here!

"Reed thinks I should stay near home just in case I go into labour," I argued, as Al pulled me to my feet and steadied me.

"You need to get out of this house. I don't care what Reed says. You need fresh air. That baby won't pop out because you decide to go for a walk."

"Sure, let's take the beached whale out for more food," I whined, even though I was secretly dying to try out the Sunday brunch at the Silver Springs Golf and Country Club.

Alder likely arrived this morning before I woke, so he could clock in early for his daily 'whale watching' appointment while Reed was at work. My brothers had taken house arrest to a very different level.

"You're not fat, Viola! I don't ever want to hear you call yourself anything but beautiful," he chastised me. "You're carrying my first nephew in there."

"My bladder is well aware of that fact, but I'm still huge."

"So what!"

Alder waved his arms erratically, like he was having some kind of fit. However, men should know never to insinuate that a woman is bigger, even if she was only pregnant. It was not polite to comment on a woman's weight.

"So, you agree?"

He groaned loudly in despair.

"That's not what I meant, but what do you expect? You're having a baby. You've been growing a living, breathing human inside of you.

Of course you're going to gain some weight. Now get dressed and meet me downstairs."

I finally gave up, knowing that anything I say against my current appearance will be refuted by Alder until he's blue in the face.

"Whatever. Let's go and stuff our faces with Belgian Waffles and whipping cream."

My nerves were getting the best of me as we pulled up to the gate at the Country Club. It had been a couple weeks since I had left the house, mainly because I didn't want to face anyone in my current state. Pregnancy wasn't something to be ashamed of, but sometimes I felt the judgement in people's eyes. It was probably all just a figment of my imagination, but it was something that bothered me. All my siblings came to Reed's place to visit me, and even though I was not permitted to go back home, I was not lonely.

Alder drove straight up to the front entrance and parked by the valet. A teenaged boy, smartly dressed in khaki pants and a green polo shirt with the Country Club logo, opened my door and held out his arm to help me out of the vehicle. I was taken aback and almost brought to tears by the tender way he held my arm as he skillfully hoisted my huge body out of the car.

"Thank you," I sniffed.

Damn hormones.

"You're very welcome, and congratulations."

"Thanks." I was sure my cheeks have a bit of colour, as I had never been the one to handle any sort of special attention well.

Alder came around the vehicle and handed his keys to the teen along with a ten-dollar tip. He held out his arm and waited for me to grasp it. Once I threaded my arm over his elbow, we walked to the hostess stand so that we could get ourselves a table.

"Was that your stomach that just roared like a lion?"

If anything, this eating for two was making me ravenous, and I was looking forward to stuffing my face with a vengeance.

"Yeah." A flush slowly crept across my cheeks.

"Let's get my nephew fed then," he teased.

The sight of Mike beyond the gate with that bitch seated next to him took my breath away. My chest constricted. I could almost hear the sound of my heart breaking as I took in the scene of her and him with what looked like their parents. He hadn't even introduced me to his parents, and I was pregnant with his child. They probably didn't even know they were going to be grandparents. It had been two weeks since he last tried to call me and the first time I see him, he just had to be with her.

She was right about one thing: it was obviously going to be the Mike and Cynthia show. However, the only way they would ever get their hands on my child was if they pried him out of my cold dead fingers.

Over my dead body.

"We have to go," I grabbed my brother's arm and tried to turn him around before Mike saw me. I didn't want to give him the satisfaction of parading his fiancé in front of me, showing me how he had moved on.

"But we just got here." Alder complained, then followed my line of sight and sang a different tune. "Never mind. I'll cook you waffles at home."

A sharp pain sliced through my side, doubling me over. The baby was not due for a couple weeks, so it took me by surprise. It didn't feel like the Braxton Hick's I had been experiencing over the last couple weeks. This one was stronger, more precise.

"Vi," Alder sounded as distressed as I felt.

"I'm fine," I lied, attempting to convince myself.

"Nice try. You are totally the opposite of fine." Alder touched my shoulder, looking in my eyes. "Let's get you to the hospital."

"I just want to go home." I groaned, while holding my stomach. All I could think of was getting as far away as possible so that Mike didn't notice I was possibly in labour. I didn't need him and *her* to show up at the hospital flashing their cash, ready to take my son.

"Miss, I think you should listen to your husband."

"Does he look like my husband?" I growled, making the host hold up his hands in surrender.

"Sorry, Miss, I don't mean to offend, but are you sure that you're not in labour?"

"It's okay. I'm her brother." Alder responded. He wrapped his arm around my waist and guided me back to the valet who already had our car waiting.

Another sharp stab makes me cry out. The reality of the situation hits me full force.

"Alder, I'm scared. He's not supposed to come for a couple weeks."

"Everything is going to be okay. Maybe you're just having more of those Braxton Hicks contractions or whatever you called them." He smiled, trying his best to reassure me, but it didn't hit his eyes, so I knew he was just as scared as I was. "I still think we should go and have you checked out."

I nodded. "Okay."

We were in and out of the doctor's office in under an hour. My doctor confirmed that I was indeed experiencing more Braxton Hicks. She also advised that I keep a close watch on things because I could go into labour any day now. I didn't even know how Alder knew anything about the Braxton Hicks, but once he mentioned the possibility, it calmed me. In my moment of panic, I forgot about everything I had read in the numerous books I had regarding this pregnancy. It obviously didn't matter what you read, when the time came, you needed to be prepared to expect the unexpected.

After the doctor, Alder drove me home in silence.

MIKE

When I showed up at Silver Springs for Sunday brunch, I was under the impression that my father wanted to mend fences. What I didn't expect was for the Miltons to be included in the meal. Twenty minutes later, I couldn't understand how I allowed them to persuade me to stay and sit through another shitty brunch with the rents and psycho Barbie from hell. Yet here I was, fending off her putrid manicured claws from sinking into my flesh and latching on like a barnacle. I was liable to become infected with some alien incurable disease.

Seriously, was I that lonely?

It had been over a month since I saw Viola; a couple weeks since I had gotten the hint that she no longer wanted me in her life. The only reason I was here was because my father convinced me that he was ready to have a decent conversation about the future of the family business. He led me to believe he was actually going to consider my thoughts on my brother Victor being trained to take over the mantle. His exact words were "we need to sit down and discuss your brother's role in the future of the company."

Instead, I was sitting at a table with the family I barely spent time with and the family that I never wanted to spend time with. My father had barely uttered a word to me beyond telling me that I was late, yet again. Then he proceeded to have the most aggravating conversation about the recent lack of policing in affluent neighbourhoods.

In my opinion, rich people spent too much time complaining about the number of non-local vehicles driving through their streets and forcing the city to install no left turn signs that police then have to write tickets for, instead of focussing on things that are actually important, like reducing crime rates or getting drugs off the streets. Fentanyl, the drug Reed's twin overdosed on, was still a problem in the city, among other dangerous narcotics.

I wished I would have taken another shift like Reed did this morning. I needed to have his back instead of indulging my father's sick fantasies of merging our families. Something was wrong with my partner, but he had yet to confide in me exactly what was happening with him. Most of our conversations have been kept to the job since everything went down with Viola. I lost more than my girlfriend and a child that day. Reed had been more like a brother for the past seven years.

Cynthia droned on and on about her latest philanthropic cause, while I prayed for some sort of miracle. I was five minutes from faking an emergency call, when suddenly, I was drawn to some kind of commotion at the gate. Being in law enforcement, I immediately assessed the risk. From the back, I could see long dark hair hanging to the middle of her back. She turned slightly to the side, giving me a glimpse of her side profile.

What was Viola doing here?

This being the last place I expected to see her, I double guessed my first identification, so I tried to get a better one. I wanted to go over there, but I didn't want to look like a weirdo if it wasn't her. Cynthia, not appreciating my distraction from her incessant boast, snapped her fingers right in my face and almost beaned me in the nose, to get my attention. When that didn't work, she grabbed my chin and pulled it in her direction. I gently grasped her wrist and removed her hand from my face.

"Don't touch me," I gritted between clenched teeth.

She gasped in an attempt to draw attention, and once she was sure she had it, she laid into me. "I don't understand what's so important over there that you have been completely ignoring me."

"Enough of this. We've already had this discussion a million times Cynthia," I said to her. "Or do I actually have to spell it out for you. I. DON'T. WANT. YOU."

"Junior, I think you should apologize to Frank and Marietta for insulting their daughter and them by proxy."

If he wanted an apology, he would get one. It just wouldn't be the wordage that he wished for.

My father could suck it, for all I cared.

"Mr. and Mrs. Milton, I apologize for my father's behavior. I've told him and your daughter on several occasions that I have no intention of marrying your daughter or joining his investment firm. In fact, I'm in love with someone, and she's having my baby."

The woman, who looked identical to Viola from behind, was heading in the direction of the valet. It had to be none other than her; I would recognize her voluptuous curves anywhere. They had grown exponentially in the last month. I missed out on a lot. Suddenly, she stopped walking and hunched over holding her stomach.

Was she in labour?

Suddenly I heard the unmistakeable sound of her crying out in pain.

I had to go.

Pushing my chair back suddenly, I launched to my feet, prepared to chase after my future.

The future not currently seated at this table.

"You will sit down and finish this meal." My father commanded.

"No, I will not be sitting down. I will not subject myself to another moment of this farce. I won't in a million years entertain the possibility of marrying Cynthia, even if she was the only woman left on the planet."

"But Mikey." Cynthia stumbled to her feet, swaying. This morning's excessive alcohol consumption impeded her mobility just as much as it had loosened her mouth.

A mimosa didn't mean ten.

"Cynthia, sit back down," her mother directed. "I will not have you making a fool out of yourself in front of our friends."

Her mother surprised me with the first statement, and then redeemed herself as a shallow self-centred Country Club robotic wife, reminding me why I was never marrying into this society. None of these women could ever compare to my Viola. I wished I wouldn't have let my family wreck the only good thing in my life. This was the last time I would let them have any say in my life.

"You will not leave this table to go after that trollop," my father boomed, grabbing my arm.

"What are you talking about?" I growled and wrenched my arm out of his grasp.

"Your little bastard oven. Did you really think I'd accept a low bred mutt like her into this family? When I found out her brother played hockey for the University, I made some calls. His coach mentioned something about looking after his sister while their brother was at work because she was close to having her first child. I put two and two together, then sent him tickets for Sunday brunch knowing he would have no choice but to bring her here."

"What the hell have you done this time?" I demanded with my teeth clenched.

"Exactly what you didn't have the balls to do son. I've cleaned up your mess. Now that your dalliance is well on her way to cutting you completely out of her life, you can take your rightful place at the company without anything holding you back." My father boasts. "Now stop making a scene and sit down."

"You really are a sorry son of a bitch," I yelled at my father, drawing the attention of surrounding spectators. Looked like the Sinclairs were this morning's entertainment.

"Robert Michael, watch how you talk to your father," my whatever she was reprimanded.

"He's no father of mine," I responded, then added another nail to my coffin. "He's so pathetic that he couldn't even get his other two children to join us for brunch. Or was the reason they never joined due to the fact that you weren't their mother?"

She gasped, hand flying to her chest for dramatic effect. She should have been on stage with the amount of theatrics she displayed.

"Go ahead, play the victim," I addressed her. "Apparently you're good at that."

"Don't talk to your mother like that."

"She's not my mother."

The only thing that surprised me through this whole ordeal was that I didn't feel an ounce of regret or even the need to apologize to my so-called parents. Their callous and manipulative nature had finally caught up to them and pushed me away forever.

"You ungrateful little puke, if you leave, you are no longer a part of this family," threatened my father.

At least I can be thankful that he taught me one thing during his sorry sad excuse of a parental reign. He taught me how not to treat my child. I was going to be the best damn father Viola allowed me to be.

"That's fine by me," I responded.

Then I experienced the most satisfying moment in the history of my relationship with my parents.

I walked out of their lives.

VIOLA

A COUPLE HOURS AFTER REED WENT TO WORK, ALDER waltzed in the door without a care in the world. Me, I was fit to be tied. This babysitting my brothers were doing was really getting to me. When Reed couldn't be here, Alder or Ash was.

"You really don't need to be here, Al," I whined, exhausted with everything.

"Actually, I do," he responded with his classic smirk.

"You guys act like no woman has been pregnant with a baby in the history of the world," I joked.

"None of my sisters have had a baby, and I'll be pissed if something happens to you while you're alone in this house."

"Nothing's going to happen." I laughed. "Besides, I'm not even due for a couple weeks."

"And until then, you'll have either Reed, Ash or me here to watch your every move," he confessed.

"Come on," I complained, even though part of me was happy to have all attention from my family. It had been five months since I had seen or talked to my father, and I missed him every day. With everything going on I was grateful I had my siblings' support and I wasn't left completely on my own.

"We've got to look after you and the munchkin you're bringing into the world. This is my first nephew, and I can't wait to teach him hockey and whatever other sports the little guy will be into," he continued, trying to get me to forget my ire over being coddled.

He might have succeeded a bit by talking about all the things he wanted to teach him. I couldn't help but think that Mike should be the one doing all those things with our son.

"Between you and Reed, my son will be shooting bullets and pucks by the time he takes his first steps," I teased.

"You played hockey; he'll play hockey."

"I only played until high school."

"So what."

"Maybe he won't play at all."

"Yeah right. With an uncle like me? He'll be skating circles around everyone on the ice by the time he's three," he throws his head back and laughs. "I'll have hockey equipment on him when he's four. Mark my words."

"You need to get your woman to pop out some hockey players for you."

"Maybe," he responded, a wistful look crossing over his face.

My phone rang, interrupting my thoughts.

"Hold that thought."

I picked up the phone and glanced at it. Ivy's smiling face greeted me from the screen. Alder took one look at it, shook his head and got up out of his chair. "I'll be right back," Alder called out as he went down the hall to the bathroom.

I didn't blame him for leaving the room. With Ivy, who knew how long this conversation would take.

"Hey Ives, I can't talk too much girl talk because Al is here."

"I don't give a shit if Al's there, you're mine now," she responded with glee. "Besides, we have lots to discuss."

"Oh, do we?" I laughed.

There was a contagious sort of contentment that Ivy spread into the world. Even though she was having a hard time with her life, she usually could find the best way to make another person smile. Maybe her outlook on life would rub off on me and I would feel better about everything. I still hadn't talked to Mike, and honestly I didn't think I would for a while.

"We do!" she squealed through the speaker on my phone. "So, what are you going to dress up as for Halloween this year?"

"A beached whale," I responded, because that was how I felt right now with the huge baby inside me just waiting to get out.

"Vi! Don't be so hard on yourself," she clucked her tongue. "You're so cute with that baby bump."

"The baby is due in a couple weeks, so I doubt I'll have time to dress up like anything."

"Whatever, Vi. You'll be dressed up, mark my words," she laughed. "So, what the heck is Al doing there for?"

"You know how overprotective Reed is," I responded, avoiding the portion of our conversation aimed at my non-Halloween costume wearing ass.

Ivy giggled.

"You mean how psycho he is about our safety, or how overbearing he is about our lives? How he treats us all like his children even though there isn't many years between us"

"All of the above," I responded. "Well, he's bound and determined for me to have around the clock babysitters until the baby is born."

"He loves you." Ivy assured me.

"I know he does. I think he's feeling guilty about what happened between Mike and me. He is caught between the two of us, his partner and his sister. Even though I would never expect him to choose, he's scared of messing things up," I sighed. "I think something is going on with him too. Something in his personal life that he wants to share with the rest of us, but something that we might judge him for. So, there's an effect on his behavior from that misplaced guilt too."

The phone slipped out of my hand and fell on the kitchen island when I was startled by a loud crash outside on the street. I slowly slid off the chair, waddled to the window and looked out to see what happened. It appeared that the driver of an old blue rusted out Chevy truck had lost control and plowed into Alder's car. Reed's neighborhood was relatively quiet most of the time so a car crashing out front was unheard of.

"Al, someone just ran into your car!"

I felt bad that his car got damaged, but morbidly, I was thankful that some complete nutso crashed into Alder's car to distract me from Ivy's phone call. Now she would have something different to discuss than my costume for this year's Halloween. It was completely absurd to have a conversation about my choice of Halloween costume for this year when my due date was close to Halloween. There was no way I would be walking around trick or treating with a newborn strapped to my chest.

"What?" Alder came running around the corner while buttoning his jeans.

Eww.

"I said, some asshole just rammed his Chevy truck into the back end of your Civic," I replied

"Fuck," Alder exclaimed, then came over to the window to see what I was talking about.

Alder pulled out his cell phone and called emergency services. I could only hear one side of the conversation as I watched what was going on outside.

"Al, the driver just kept going and didn't stop until he crashed. It was like he hit your car on purpose or something. There was no brake involved, just acceleration," I told him.

"What's going on Vi?" I could still hear Ivy over the speakerphone.

"Ivy, are you still there?" I was surprised to hear her, since I had completely forgotten her on the line.

"I'm here," she answered.

"I don't know why, but someone just crashed into Alder's car outside. Al just called the police, so hopefully they'll be here soon." I yelled back. I didn't feel like waddling back to the island to grab the phone. Plus, I wanted to see what else the Captain of Crazy Town was going to do.

Reed lived on a quiet street in a nice residential neighbourhood. Things like this just didn't happen here. We weren't near a bar, so there was very little risk that a drunk driver would accidentally sideswipe your vehicle parked on the street. Watching this guy, as he got out of his truck, it was obvious that he had been drinking. There was no reason for him to have hit Al's car. It wasn't hard to avoid with its bright orange paint.

The man hit the ground running. He was on a mission, and it appeared that his destination was Reed's house, for some crazy reason. He bobbed and weaved over the grass as cut through the yard diagonally. He hit the front deck with a thump. In his haste, scrambling up the steps, he almost fell over as he tripped on a few. It sounded like a herd of rhinos trying to scale a building.

Pounding on the side of door with all of his might, he screamed and demanded entry. The door, with its stained-glass window in the centre, was not infallible. Pretty soon the guy would decide we weren't answering and smash the window to get in. He seemed pretty determined to gain entry.

"Where is she?" he bellowed, looking around the kitchen. The unknown crash bandit suddenly pushed in the door, knocking my brother to the side.

"Where's who?" Alder asked.

"My woman, that's who. I know she comes here with some guy that looks like you."

"Sir, please calm down," I instructed him in a gentle voice. I didn't want to get him any more riled up than he already was. "We don't know who you're talking about. We're the only ones in the house."

I walked away from the window to grab my cell phone off the counter, and by the time I got there, the man was two steps away from me moving with purpose, his wild eyes swinging around the room. Walking around the other side of the island, I placed my stomach towards the counter to shield my baby from the guy, just in case he hit me by accident.

"You lie!" he pushed past me, knocking me off balance. Air whooshed out of my lungs when my stomach suddenly hit the island.

"Hey, fucker, that's my pregnant sister you just pushed," Alder yelled, grabbing his arm before he could run up the stairs.

"I know the little slut is here and I'm not leaving until I find her. "The intruder ripped his arm out of my brother's hand and asked, "Where are they?"

This dude was like a broken record.

"Whoever you're looking for is obviously not here," Alder explained. "We've called the police, and they will be arriving soon. I suggest you go back out to your truck and maybe the arresting officers will go easier on you. They might not press charges for forced entry."

"I know you're hiding them. You and the guy who lives here that looks like you. Are you both fucking her?"

"We're not hiding anyone here," I repeated. "Listen to my brother. They might go easier on you if you're not in here. You broke into the house of a cop. You don't want to be here to explain why you pushed into our house for no reason."

"Vi, why don't you go wait upstairs for the police to get here?"

"I don't want to leave you alone." I responded, moving further into the living area.

Alder grabbed his arm again and tried to shift him toward the door. He was trying to get the guy further from me so that I could go and wait somewhere safer, but he was resisting. Even in his drunk state he still had some gumption and was fighting back with all his might. He slipped out of Alder's grasp, and whipped around, instantly going on the offensive.

In my far-off corner of the living room, I predicted this was not going to end well for the drunkard. I only hoped the police would arrive before anything happened to my brother. Neither of us knew what the guy might have on him. He could have a concealed weapon or a tainted needle from drugs. It wasn't like this crazy dude was going to answer any questions regarding what he was hiding on his person.

He curled his hand into a fist and aimed for my brother's face, but when he swung, Alder ducked. Angered, he launched at my brother, and then there was a scuffle. There was a scuffle. They exchange punches while each one tried to get the upper hand. With his level of inebriation and Alder's training in self defense, he was sorely outclassed, but it didn't stop him from trying to take Alder out.

Alder's fist hit the bridge of the guy's nose. Blood splattered all over the kitchen floor. The perp swung, his hit barely grazing my brother's shoulder. With the intruder's body to the side and slightly vulnerable, Alder followed with another punch, effectively knocking him out. The man slumped to the floor like a sack of potatoes.

Once the intruder was laid out, Alder got him restrained. He was looking around for something to tie his hands together with when I remembered the extra pair of handcuffs Reed kept in the drawer in the table by the front door entry way. Considering the amount of excitement, I wasn't surprised that I had forgotten we needed a way to keep him contained while we waited for the police to arrive.

"Reed has another set of cuffs. Hold him still and I'll go and get them."

"Go careful, there's no need to hurry. He's out."

"You're still holding him?"

"I'm securing him just in case he comes to and starts swinging," he explained.

I watched as Alder pressed his knee into the intruder's lower back and held his hands in place behind him. When he nodded, I walked as fast as I could to retrieve the spare cuffs. A sharp pain rolls through my stomach when I reach the entry way. If I had ever been stabbed, I would imagine that would be what it felt like. After taking a few deep breaths, the pain subsided a little. I reached into the drawer and pulled out the cuffs. Thankfully my brother Reed, the ever-ready cop, was always prepared.

A few moments later, when I returned, the dude was still passed out on the floor. My brother reached over and grabbed the cuffs from my outstretched hands.

"Remain on the other side of the room Vi," Alder instructed. "At least until I have him completely secured."

As I waited off to the side, the frequency and the duration of the contractions became longer, falling into a more regular pattern. In that moment I realized they were probably not Braxton Hicks. My heart leapt into my throat.

What if hitting the island hurt the baby?

"Alder," I cried out. "I think that something's wrong with the baby."

Leaving psycho dude to his own devices, knocked out, with his hands shackled behind him, my brother made his way back to me. The way I watched Alder secure him and had him handled was indicative of the life our family lived. I had always been proud of the life that most of the men in my family, and some of the women, lived. There was no doubt in my mind which way Alder was leaning for a career, and he had my utmost support.

"Where does it hurt?" he asked.

"There's a dull ache in my side," I responded. My mind raced with all the negative consequences.

What if I never got to meet my son?

What if this was always supposed to happen because Mike didn't want me or the baby?

Did I deserved it for being an irresponsible mother?

A sudden gush of water down my legs. The floor became wet and slippery; I had to step to the side to avoid falling.

"Al, I think my water just broke," I informed him.

"Are you sure you didn't just pee yourself?" He tried to make light of the situation, but it only enraged me more. I didn't have the patience to deal with his jokes while I kept feeling like I was being squeezed around my middle by a boa constrictor decided to use me for its next meal.

"Fuck off," I groaned, as another spasm took my breath away.

"What's going on Vi?" Ivy yelled through speaker phone.

"Al knocked him out and got him restrained with Reed's spare cuffs, but now I'm having contractions and my water broke."

"The ambulance is on the way, babe, you'll be okay," Ivy assured me.

"Sweetheart hang up the phone with me and tell Alder that the cops and ambulance are on the way. I'm gonna call someone to take me there to meet you. You're going to be okay. The baby's going to be okay. I love you."

"I love you too, Ives." I sniffled again, and then disconnected the call.

"See, it's going to be okay, Vi. The ambulance is already on the way and we're not too far away from the hospital. If we can't make it there, I will deliver the baby myself," he assured me, repeating some of the things Ivy had already said over speaker.

"Like hell you will," I responded. There was no way I was going to allow Alder to look or get his hands close to anywhere down there. I wouldn't even want my best friend or even Mike to deliver this baby. We had no choice but to make it to the hospital on time.

Even if I had to resort to crossing my legs.

"I will do what's necessary to save you and my nephew," he responded. "I never should have opened that door. This is all my fault."

He placed a towel on the chair and braced my arm as he lowered me down. He obviously wanted me to be comfortable while we waited for the ambulance.

"Al, I didn't even ask if you're okay." I felt like a complete bitch, not asking him if he was okay. He had just had a fight with some weirdo that had crashed into his car. Of course, he wasn't okay, but knowing him, he would put on a brave face and just blow it all off.

Hockey players…knock out their teeth and they'll swish their mouth with Gatorade, stop the bleeding and then get back out on the ice and score the next goal to win the game.

"Nothing I can't get looked at when we're at the hospital. No big deal. Just some bumps and bruises. Psycho car crasher is the one who's going to have a hard night."

What seemed like hours, but truly only minutes later, we finally heard sirens in the distance. Law enforcement officers ran up the sidewalk with their guns drawn. The door was still open, so they easily gained entrance.

With the number of officers responding, there was no doubt in my mind that Reed's house was listed as belonging to a police officer. When we called to report the break in, they likely sent more back up just to be safe, not knowing the situation.

"Officers, the man who broke into my brother's house is knocked out over there by the fridge with his arms held back in my brother's spare hand cuffs."

"Thanks, man. Is everyone okay in here?"

"My sister got knocked into the kitchen island by that punk when he tried to push by her so he could get further into the house. She started having contractions and then her water broke. We'll need either the ambulance or a patrol car to take her to the nearest hospital."

"Sure, no problem. We can call another ambulance for this guy here, and you guys can go in that one."

MIKE

Reed's phone was blowing up on the dash, but he continued to ignore it because we were patrolling through a high traffic area with a lot of crime. He needed to keep an eye on our surroundings while I drove just in case he spotted anything that required our attention. We both needed to be on the alert just in case something happened. Thankfully we had made it through half of our shift already with nothing serious coming over the radio. At the beginning of our shift there were a couple drunk and disorderly calls, and a shoplifter at the drugstore.

"Reed speaking," he answered.

He listened intently to the other side of the conversation while I continued driving.

"What?"

I tried to keep my eyes on the road, but I couldn't help wondering who he was talking with and what was going on. His facial expressions kept changing as he tried to understand the other side of the call.

"Ivy, slow down," he instructed.

Another Ivy catastrophe…

Who knew what was going on in her life? Since the moment I had been introduced to her I knew she was a bit of a wild child. Ivy was like a hurricane who blew in, threw some shit around and then left with you even more confused than you were when she first arrived. When Reed introduced us, I thought he had lost his mind. He knew I avoided drama like a rattlesnake on a hiking trail.

Lucky for me, Viola was nothing like her sister, she was calm and collected, a planner, all organized and detailed.

"What the fuck happened to Al's car?" He yelled through the phone "In front of my house? Who?"

He went from confusion to worry, then straight to terror. I couldn't hear the other side of the conversation, but I immediately feared the worst. I hadn't talked to Viola in over a month, and she was due to have our baby in a couple weeks. It was more than obvious that she had every intention of doing everything without me, which hurt like hell. My first son was going to be born without me, all because of my meddling parents, a psycho ex-girlfriend that wouldn't take a hint and my inability to be honest to everyone who mattered about my familial background.

Countless times, Vi asked me about my family and why they were never around. Even with her strained relationship with her father, she couldn't understand how I had two siblings that I never spent any time with. She felt that the distance her father put between them only made her relationship with her brothers and sisters all that much stronger. For the same amount of times she asked, I made up excuses, rather than telling her my family was controlling, manipulative, and most of all not to be trusted. I should have told her that no matter what happened, she and the baby were the only family I would ever need.

"No, you don't need to call Mike. I've got him right here in the patrol car with me." Reed said into the phone. "We'll be there as soon as we can."

He held the phone away from my ear, turned to me and said, "Viola's in labour. We're going there now."

"She can't be having him now, it's too early," I responded.

He shook his head but didn't reply.

"What?" I asked.

He held up a finger and turned his attention back to Ivy.

"Ives. We're on the way there now. Tell Viola that Mike's on the way and not to worry about anything. She wasn't dealt a shitty upbringing to be given heartache in the end." He took a deep breath, and in that moment, I knew he was trying to be strong for his sister. Every horrible scenario was running through my mind and I needed to know what was going on. "Okay, yeah. Tell her that I love her, and I'll be there soon."

"What aren't you telling me?" I asked again, not really knowing if I wanted the answer.

"I think we should get to the hospital first and I will tell you everything once the vehicle is parked," he responded. "I don't want us to have a wreck on the way to the hospital because you're not focussing on the road.

Once we hit the next intersection, I immediately changed directions and accelerated. I needed to be there for the woman I loved.

"Please," I begged. "Just tell me if my family is going to be okay."

I loved her. She had to be okay because without her I was nothing.

"Knowing Vi, they'll be just fine. The important part is that she's in the ambulance on the way to the hospital and Alder is with her."

The trip to the hospital took less than fifteen minutes but felt like a lifetime. The whole drive I kept thinking of what I would say to the woman that I loved, besides apologizing for everything that she had gone through without me.

The only thing that was concrete in my mind was that I was never letting her go again.

VIOLA

SHARP PAIN LANCED THROUGH MY STOMACH AS another contraction followed close behind, making me clench Alder's hand in a death grip. Stories of labour lasting hours made me respect all the mothers willing to put themselves through moments of misery for that tiny little bundle of joy.

"Al, I can't do this!" I yelled, grabbing his hand as another contraction ripped through my body and I tried not to push.

"You can do anything you set your mind to, imp," he reassured me, rubbing circles on my back like the nurse had directed him. It did very little to mask the pain I had been experiencing, but I refused to let him know in fear he would be disappointed.

Reed and Ivy had been the ones to attend my birthing class, so Al was completely out of his depth. I wanted to laugh, even though I felt like crying. He was being a trooper and I couldn't love him more for it. A sudden wave of emotion crashed over me as I realized just how great my siblings were. My father may be a complete disappointment, but at least I had them.

"Thanks for not leaving me here to do this alone," I said to Al. "I don't want to be alone." I sobbed.

"Imp, you're never alone. We're all going to be here for you and this little guy."

My body continued to betray me in every sense of the word. No matter how many books a person read, they would never be prepared for the level of pain experienced during childbirth.

The pain was excruciating and all I wanted to do was yell at Mike for doing this to me, but he wasn't here. It was completely and utterly irrational, because we both made the choice to sleep together, but he was supposed to be here. My brother Alder, by the ashen look of his face, definitely didn't want to be here. Then again, none of my brothers could stand any of us girls being in pain.

"I still need to be able to play hockey this season, Vi."

"Does it look like I care?" I gritted through clenched teeth.

"You should, I'm your brother."

I barely registered Alder trying and failing to remove my grip, but when the contraction finally eased, I relaxed my hand and he sighed in relief.

Oops.

"Sorry," I apologized, giving him my biggest smile and batting my eyes.

"You have a great excuse to break my hand, just…please don't," he responded.

Just when I thought I would be doing this without him, the door opened, and Reed shoved Mike through the door. It had been a week since I saw him at the Country Club with Cynthia. He looked like someone kicked him in the stomach a couple of times and then forced him to hike ten kilometres to come see me.

"I don't want to see any of this shit cause I'm too squeamish, but I think this guy would like the chance to watch his son be born." Reed motioned to Alder, "Let's go join the rest of the clan in the waiting room. I have someone that you should meet."

"Yes!" Alder pumped his fist and headed toward the door, then glanced back at me, "Sorry. I guess I should have asked if I was excused, but I really don't want to be around when they flip up that sheet. There are just some things a brother should never see, and I don't want to have nightmares for the rest of my life, thank you very much."

When the door closed, I glanced over at Mike.

The nurse glanced at me and seeing my face, asked, "Honey, do you want this man in here?"

I looked at Mike one more time, and the expression on his face broke me. He actually wanted to be here.

"It's okay, he's the father," I answered.

Mike breathed out a sigh of what I could only think was relief and he immediately looked like the weight of the world had been removed from his shoulders. Without a word, he walked over to the bed and reached for my hand.

"Hi," I said to him, hoping he would say something.

"Hi," he responded. "Are you okay?"

"I'm okay now that you're here," I confessed.

"I didn't think you'd want me to be," he replied, pushing my damp hair out of my face.

"I'm just so mad at everything," I replied with a tear running down my face.

"I know babe, I know," he responded. "If you let me explain, I want to make it up to you."

"I don't know if I can do this."

"You're the strongest woman I know. I couldn't imagine a better mother for our son."

"It's time for you to push, Viola."

He was finally here.

My first child; our baby boy.

The only feature he had of mine was my eyes.

Everything else belonged to Mike: a full head of dark wavy hair, nose, lips and chin.

Even after the pain of delivering this little man, I wanted more babies in the future.

We named him Malakai Robert. I wanted to keep with the Sinclair tradition of naming the first-born son Robert Michael, but Mike wanted it to end with him. So, we settled on still following tradition, but doing it our way.

The moment the nurse placed him on my chest I knew my life was complete. Finally, I felt closer to my own mom that I ever had before.

The only person missing was my father, but I doubted I would see him. Considering he hadn't talked to me for the duration of my pregnancy, he likely wrote me off months ago. It didn't make the pain go away, but I had something more important to focus on.

The moment I heard our son's cries, I knew it was worth it.

Mike was my rock through the whole delivery. I was sure my colourful language would scare him away. All the verbal abuse, including me yelling at him for making me push a baby the size of a watermelon through a hole the size of a lemon.

Everything I had ever gone through up until this point was worth it: all the late nights worrying about how much my future had changed, my father's disappointment, the judgemental stares from the faculty at Sacred Heart, my inevitable exile from Sacred Heart, etc.

The only thing I wasn't sure of was my relationship with Mike. We were forever connected by this innocent little baby. Sure, once he was eighteen, he would likely move out of the house, but that didn't stop Mike and I from having to interact in relation to the child we created together.

When I looked into his eyes, they were full of thought, but I didn't have a clue what he was thinking about.

If only he would tell me.

MIKE

"Where is she?" a loud, familiar voice boomed down at the maternity floor reception desk.

"That sounds like dad," Alder confirmed my suspicion. We were all in the waiting room while the nurses got Viola cleaned up and the doctor examined our son.

Reed stood up, but I held up my hand to stop him.

"I need to talk to him before sees Viola," I said. I was either signing my own death warrant, or pink slip, only time would tell.

"Are you sure you want to do that?" Reed asked. "He sounds pretty riled up over there."

"He's not going in that room, until I'm positive of his intentions." His eyes widened with the knowledge that I was making a move to go talk to his father. "There's also a question I need to ask."

"Your funeral," Reed replied.

We actually had come a long way in regard to my relationship or lack thereof with Viola. He now knew the whole story about Cynthia and my manipulative parents and considering he had shoved me into the room with Viola. Although he supported his sisters wishes regarding our separation, he believed that nothing was going on with Cynthia and I was in love with his sister.

"Where's my daughter?" Richard King, the Chief of Police, and Viola's father, asked again.

"Sir, please calm down," I heard one of the staff reply as I got closer to the desk.

"Chief," I called out. "Can I have a word?"

He turned in my direction and I took in his appearance. His normally calm and collected demeanor had been replaced with a disheveled suit, wrinkled tie and erratic behavior.

"I don't have time Sinclair," he responded gruffly.

"Actually, sir, I would appreciate it if you could talk to me before you go and see Viola," I replied. If he was just going to stress her out more, I wasn't going to let him in there. He could fire me for all I cared.

My family was everything to me.

"What business is it of yours?" he asked.

My heart raced as I ran my hand through my hair.

"Sir, I have been meaning to have this conversation for a while, but considering your estrangement from Viola, I didn't think it was appropriate for me to approach you without her permission," I responded.

"Why would you need my daughter's permission to talk to me? I also don't see the point of this conversation when I need to get to my daughter," he said.

"Your access to Viola's room is dependant on this discussion."

"Look, Sinclair, I don't know who you think you are, but you're not going to dictate whether I can see my own child or not."

"She may be your daughter, but she just gave birth to my son and I will not have you in there upsetting her anymore than she already is."

"You're the prick that got my teenage daughter pregnant?" The Chief yelled, placing his hands on my chest and pushing me back in the direction of the waiting room. His tirade was drawing the attention of the patients and staff near us.

"Dad!" Reed called out as he came running, likely to ensure I didn't get knocked out.

"Reed, how could you let your partner defile your sister?"

Reed looked like he was simultaneously slapped and grossed out. If the situation had warranted it, I would have let the laugh that was building slip out.

"Whoa, Dad, seriously?" Reed addressed his father. "If you keep acting this way the staff will have to call security. Think of how that will look."

"It is your responsibility to look after your siblings."

"All of my siblings are now adults, and although I love them with everything I have, I cannot dictate their actions," he responded.

"That doesn't mean you stop taking care of your siblings," the Chief's argument fell on deaf ears.

"Mike, it looks like you've got this under control. I'm going to head back over there before I have to have another conversation about my sister's sex life with my dad." Reed saluted me jokingly and then sat back down with his siblings.

"Out of my way, son."

"Not until I learn of your plans." I stood my ground.

During the months that Vi lived with me, I could tell she was saddened by her father's ultimate rejection. She had learned to deal with the day to day because she was away at boarding school. When she had come home on the weekends, her time was spent with her sister or her friends, so she didn't have time to feel the absence. Then she was all at once: kicked out of the only home she had ever known, expelled from school, and forced to move in with a man who may have been the father of her unborn child, but was still essentially a complete stranger.

"I just want to see my daughter."

"Viola has been through a lot today, and I would just like to make sure that your intentions are aimed at being supportive rather than ready to break her more than you've already done."

"I've made some mistakes," he began. "I'm here to ensure that I don't make any more in regard to my family."

Richard King, the large brute of a man in a dishevelled suit, deflated in front of my eyes. For the first time in all the years I had known him, he was no longer this untouchable, larger than life man. He was fallible, just as we all were some point in our life. Most of all, he was a father, who upon realizing he had messed up, wanted to fix things with his youngest child.

Realizing that I myself had messed up significantly in the past couple months, and was now the father of his grandchild, I couldn't keep them apart if what he was saying was true. If I knew anything about him, I knew he was good at his word, so there was no reason to stop him from going in there.

"Now that you've calmed down, I don't see any reason you can't go in there," I responded, completely surprised by the method in which I talked to my superior and the father of the woman I wanted to spend the rest of my life with. "I'll go see if I can go find our son, so everyone can meet him."

"Thank you," he replied, looking humbled, as he headed in the direction of Vi's room.

I turned and faced the people in the waiting room, who all looked floored by what they had just witnessed.

"Holy shit, did that just happen?" Ash asked Alder.

"Yup, I think it did," Alder chuckled. "You've definitely got some balls, man," he then told me. "You must really love my sister."

"I do." I responded. "In fact, if you'll allow it, I'm going to marry your sister."

"Fine by us," Ash replied, not waiting for anyone else to answer.

"Welcome to the family," Alder agreed.

"You were already my brother," stated Reed.

"Eww, your brother knocked up your sister," Alder guffawed.

"Grow the fuck up," Reed replied, punching Alder in the shoulder. "That shit's not funny."

"Oh, but I think it is," Ash replied.

∼

I WAS OFFICIALLY A FATHER.

The nurse placed my son in my arms, wrapped up like a cute little blue burrito. Kai was fast asleep, probably tuckered out from the big day. If I was able to talk his mother into coming home and living with me, this may be the only calm moment for the rest of my life. The moment I held him I knew I would there was nothing I wouldn't do for my child.

I would die for him.

Now I needed to get my family back together under one roof. I pulled out the engagement ring my grandfather gave to my grandmother when they got married. Thankfully he gave it to me that last time I was at the house, because I would never go back there again. My dad was keeping it in his safe for when I got married to Cynthia, but that wasn't happening. Pops must have known what my plan was because he disappeared just before I left the house and slipped it in my pocket. It was like he knew I needed it and wouldn't have had a chance to retrieve it from my father without a fight.

I loved that man. He was the only person in my family who really got me. It might have been because his brother spent his whole career in law enforcement. Pops would be the only one out of my family that my son would know, unless my siblings and I mended our relationships. The pessimist in me doubted that would happen any time soon.

I took one more look at my son and headed back in the direction of Viola's room. I needed to check to see how it was going with her dad, then I had a very important question to ask her.

Hopefully she felt the same way.

VIOLA

A LIGHT KNOCK ON THE DOOR FRAME DREW MY attention and made me glance over to see who was visiting. Dad stepped into the room and I braced for the lecture of my life. Considering the last time that I saw him, he was kicking me out of the house, I expected more of the same. For the couple months after I left, I tried calling multiple times, but he never picked up the phone. Eventually, I accepted the loss of the only parent I knew.

"Forgive me, sweetheart?" he asked, blowing me away.

"What?" I choked out.

"I was wrong. I shouldn't have kicked you out of the house at one of the most stressful moments in your life."

I regarded my hands securely folded in my lap as he continued. They needed to be the most interesting thing I would see for the duration of his apology. I knew if I looked him in the eyes I would start bawling like a baby. These damn pregnancy hormones were driving me batty and I felt even more out of control since the delivery. Kai had been taken for a check-up by the doctor following my delivery, so I didn't get a lot of time with him. That was likely contributing to my rollercoaster of emotions. If Mike hadn't promised he would be back once the nurses were done cleaning me up, I would have been freaking out over that too.

"I should have been understanding. I should have taken care of my baby when she found out she was having a baby. Instead I made the biggest mistake of my life and turned my back on you."

"I never wanted you to be ashamed of me, Dad."

"I wasn't. If anything, I was scared."

Even though he didn't shower me with a lot of attention and love, I never thought he was weak. In a dangerous situation my father would be the first person running in the door, while everyone else exited in the other direction. Never in a million years would I have thought he would be scared.

"You were scared?"

How could my father be afraid of anything?

"More than anything in my life, and I've been shot at more than once. You look so much like your mother that you could have been twins. I worried that you would be dealt the same fate, so I pushed you away."

"I understand." I sniffed.

"You know, when your mother died, a part of me went with her. Then I was left with a precious little baby girl and six more children waiting at home for me to raise on my own. Then when you were eleven, my eldest succumbed to years of addiction, which broke me just as much as losing my wife. I didn't know what to do, so I distanced myself from you all and built a wall with my grief. I threw myself into work, ran my household like it was a precinct, and until the day I threw out my baby daughter because she was pregnant, I thought I was doing okay."

Mike returned with our baby boy in his arms, all wrapped up in a blue blanket, wearing a matching blue toque. I was itching to hold Kai again, but this conversation was important to me. Maybe with Mike in the room I would finally have the strength to tell my dad some of the things I felt as a child.

He might be able to gain some perspective.

"I never felt like I wasn't loved, and if you ask the others, I think they would agree with me."

"That wasn't my intention. I think you might have had it harder than the others because as you grew, you reminded me so much of your mother. More so than your sisters, which was surprising considering Fern had actually spent time with her."

"You were hard on us. It is somewhat understandable since you were a single parent with seven children under the age of eight. I doubt we were easy to care for. I'm positive most of your grey hair is from Ivy, though."

He laughed.

"That being said, I can't keep being angry with you, or the hand that I was dealt."

"Could you ever find it in your heart to someday be able to forgive an old man for his shortcomings?"

"There's nothing left to forgive, Dad."

Something about giving birth to my son changed the way I looked at my father. If anything were to ever happen to Kai or Mike, I would be an empty shell of myself. That was just what my father had been for the past eighteen years.

An empty shell.

The day after I was born, his wife died. Eleven years later, his eldest son overdosed. I experienced it too, but I would be a fraction of what I was now if I had lost my husband and child. There was something about losing those who you were responsible for. It didn't mean that he loved my mom and Rowan more than I did. He just loved them differently. He was supposed to spend the rest of his life with his wife, and a child was meant to outlive their parents.

"Thank you, sweetheart. You don't know how much I wanted to hear those words from you. I promise you won't regret it."

"I know I won't. I've missed you."

He wrapped his arms around me and gave me a gentle hug, then stepped back.

"Where have you been living?"

I glanced down at my hands again. "I'm living with Reed right now."

"We can't have that. I think you and the baby should come home with me. In fact, I want you and my grandson to come live with me."

Mike interrupted, "Sir, actually I was hoping Vi would come home with me. I would like my family to be together."

My heart thumped in my chest. "Really?" I asked.

Mike ignored me for a moment and turned to my father and said, "Sir, would you like to hold your grandson?"

"I would love to," my dad responded.

Mike placed Kai in my dad's arms, and then kissed my temple. "Really," he whispered in my ear.

"What did you name him?" my dad asked us while looking down into Kai's beautiful blue eyes.

"Malakai Robert Sinclair," I replied.

"That's unique," he responded.

"We have a tradition in the Sinclair family. The first-born son is always named Robert Michael. I wanted to break the tradition, but Vi thought it was important to continue, so she put a bit of a twist on it."

"It's a nice strong name."

"We'll probably call him Kai most of the time," I piped up.

"He's beautiful, Vi," my father told me as he stroked Kai's cheek.

Reed knocked on the door and came inside. "Dad, if you have a moment, there's someone out here I want you to meet."

"Is that okay with you, sweetheart?"

"Sure, I'm kind of tired."

"I'll stop in before I go home."

"Okay," I replied.

"Reed has someone for him to meet?"

"He probably means Kalista," he responded.

"Who's Kalista?" I asked.

EPILOGUE

"Sweetheart, the sitter is here," Mike called from downstairs.

"Be right there!"

If anyone would have told me I would be a mother and married the same year I graduated, I would have laughed in their face. I had a five-year plan, and nothing was supposed to derail it. However, over the years I had learned my obsession with planning was an attempt to gain some semblance of control over my life. When I became pregnant with Kai, everything changed. Overnight I realized that as much as you planned, something could throw a wrench in it.

Kai would forever be my best form of chaos.

Tonight, was our fifth anniversary, and this was our first night out since our youngest, Maci was born. I was finally down to my pre-baby weight and had put on a gorgeous red halter dress that Ivy helped me pick out earlier in the week. Mike was used to me lounging around in sweats or shorts and a shirt, so I hoped this change would blow him away. I giggled when I thought about how she persuaded me to purchase it because she said it would have him begging me for another baby in no time.

Despite our rocky beginnings, I was still as in love with Mike as I was the day we were married. He had given me three children. Our eldest, Malakai turned five a month ago, Maya was almost four, and our youngest, Maci was just seven months old. Tonight, before he started begging for a fourth, I was going to tell him that we could start trying again. I loved growing up surrounded by lots of siblings, and I wanted my children to have the same relationships.

In fact, just this morning, following an all-out brawl between Maya and Malakai, over his race car track of all things, my eldest son informed me that I needed to go to the hospital and pick up a baby brother for him. Apparently, he thought that if we had another boy that he would have some respect for locomotive engineering. I didn't have the heart to break it to him that even if we had another son, that wouldn't guarantee he would be interested in trains. His new brother might want to be a cowboy or maybe he would play with dolls like Maya did.

Whatever my children's interests were, they would be fully supported by me and their father.

Mike had no interest to maintain his relationship with his parents, so I was fully prepared to give him as many children as he wanted, and I was physically able to have. We started young, so I had quite a few childbearing years remaining. I was only twenty-three and already had three children, so what was a couple more?

It was unfortunate that Mike's parents hadn't accepted us, but as far as both of us were concerned, it was their loss.

They still believed he was throwing away the chance at an advantageous union between him and Cynthia. After the birth of their first grandson, and someone to carry on the Sinclair name, we had hoped that his parents would eventually accept us. They were like massive boulders too stubborn to shift. Two days before our wedding, to which they were invited, his mother summoned me to an afternoon tea at the country club. When I accepted her offer, I was excited that we had finally persuaded them to be in our lives.

After all, I still sometimes yearned for a maternal figure in my life and the possibility of having his parents in our lives was exciting.

However, that all changed in the blink of an eye. When I arrived at the club, I was immediately hustled into a back room. Their lawyer proceeded to persuade me to sign a prenup. When I refused to bow to their wishes, she threatened to call the police and claim I had been stalking and harassing them. I told them to go ahead and do whatever they deemed necessary, essentially calling their bluff. I also informed them that if they didn't allow me to leave that I could have them charged with forced confinement.

What I didn't know at the time, was that she had already called the police prior to rushing me into the back room. Estelle had concocted an elaborate story involving unauthorized surveillance, threats and property damage. She had hoped my being at the country club would be further proof of the so-called harassment. The whole ordeal involved hysterical pleas to have me removed from the grounds. Neither Mike nor I maintained a membership at the country club, so they didn't have my name in their records. I was surprised that they overlooked my last name though because the only Kings in our city were members of the Chief of Police's family.

To their surprise when security called the police, Reed and Michael were dispatched to the call. Mike convinced them it was in their best interests to drop the false charges, as he could use all the secrets, he had to do more damage to their reputations. The day of our wedding, his grandfather and siblings were the only ones who attended. Prior to the reception, his grandfather heard of his son and daughter-in-law's plan, so as a wedding gift, he activated his living will, naming my husband sole beneficiary and principal owner of Sinclair Investments.

It was never Mike's dream to work at his family's investment firm, so as soon as his sister Claudia finished her Master's in Business Management, he hired her to fill the role. He still owned the company but ensured both of his siblings that they would have employment for the rest of their lives. Before Kai was born, Mike bought a large plot of land near my childhood home, just outside the city. Mike hired an architectural firm to design and build our house, but when he found out about his inheritance, he changed the plans entirely to include ten bedrooms.

When he told me, the house would have ten bedrooms I just about lost my mind. Then I realized the one thing I wanted more than anything was a huge family to fill those rooms. If we didn't manage to fill them, we would have guest rooms for my nieces and nephews to visit and later our grandchildren. In addition to the home, we added a one-bedroom pool house that reminded me of a small condo. His grandfather currently lived there, and we had homecare come in once a week to ensure we hadn't missed anything in regard to his health care needs. He was welcome to stay there until the time came when he chose to live in a senior housing facility. For now, he enjoyed his time with his great grandchildren.

The dark coloured brick exterior looked like each of the bricks were laid one at a time. The dark black door for the front entry had a large brass coloured metal knocker. White wainscoting lined the walls throughout every room of the house, which gave it an older style feel. Each room had white or grey paint on the wall above the paneling. We both agreed that once we had more children, they could choose their own unique colours to go along with their personalities.

Mike's nephew Gabriel, Victor's son, who was two years younger than Kai, often came over to spend time with our children and his great grandpa. Family was still as important as ever, and even if we didn't get along with his parents, we wanted our children to know their cousins. Sometimes we would have all nine of the King grandchildren here and the house would be full of laughter. It was crazy, but I couldn't wait to add to the ranks.

Just before we drove away from the house I turned to Mike. "You might want to enjoy how I look right now because next year, if we're lucky, I'll be the size of a house again."

His eyes widened, then once he comprehended what I meant, his smile lit up the cab of the truck. "Now I don't want to go to supper. We could be up there in our bedroom trying right now."

"Or we could drive to a make out spot like a couple of teenagers and test out the back seat."

"Sure, let's fog up some windows," he agreed reaching across the seat, yanking me closer to him so I was sitting in the middle next to him. He crushed his lips on mine in the most possessive kiss imaginable. It brought me back to when we first got married and couldn't keep our hands off each other.

It was still like that sometimes, but it was harder to find our special sexy times with three small children. The shower in the bathroom gets more use than the bed these days. With my legs settled on either side of the gear shift, he ran his knuckles over the inside of my knee causing a gasp from me.

"Not here," I breathily told him.

"Right." He winked, then placed his hand on the gear shift in between my legs. "You might have to open wider, sweetheart."

"So romantic," I teased him and widened my legs.

Makenzie Rachel, or Mak as Kai affectionately called her, was born a little over a year later in December.

And we didn't stop there...

NEXT IN THE SERIES...

Do you want to know who Kalista is too?
Keep an eye out for Book 2.

ABOUT THE AUTHOR

Katya Ensmore is an independent Canadian author who loves all things supernatural. She has been writing stories since she was a child, but only recently decided to devote time to completing a novel. She currently has several works in progress with hopes to publish more in the near future.

When she is not spending time with her huge Great Dane fur baby aptly named Khaos, she can be found reading or writing.

Manufactured by Amazon.ca
Bolton, ON